S0-AUZ-353

DONALD MOFFITT

THE GENESIS QUEST

DONALD MOFFITT was born in Boston, and now lives in rural Maine with his wife, Anne, a native of Connecticut. A former public relations executive, industrial filmmaker, and ghostwriter, he has been writing fiction on and off for more than twenty years under his own name and an assortment of pen names. His first full-length science-fiction novel and the first book of any genre to be published under his own name was *The Jupiter Theft* (Del Rey, 1977).

ALSO BY DONALD MOFFITT
Published by ibooks, inc.:

Jovian

COMING MAY 2003
Second Genesis

THE GENESIS QUEST

DONALD MOFFITT

ibooks
new york
www.ibooks.net

DISTRIBUTED BY SIMON AND SCHUSTER, INC.

A Publication of ibooks, inc.

Copyright © 1986, 2003 by Donald Moffitt

An ibooks, inc. Book

All rights reserved, including the right to reproduce this book
or portions thereof in any form whatsoever.
Distributed by Simon & Schuster, Inc.
1230 Avenue of the Americas, New York, NY 10020

ibooks, inc.
24 West 25th Street
New York, NY 10010

The ibooks World Wide Web Site Address is:
http://www.ibooks.net

ISBN 0-7434-5833-8
First ibooks, inc. printing March 2003
10 9 8 7 6 5 4 3 2 1

Cover art copyright © 2002 Stephan Martiniere
Cover design by Mike Rivilis

Printed in the U.S.A.

Prologue One
MESSAGE

One entire hemisphere of the little moon had been turned into an ear. The great radio bowls spread to the sharp curve of the horizon like the lacy skeletons of sea creatures left behind by some unimaginable tide, their serried ranks bristling against the airless black of the sky.

It was still some hours before worldrise. The stars were huge and brilliant across the empty night. The listening was still good. The immense shells yearned toward the void, collecting the random crackle of radio noise from beyond, as they had done now for half a thousand years.

Without result.

In the observatory dome rising at the center of the tremendous array, the project director refocused two or three of the eyes he had been keeping on the control panel and indulged himself for a moment with a full-circle view of the surrounding system. He never tired of the sight, though he had been here from the beginning, watching the field of antennae grow outward for nearly half his lifetime.

One of the bowls in the middle distance was being serviced, he noticed. He could see the tiny outstretched shapes

1

of space-suited technicians crawling over the vast curved surface like so many animated snowflakes. That one bowl was out of order didn't matter. A few inactive bowls out of all those thousands could not affect the total picture.

He touched limbs with his visitor from the Father World and said soundlessly, "It will be in a moment now."

The visitor wore a radio sleeve and was doubtless in communication with whatever touch group he represented on the home planet. There was the familiar delay of a couple of seconds while the transmission was relayed to the other side of the moon and bounced down to the planetary surface and back, and then, through the limb he had linked with the visitor, the project director felt the faint ghostly feedback from all those absent voices.

The visitor was too courteous to express the skepticism of his touch brothers overtly; but he couldn't entirely suppress his own involuntary reaction to it.

"You've listened to thousands of stars," he said aloud, "and found nothing?"

"Tens of thousands, actually," the project director said good-naturedly. "One at a time, within our own galaxy. But now we're about to listen to two hundred billion stars at once."

"How can you do that?" The visitor let an eye or two wander to the endless thicket of antennae outside. "Even with this marvelous facility. How can you possibly sort them out?"

"We don't have to sort them out. The galaxy that we have chosen as our target is so far away that we may consider it as a single radio source. In effect, we will accomplish two million years of listening in an hour. All we have to do is to search the preferred wavelengths until we find one in which a modulated signal outshines the background noise by a significant factor."

"And then?"

"And then we shall know that life is possible elsewhere. That we need not be alone in the universe."

At the prompting of his radio sleeve, the visitor said apologetically, "But what's the good of it? You can't answer such a signal."

"True," the project director conceded. "Any message we received would necessarily have been sent tens of millions of years ago—not the mere tens of thousands of years for signals from our own galaxy's farther stars. Any conceivable reply we might make would take additional tens of millions of years to bridge the gulf. By that time they—and we—likely would be long extinct."

"Then why bother?" the visitor persisted.

The project director had answered such questions many times over his centuries of stewardship. Demands on the time of the great radio telescope grew ever more insistent as the race expanded into space. There was competition from other astronomers, other project directors, each with a convincing claim to priority, and soon, with the interstellar probes about to be sent to the nearer stars, the magnificent instrument would be pressed into service as a communication device. The director had fought jealously to protect the fraction of time devoted to the search for intelligent life. One day, he knew, he would have to face a convocation of his fellows and defend the whole monumental enterprise all over again.

For now, he said simply, "We would have much to learn from the very existence of such a message. And more, doubtless, from the message itself."

The visitor listened to his sleeve for a moment. After a suitable interval he posed the question in his own voice, a little less rudely than it probably had been asked. "And how will you know that you have not been deceived by natural phenomena, as you were before?"

The director sent a ripple of laughter down his arm. "One of your touch brothers is very astute. The incident he refers to took place in the early days of radio astronomy, when our observations were still planet-bound. I was hardly past my apprenticeship at the time. A stellar radio source was found whose pulses were so regular that it was thought at first to be an artificial signal. Today, of course, we know about such things as neutron stars. We won't jump to *that* conclusion again."

"And if you find nothing at all?"

"Then we'll try another galaxy."

Across the dome an aproned assistant waved a signal, and the director forestalled more questions by saying, "We're aiming now. Look outside. It's a sight you won't want to miss."

Beyond the transparent wall the surface of the moon seemed to writhe like a live thing as the closely packed bowls all turned simultaneously to face in a new direction. The silent rumble of the vast collective movement could be felt through the floor of the observatory itself.

And the world changed, never to be the same again.

The first signals were detected almost at once. They were found mostly in the part of the spectrum between the hydrogen and hydroxyl radical lines, where theory had long predicted that water-based life would be apt to concentrate its communication efforts.

An excited assistant hurried up. "We're locked onto them now. There's remarkably little frequency drift.

4

They're also utilizing the first harmonic of the hydrogen frequency."

He passed over a touch pad that was beating rhythmically with repeating data. The director pulsated with emotion. "The very first time!" he murmured to himself. "We've found them the very first time!"

He'd forgotten completely about his visitor, who was still sharing his thoughts through a patch of contact. A diffident query reached his consciousness: "Can you be sure?"

"Eh? Yes. It's unmistakable." He thrust the throbbing datapad at him. "Have a look at this. It's the first ten prime numbers—counted out plainly in a steady rhythm and sitting in the middle of what looks like an ongoing message in binary code. That's to get our attention. It's their beacon. I'm willing to bet that it's repeated every few minutes."

And then the director linked with assistants and with data input devices and became very busy. The visitor discreetly withdrew a short distance.

Several hours later, when the excitement had died down somewhat and matters could be safely left to the scribes and the mechanical recorders, the director belatedly remembered his patiently waiting visitor—remembered, too, that every conceivable touch group on the Father World would soon be vying for a say in the allocation of resources—and apologetically groped for contact again.

"We've only begun the job, of course. We astronomers will go on recording as long as the message lasts and continue refining our techniques in case we're missing anything. And we'll try to learn more about the signal source itself—its orbital motion and so forth—through Doppler analysis and other methods. But now it will be the task of others—our greatest group minds—to interpret this ... gift from the stars."

"What can you tell so far?"

"They must be a very advanced race. Our entire civilization does not generate enough power to broadcast such a signal across so great a distance and with so high an information rate."

"But what are they *like*?"

The director thought it over. "To begin with, their arithmetic is to the base ten, so they must have ten limbs like ourselves."

"That much is obvious," the visitor said with a trace of impatience. "Any intelligent life form would necessarily resemble us more or less."

Not wanting to give offense, the director said cautiously, "I've heard religious people advance the argument that sentience cannot exist except in the image of the Father-of-All."

"No, no, I'm talking about the scientific argument. That whatever evolutionary path life takes to arrive at intelligence, it will need tool-handling limbs, vision, a sense of touch for cooperative communication. And an efficient body plan presupposes radial symmetry and a diffuse neural network with most of the brain at the center of the body, where it's well protected and where it can send impulses to all the extremities with minimum delay."

"Yes, I'm familiar with the thesis."

"A similar case is made for the evolution of Language. Certain it is that Language seems to be inborn in children—it's found even in those unfortunates who somehow escape the harvesting nets and grow in isolation before they can be ingathered—though of course they need to catch up to their new touch brothers."

The director used a lee eye to steal a glance at the field of antennae. "I doubt that the message will turn out to be in anything as complex as Language. Across intergalactic distances, the information density would be too low. I more likely we'll find that it's in some sort of symbolic code that translates to one of the simpler senses, like hearing or vision."

"Then how will we ever understand the senders?"

"You'd be surprised at how much hard information can be conveyed that way. Enough so that we can infer some of the rest."

Together they watched the rippling patterns on one of the console's touch screens. Even with vision alone, you could easily make out the regular structure of the transmission. On impulse, the director reached out and absorbed a brief section of the transmission directly, sharing it with his visitor through their linked limbs.

The transmission meant nothing, of course: It was devoid of affective content. But in the simple pulses, the director imagined that he could sense the shadow of ... something. These patterns were an artifact of intelligent life, after all.

"There's no sign of a repeat yet, except for the periodic insertion of the prime number sequence. The message must be a very long one—perhaps one that will take years to complete."

Like the director, the visitor was moved to awe by some portent he could sense beyond the unadorned vibrations. "What can it be that they've sent?" he asked uneasily.

"Perhaps," the director joked in an attempt to relieve the sudden tension, "they sent themselves."

And that, in fact, was what turned out to be the case.

PART I

Chapter One

Why am I different?" the boy, Bram, asked.

Voth, his adoptive tutor, stretched to three times the boy's height on the five lower limbs that supported him and spread his crown of slender petals. "I have told you many times," the old teacher sighed from somewhere within his maw.

"Tell me again," the little boy persisted. He sat cross-legged on the yielding floor of the cluttered beehive chamber that served as nursery and classroom, surrounded by wooden blocks and bright spongy pyramids and touch objects of various shapes, and looked up expectantly into two or three of the five mirror eyes spaced around Voth's waist at the forks of his upper limbs.

Patiently, the flowerlike being settled a bit closer to the child's level and bent toward him. The pliant upper limbs opened out wider to show still more of the velvety inner surfaces whose rich plum shades contrasted so vividly with the yellow of the smooth, waxy outer integument that the Nar presented to the world.

"Because," Voth said carefully and distinctly in the deep

10

thrum of the Small Language, "you're made of human stuff, like other human folk, and your touch brothers are made of Nar stuff, like me."

The little boy considered the matter, his dark eyes wide and grave. He was five in the problematical human years—a little less than that in Nar reckoning—wiry and big-headed, with a mop of russet hair. He had always thought of himself as "Bram," though it was only a pet name in the Small Language and he owned a perfectly good human name with three words in it.

"No," he said, frowning. "That's not what I really, *really* meant. I meant, why is human *stuff* different?"

He contemplated his own skinny bare limbs and wiggled his toes experimentally, then transferred his gaze to the graceful ten-limbed shape of his mentor. Like the other members of the dominant life form on the planet, Voth was a decapod, built on a body plan of two five-pointed stars joined at a common waist. Evolution had elongated the stars and stretched them upward and downward for height and mobility. The sensible radial design was not quite a mirror image; the lower star was thicker and fleshier, and the five vestigial eyes at its crotches were lensless, though still light-sensitive for whatever endocrine processes were affected by light. The upper structure was more supple and willowy, its divided tips more adroit at handling things.

Now one of those supple limbs descended to Bram's shoulder, velvety side out. The tiny cilia of the warm surface tickled Bram's skin as they rippled in a reflex of frustrated communication. The Nar frequently thought aloud in the Great Language when they talked in the vocal mode, just as humans often made involuntary hand and body gestures while speaking. Except that with the Nar it was

11

the other way around: the Great Language was richer and subtler than speech. Bram, though only five, was better than most at picking up traces of meaning and emotion from skin contact, and he could tell that Voth was sad.

"Because," Voth said patiently, "human stuff started out on another world."

"Like Ilf?" the boy asked, naming the principal inhabited planet that swung around the sun's companion star. Ilf was only a few months distant in the great living spaceships—less by fusion-fission drive—and there was a lively commerce between the two worlds.

"Well, like Ilf," the old decapod conceded, "but much, much farther away."

"How far?" Bram demanded.

"Very far. Too far to see."

"Even through a telescope?"

"Even through a telescope." They had played this game many times before.

"I bet I could see it if I had a really *big* telescope," Bram said stubbornly.

"No, not even then."

"A really big, big, *big* telescope!"

"No, little one, it's not possible," Voth said, reverting to Inglex, which with Chin-pin-yin was one of the two principal human languages. Even when they spoke to each other in the Small Language, the Nar used a lot of human loan words.

"But why not?"

Bram could feel the agitated writhing of the hairlike filaments against his shoulder as the decapod debated with himself whether to go further with his information this time. Without looking, he knew that bands of deeper purple were marching up the underside of the tentacle, and he could detect a faint smell that he would have described as lemony if he had ever seen a lemon.

"Bram, you must understand just how far away the world that human people originated on is. If we could see the light from its sun, we would be seeing light that left there more than thirty-seven million years ago. We Nar didn't even exist then. We were just little primitive creatures as big as your hand that lived along the seashore, and we were just learning to walk upright on our lower five. We—" Voth hesitated. Bram felt a tingling sensation on his shoulder. "We think that human beings don't exist there anymore. And if they did, they would have changed into something else. For all we know, their sun itself could have stopped existing thirty-seven million years ago."

"Well, then," Bram said with five-year-old logic, "why don't we go there to find out?"

The feathery touch of another tentacle brushed his cheek. "People and things could never, ever travel so far," Voth said. "If it takes light thirty-seven million years to get here from the human sun, it would take a full-grown spaceship seven times as long to go there. Can you figure out how long that is?"

Bram screwed up his small features. "Two hundred and fifty-nine *million*," he finally announced.

"Very good, Bram."

"Well, then, why couldn't we go in a rocket?"

"It would take almost as long, and besides, a fusion-fission ship is too small to live on for any length of time. And if you could live two hundred million years, you'd forget who you were and why you went. No, it's just not possible."

"Well," Bram said, pouncing triumphantly, "how did human people get *here*, then?"

13

There was a cautious circularity of cilia movement. "Didn't one of your gene mothers ever discuss it with you?"

Bram dropped his eyes and traced a geometric figure on the floor with his big toe. "I asked mama-mu Dlors about it once, and she said I'd understand when I got older."

"I see. I think you're old enough to understand now, Bram. That was a very intelligent question. The answer is they didn't."

Bram warmed to the praise. "But human *stuff* did, though? And then you grew people out of it, the way you grow potatoes and spaceships and things?"

The old decapod's crown quivered in a manner that was equivalent to a man's shaking his head. "No. I told you that people and things can never travel so far. But information can—information in the form of radio waves, spreading outward at the speed of light. Before they vanished from the universe, human beings had achieved the power to tame whole suns and use their energy to shout across the space between galaxies. They told us many useful things. And one of the things their message contained was a—a sort of plan. A plan of how to make a human egg."

"They must have been very smart," Bram said with a yawn.

Voth squeezed Bram's shoulder gently. The four star points that were not occupied stood straight up in the air and drooped symmetrically outward in a formal gesture of respect.

"They were a very great people at the height of their powers," Voth said. "We Nar were fortunate that during the years the human message was being broadcast, we were in the early stages of our own space age. We had already begun to colonize the worlds of the lesser sun, and we had

14

sent our first primitive boron-drive ships to the nearest star outside our system, almost a whole light-year away. So we had a large enough radio ear already in place—a field of thousands of receivers covering a hemisphere of one of our smaller airless moons. We knew something of genetic engineering even then, but the human message was a revelation. As were the genetic building blocks the humans gave us— useful things like terrestrial starches and woody stems that made it possible for us to expand more quickly and cheaply into space. Within a single Nar lifetime, the whole direction of our civilization had changed. We had the beginnings of abundance. And then, half a Nar lifetime ago, we were ready to try to recreate man himself. I was fortunate to be a part of that new beginning, though I was but a small finger of the bioengineering touch group entrusted with the project. Yes, little one, we are very grateful for human beings."

Bram's attention had wandered. He rubbed at a sleepy eye with one fist. "Voth, can I play with Tha-tha?"

The tentacle whose tip rested on Bram's shoulder uncreased all the way up and enfolded the boy in its comforting mantle. "First I think you had better have your nap."

"Tha-tha's very nice. He's my favorite touch brother."

"Yes, he is nice. He'll grow into a fine person one day."

"Will he still be my friend when we grow up?"

Again there was that sensation of sadness from the downy undersurface of Voth's limb. "Touch brothers are always friends. For as long as they live."

"Will I be able to speak the Great Language to him then?"

"Let's not talk about that now. It's a very complicated subject."

"Sometimes he forgets to talk the Small Language and he just hugs me and I can't understand him."

"Don't worry about that, little one. I'll speak to Tha-tha. Young creatures are sometimes forgetful."

"Voth?"

"What, child?"

"Does Tha-tha have a gene mother too?"

A startled ripple traveled down Voth's tentacle. "Well, yes, of course. All Nar had mothers."

"I asked him, but he didn't know."

"He wouldn't remember. He was just a little swimming thing. After sentience, of course, he was raised by me and my touch brothers." The edges of the fleshy mantle curled in a way that Bram had come to recognize as the usual grown-up reticence, like when he asked mama-mu Dlors where they grew babies.

"Where do all the lady Nar *go*? You hardly ever see them, the way you see human ladies all the time, and then they're all old. And you never see a little girl Nar."

"That's enough for one day," Voth said firmly. "Time for your nap."

Bram allowed himself to be guided past the toy box, past his own little desk with the styluses and reading screen, past the miniature star-shaped whole-body reader that his touch brothers stretched themselves out on for hours at a time, to the cot in the corner, which still had his baby touch objects and alphabet letters dangling over it.

"Some day," Bram said as Voth started to tuck him in, "I'm going to go back to the world that human people started out on and see what it's like."

"Hush now, and go to sleep. I've told you it's not possible."

"I'll find a way to go anyhow," Bram said.

The old decapod gathered the boy compassionately in

16

his petals. "Oh, Bram, you are a child!" he said. "You will understand when you are older!"

Wrapped in the warm velvety cloak, Bram felt the waves of soft bristles caress him as Voth crooned to him in the Great Language. The meaning was muzzy but comforting, like a lullaby hummed without the actual words.

"You'll see," said a sleepy little boy.

Dlors was pouring a drink for her new friend, Arthe, when the door rattle made a diffident noise.

"Stay where you are," she said. "I'll get it."

She rose from the low orange pouf she had been sitting on and set the pitcher of iced and flavored distillate down on the fragile wooden stand between them. Arthe had made the little five-legged table out of vacuum-poplar; he was handier with edged tools than Bram's gene fathers had been.

"If it's Lan and Elaire, send them away," Arthe groaned. "He'll only want to drone on for hours about that mote drama he's got himself a part in." The thirtieth-century mote dramas of Jam Anders that were now being deciphered were the latest fad in the human community. Arthe's tastes in theater were more conservative, running to the neo-Shakespeare movement.

"Quiet, they'll hear you," Dlors said.

She went to the door, a wooden oval set in the nacre of the curving wall, and opened it. The tall spindle shape of a Nar was there, its tentacles raised and clustered with their waxy sides out in a mode of nonpresumptive courtesy.

"Oh ... Voth-shr-voth," she said. After a moment she remembered her manners and held up her hands, palms outward.

The decapod unpeeled two of its limbs and touched her palms in formal greeting.

"Good evening, Dlors Hsin-jen Jons," the being said in mid-Inglex. "May I see Bram?"

"Yes . . . of course. I'll get him. I wasn't expecting you at this hour."

"Forgive me for intruding on your Tenday." The hidden baritone vibrations were a little muffled by the palisade of tentacles. "There is a place I must take him to this night if you do not mind giving up his presence for a short time."

"No . . . not at all. I mean, he was going to go to bed soon, anyhow. He's a funny little boy. He can sit in his compartment for hours, playing by himself and making up games. He doesn't have any near siblings, you know—not here, anyhow, though there's a sixteenth-sister and some thirty-seconds elsewhere in the Compound."

"I will try to have him back in a few hours," Voth said gravely. "Perhaps he might sleep a little later tomorrow."

"I'll tell you what," Dlors said brightly. "Why doesn't he just stay with you tonight. I mean, he'd be going in the morning anyway, and that way there wouldn't be any problem."

The flat petals creased slightly at their midline. "His touch brothers will be pleased."

He followed her into the ribbed pearly chamber, mincing along on the stiffened tips of his lower points to match her gait. The Nar had no skeletons, but their hydrostatic support system enabled them to put a knee anywhere.

"Arthe, this is Voth-shr-voth, little Bram's mentor," Dlors blurted. She looked hesitantly from one to the other. "I'll get Bram," she said, and hurried out.

Arthe, sprawled in a fan-back seat, did not offer to rise. He took a sip of his drink as Voth started to unfold. Voth's partially extended petals closed again, though staying politely flared at the tops.

"I know of your work as an architect, Arthe Wulter Collin," the decapod said. "It is of interest."

Arthe's face flushed with pleasure, then tightened again. "It's not very practical, though, is it?" he said. "Not when you can biosculpt large structures cheaper than you can knock them together out of materials. And can't get enough of the materials, to boot. No, my real work's at the ethanol plant. Architecture's only a hobby." He took another sip of his drink. "All us humans have hobbies."

"The creation of habitats is not merely practical," Voth said. "We, too, see it as an art. And architecture is a human art. It is encouraged. Arthe Wulter Collin, you should go to your touch brothers and tell them of your need for materials."

"Haven't seen 'em for years," Arthe said. He changed the subject. "Come to take the kid someplace, have you?"

"He has expressed an interest in stellar objects," Voth said. "The lesser sun sets early at this season, and this will be a good night for viewing."

"Stargazing. Ah, well, I guess it's a stage most kids go through. I went through it myself. But there's not much use for human star travelers. Not when we wouldn't live long enough to reach most of the places you'd go to."

"No, but there is work for human astronomers. And some day, human beings will be with us at our farthest extent, though it will take many stages, many lifetimes, both human and Nar." The voice within grew more muffled. "We Nar have our limitations too."

"Ah, well, let the boy dream. When he grows up, he

might want to settle on Juxt One—if he's willing to spend ten years of his life getting there."

"You are fond of Bram?"

"He's a nice little kid. Quiet. No trouble."

Dlors came from an inner chamber, leading Bram by the hand. "I dressed him. It's a little chilly," she said. He was wearing a belted tunic of felted polymer with wide, elbow-length sleeves.

Seen together, the two showed little resemblance, though Dlors was his principal gene mother and the woman who had borne him. Her round face, thick blond hair, and blue eyes with their epicanthic folds were at odds with his dark, serious eyes and fine-boned facial architecture, though there was a premonition of Bram in the shape of her chin and the long sensitive hands. Before her figure had grown a bit too comfortable, Dlors had been a dancer, part of a company that had attempted to reinvent ballet.

"Voth!" Bram cried. He ran to the decapod, who swept him up in a nest of petals and gave him a hug.

"How would you like to stay up late tonight, Bram?" his custodian asked.

They were in a bubble car high over the coastal megacity. Bram twisted around in his seat to see the human compound, a pebbled polygon of dim chalky spherules and knobs interspersed with the queer new boxy shapes of the wood and stone buildings that the Reconstructionist architects, Arthe among them, were starting to put up. At this height and distance, the lightpoles at the squares and intersections were mere incandescent filaments. Bram tried to pick out his own home but could not.

Below the speeding bubble car and stretching far into

the distance, the coastal flats were cobbled with the tall calcified spirals of the Nar structures, connected by a lacework of fairy bridges and cambered roadways and beginning to glow with their own bioluminescence now that the sky was darkening. Glittering motes of light moved along the grid, and in the sky above, strings of illuminated bubble cars crawled along their invisible threads like translucent beads.

The real sun had set long ago, and the lesser sun was low over the edge of a glassy black sea, a brilliant topaz point that made the coiled spires of the city cast ghostly shadows across the miles. The brighter stars were already twinkling in the deepening sky, and the enormous blob of light known by Nar and humans alike as the Bonfire, with its bridge of blue stars and starfog, was growing brighter, dominating the night sky.

"Do you know what that is?" Voth said, sitting beside Bram with his lower limbs coiled into a ball that would fit in one of the cuplike seats.

"Sure, that's the Bonfire," Bram said. He was perched with his knees drawn up in the center of a seat that was too big for him, his attention transferred to the other passengers in the bubble car. They were mostly Nar, though there were a few humans who were traveling alone. One of them, trying to preserve his dignity in the yielding bowl that left his sandaled feet dangling, was a bald middle-aged man with a self-important expression. He carried a transparent portfolio stuffed with body-reader holos that proclaimed him to be one of those fortunates chosen to be an intern in some Nar enterprise.

"Can you guess what the Bonfire is made of?" Voth asked.

Bram squinted at the bright fog with its central blaze of

light. "It's clouds," he decided. He had an inspiration. "Of thousands and thousands of little biolights all coming together in the middle and getting squashed."

"It's made of stars, Bram. It's a collection of stars called a galaxy. And it's very close, as galaxies go."

The little boy gazed at the sky's other glory, the long luminous streamer with its embedded blue sparks that seemed to pour itself into the Bonfire.

"I guess I can see that, sort of," he said. "Where Skybridge comes out of it."

"Good guess, Bram," Voth said with an encouraging pat of a tentacle. "But actually, Skybridge is an arm of our own galaxy, and those stars you see aren't really in it. They're closer to us than Skybridge or the Bonfire—close enough to see them as individuals. A long, long time ago, we think, the Bonfire brushed past our own galaxy and pulled it out of shape and tore millions of stars away from us. Millions more young stars were born because of that encounter, and that's why Skybridge seems blue."

It was a marvelous idea. "Does our galaxy look like the Bonfire?" Bram said.

There was a startled twitch from Voth. The tentacle that rested lightly on Bram's forearm under the wide tunic sleeve generated a sensation of respect.

"That was a very big leap of the imagination, Bram. No, our galaxy managed to keep its shape better than the Bonfire did. We think it's a spiral—somewhat elongated and with sprung arms. But it must be a beautiful sight from outside." He hesitated. "We know that because the humans, long ago, had a name for it. They called it M-51, the Whirlpool. It was prominent among the sky objects described by them in their great message, part of a sort of orientation chart to help the recipients of that message pinpoint the human galaxy." He hesitated again. "You see, the message was not aimed directly at us. It was aimed at a great cluster of more than a thousand galaxies, to improve their odds. We happened to be in its path."

Bram hardly noticed the last part of what Voth had told him. A great rush of excitement had driven all thoughts but one from his head. He struggled with the new idea. "If—if they can see *us*, then we can see *them*!"

"Not *can* see us, Bram," Voth corrected. "*Could* see us. More than thirty-seven million years ago. And we can see them only as they *were*, thirty-seven million years ago. And not their suns or their worlds, only their galaxy—just as they, no matter how mighty their science, could not have seen any of the suns or worlds we now dwell on but only the object they called the Whirlpool. You remember what I told you about that before?"

The tremendous thought swirled round in Bram's head. "What does the human gal—galaxy look like?"

"Very much like ours. It's a spiral too."

Outside the crystal dome of the bubble car, full night had fallen. The lesser sun was finally below the horizon, and the three visible moons shed nowhere near as much light. The world had turned into a carpet of dappled silver overhung by a great black bowl pierced by stars.

"You're going to see it tonight, Bram," Voth went on. "Now that we're approaching the season when the lesser sun moves to the daytime sky, it's possible to see man's galaxy from a planet-based observatory. That's where I'm taking you now."

They had reached the mountains. The bubble car slowed on its gossamer cable as it drew near to the thick, squat pylon anchored in the slopes. There was a rustle of movement as the passengers began to uncoil their limbs and flow toward the exits. The bald-headed human with the holo portfolio slid from his cupped pedestal and stood up, glancing around the car to see if anyone had noticed his brief lapse of dignity.

Bram's attention was elsewhere. He was still looking out at the stars. They held a new meaning for him now.

The director hurried on arched legs toward them over the vast darkened expanse of the observatory floor, giving a welcoming hoot in the Small Language as he came.

"It is good of you to have us here, Director," Voth said aloud, for Bram's benefit, as the two decapods touched tentacle tips. The amount of fleshy interface was small, just enough surface area for the social amenities.

"Nonsense," the director said obligingly in the Small Language after a moment of silence in which he must have been speaking to Voth solely in the tactile mode. "We're always augmented by your presence, Voth-shr-voth. Is this the young person you spoke to me about?"

Bram politely presented his palms as the director, without moving physically, shifted his body-face toward Bram. The Nar never actually had to turn around the way humans did, though most of them had a preferential front. Bram, unlike a lot of human grown-ups he knew, could always tell which of the five sides of a Nar was facing "forward." The eyes in that direction seemed to have more expression, and, of course, there was more limb activity.

"Yes, this is Bram," Voth said, again supplementing his speech with words. "Bram, say hello to Pfaf-tlk-pfaf."

The director pressed a pair of dry, lifeless tentacle tips against Bram's palms. Most Nar found it hard to believe that humans got any input from the Great Language and involuntarily held themselves stiff until they got to know an individual human being well.

"Hello, young Bram," the director said in stilted Inglex, repeating it unnecessarily in Chin-pin-yin: "Ni hao, Bram-xiao."

"I am augmented to mesh, Pfaf-tlk-pfaf," Bram said respectfully, speaking in the pure Small Language with no human admixtures.

The director was half a tip shorter than Voth, and his outer skin was a younger yellow. "So you're the youngling who is interested in galaxies?" he said.

"Yes, Pfaf-tlk-pfaf," Bram said.

"We'll have something to show you shortly. In the meantime, why don't you have a look around the place? Jun Davd here will show you around."

A very tall human person with white hair and umber skin had appeared at the director's side. "Hello, Bram," he said with a nice smile.

Bram smiled back. He wondered how Jun Davd knew his name. The tall man took him by the hand and led him away. Voth and the director were deep in conversation, their tentacles melded up to what in human beings would have been the elbow, and the bifurcate tips of a second pair of limbs were beginning to quest toward contact.

"I hope I haven't disturbed your routines," Voth was saying, still speaking the Small Language in rough parallel to his real conversation. Nar did that all the time in the first stages of establishing intimacy. It was a throwback to a less civilized epoch of Nar development, when two primitive decapods, meeting for the first time on some tidal flat, would literally have sounded each other out before entrusting their tender inner parts to a stranger.

The director's Small Language was full of slips and elisions now that he was no longer vocalizing primarily for Bram's benefit. "Not in the least, Voth-shr-voth . . . scheduled anyway . . . optical monitoring . . . prime interest object . . . after all, first best proof . . . search . . . intelligent life . . . universe."

Voth replied, still eliding hardly at all: ". . . still kind of you to indulge us, Director. I am old . . . soon time to mate and die . . . I have adopted many human children over the centuries, but none has affected me as deeply as this boy, Bram. Perhaps–" There was the steam whistle sound of a Nar laugh. "Perhaps it is a side effect of beginning endocrine changes . . . prepare for maternal behavior–"

He broke off as he realized that Bram was still within earshot. Bram felt a tug on his hand. "Come on," Jun Davd said gently.

Bram didn't exactly understand everything that Voth was saying. He knew that Voth was talking about his own death. But there was no sadness in it. Instead, there was a sort of joy. The Nar didn't fear death the way human persons did—maybe because they lived for a thousand years or more. Whatever sadness there had been in Voth's tone had been reserved for Bram. But that was silly, Bram thought. *He* wasn't the one who was growing old.

"Have you ever been in an observatory before?" Jun Davd asked.

Bram shook his head.

"Most of the really important work is done in space or on the airless moons," Jun Davd explained. "But there's still plenty of work for a planet-based observatory. This is one of the biggest."

Bram could believe it. He and Jun Davd were mere specks in the immense perforated ball of the main chamber. It must have taken years to grow. Echoes bounced off the distant walls, and huge, spidery steel and polycarbonate structures rose out of the shadows. There were human figures in white smocks here and there, but most of the personnel were decapod. Jun Davd hurried Bram past a group of scientists having a conference; one of them was stretched out against the tilted star-shaped surface of a body reader, absorbing input from some instrument or other, while three more Nar, two of them wearing optical girdles, linked tentacles with him.

Jun Davd brought Bram to a halt on a balcony above a tremendous bowl of blue jelly. A great latticework cylinder enclosed them. Suspended high above the center of the bowl, almost close enough to touch, was a silver sphere the size of a young house.

"This is the big eye, Bram," Jun Davd said proudly. "With it, we can see far into the universe. There are bigger eyes in space—thin films stretched across thousand-meter hoops out there where gravity can't make them sag, but even so, they're not as good in some ways as this one. And they never will be until somebody figures out a way to develop a big bioreflector that will live in vacuum."

It really looked like an eye, Bram thought, with the small black circle stating out of the middle like a pupil. He said so to Jun Davd, who laughed.

"Oh, it's not an eye like yours or mine, Bram. That round thing in the center isn't a part of the living stuff. It's a well to let light through. There's a sheet of charge-coupled devices growing underneath in a nutrient solution. The eye itself is made of millions of tiny facets built up of alternating layers of cytoplasm and guanine crystals—on the same principle as the mirror optics of the Nar eye and the eyes of the other advanced life forms on this planet. In fact, Nar genetic material was the starting point. The layers have different refractive indexes. They're built up in stacks, each a given fraction of a particular wavelength of light. The eye responds to external stimuli and looks at what we tell it to."

"Could you ask it to show us something now?"

"Oh, no," Jun Davd said hastily. "I'm not allowed to touch it. You have to have an apprenticeship of a century or more to reach that level." He ran a hand ruefully through his white hair. "I'm not old enough to qualify. I'm afraid I never will be." He gave Bram his nice smile again, white teeth in a dark face, "I can show you something through the small refractor, though."

"Can I see Ilf?"

"Ilf's already set, I'm afraid. Along with its primary, the lesser sun."

"Oh." Bram was disappointed.

"You don't need a telescope to see Ilf, you know. At least, I'm sure *you* don't. My old eyes can't quite manage it anymore, It's the dimmer of the two stars near the lesser sun. The brighter star is the gas giant. They both shine brighter than they ordinarily would at that distance—almost as bright as some of the planets that belong properly to our own sun—because they reflect the lesser sun's light. You know they're planets, not stars, because sometimes they're on one side of the lesser sun and sometimes on the other. You see, in a double star system like ours, even the smaller sun can hang on to its own planets if their orbits are close enough and the bigger star is far enough away."

Bram paid courteous attention. When Jun Davd finished, he said, "I look for Ilf all the time. Voth showed me where it was. But he says that pretty soon I won't be able to see it anymore. Not till next winter, anyhow, I guess I was too little to remember about that from the year before."

"Why do you want to look at Ilf through a telescope, Bram?" Jun Davd asked.

"I thought maybe I could see people on it."

Jun Davd didn't laugh this time. "It's too far away to see the people walking around. It would look sort of like a big fuzzy ball."

"Could I see the people on Jumb? Jumb's closer."

"I see you know your subject, Bram," Jun Davd said gravely. "You're right, Jumb *is* closer. It's one of our own gas giants. Actually, there are no people on Jumb itself. They live on its moons."

"*Could* I?"

"No, Bram, I'm afraid not. Jumb would look like a fuzzy ball, too. Why are you so interested in seeing the people?"

Bram shuffled his feet. "I don't know."

"Come on, let's have a look anyway. Jumb's in the sky tonight, at least." He took Bram by the hand and led him to a small auxiliary structure growing out of the main ball.

Bram was somewhat mollified after having a look through Jun Davd's telescope. It was more like what he thought a telescope ought to be like, with a big long barrel and an eyepiece that you looked through squinty fashion, with one eye closed. Jun Davd showed him how to look through it after clearing away some equipment that, he said, had done enough work for now.

"Don't stare too long, Bram," he said. "Take short looks. Here, I'll set it up for you."

At first Bram didn't see anything. Then there was Jumb, no longer the familiar brilliant point of light in the sky but the fuzzy ball that Jun Davd had promised, as plain as anything once he got used to its jumping around like that.

"Do you see the moons, Bram?"

Bram caught his breath as he spotted the cluster of bright dots swimming next to the mottled face of the gas giant and realized that they were little worlds, worlds with human and Nar people living on them. There was a round black speck pasted on Jumb. After a moment his eye turned it into the shadow of another moon that he couldn't see, and in a bright flash of intuition he suddenly could appreciate the scale of what he was seeing.

"Would you like to see Juxt One, Bram?" Jun Davd asked. "There are people living there, too, almost a light-year away. Next to this world and Ilf, there are more human beings living there than any other place in the universe—thousands of them."

Bram tore his gaze away from the eyepiece and nodded dumbly.

"I'll have to show it to you on a screen. We can't see the actual light directly through a telescope like this, of course. I'm going to tap into a relay from the orbiting multiple-mirror telescope. They keep an eye on it all the time for the laser message traffic."

Jun Davd busied himself with a terminal that had been fitted out with buttons for human use. "All the mirrors gather photons and combine them into one computer-enhanced image," he said. "Human engineers contributed a lot to the system. We're considered to be very mechanical-minded, you know." There was a hint of the proprietary in his tone.

The screen lit up with a rather diffuse round glow, but Jun Davd seemed very pleased with it. "Watch," he said. He manipulated his terminal, and the glow seemed to coalesce and dim. It moved sideways off the screen, and after a moment a tiny irregular blob of light moved to the center of the screen from the other side.

"There you are, Juxt One!" Jun Davd said triumphantly. "You know, Bram, the Nar were awfully lucky in their choice of a planet to evolve on. They were able to learn star travel by easy steps. First, being part of a double star system with a companion only light-hours away. A companion star with its own habitable planet, Ilf, and a gas giant with seven decent-size moons more or less within the ecosphere. And then, when they were ready for the next big step, being blessed with another star system less than a light-year away. The average stellar distances in this part of the galaxy are four or five times that. But even a human being can get to Juxt within a reasonable fraction of a lifetime."

"Jun Davd, are there any human beings farther away than Juxt?"

"Hmm, yes, we've spread with the Nar to four or five of the nearer stars. And I'm sure that future generations of human beings will spread still farther from those foci. The Nar themselves now occupy a volume of space with a diameter of about a hundred light-years, and that's about the limit for them, even with their longer lifetimes. But as their outposts continue to develop the way Juxt One has, they'll serve as jumping-off points too. Why, in a million years they could even expand through the entire galaxy! And you can rest assured that wherever they go, they'll take human beings with them. Or grow a new crop of us."

"I'm going to go *myself*!" Bram exclaimed. He found Jun Davd's words disturbing, though he could not have said why.

Jun Davd smiled winningly. "Bram, Voth-shr-voth says you're very good at arithmetic for your age. Do you know how big a million is?"

"I guess so," Bram said unwillingly.

"Except for Juxt One, and maybe Next, you'd have to spend most of your life journeying even to the nearer inhabited stars, with no company except your ship-brothers. Almost all of the humans who live in those places were born and grew up there."

Bram wished he could close his ears and not hear what Jun Davd was saying, but he didn't want to hurt Jun Davd's feelings, so he gave him his full attention and said nothing.

"But the next best thing to going to the stars," Jun Davd went on, "is studying them. How would you like to be an astronomer when you grow up?"

"I guess it would be okay," Bram said.

"Voth-shr-voth thinks it might be a good profession for you."

Bram was surprised to hear that. Voth's own field was genetics, and if Bram had ever visualized an adult career for himself at all, he would have supposed that Voth would wish to take him under his own arm.

"Well, think it over," Jun Davd said. "You're welcome to come back and visit any time. We can talk, and we can look at the stars together. Would you like that?"

Bram nodded vigorously. "Yes," he said, meaning it.

There must have been some kind of signal then, because Jun Davd raised his head and said, "They're ready for us."

He brought Bram back to the balcony circling the big eye. The director and Voth were waiting there, along with a couple of young Nar assistants. The assistants must have just finished their lunch; one of them was bent over a piece of equipment, and Bram could see down along the insides of his tentacles, where successive waves of cilia marched systematically toward the central maw, brushing crumbs and food particles inward. No Nar would speak in the Great Language until he had finished grooming himself this way; it would be, Tha-tha had once explained, like a human person talking with his mouth full, very impolite. It was surprising, Bram thought, how dry and fluffy a Nar's inner surfaces could be within a minute or two of eating.

The director gave Bram a nod—actually a susurrated recognition signal in the Small Language—and said something to the assistant. With a last hasty sweep of food fragments, the assistant pressed a tentacle tip against a ciliated touch bar. There was a rumble of moving machinery overhead. Bram retreated to the shelter of Voth's folding petals. He looked around for Jun Davd, but the white-haired apprentice had melted away.

Down below, with shocking suddenness, the great bowl of blue jelly quivered once and turned a silvery white. It seemed to come alive like some kind of a creature trying to climb one side of the bowl to get at them. Bram wondered what would happen if someone fell into it. He shrank closer to Voth, and the soft mantle that wrapped him sent out waves of reassurance.

"Get me a focus star," the director said in the Small Language. "Let's use the point star in the constellation of the Boat."

The huge sphere suspended across from Bram seemed to writhe and shimmer. Bram jumped. And then the night sky appeared realistically within a hoop on the balcony. The director touched tips absentmindedly with Voth, and Voth translated: "We've put a secondary focus up here for the moment and generated an amplified image on the screen for the lad. But it's not really suitable for very faint objects. Once we zero in on our target, of course, the real work will go on below."

"What does he mean?" Bram whispered.

"He means that we'll see what the big eye sees," Voth whispered back, "but it will be by secondhand light."

The assistant had one of his waistline eyes screwed up against a tube. The bright star in the middle of the hoop bobbed around, then settled down and began to drift off-screen. A collection of indistinct lights swam into view on the screen, and the director took over the controls from the assistant.

"This was their local group of galaxies," the director said. "It's smaller than our own local group. Basically it consists only of two spiral galaxies bound gravitationally to one another, each with its attendant swarm of satellite galaxies."

He made a fine adjustment, and the image sharpened. Bram could see the two spirals, like tiny glowing coiled springs, surrounded by hazy dots.

"They had a name for our own local group, or rather the constellation it appeared in from their point of view," the director went on. "They called it the Hunting Dogs."

Bram whispered to Voth again, and the director said, "That's all right, youngster. What did you want to know?"

"What's a dog?" Bram said in a small voice.

"It was another life form that the humans bred for companionship and various simple chores. We gather that it was intelligent but not as intelligent as Man."

"Did they make them?"

"We don't know," the director said impatiently. "We think they may have been adapted from an existing life form."

"There are dogs mentioned in human literature, Bram," Voth said. "You'll read about them when you grow older."

"The human radio beacon was not aimed at us here in

the Dogs," the director continued. "It was aimed beyond us at a very large cluster of galaxies in a constellation they called Virgo." He paused. "Virgo was their term for a being who has not yet attained the female reproductive stage." There must have been some kind of a warning signal from Voth; Bram could feel its echo in the swish of cilia in the arm that enfolded him. The director hurried on. "The Virgo cluster of galaxies consists of well over a thousand galaxies, and we believe it to be the center of a supercluster of which our local group and the human local group are outriders. So the humans did a very intelligent thing. Can you guess what that is?"

"They wanted to send their message to a whole lot of galaxies all at the same time," Bram said promptly.

"Exactly right, young Bram," the director said with a pleased expression. "You were right about him, Voth-shr-voth." The two mirror eyes aimed in Bram's direction turned blue again. "That beam of radio waves will keep spreading outward for tens of millions of years, and they wanted it to encounter the greatest possible number of galaxies. Here, I think we can hold this image while I show you the Virgo cluster. It's in our daytime sky now, on the opposite side of the world, but one of our orbiting telescopes will have it in view."

He spoke to his assistant. A moment later, to Bram's consternation, the wriggly glowworms on the screen snapped out of existence, and the hoop was filled with a spectacular shower of sparks and flares.

"The richest imaginable target," the director said. "That one elliptical galaxy in the center alone contains three thousand billion suns, compared to our paltry two hundred billion, in addition to a halo of ten thousand globular clusters. The humans, long ago, would have had much the same view we're seeing now, but from almost twice as far away. The human radio waves haven't reached it yet. They won't for another thirty million years."

To Bram's relief he switched back to the other side of the sky. The human galaxy was still there, one of those bright midges.

"The larger of the two is the one they called Andromeda," the director said. "It's the other one we want."

The image centered and grew in swoops, becoming alternately blurred and sharp as the director adjusted his focus. At last it filled the hoop, a jeweled whorl with an incandescent center. Bram remembered that the jewels would be foreground stars, but that did not detract from the splendor of the vision. He drowned himself in it, lost in wonder.

"We're seeing their galaxy almost head on, as they must have seen us." The director's voice seemed to buzz from a distance. "That was a piece of luck for us. They were very sensibly transmitting in a direction at right angles to the plane of their galaxy, and for our part, we didn't have to look through our own spiral arms. We were in the early stages of our own project to search for life in the universe. We'd already tried hundreds of individual stars in our own galaxy, without success. The giant radio array on our fourth moon was newly in place. And then the project astronomer suggested that we try listening to whole galaxies instead of eavesdropping on stars one at a time. His reasoning was that an entire galaxy would be within the field of view of the array and could be considered as a single source. If an artificial radio signal was on the right wavelength and powerful enough, it would outshine all other radio energy on that particular frequency. We would be listening, in effect, to two hundred billion stars at once."

The director touched Bram, remembered that he was a human child, and withdrew the tentacle. "The human signal was detected almost at once, in the middle of what proved to be a fifty-year cycle," he went on in a Small Language patois that was heavily laced with Inglex. "Ironically, it was not the human galaxy that the radio telescope was aimed at. It was Andromeda. Andromeda was a more attractive target. It has more stars. But Andromeda proved to be close enough. At thirty-seven million light-years, even the tightest of beams spreads out quite a bit. The energy that would have been required to transmit such a signal was enormous. We think they must have enclosed a star and turned it into a modulated radio emitter. We can't imagine how they were able to do such a thing, or what motives inspired them to allocate such a wealth of energy to their testament."

Voth's grip tightened on Bram. The director's voice had pity in it. Bram tore his eyes away from the coiled blob of light on the screen and looked at the director, who stood tiptoe in a quintuple arch, the petals of his upper structure radiating tact.

"For testament it proved to be," the director said. "Over the next century, a complete cycle was heard and then half of another repeat with new data added, and then it stopped. Stopped in midsentence, as it were. And in the centuries since, the signal never has resumed."

He sighed. "We never found evidence of intelligent life in the universe again. Perhaps it's an extremely rare event. There's us and there were the humans, so far away, and now they're gone."

Bram could tell the precise moment when he was seeing the human galaxy by secondhand light. There was a brief winkout and an almost imperceptible change in image brightness, and then the picture of that vortex of stars stood motionless and lifeless within the hoop as some computer downstairs compensated for the bobbing image and held the cheating replica steady in its frame. The director said something to one of the assistants with a brief clasp of tentacles, and the assistant went pinwheeling down the steps.

"No," Bram burst out. "We're *not* gone, and someday we're going to go back!"

"Bram!" Voth said, shocked. "Don't contradict Pfaf-tlk-pfaf."

"It's all right, Voth-shr-voth," the director said. "I understand." To Bram he said kindly, "Didn't Jun Davd explain about stellar distances? In time, in millions of years if we last that long as a species, we might conceivably explore our galaxy. But we can never cross the gulf between galaxies."

"We can," Bram said, starting to cry. "Yes, we can."

"He's cranky," Voth apologized. "It's past his bedtime." The warm petals caressed Bram. "You must give up these thoughts, little one," came the soft whisper. "Be happy in your life here."

He picked the child up. "Say good-bye to Pfaf-tlk-pfaf," he said.

"Good-bye, Pfaf-tlk-pfaf," Bram said obediently.

"Good-bye, Bram," the director said. "Come see us again."

As Voth was about to leave, the assistant whom the director had dispatched downstairs returned with a little horny flake smaller than Bram's fingernail.

"This is for you, Bram," the director said. "We thought you might like to have it. It's a little patch of the charge-coupled surface that was changed by light from the galaxy you saw. Perhaps, just perhaps, one of the photons that crossed that thirty-seven-million-year gulf came from the human sun."

CHAPTER 2

The young man and the young woman hurried across the plaza to catch up to the stragglers who were still trickling into the great humped vault of the auditorium. It was a glorious summer evening, with the air so clear and pure that even the lesser sun could not drown out the brighter stars. The Bonfire was visible as a pale wash against the heavens, fed by the gauzy streamer that was Skybridge.

"We'll miss the beginning," Mim said, hauling Bram energetically by the arm. She was a small vivid girl with a tiny waist and choppy black hair and a pale face that made her dark eyes more emphatic.

"No, we won't," Bram said. "They're still going in."

He had almost finished his growth that year; he had turned into a lean, long-boned youth with perhaps another inch or two of height to go. He had kept the slender hands and feet of his childhood and retained a tumble of brown hair that kept falling into his eyes because it was still too fine.

"Anyway," he finished, "I got here as soon as I could."

"Where were you? At that observatory again?" she asked, her eyes still fixed on the distant goal of the entrance. She gave his arm an impatient tug.

"Yes," he said.

He left it at that. He was not ready to talk about it yet. He had a lot of thinking to do before he made his decision.

They joined the fringe of the crowd that was climbing the broad spiral ramp. Bram glanced around at the throng. A lot of people had made a special effort to dress up for tonight's event in bright, festive clothes—multicolored tunics, gaudy jerkins showing puffed sleeves, kirtles with scalloped hems or complicated flounces, slinky gowns beaded with lenticular eyes that winked on and off, and even a few togas inspired by the previous Tenday's performance of Julius Caesar. Bram felt out of place in the old mono he had been wearing all day.

Even some of the Nar who were sprinkled throughout the assemblage had made an attempt to dress in imitation of human styles. Bram saw iridescent kilts draped around decapod waists, belted just below the row of primary eyes, and five-holed ponchos that must have been uncomfortable around the tentacle roots and that certainly must have interfered with intimate conversation.

"Just think of it!" Mim said, her face glowing. "The first performance of the Ravel quartet! And played on real wooden instruments instead of a synthesizer!"

Bram smiled weakly, trying to muster a show of enthusiasm for Mim's benefit. He liked music all right—especially the kind where people got together and sang—though he found it hard to understand some of the reconstructions and experiments the music department came up with. The Ravel quartet, he gathered, fell somewhere within the

41

twentieth-century hiatus or close to it. But he was willing to sit tamely through an evening of cacophony to stay in Mim's good graces.

"It's a joint project with the physics department," Mim prattled on cheerfully. "We've been working on it with them for almost three years now."

Mim was a music student and used the possessive "we" in talking about all of her department's activities, though she could hardly have been more than a novitiate when the Ravel quartet had been unearthed in a mass of unprocessed data. Bram didn't know whether to envy the music students or feel sorry for them. On the one hand, they had chosen a field of endeavor that the Nar could not dominate. On the other hand, they had forever ghettoized themselves within a synthetic human culture and withdrawn from participation in society as a whole.

"It sounds very interesting," he said with careful tact.

"Interesting?" she teased him. "You're hopeless! It's a breakthrough! We've got the *notation* for hundreds and hundreds of musical compositions, of course, and we've always been able to use a synthesizer to approximate the *sounds* of the most common musical instruments from the few recorded samples we've analyzed—the two Brandenburg Concertos, for instance, and the Beethoven symphony. We don't know what a piano looked like, but we know that violins and cellos were hollow resonating bodies made of wood. The physics department worked out the acoustics and made some prototypes on computerized lathes. It's going to be a whole new era in music. Direct production of sound! No more keyboards between you and the notes. I'm thinking of changing my field of study."

"What's the point?" he said. "Wooden instruments already exist." Arthe had one that he had carved himself out of vacuum poplar, and he used it to accompany himself in songfests.

"Those simple strumming things!" she exclaimed impatiently. "You don't understand. We've worked out the physics of the *bowed* string."

"What's that?"

"You scrape an abrasive element across a taut string and get a continuous vibration."

"Sounds unpleasant. Like a fingernail on slate."

"It's more *expressive*! Oh, you're being impossible, Brambram. I've heard it at some of the rehearsals. Four of our best virtuosos have been practicing with the new instruments for *months* now! Just wait till you hear them!"

Bram retreated hastily. The one thing he did not want to do was get Mim annoyed with him. He thought she was the most exquisite creature he had ever met. She was a year older than he was, and he had hardly been able to believe his good luck when she had shown an interest in him; not when she was surrounded by older fellows who had already chosen their careers and had important things to talk about. He was desperate to impress her. Sometimes, though he had no idea if their gene maps were compatible, he had fantasies that she would choose him to bond with her.

"Oh, look!" she cried as they spilled through into the inner amphitheater with the mostly human tide. "Isn't one of those Nar waving at you?"

Bram looked across at the upper level of curving tiers and saw Tha-tha with a group of older Nar. One of his tentacles was raised in imitation of the human gesture. Bram waved back.

"Who was that!" Mim said.

"One of my touch brothers," he said. He felt embarrassed, and he didn't know why.

43

"I seem to see less and less of my own touch brothers these days," Mim said. "We try to keep up but—you know!" She shrugged. "They don't really understand what I'm *doing*! Oh, they know that music is important to us humans, and they have an abstract grasp of what it's all about, and they *say* all the right things. I *know* they have a sense of pitch—at least they can sing a simple tune on key, sort of. But I always have this feeling that they're, I don't know, *indulging* me. You know, like when you're a little kid and you take off your clothes and you stretch out on a body reader and you let it tickle you all over. Did you ever do that? And you tell your tutor that you're reading and you make up a story, and he makes believe you really *are* reading. *That's* what it's like."

Bram nodded. "I know what you mean."

Except for Tha-tha, he was no longer close to any of his touch brothers. As their command of adult speech had become surer, they had grown beyond him. They still made an effort to see him occasionally, but more and more they presented their smooth outer surfaces to him and spoke to him in the Small Language as if he were a fingerling. Only Tha-tha, once in a while, still unfolded to him and shared something of his increasingly incomprehensible Nar life with him in the familiar bastard blend of Small Language, inarticulate physical contact, and pidgin Inglex that had served them while they were growing up together.

Tha-tha, Bram knew, had given his life to the tactile art form that, for the Nar, was poetry, symphony, and saga all rolled into one. Tha-tha's teachers thought he had talent. He might make a name for himself someday. But there were no words for the things that fired Tha-tha's imagination in the masterpieces he admired or for what he was trying to accomplish himself, though he tried diligently to find analogies to make Bram understand.

Bram's relationship with Voth was growing more formal, too. Voth was still bound to him as tutor and guardian and still took an affectionate interest in him. But the physical signs of his approaching reproductive stage and ultimate dissolution were already beginning to show; the change couldn't be more than a decade or two away now. Voth was becoming increasingly autumnal, preoccupied and mellow.

Partly, Bram told himself guiltily when he thought about it at all, it was his own fault. When you got older, there were just so many things to *do*! Human friends to spend time with, places to go, things to see. And there was Mim.

"There are two seats over there," Mim said, pulling him by the hand. "Hurry up before somebody else takes them."

They squeezed their way down the rows of extruded benches and sat down. The cavernous space, all bleached undulating surfaces that grew into each other, was crammed with more than two thousand humans—an impressive percentage of the human population of the megacity—and probably two or three hundred Nar. Some dozens of both phyla in the audience had come from other cities on the continent for this premiere performance.

"Look," Mim said, her eyes on the raised elliptical stage in the center of the auditorium.

Bram dutifully followed her gaze. The musicians had not yet arrived, but their instruments had already been set up. Bram saw four unimpressive wooden boxes resting on low tables, with a stool behind each one.

"The big one's the cello," Mim said. "The two small ones are the violins, and the medium-size one is the viola."

He and Mim were sitting high enough up so that he

could see the tops of the boxes; each had an oval hole in the lid and a couple of dozen wires or strings stretched between a curved bridge at one end of the box and a row of pegs at the other. A peculiar-looking three-toothed metal rake ran on a sliding track over the strings, just forward of the pegged end; it was connected by a system of levers to a set of seven foot-treadles.

Most puzzling of all was the pair of devices laid out on each stool. Each consisted of a small wheel mounted in a kind of haft that ended in a trigger grip. A cord snaked from the handle to a power source. The odd object reminded Bram of one of Arthe's power tools for woodworking.

"Where are the keyboards?" Bram said. He was thinking of the symphony concerts he had attended, big affairs requiring ten or fifteen musicians. The cello—or cello "section," as they called it for symphonies—was always controlled by a musician at a synthesizer keyboard, as were the violin and viola "sections."

"Didn't you listen?" she exclaimed in exasperation. "There *are* no keyboards! This is *real* music!"

Bram shrugged. The symphonies had seemed real enough to him, but he was not about to risk an argument with Mim.

Mollified, she went on. "Each instrument has twenty-one strings—one for each of the seven notes of the diatonic scale over a three-octave range. There are three frets for each string. For naturals, sharps, or flats. So that by pressing the proper foot pedal—with your heel to lower a tone or your toe to raise it—you can get the complete chromatic scale." She frowned. "In equal-temperament tuning, of course. Actually, for example, an F sharp and a G flat aren't exactly the same note. We think Original Man must have had some way of getting around the problem. But the department's working on it."

"Sounds awfully complicated. Why not a separate string for each note?"

She was pleased at his interest. "That was one of the original proposals. But they decided it would make the instruments too cumbersome, too unwieldy to play. You'd be surprised at how nimble a real virtuoso can be at operating those frets. Of course, there are some double and triple stop combinations that are impossible, but we edited the score slightly where those cropped up. I don't think Ravel would have minded."

The musicians were filing on stage now, four men in roomy drawers and sleeveless singlets that wouldn't hamper their arm movements, and the audience burst into applause. The Nar in the upper tiers courteously imitated the motions of clapping, though they produced no sound.

Mim leaned closer to Bram, her mouth next to his ear to make herself heard amidst the tumult, and he could not help thinking about how pleasant it was to have another human body pressed against his. Even though, the bitter thought intruded, it provided only the illusion of communication, not the real thing that the Nar had.

"Somebody on the committee," she finished hastily, "even made the suggestion that Original Man might not have used frets at all. That the instrument he called a violin, whatever it looked like, might have had only three or four strings and that he produced the full range of notes by finger action. But that's ridiculous. How could you produce all the notes accurately in a rapid passage without frets? It would take years of practice."

The applause died down as the musicians picked up the little motorized disks and sat down. Bram recognized the cellist. He was Olan Byr, the concerto specialist. Most virtuosi gave a lot of solo concerts, leaning heavily on the ancient piano repertoire interlarded with one-man assaults on orchestral favorites. But not Olan Byr. His trademark was instruments that played only one note at a time, like the flute or the violin or the horn. His public adored him. He had spent hundreds of hours analyzing the sine waves of all the old instrumental samples in the archives and programmed his keyboard to produce sounds that, it was sworn, could be matched by no other living musician. He had disappeared from public view some months ago, and now the mystery was solved. He had been practicing on these queer, new, crude instruments.

The music began. Bram was pleasantly surprised. After the first gossamer moments he decided that it was going to be pretty, after all, and he settled down to enjoy it. Mim turned an I-told-you-so face toward him and squeezed his hand.

Partly it was the music itself that stirred him. It was nothing like the robust energy of Beethoven or the simple modal harmonies of the twenty-sixth-century neoteric composer Nakusome—up until now two of Bram's favorites. Ravel was complex and elusive, full of shifting tone colors and tenuous harmonies that made sprays of pure sound. It had been part of a short-lived movement going by the odd name of Impressionism, Mim had told him. Bram could not understand why it had lain in storage for so long.

But it was the performance that really astonished him. He could hardly believe that these sweating, athletic men in their singlets, wielding their clumsy motorized disks with two-handed agility, were producing the shimmering fantasy he was listening to. The expression and the loudness, he supposed, could be varied by changing the speed of the spinning wheel and the pressure applied to the strings. In addition, he noticed that Olan Byr in particular had worked out little tricks of technique, like touching the strings with the wheel at an angle or letting the wheel bounce lightly off the string. At several points he and the other players, without letting go of the handles, actually plucked the strings with extended forefingers, then returned smoothly to the "bowed" mode. The few wrong notes or occasional ugly scrapings hardly mattered. The performance was a miracle. There was a life and immediacy to it that could not be matched by computer-generated sound, no matter how perfect.

The audience shared his perception. At the finish of the quartet's final section they stood up spontaneously, clapping wildly and cheering. Bram clapped with them till his hands hurt.

Mim's face was radiant. "Weren't they wonderful?" she shouted in his ear. "Didn't Olan have a marvelous legato?"

Bram didn't know what a legato was, but he agreed that the concert had been wonderful. Was this the kind of music the human race had enjoyed thirty-seven million years before? Clearly, human beings were still groping their way toward the legacy of Original Man. How much more still lay neglected in the archives? Tonight's performance proved that they hadn't yet assimilated it all.

At last the audience reluctantly let the musicians go and began to file toward the exits. Mim took Bram by the arm.

"Come on," she said. "There's a reception. The biology department's supposed to have some sort of surprise. And you'll have a chance to meet Olan and the others."

"The first terrestrial life form was the potato," the portly man in the green toga was saying. "So of course the Nar had considerable experience working with potato genes before going on to attempt the recreation of other earthly organisms. By the time they got around to resurrecting *us*, a firm foundation was laid."

He was holding forth to a considerable audience. His listeners hung on his every word, clustering closely in a semicircle that blocked the way to the long table with the goodies.

"So," he continued loftily, "we had several centuries worth of experience to draw on. To this day our beginning agriengineering students generally start with the potato. It's extremely easy to clone."

Bram and Mim edged through the crowd, trying to reach the table. Mim was distracted. She kept looking for the musicians, but they hadn't put in an appearance yet.

"Who's that?" she whispered.

Bram was surprised at her ignorance. "Willum-frth-willum," he said. "The overman of the bio department."

"Oh," she said, impressed. Only a handful of humans could claim Nar honorifics in their names. "I know who he *is*," she said defensively. "I just didn't know that was *him*."

"He was an associate in the Nar touch group that worked out the nucleotide sequence for the synthetic monofilament virus," Bram said, showing off his knowledge. Voth's touch group had been part of the same team. "But he gave it all up to run the human department here in the Compound."

"Oh," she said. "He didn't turn Schismatist, did he?"

Bram had no interest in politics. "No, he's a true-blue Partnerite. I guess he just wanted to be a big wiggler in a small pool."

Willum-frth-willum had paused to select some kind of biological artifact from a basket proffered by one of the student helpers. The object was a bright red globe with a little cluster of green tentacles on top.

"There are plenty to go round," the overman said. "So help yourselves."

"Excuse me, but that doesn't look like any potato variation *I've* ever seen," said one of Willum-frth-willum's admirers, a mauve-dyed woman in a five-pointed yellow cape that made her look like a wilted Nar.

"It's not," the portly man said smugly. "We worked backward from potato genes to create another plant in the same family. The nightshade family, as the archives call it." He paused for dramatic effect. "We believe it's a 'tomato,' or something very close to it."

"Excuse me," said a worried-looking man with the bent shoulders of a scholar, "but isn't that *'deadly'* nightshade?"

"The ripe fruit's quite safe, I assure you," Willum-frth-willum said with a condescending smile. "The alkaloids in this particular family are concentrated in the foliage. In fact, we've been isolating medically useful alkaloids from altered leaf protoplasts for several generations—things like atropine and scopolamine and the belladonna that some of the ladies use to make their eyes more beautiful. At present, we're working to duplicate another potato relative—an herb called tobacco, which seems to have disappeared after the twenty-third century but which some of the earlier literature describes as beneficial."

"What did you call it?" somebody called out. "A tomato?"

"Yes."

"Well, whatever it is, we're all indebted to the bio department," the mauve-haired woman said firmly. "Any addition to the human diet is welcome. Food seems so *dull* and *repetitive* sometimes! Not," she added hastily, "that the bio department hasn't done *wonders* during our lifetime!"

"You must remember," Willum-frth-willum said rather

stiffly, "that my predecessors and I have been limited to the genetic codes for the thirty basic human food crops that were originally transmitted some centuries ago. Thirty, that is, if you want to include bacterial protein and heterochronic eggs. I'd also like to point out that we've mostly been on our own in these projects. The Nar regard the human diet as adequate. Adding novelties to it has a low priority for them."

"Yes, yes, of course," the mauve-haired lady agreed. "We're all very grateful, as I said."

About a dozen people had acquired the red globes from the baskets being circulated by the students, and were holding the strange fruits doubtfully.

"How do you eat it?" a brave soul inquired.

"Just bite into it," the overman said. "It's an acquired taste, I'm afraid, but our culinary experts think it might be useful in cooking."

"I'll get you one," Bram said to Mim, and plunged into the crowd. He came back a moment later with two of the fruits.

She took a suspicious bite and made a face. "It tastes a little . . . I don't know . . . acid," she pronounced. "I was expecting it to be sweet."

Bram bit into his own tomato. To his embarrassment, it squirted juice and little seeds that dribbled down his chin. Surreptitiously, he wiped it off with the sleeve of his mono, but Mim didn't seem to have noticed his clumsiness. She was looking around again for the musicians.

He got two goblets of some pale fizzy stuff, at the risk of being told by the gray-haired lady who was ladling it out that he was too young for the spiked punch, and he and Mim drifted away from the buffet into the thick of the party. He could hear the arguments about the tomato going on in his wake: "... think they must have made a sort of wine out of it." And: "... know for a fact from a mid-Inglex reference that they used it in their social rituals, like throwing it at the stage to indicate disapproval of a theatrical performance."

Mim, still looking around, collided with someone disengaging himself from another group, but held on to her drink without spilling it.

"Oops, sorry," he said, apologizing first. He was a stocky, muscular man with blue-black locks and thick, cursive features.

"Hello, Dal," she said. "This is Bram."

"Hello, Bram," the man said without much interest. He turned back to Mim. "Did you get your tomato?"

"Yes. How about you?"

"I'm going to wait. Till I see if there are any survivors."

Mim laughed, and a jealous stab went through Bram. Dal was older, established, confident-looking, and he seemed to know Mim very well.

"How did you like the music tonight?" Dal asked her.

"It was a tremendous success. It's going to start a craze for Impressionism. I'll bet all the composers will be writing in that style for *months!*"

"My impression exactly. Why do you suppose it stayed on the shelf for so long?"

Bram felt ignored. He tried to look knowledgeable and interested as they talked on about music.

"I suppose they didn't realize it *was* music at first, and then it got put aside and lost for a while," Mim said seriously. "Repetitive patterns and voice imitations wouldn't have been easy to pick out of all the coloristic effects, would they? That's why music began with counterpoint. Original Man was clever. The first music he sent was Bach.

The Art of the Fugue. Even the Nar recognized it as some kind of art form." She gave a tinkling laugh that squeezed at Bram's heart. "I believe they first tried a readout on a touch machine. Then somebody noticed similar patterns of imitation and repetition in the fugal movement of the recorded transmission of the Second Brandenburg, and they assigned pitch and duration to the symbols. After that, decoding Beethoven was easy."

"Is that from the music history course, little Mim?" Dal teased her.

She blushed, and Bram felt younger than ever compared to a rival who could make Mim, with her formidable mettle, do *that*.

"Yes," she admitted.

Dal let her off the hook, treating her as a grown woman again. "Is there any more Ravel waiting to be reconstituted, do you think?"

"No, that was the only sample."

"Pity. I'm going to need some incidental music for my new verse play. Something novel. A Ravel that no one's heard yet would have been perfect."

"You could arrange with the music department to have something composed in the same style."

"Yes, I could do that." He didn't seem pleased by the idea.

A florid man from the adjacent group had been eavesdropping. "What are you going to spring on us this time, Dal? Are you going to try to top *Quixote Sobre Las Estrellas?*"

Dal laughed. "No, I'm staying in the mainstream. If Inglex was good enough for Shakespeare and Jarn Anders, it's good enough for me."

Bram thought that Dal sounded piqued. The neo-Cervantist play had been the hit of the season. It had been written entirely in Spanish, a proto-Inglex dialect that not more than a few dozen people in the audience understood despite all the twenty-first-century loan words that had given it a second rebirth in mid-Inglex. The play had been a huge success nevertheless; the force of the performance had carried it along even when the meaning was obscure.

"Glad to see that you're taking it so well, amigo-san," the florid man said mockingly.

"I agree with Dal," said a thin woman in a long skirt and dickey. "Basically we're firmly rooted in the mid-Inglex culture, anchored by Shakespeare and Chaucer at one end and Anders and Tsukada at the other. That's our seedbed. Our own culture—what we've produced in the last twenty generations and what we'll produce in the thirty centuries to come—will flower from the diversity that's been laid down for us."

"I'd hardly call Jarn Anders a mid-Inglex author," put in a long-nosed, saturnine man in a kilt that did not quite conceal the beginnings of a potbelly. "Properly, he belongs to the beginning of the transitional—Inglex period. And Chaucer? Really, Alis, my dear! He came with a translation, like *Beowulf* and the rest of the pre-Inglex samples."

"You know what I mean, Pers-Morley," the thin woman said impatiently. "I'm saying that Inglex hardly changed at all after the last great influx of Japanese and Chinese and Arabic and Spanish loan words in the twenty-first and twenty-second centuries. And that it held onto its roots—because Shakespeare and the King James Bible continued to be the standard for the proselyte Inglex-speakers who were being absorbed into the growing stream. Already by their twentieth century, Inglex was the second most widely spoken language in the human culture, and other speakers accommodated themselves to it rather than the other way around. It was the language of commerce, and even the Sovs, a great rival power of the time, taught their schoolchildren to speak it. And of course, by that time printing and the electronic media had pretty well frozen it into a semipermanent matrix that could have been understood by any Inglex speaker from"—she glared challengingly at the potbellied man—"Chaucer's time to—to the last centuries we have a record of."

Mim nudged Bram. "That's Alis Tonia Atli. Isn't she wonderful? She wrote the most *beautiful* historical romance about early times, the first breeding generation when there were only a few score people in the world. *The Fledgling Hearts,* it's called. It's sort of like *Romeo and Juliet,* about two lovers with *totally* incompatible gene maps who aren't allowed to contribute to the same genome and live on in it. It's on lit net—you really ought to punch yourself out a copy." She glanced admiringly at the thin woman. "There are some who say that she's a militant Resurgist, but I don't care."

"She sounds very brilliant," Bram said miserably. He could feel himself shrinking into insignificance in this company. But at least the muscular playwright, Dal, had turned his attention away from Mim.

"What about Chin-pin-yin?" somebody protested to Aris. "Chinese, they called the twentieth-century form. That was the *most* widely spoken human language. You can't ignore it. Original Man certainly didn't when he made it a part of us. All of us speak it to some degree."

"It may have been the most *prevalent* human language," Alis conceded, "but it didn't travel well. By the time a phonetic notation came along to freeze it into the form we know today, it was already top-heavy with circumlocutions borrowed from western concepts. The grammar's

56

simple, granted—simpler for us to learn as children than Inglex. It's marvelous for telling stories and for being ambiguous when you don't want to come right out and say something. But the number of word roots was too limited for the technological age, even with a lot of ingenious coinage, and with the mass education that came along in the twentieth and twenty-first centuries, the whole society became bilingual. The second language of choice, of course, being Inglex. Inglex simply swallowed everything up. And with Inglex went the western culture that had produced it."

"Alis is right," a new voice said. Bram recognized Olan Byr. The cellist had changed from his sweaty singlet to a crisp blouse and pantalets. His dark hair was wet. "The same principle holds true for music. The western forms simply absorbed the eastern forms. By the time of the period she's talking about, Japanese musicians were abandoning *gagaku* music in favor of Mozart string quartets, committees of Chinese composers were writing piano concertos in the western romantic idiom, and India was contributing symphony conductors to the Inglex-speaking world."

"Hold on there a minute, Olan," said a young man who looked like one of Mim's music-student friends. "You can't write off everything else that way. What about Balinese music? Arab music? Indian *gita* and *vadya*, for that matter. We don't have many samples, I admit, but—"

"My point exactly," the cellist said. "We *don't* have many samples. Oh, our designers made an *effort* to transmit a broad spectrum of human culture, if only to define the full range of what was human. Just as, for the same reason, all of us contain a panracial assortment of genes. But pentatonic scales and ornamented monody and Arab *maqams* that stray from the natural harmonics were cultural dead ends. Frozen artifacts."

"Hold it right there, Olan," the young man began hotly. "The number of mathematical combinations possible in a typical *maqam*—"

"No, you hold it," the cellist went on smoothly. "At your age I was convinced that there was an unrealized universe in the Robertsbridge Codex, our only example of primitive organ music. But the point is that the universe *was* realized by Bach. In the same way, your pet eastern scales and rhythms are *already* in our mainstream as exotic elements. No, my young friend, our cultural center in music will always hover around Bach and Beethoven, just as in language it will always hover around Shakespeare. That's why we *do* have so many samples of *them.*"

Mim, who had been listening with growing absorption, broke in. "And there's so much that's missing, even there! We have only *eight* Beethoven sonatas! We know there were at least thirty-two. We've got *twelve* preludes and fugues from *The Well-Tempered Clavier.* We know there were forty-eight. We—" She broke off as she saw all the eyes looking at her.

"No, go on, Mimsy," Olan said. He helped her out. "We have only *one* Beethoven symphony because it takes more data bits to transmit an orchestral score than a piano piece or a string quartet. That's why I've orchestrated all the sonatas."

Mim might have been a little flustered by the glittering, older company, but she was not shy. Bram felt a thrill of admiration as she held her own.

"I was just thinking," she said sadly, "of all the treasures we'll never know."

"We'll make new treasures of our own, Mimsy," Olan said. Bram did not care for the way he smiled at her.

"You musicians think you have reason to feel sorry for yourselves?" The speaker was a weedy red-haired individual who evidently had spent some time around the punch bowl. "How would you like to be a painter? *We* have nothing to go on except cartoons—about two thousand digital excuses for line drawings to represent fifteen thousand years of art, from the cave paintings on! That comes to about thirteen per century. With digital codes for approximate masses of color, very helpfully keyed to wavelengths of light—never mind what kind of a sun we're living under! And then, just to break our hearts, the Big Twelve in full color transmission! One Giotto, one Rembrandt, one van Gogh, one Picasso, and so forth. All chosen by committee and guaranteed to be Great! In all the marvelous wealth of detail that a couple of thousand scanning lines can achieve. If you don't care about small details like brush strokes, that is."

He touched off another argument. A partisan of Homer started to complain about the fact that the *Odyssey* had been transmitted only in Inglex translation, though it was possible to read *The Divine Comedy, Faust,* and *Don Quixote* in their original languages. "Surely Homer is one of the great engines of our culture, just as Dante, Goethe, and Cervantes are!" he appealed.

Mim took the opportunity to pull Bram closer to Olan Byr. "Olan," she said, "this is my friend Brambram."

Olan was gracious. "How do you do, Bram. You're not a music student. I'm sure I'd know you. What's your field of interest? You're not interning in lit, are you?"

"Well, I haven't exactly settled on anything yet," Bram said self-consciously.

Olan raised his eyebrows in surprise. "Well, there's no hurry, of course. Our music students seem to find themselves rather early in life, but Dal Terson, just to take one example, knocked around for years before he decided that he wanted to be a playcrafter."

"I'm—I'm sort of interested in astronomy," Bram said with a sidelong glance at Mim.

Olan's face lost some of its geniality and became merely polite. "Oh, science," he said. "Well, there's nothing wrong with that. The science devotees have made any number of valuable contributions to the human family. The tomato, for instance."

"Yes, everybody's talking about those," Mim said helpfully.

"Just so. If you *are* interested in science," Olan said kindly, "why don't you go in for bioengineering? Astronomy is so . . . so *abstract*. You could apply for an internship in Willum's shop. Frth-willum, as he styles himself these days. I'm sure he'd fit you in."

Bram knew what Olan really meant. Astronomy was a Nar science. With its expensive toys and space-based establishment and millennia-long projects, there was no analog for it within the human community. Biology was a Nar science, too. Everything was. It was a Nar world, after all. But human beings were free to build little kingdoms within it, kingdoms in which the Nar were not especially interested. And Willum-frth-willum's bioengineering sideshow was one of those.

Mim had missed the point. "Bram's tutor-guardian is Voth-shr-voth," she said, giving Bram a dig in the ribs. "He thinks very highly of Bram. I'm sure Bram could get a place as a human apprentice to Voth-shr-voth's touch group if he wanted!"

"Well, there you *are*!" Olan said with a blinding artificial smile. "A few years or a decade under Voth, an accomplishment or two of your own, and you could come back here with an honorific and have a brilliant career still ahead of you. It's not unheard of."

"I suppose not," Bram said gloomily. The image of Jun Davd had come to him, older and more bent after all these years and still an apprentice at the observatory. Jun Davd had given him much the same advice that afternoon.

"I'm a poor example for you to copy, Bram," Jun Davd had said. "It's true enough that you have the aptitude. I've watched you since you were a wee wrig, coming here whenever you could get someone to take you on the bubble car and begging for telescope time so that you could have a glimpse of that fuzzy patch in the sky that the protohumans called the Milky Way. And you absorbed everything I taught you. But I haven't seen much of you the last couple of years, and maybe that's a sign. You're getting older, and maybe it's time for you to put away childish things." Jun Davd had smiled sadly. "That's all it is, Bram, this passion for the glory of the heavens, though I've given my own life to it. It leads nowhere in the end. A human apprentice is nothing but a helping cilium here, and there are no facilities for humans in orbit. But if you apprenticed yourself to the bioengineering touch group, you'd have your own guardian, Voth-shr-voth, to take you under his mantle. Voth encouraged your interest in astronomy because he thought it would make you happy, and as a Nar he doesn't see much practical difference between what you can accomplish here during a human lifetime and what you could accomplish with a boost from him. But he's wrong. The Nar don't understand *everything*. A ripple to them is a wave to us. You've become a young man. You'll be thinking about permanent pair-bonding soon, and you'll want your mate to be proud of you in the human community we all have to live in, like it or not. And you have a chance of accomplishing something more

61

tangible in bioengineering than you do in astronomy—something people can understand. Whatever Voth-shr-voth may have said to you, I know that he would be as pleased as a fingerling with a new touch toy if you'd only go to him and tell him you wanted to be apprenticed to his group."

And Bram, one hand in a sidepocket fingering the talisman he had saved all these years—the flake of charge-coupled material that once might have been struck by an actual photon from the Milky Way—thought guiltily of Mira and admitted to himself that yes, he did want to impress her.

Now Mim, at his side, was smiling up at Olan Byr, whose attention was wandering as he listened with half an ear to a dialogue a few feet away about the string quartet performance he had given tonight.

"Hey, Olan, come over here and settle this," a voice called out. "Can you double-stop an interval larger than a minor third with one spin-wheel?"

"Excuse me," Olan said with a little pat on the arm for Mim. "Nice to have met you, Bram."

He turned away to join his colleagues. Mim followed his progress with shining eyes. "Olan's agreed to give me cello lessons," she said. "Isn't that wonderful?"

The reception seemed to drag on interminably. Bram trailed faithfully after Mim, enduring all the bright, earnest chatter, saying little, and waiting till he could get her to himself.

Once they were intercepted by a wispy woman who, Mim told him later, was one of her minor gene mothers. "Oh Mimsy-mim, you're growing into quite the beauty, we must get together for a long chat soon, who's your handsome friend, is he a music student, too?" A number of times they found themselves part of one of the noisy student groups that revolved around centers of mutual babble. A sleek older fellow with experienced eyes, who seemed to know Mim altogether too well, invited them to go with the bunch to the beach for a night swim—though only a bare nod included Bram in the invitation—and Bram was relieved when Mim declined, saying that she wanted to stay a while longer at the reception.

A few Nar prowled through the human crowd, their clustered tops swaying high over the human heads, stopping here and there for conversation and ignoring the refreshment wells that had been set up for them next to the buffet. Tha-tha paused to talk to Bram and to introduce him to one of the older decapods who accompanied him. "This is Chir-prl-chir," he said in the Small Language, framing the spoken name with a gesture of respect that revealed complex ripples and color changes surging across the inner surfaces of his arms. "He is one of the greatest of living touch composers; it is an honor to serve as his amanuensis. I persuaded him to come to this concert so that he might experience something of the human art of music."

Mim was magnificent. Not at all awed by Chir-prl-chir's eminence, she did her best to explain what the Ravel quartet was all about.

"Extraordinary!" that imposing being said when she finally ran out of breath. "To think that a few dozen pages of written notation, filtered through the sensibilities of the performing artists, could result in an aesthetic experience that approximated the intentions of the original composer!"

"Before the technological age," Tha-tha explained in Inglex, "the great artistic works were preserved by living mnemonic touch readers who passed them on from generation to generation. Now, of course, we have tactile recorders and touch transcriptions. But Chir-prl-chir is old-fashioned. He doesn't trust a computer to capture all the nuances. That's why he prefers to rely on the living arm of a scribe."

"It was the same in the history of human music," Mim said bravely to the decapod composer. "Until a written notation became universal, music was generally passed on from person to person."

"The case isn't the same," Tha-tha said. "What our tactile recorders do is closer, in essence, to your sound recordings of an actual *performance*. That still leaves the mystery of how a few scratches on paper can express such emotion."

Bram sneaked a look at Mim. He hoped she hadn't thought the remark sounded condescending. She didn't know Tha-tha as well as he did.

Then Chir-prl-chir, with the kindest intentions, made it worse. "The greater mystery," he said, "is how such a small amount of sensory input—from a fingerpoint-sized area of cilia within the human ear—can result in the profound subjective impressions that human beings evidently experience when hearing music."

Bram fidgeted through what remained of the exchange. His discomfort was somewhat offset by the fact that Mim was obviously impressed by the introduction to the great Chir-prl-chir, though it was secondhand through Bram's childhood touch brother. Now, Bram thought fiercely, she'd have to take him more seriously.

At last Tha-tha excused himself, with a promise to look Bram up soon, and Bram had Mim to himself. With great cunning and deviousness he found the two of them a quiet place to sit: an outdoor bench on one of the upper galleries that overlooked the ocean. Behind them, the rows of fili-greed doors threw long oval splashes of light across the semidarkened veranda. A murmur of voices came from strolling groups below. The sky was huge and luminous in the half night, and the bright dot of the lesser sun cast complicated shadows across the rooftops of the human quarter. Beyond, the beach could be seen sloping in ser-rated planes to the silvered water.

"They can't really understand," Mim said.

Neither can we, Bram thought, but he kept it to himself. Instead, he searched awkwardly for something to say that would make him sound knowledgeable.

She gave him the opening. "Isn't it beautiful tonight?" she sighed. "I've never *seen* so many stars out during a half night. There must be dozens."

"See that bright one? Shield your eyes from the lesser sun. That's the prow star of the Boat constellation. If you hold out your other hand at arm's length, at just about one thumb width above it and a hair to the right, that little patch of sky is where the home of Original Man was. Ravel lived right where you're looking. So did Bach and Beethoven and the rest of them."

"I don't see anything."

"No, you can't. But that's the exact place. You can see the galaxy through a telescope. It's a beautiful sight. A sort of pinwheel of stars. I've seen it lots of times."

"Is that why you go to the observatory all the time? To look at it?"

He felt his face grow hot. "I don't go there much any-more. I used to go there a lot when I was a little kid."

She didn't make fun of him. "It's a strange idea, Bram-bram. I never thought of it that way before. That it was a *place*. I mean, you know they must have been alive and walked around, but it's always been a sort of, I don't know, a myth."

Encouraged, he went on. "What if you could go there? I wonder what you'd find."

"Oh, Bram-bram, where do you *get* these ideas?"

"No, I mean it. What if you went there, and some of the human worlds still existed, and you found . . . " He cast about for a clincher. "And you found some of that missing music you thought was gone from the universe! One shelf and you'd double what you have now! And what if there was just one picture book full of paintings for that artist fellow? And one more Shakespeare play or Milton poem or King James Bible? The whole lost heritage of the human race could be there waiting."

He had caught her imagination. "Yes!" she breathed. "What a thought!" Then she shook her head. "But it's no good dwelling on daydreams. We've got to be satisfied with what we've got *here*. The god knows, we've got enough to keep us busy for lifetimes. And we'll have our own Bachs, our own Miltons. Maybe some of them are inside at the party right now and we don't know it yet."

Bram knew she was thinking about Olan Byr, and it was a dagger in his heart. "No, listen," he said recklessly. "What if the whole human race just decided to pick itself up and go home?"

"You're a poet, Bram, and it's a beautiful vision." She touched his arm. "But once I saw an old woman who went to Juxt One as a girl and didn't like it and came back—and her whole life was gone. I want to live, Bram, not just use up my life."

If Bram had been in a fit state to be analytical, he would have noticed that Mim had stopped using the babyish form of his name at the same moment he had confided his babyish dream to her. As it was, he was aware only of her near-ness and warmth and the great dizzy expanse of sky with its smidgen of stars. He took her hand and found it respon-sive. "Mim," he began.

The doors behind them flew open, spilling light across the terrace. A lanky shadow fell across them, and Bram turned to see Smeth standing there, balancing a glass of punch and a plate of suncrisps and beanpuffs.

"Hi there, Mim! What are you doing out here?" Smeth said. "Oh, hello, Bram." His tone suggested that he was do-ing them a favor.

Mim let go of Bram's hand. "I thought you were too busy to waste time on frivolous things like concerts and parties," she said with more banter in her voice than Bram thought was necessary.

"Oh, I thought I might as well hear the result after all the work our team did on it," he said. He sat down beside them uninvited, the plate of snacks resting precariously on one bony knee.

Bram regarded Smeth without enthusiasm. He found Smeth insufferable for a number of reasons, not the least of them being that Smeth was three years older than he was, had treated Bram like a kid when they had gone to middle school in the Compound together, and thought he knew everything. Now Smeth was in his first year as a physics intern.

"How did you like it?" she asked.

"Lot of scraping," he said. "But from a scientific point of view, I guess it counts as another success for the physics department."

Mim's eyes flashed dangerously. "Don't you think that Olan and the other performers might have had something to do with it?"

Smeth waved a negligent hand, almost upsetting his glass. "Oh, that part of it? Well, sure, we needed competent technicians to carry out the final stages of the project, but all they did was to verify our theoretical findings." He preened himself. "Do you know that the suggestion about using wound strings for the lower tones was mine? Even though the whole team got credit for it, of course. You see, you can only go so far with composite materials. In using a range of metals and polymers, the coefficient of inharmonicity is proportional to the modulus of elasticity divided by the square of the density. The math can get quite complicated."

"Perhaps you'd care to explain it to us," Mim said, her voice deadly calm.

Smeth did so, at length. "So you see," he finished with a flourish, "the problem was one of adjusting the mass of the lowest string to the harmonics based on whole-number multiples of the fundamental component, and the winding solved that quite nicely." He popped a beanpuff into his mouth and began working on it.

Mim exploded. "That's the most arrogant, conceited piece of nonsense I've ever heard!" she sputtered. "You think you can reduce everything to—to *numbers!* You probably *dream* in numbers! What about emotion, human feeling, sentiment?"

Smeth was unruffled. "That's irrelevant for a scientist," he said with his mouth full. "We don't deal in human feelings."

"Everybody has feelings," Bram said, coming feebly to Mim's defense. "Whether they're human or Nar." He thought of Voth taking him to the observatory when he was small, and of the director going out of his way to humor a human hatchling with an inarticulate yearning. "Nar scientists think emotions are important."

"Yes, you should listen to Btam," Mim said. *"He* wants to be a scientist. An astronomer. And *he* hasn't given up on his feelings the way you have!"

"Oh, astronomy," Smeth said with a condescending smile. "A descriptive science. In physics, we're *doing* things. Things that are important even to the Nar."

"You can scoff all you want to, Smeth Norv-Tomas Claster," Mim said with her pert chin thrust out. And then, to Bram's horror, she began spilling out his most precious dream as if it were an itinerary for a day at the beach. "But Bram said the most beautiful thing to me a moment ago. He showed me the place in the sky where Original Man lived, and he said what if someday the whole human race were to pack up and go home, back to the star we came from. And find our heritage again. What good is science *for* if it isn't to give us dreams like that?"

Smeth gave them a superior smile, full of what seemed to Bram to be more than the normal number of teeth. "In the first place, we didn't 'come from' someplace else. We were created *here,* right in this solar system, out of laboratory chemicals, from a recipe which may or may not have been identical to the genetic code of the senders. In the second place, the notion of traveling to another galaxy isn't science, it's sheer mush-minded fantasy. It's not exactly the same as traveling to a star a few light-years away. Or even a few tens of light-years away."

"Bram didn't mean it *literally,*" Mim said with misplaced protectiveness. "It's just a beautiful thought. And you're horrid for making fun of it."

The smirk on Smeth's face made Bram throw caution to

the winds. He remembered the long discussions with Jun Davd about the wonders of the cosmos, the startling ideas that Jun Davd had stuffed his head with—ideas far beyond the normal curriculum for his age at middle school in the Compound.

"Maybe you haven't heard of a little thing called relativity," he said with a bravado he was not feeling at the moment. He spoke mostly for Mim's benefit. "The faster an object travels, the more slowly time passes for it. If a spaceship traveled close enough to the speed of light, it could cover *any* distance in practically no time at all."

"Have you worked out the math?" Smeth said.

"Well, no," Bram admitted. "Not exactly."

Smeth whipped out an inkcap and fitted it over his forefinger. He set his plate of food down on the ground, and from a bulky wallet clipped to his lab frock he produced a note roll and tore off a ragged length.

"All of the relativistic effects," he lectured, "depend on something called the gamma factor. It can be expressed as one divided by the square root of one minus the square of velocity divided by the square of the speed of light." He scribbled rapidly on his knee, using the stray light from the pierced door behind him. "As anyone with even an elementary knowledge of algebra can plainly see, the relativistic effects are insignificant until you get very, very close to the speed of light. At ninety percent of the speed of light— if there were any way of attaining it—the time dilation effect would only be a little more than two to one." He scribbled some more, then raised a shaggy head. "At *ninety-nine* percent of the speed of light, the time dilation effect is about seven to one. How far away is this galaxy of yours, Bram, my boy?"

Bram reddened. "Thirty-seven million light-years."

"Congratulations. You'd get there in about five million years of shipboard time."

Bram could not look at Mim. "You'd just need a higher speed, that's all," he said.

"Oh, ho, listen to him!" Smeth crowed. "You want a higher speed? Okay." His long skinny forefinger traced a new set of marks on the scratch scroll. "You're traveling at ninety-nine and nine-tenths the speed of light. I don't know how you're doing it, but you are. And the gamma factor works out to twenty-two point thirty-seven. Which means that you get to your 'home' galaxy in a little matter of one million six hundred fifty-four thousand years. But in the meantime, another thirty-seven million years've elapsed in this pet galaxy of yours. How long did it take *Homo erectus* to evolve into *Homo sapiens?* About a million years? How long did Original Man exist as a species? About one-tenth of a million?"

"All right," Mim said. "We get the idea."

"I'm not finished yet. Where are we going to get the energy to accelerate Bram here to that close to the speed of light? To say nothing of the rest of the human species. How much do you weigh, Bram?"

"Knock it off, Smeth," Bram said, his face burning.

Smeth was enjoying himself. "And we'd better give you some air to breathe, and some snacks to eat along the way. Call it a million-ton payload. Hmm, we'd better assume that we have a magical space drive that converts matter *entirely* into energy. And that *all* that energy goes into moving the ship—no fraction of it wasted for reaction or for cooking the passengers! That's simple. We'll just use the energy to push against the universe so that all the energy will appear in the ship." His finger flew across the page. "At ninety-nine point nine percent the speed of light, figuring the mass ratio at two divided by a factor of one minus the velocity divided by the speed of light, we get a figure of about two thousand times the mass of the payload, and when you convert all *that* into energy—" He tore off the end of the scroll and raised his head with a friendly sneer. "—you find that Bram's little excursion would take more than the total amount of energy that the entire Nar civilization has produced in the last thousand years."

While Bram shriveled in his seat and wished for the ground to swallow him up, Mim shot a suspicious glance at Smeth and the ribbon of paper he was dangling.

"Don't be obnoxious," she said. "I don't believe you figured all that out while you were sitting there talking to us."

Smeth didn't have the good grace to be crestfallen. He grinned with delight. "You're right. My study team's been splashing the waves on the subject for a couple of days now. None of the ideas that came out of the brain sessions were as wild as Bram's, though. I'm not supposed to say anything till the official announcement."

"What are you talking about?"

"Our team's been chosen to assist in a tremendous new multidiscipline Nar project. We're going to be attached to one of their physics touch groups."

"Oh, Smeth, that's a tremendous honor," Mim said, her antagonism forgotten. "And you're still a junior. What's it all about?"

Smeth frowned. "We don't know ail the details yet. It has something to do with space travel. The Nar have decided to take the next big leap. The project's going to take fifty thousand years or more to come to fruition, so some of the fellows think they're planning to reach the center of the galaxy. For some purpose that's terribly important to them as a race." He lowered his voice. "About two Tendays ago, they had a world meeting. Millions and millions of them linked, petal to petal, with all the separate assemblies connected to other assemblies all over the planet by body-reader transmissions. All the other planets and moons in the system were linked too, with allowances made for the communications delay. I guess Juxt One won't get the consensus for almost a year, by laser, and the other stellar settlements even later, but they're going ahead with the first steps without waiting."

"Fifty thousand years!" Mim said. "Even the Nar don't think that far ahead."

Smeth scratched his head. "Even the active phase of the project is going to take half a Nar lifetime. Hundreds of years. At least that's what they figure."

Bram offered his hand to Smeth. "Congratulations," he said stiffly.

"Thanks, sprout," Smeth said.

"What about the project on the physics of brasses and woodwinds that your team was going to do next for the music department?" Min asked.

"We won't have time for silly stuff like that now. The music department's on its own."

"Couldn't the Nar project wait another year for you to join them? If it's so long-range, your team's little contribution couldn't matter that much. Isn't human culture more important?"

Smeth didn't care for the "little contribution" phrase. "You don't say no to the Nar," he said irritably. "Besides, they value human insights. They recognize the fact that we conceptualize differently than they do, and that's important when you get to abstractions like quantum gravitonics and supersymmetry."

"None of it's going to make the slightest difference to anyone who's alive now. Even our children won't live to see any results."

"The same goes for some of the Nar who're going to work on the project. The important thing is that we're all going to play a part in a major purpose of this civilization."

"Which is?"

Smeth was reduced to sputtering. "I *told* you! It has something to do with the diffusion of intelligent life throughout the galaxy! At the present rate, that could take thirty million years. That's according to one computer model, anyway. But if this new Nar project is the signal of a basic commitment to such a goal, it could be done in as little as one or two million!"

"And you say that Bram's ideas are farfetched," Mim said with a toss of her dark hair.

Smeth recovered his infuriating composure. "Bram isn't *doing* anything about his ideas, though, is he?" he said with a toothy smile. "You're just pedaling water, aren't you, sprout? You're already a year past middle school and you haven't even decided what floater you're going to swim for, have you?"

Smeth and Mim were both looking at him. A million wordless images churned round in Bram's head, but the most satisfying one was the image of punching Smeth right in the middle of his toothy, condescending smile.

The terrace doors flapped open, emitting a burst of light that contained a small party of humans. A woman was hanging on to a man's arm and gushing, "Oh, you're being much too modest, Jorby, darling. Everyone knows you're the real brains behind the retrogenetics group. Willum may take credit for tomatoes if he wants to, but it's you we're all indebted to." The party swept past, headed toward one of the parapets overlooking the ocean.

Mim and Smeth were still looking at Bram. He cleared his throat. "As a matter of fact," he said, "I'm seeing my foster tutor tomorrow. Voth-shr-voth. I'm sure you know who *he* is! We're going to talk about my being taken into his bioengineering touch group, with him as my sponsor."

As soon as he got the words out, he felt as if he had been emptied of a flood, a warm tide that had rocked him since babyhood. He squared his shoulders and lifted his chin and looked Smeth straight in the eye.

"That's wonderful, Bram," Mim said. "What a plum! Why didn't you say something before?"

Smeth swallowed manfully and stuck out his hand. "My turn to congratulate *you*, sprout. I knew you had it in you. Of course, it's *applied* science, not pure research. But a lot of privilege goes with a billet like that. You'll be walking on all points, boy. You're a solid citizen now. They'll be lining up to compare gene maps with you."

Bram blushed and avoided looking at Mim. His gaze wandered to the sky and its handful of stars. He found his little patch of nothingness by the prow of the Boat and weighed it against the real world he was going to play his part in.

Why, he thought, wasn't he happier about his decision when every voice of reason said he ought to be envied?

Voth rose to greet him, laying aside the micromanipulator and feedback glove he had been working with. The attendant who had shown Bram in blossomed respectfully at the top and backed out of the chamber. At least, a human being might have described it as backing out: The Nar never needed to make a fuss about distinguishing front and back, having five choices in the matter at any given time.

"I am pleased that you have come, Bram," the venerable decapod vocalized in a deep baritone that seemed to have become more mellow, almost like the wooden cello contraption that Olan Byr had played the night before.

"I am pleased to be here, Voth-shr-voth," Bram said in the Small Language, like any deferential fingerling approaching from a distance.

Without thinking about it, he lifted his arms in a dancerlike movement and rotated them palms outward in the childhood gesture he had acquired in imitation of the touch brothers he had spent so much time with.

Bram studied his old teacher, noticing with a pang the physiological changes that were overtaking Voth as he hastened toward the final, reproductive stage of his life. The yellow petal-limbs had darkened noticeably at the edges and along the center creases, and the secondary lensless eyes in a row between the walking limbs were turning cloudy. Though he was still male, he would be ready for the mating pools within Bram's lifetime. That was a hard thought to accept.

"Come closer, little one," Voth said. "Though you are not so little anymore."

Bram tore at his shirt. With a glad cry, he sprang forward. Voth peeled his tentacles down almost to the waist so that he was not much taller than Bram was. Bram spread his arms wide and felt the frondlike nest close about him. The waves of the Great Language enclosed him, and he could dimly comprehend the broad outline of their meaning, assisted by the muffled voice at his ear.

"We'll work together, eh, my boy? You and me and my touch brothers and their protégés, and you they shall treat as my son."

CHAPTER 3

The little five-legged transport beast skidded to a stop at
the biocenter entrance ramp and lowered its central cup to
dismounting height, its stiltlike legs bent into a picket of
stiff arches. Bram emerged from the one-man howdah and
slid to the ground. The pentangular creature waited for its
payment, quivering with expectation. Bram dug into his
shoulder pouch and tossed it the three polysugar bars that
the distance had called for. It gobbled them up and hung
around for more. Bram relented and gave it another one,
then slapped its cool flank and sent it trotting back to the
central stable.

He stopped for a moment at the foot of the ramp to gaze
upward at the tip of the gleaming white orthocone that
housed the main body of the institution. It was over a
thousand feet high, a slender unbroken tusk that domi-
nated the district for miles around, and it was still growing
at the base. It was awe-inspiring to think of how old it
must be.

Then, conscious of the rising sun, he joined the crowd—
mostly Nar—that was hurrying to work across the bridge

that curled over the surrounding moat of nutrient solution. The waters were an achingly beautiful blue, garnished with bright ornamental floaters, and Bram had to fight the impulse to loiter for a while at the balustrade.

Really, he thought, he ought to move closer to his work. There was a small cluster of human housing nearby, mostly young singles who worked in the neighborhood, with adequate vending stations for the basic necessities. If he lived there, he could walk to his job every morning and not have to spend time and allowances riding.

But then he'd be farther away from Kerthin. She'd never consent to living outside the Compound even if the two of them decided to make their relationship permanent.

He quickened his step, throwing off the thought. A dignified Nar who was festooned with message bandoliers and carrypods "nodded" to him with a perfunctory flexing of his tentacle tips; Bram recognized him as an affiliated project director from one of the upper septa and returned the greeting with a two-handed spreading of fingers.

The bridge debouched into the lowest usable septum of the nonliving part of the orthocone. It was an enormous, sweeping chamber with an avenue of clerical pavilions and reception booths around the outer perimeter. A central well looked down through two or three siphuncle holes to the chamber where the orthocone creature now resided, with a stout railing as protection against any random heavings of those thousands of tons of living flesh. Not that there was any danger of the creature breaking through to this level. It had lived here a couple of centuries ago. It would no longer fit through the siphuncle; at most a small hillock of itself might bulge through the opening. When it was feeling blue or threatened, the best it could do at this stage was to retreat to a larger, more recent septum one or two levels below. Now it was almost finished secreting its latest bottom story, and in a few more decades the bio institute would be able to expand one more chamber downward.

Bram ascended a ramp to the buttressed gallery that had been erected over the central well and waited with the crowd for an elevator car to come down the spiral. In the dark chasm below he thought he saw a suggestion of gray, oily movement, but it might have been his imagination. One of the cars, a pearly ovoid that matched the biological building material of the chamber interior for esthetic reasons but was actually a manufactured polycarbonate, whirred down on its helical gears. Bram got on with the rest and rose through the spiral from septum to septum until he came to a level about halfway up the orthocone. He stepped off and proceeded through a maze of foamed corridors until he came to Voth's worksuite, a spacious, sunny series of compartments whose tall oval windows, cut out of the shell material, provided a spectacular view of the city.

A small subgroup of junior associates was already at work, having an early-morning conference. Three of them were crammed at the entrance of a crescent desk, arms melded, a litter of touch pads scattered over the desk top. Bram waved at them as he walked by and got a frondlike flutter in return—one raised member serving for all three. Voth was not in yet; at least he was not visible in what could be seen of his chamber through the doorway. Bram proceeded to his own cubbyhole, a dusty space cramped by stacks of improvised shelving that contained piles of old records and reference materials that he kept promising himself he would sort out someday. The crescent desk wasn't really a comfortable height for a human being, but it sat right up against one of the huge airy oval windows, and he enjoyed the openness of it—the feeling, when he turned from his work to take a brief break, of hanging in midair over the bustling, miniature activity of the city below.

He sat down inside his desk and leaned back in the human-style chair that Smeth had helped him lug up here—how long ago?

Seven years.

The first four of those years had been spent mostly in intensive study. Oh, Voth had put him to work from the very first day, giving him little problems to nibble around the edges of—problems that were always just the smallest distance beyond his reach. He'd had to bone up for everything, step by tiny step. But there was always a reward at the end of each step. Nothing was abstract. He was always learning something he needed to know, something he could use.

It was a good way to acquire an education.

Voth himself had been his tutor most of the time. With infinite patience, Voth had given freely of his dwindling life span, when he might have used those thousands of hours in the winding up of his own life's purpose, in the grand summing up that the Nar set so much store by.

But Voth had also sent him to others, both Nar and human, for some of the specialized knowledge he must have. Mathematics, in particular, had been taught by a succession of human tutors. Nar and human brains were wired differently when it came to numbers. In particular, the Nar had the faculty of perceiving whole orders of mathematical operations directly, by totting up in computer fashion millions of digits at blinding speed on their ciliated undersurfaces. Mathematics was simply another sensory experience for them, generating higher orders of abstraction in the brain. In an analogous manner, a musically talented human might directly perceive the sensory information contained in a sound recording, deduce from it the organizational principles known as musical form, and, if sufficiently talented, even be able to reproduce exactly such details as harmony, counterpoint, and orchestration. The Nar faculty wasn't precisely a matter of counting on their "fingers," either. Specific areas of cilia didn't seem to be involved. A Nar could temporarily remove a tentacle or two to talk, eat, or scratch while the process went on. In the same way, the musical human might hear his symphony on an inferior loudspeaker, with part of the information missing, and still arrive at the same results, note for note. A more serious difference between Nar and human Conceptualization was that imaginary numbers had no meaning for the Nar; instead of the idea of the square root of a negative number, they thought in terms of a sort of inside out number that, in operations involving hybrid complex numbers, made both the imaginary axis and the real axis simultaneously and equally concrete to them.

But Bram, his tutors informed Voth, had a rare talent for Nar conceptual thought. Perhaps it went with a high level of empathy. Bram had a greater affinity for the Great Language than any human Voth had ever known. He could even use the star-shaped touch readers in a primitive fashion—at least to point himself in the right direction for searches of indexed material—and he could plug himself into the periphery of a group conference and get something out of it beyond the shorthand information contained in vocalized talk. By now, Voth's touch associates had grown used to the human adoptee who sometimes squeezed into a packed meeting, and they often drew him inward with two or three casual tentacles.

Seven years.

For the last three of those seven, Bram increasingly had

been doing solid, useful work that was beginning to come to the attention of other touch groups in the institution. Learning never ended, of course, but now he was spending four-fifths of his time on subprojects. Word of his subtle metamorphosis to graduate status had even filtered down to the human community. It was Smeth who had made Bram realize this.

"I hear they've given you the responsibility for tailoring one of the synthetic genes in the new viral monofilament project, Smeth had remarked one day when they had bumped into each other in the washroom of the bachelors' lodge where they were both living at the time. "Keep it up, old son, and you'll be another Willum-frth-willum by the time you're thirty."

"It's only a modification of one of the genes they're using now," Bram had told him. "They want to change an initiation codon to provide an extra loop. Where did you hear about it?"

"Oh, they're raving about you. You're a real pet. A shining example of what a human can do despite our limitations." The breezy inflection didn't quite come off. "One of the Nar at the biocenter has a touch brother in the physics group our team is assigned to. I'll tell you this, old son, it'll be all over the batch house by tomorrow."

Smeth hadn't changed much in the seven years except to get a little skinnier and a lot more pedantic. He had tried a beard for a while, but someone had told him it made him look scruffy. He had run twice for the presidency of the physics society and was sanguine about his chances in a third try. He could be heard in the common room evenings, talking about the need for a guild. Bram had grown rather fond of him despite his aptitude for being stuffy. Smeth wasn't a bad sort, just awkward about people. When Bram

83

had moved out of the lodge, he had even asked Smeth if he wanted to share quarters, but Smeth had declined the invitation; he preferred to live communally with the other bachelors, spending his evenings playing board games with some of the older members and practicing to become an old fogy himself.

Bram didn't see much of Mim these days—except to make a point of attending her cello recitals whenever he could. They had drifted apart after their first youthful sampling of one another and the glad, glowing year they had spent together after the long interruption that had followed the initial experiment. It had been a comfortable relationship, as easy and natural as breathing, but despite their affinity for one another they had never discussed making it permanent, had never even had their gene maps compared. It was as if each of them had approached their liaison through a long corridor with the doors left open at either end.

Mim was making a name for herself as an interpreter of string music. An explosive renaissance of string writing had been inspired by that landmark performance of the Ravel quartet so long ago. The cello and the other string instruments had been modified and simplified since then. No longer were they ugly rectangular boxes on a table, with an unmanageable number of strings manipulated by foot pedals. Now they were six-string instruments tuned in fifths, and the players held them comfortably on their laps, pressing their fingers directly against the frets. The bow had been simplified, too: It had become little more than a lightweight wand, battery-powered, with an endless-chain friction band moving around it on sprockets.

Mim was living with Olan Byr now, and everyone said they were happy together despite the age difference. Mim had not given birth herself, but Bram had heard that she and Olan had contributed short nucleotide sequences to a genetic construct. He didn't know if there was anything to the rumor.

Bram wished them well. He himself was caught up in the excitement of his relationship with Kerthin. So far he hadn't been able to persuade her to move in permanently with him, but that day didn't seem far off. They'd had an exploratory sequencing done, just for a lark, and while their gene mapping was still incomplete, they had every reason to hope that they would be allowed to contribute a preponderant number of their genes to a composite genome and rear the child as their own.

It was a sobering thought. Was he ready for a serious step like that? He stared out the oval window and told himself he was. Life was like a ride in a bubble car. You chose your car. And then you went to wherever the monofilament cable led to. He had made his choice the day he had gone to Voth and accepted the apprenticeship. He couldn't complain. The problem was Kerthin. She kept telling him he was too complacent.

Bram sighed. Kerthin was sometimes difficult, but the emotions she stirred in him were a far cry from the placid contentment he had felt with Mim.

The conference across the way was breaking up. Through the chinks in his shelving, Bram could see the three participants taking leave of one another and ambling toward their workplaces. One of the juniors poked a crown into Bram's niche and hooted at him.

"We've decided to apply a dose of colchicine to the meristematic tissue and try to force polyploidy. How are you coming with that heterochronic gene?"

Bram gave a guilty start. Time to stop daydreaming. He could have it out with Kerthin tonight. There was some sort of political meeting she wanted to go to, but maybe he could talk her out of it.

"I've already snipped a piece of the nucleotide sequence," Bram replied. "I think it will cross species if I can get my nonhistone protein to stick at the end of it. There's a place where my ribosome-recognition site overlaps your recognition codon. I should have something for you this afternoon."

"If it takes," the decapod said, "we'll have developed a new species out of the bud scales."

"Don't count on it," Bram said.

"It could be a very useful organism," the decapod said.

"Sure. A tree that lays eggs," Bram said.

The decapod recognized a human joke, gave a credible imitation of a human laugh through its vocal syrinx, and withdrew. Bram settled down to work.

An hour later he had rescued the fragments of DNA from the buffer medium where he had stored them the day before. He examined a sequence on the little vid screen where it was represented schematically. It couldn't be looked at directly through a muon scope; not if it was to be used afterward. But the chemical sensors in the tray told the computer what was going on, and the graphics were easier to work with, anyway.

The Nar did the same thing by touch, using a tactile display and feedback glove for the micromanipulators. For humans like Bram, there was a computer interface to supply a visual mode. One system wasn't basically better than the other; it was just a question of style.

The thing on the screen was a representation of one of the eight genes that made an egg divide before it could become a chicken. Or rather, it was two of the nine genes that accomplished that particular trick. One gene was within the other; it used part of the same nucleotide sequence, but began and ended in a different reading frame. The ends of the snippet of life stuff also contained, respectively, a recognition site and a codon that with a little tinkering, Bram hoped, would be capable of an interspecies masquerade.

Bram did not know what a chicken was, except that it was some kind of animal that had lived in symbiosis with Original Man. A literary friend of Mim's, long ago, had offered an ancient epigram by way of enlightenment: "A chicken is an egg's way of making another egg."

But the Nar had done away with the intermediate stage several human generations earlier—for ethical reasons. They had been horrified to realize that Original Man had intended his reborn self to eat a near-sentient life form as if it were a potato or a carrot. The Nar themselves ate no form of animal life more complex than a one-celled wriggler. So they had spent a century or two manufacturing a set of artificial heterochronic genes that made possible a self-replicating egg.

Now Bram had a sequence containing two of the heterochronic genes in his sights. On the screen it looked like an orange and blue chain of geometric shapes with blinking labels helpfully supplied by the computer.

Bram slipped his hand into a glove shaped for human fingers. The microscopic events he was manipulating showed up on the screen as abstract tweezers and suction tubes moving three-dimensionally among the abstractions of molecules. But instinct was everything, and Bram had a feeling for what he was actually doing in his invisible arena.

He skipped lunch and stuck with his work. By the time he was finished with his microsurgery, his face was streaked with perspiration and his limbs were stiff. He leaned back and stretched and looked at what he had.

The screen told him that he had successfully manufactured the chimera he wanted. The stretch of material from the heterochronic egg was spliced to the proper segment of embryonic stem tissue DNA from a space poplar. It was a good match. He still had a little patching to do at the joints—the gaps had to be filled with annealing enzymes and sealed with DNA ligase.

But what he had in front of him was a successful first step toward a poplar tree whose embryonic bud scale cells ought to be able to reproduce without maturing further.

Now came the tricky part.

He wiped the sweat off his forehead with the back of his hand. An unexpressed gene was no good to anybody. It would be the task of the Nar team to splice Bram's fragment into the total poplar genome and get it to work within a cell nucleus. He had to give them a gene that was able to switch itself on.

He increased magnification and examined the sites where the regulatory proteins would operate. He needed a nonhistone fraction whose amino acid sequence would bridge the gap between plant and animal species. It didn't have to be identical to an existing protein, though it would help if it were close, but it did have to recognize a specific DNA site and elbow aside the repressor histone. A clue to what he wanted might be found in the archives, going back to the design of the original synthetic genes for the heterochronic egg.

He took off his shirt and went over to the big whole-body reader in the center of the atrium. Nobody was using it at the moment. He didn't feel like going all the way down to the library annex where they kept a few badly maintained human-style readers that interfaced with the Nar system. With luck he could tickle enough information out of the touch reader to narrow down the index search.

He punched in the main entries on the touch pad at the tip of one of the five points of the pentacle, adjusted the tilt of the top surface for comfort, and crucified himself on the machine. He could feel the ghostly tingle of thousands of tiny bristles against his outstretched arras, bare chest, and cheek. The chemical traces that were an integral part of the Great Language's nuances manifested themselves as a series of ambiguous perfumes and passing astringencies on the surface of his skin, but he closed his eyes and concentrated on the broad recognition factors.

The machine scrolled through a menu of major subject headings. When it reached terrestrial DNA, he slowed it down and let it run through the list of the thirty basic human food crops until it came to eggs. It did not occur to him that there were no more than a dozen human beings in the universe who could do what he was doing now. It was part talent, part practice, part early conditioning, all factoring out to a rather small twig on the probability tree.

But now he was stymied. His fingers fluttered over the touch pad again and again, but he got no further. The broad bands of cilia movement he could feel against his chest kept fragmenting and marching off into a dozen directions, all of them useless. Whatever his adroitness with the machine, he still would never be a Nar. It was a little like a clumsy person using a shod foot to find the right page in a tissue-paged reference book.

Reluctantly, he asked for help. One of the Nar juniors found the information for him in a moment, using no more than a few square inches of tentacle surface.

"You kept wandering into a 'records not available' area," the Nar explained. "The manufacture of those genes goes back a long way. Lots of dead ends, lots of useless stuff thrown out."

Bram thanked him and took the reference coordinates over to the other side of the atrium for a printout. He got a thick sheaf of holos that would have translated into a series of minute-long, information-packed sessions on the touch reader. With a sigh he began the long, boring task of showing them one by one to the optical scanner of his desk computer and poring through the visual display that the interface program called forth.

It was dark outside by the time he wound up his work for the day. Through the tall oval window, Bram could see the city glowing softly. The biolights inside had come on, too, casting a shadowless illumination over everything. The building was mostly emptied out by now, a silent shell that made audible the faint hollow gurglings from below.

The biocrafting team was still at work, though, one floor down in the big lab with its special equipment. They had told Bram that his construct looked promising, that there was nothing more for him to do today, and that he could go home. But there were still some hundreds of nucleotide combinations in the chimeric stretch that might yet be profitably explored, and Bram had gotten immersed in making a start toward cataloging them.

He thumbed the face of his watch and got a shock. It was 7:85. He had promised Kerthin that he'd be home before the eighth hour. He'd never make it in time, even if he found transport right away.

Guiltily, he stacked the holos and filed them away in his desk. He switched off his visual display and got up to leave. He had to wait a long time for an elevator. At this hour four-fifths of them were out of service, having their low-density flywheels recharged in anticipation of the following day's traffic—the energy being supplied gratis by random shifts of body mass of the orthocone creature down below.

When he reached ground level, he found that he was in luck. One of the short-range transport beasts was discharging a Nar passenger at the edge of the nutrient lagoon. Bram was out of polysugar bars, but the leggy little pentadactyls carried a supply of them in a locked box that only the passenger could open, with suitable credit transfer.

Bram settled into the howdah and gave the beast its instructions with a few strokes of his fingers. Not being a Nar, he couldn't give it a door-to-door destination, but when they got to the human quarter he could steer it manually.

The howdah teetered and rose. Bram settled back to enjoy the ride as best he could while he rehearsed an explanation for Kerthin of why he was late.

There were three people he had never seen before in his compartment, sprawled about as if they owned the place. Two of them were bearded, tousle-haired young men wearing aggressively utilitarian monos. The third was an extremely thin young woman showing her ribs and hipbones in a striped stretchshirt, tights, and legsacks. The strangers looked Bram over in bored fashion as he entered, but none of them made a move to get up from their puffseats.

"Where have you *been?*" Kerthin demanded, coming toward him. "We were just about to leave without you."

Bram looked at her with pleasure, as always, no matter what her mood. Kerthin was tall, firm-bodied, and gray-eyed, her thick bronze hair braided into a heavy rope. She had strong features and smooth golden skin. She was dressed to go out, in a lightweight overmantle with a ruff collar.

"I'm sorry," he said, stumbling over the words. "We're

trying to develop a new organism, and they were waiting for a chimeric section they needed from me. I guess I lost track of the time." A returning flush of pride removed the apology from his tone. "It may turn out to be rather important. You see, it's a—"

She cut him off. "No time for that. You can tell me later." She turned to the others. "Well, what are we waiting for?"

The two men struggled up from their seating puffs without particular haste. The woman followed. None of them offered to speak. Bram looked questioningly at Kerthin.

"Oh," Kerthin said. She tossed her head impatiently. "This is Pite. And that's Fraz. And she's Eena."

Pite acknowledged the introduction with a lazy nod. He was the one with the short blonde beard. He was medium height with a thick chest and wide shoulders. He moved in a sort of controlled prowl.

The one with the scraggly black heard and the red, wide-lipped face was Fraz. The sleeves of his mono were rolled up to show powerfully thewed forearms. He didn't look overwhelmingly bright—an odd choice of friend for someone like Kerthin. "Hiya," he said. He stole a glance at Pite, as if to see that it was all right.

"Hello," Bram replied, still puzzled.

The thin young woman, Eena, gave Bram an actual smile. "Say," she said, "do you really work for the yellowlegs?"

Bram frowned at the pejorative. "Well ... I've been taken into one of the touch groups. As an adoptee of the Folk." He used the Inglexcised form of the term in the Small Language by which the Nar referred to themselves.

"Yuh?" She gave him a blank stare. "What is it you do exactly?"

"Well, I—"

"Come *on!*" Kerthin said. "We can talk on the way."

"Where are we going?" Bram asked.

"To a *meeting*. I mentioned it yesterday. Weren't you listening? Look, if you don't want to go, just say so. I'll go by myself."

"No, no," he said hastily. "I'll go." His eyes fell on the empty cups and dirty plates scattered on the floor near the seating puffs. It looked as if Kerthin had been entertaining her friends for the last hour or so with cornbrew and nibbles from the cold locker. Bram's empty stomach reminded him that he had skipped lunch; he would have given anything for a quick brew and a plate of beanwraps. Kerthin, however, was all but tapping her foot with impatience.

Bram tried to make small talk during the walk to the meeting place. "What kind of meeting is it?" he asked Pite.

"Oh, just a meeting, you know," Pite replied, his pale eyes shifting. "Politics and all that stuff."

"He's all *right*, I told you, Pite," Kerthin said. "Just a little politically undeveloped."

Pite shrugged. "Any friend of Kerthin's . . ." he said. "Look, Brammo, we humans are a minority in a society run by the yellowlegs. We got to maintain our own identity, look out for our own interests, right?"

"Are you a Resurgist?" Bram asked politely.

Fraz, walking ahead with the thin girl, gave a rude hoot of laughter.

"You were right, Kerth," Eena said. "He *is* politically undeveloped."

Bram flushed. He was beginning to get tired of Kerthin's friends. And he wasn't too pleased, either, with the form Kerthin's endorsement of him had taken.

"The Resurgists live in their own dream world," Pite said

smoothly. "They think they can dress up in their play clothes that they get from descriptions in dead books and copy all the old plays and the old music and the old political institutions. And put up one-way walls around human society and live by the sufferance of the yellowlegs in a world where the yellowlegs control all the resources. And they're willing to go on holding out their hand and begging for whatever crumbs the yellowlegs are kind enough to give them." His voice contained a chill certainty. "But that won't work. We humans are going to have to fight for what's ours."

"Fight who?" Bram said. "We don't have any enemies."

"That's where you're wrong, Brammo," Pite said. "Everybody's our enemy. The yellowlegs for keeping us down. The Partnerites for collaborating with them. The Resurgists for diverting us from the *real* struggle that's ahead. And you. For donating your talents to the yellowlegs instead of your own kind."

"Now, just a minute," Bram said. "What we do at the biocenter benefits everybody eventually, Nar and human alike. Look at mining bacteria, for example. Or fuel crops. All creating more abundance, more wealth to go around. That one-piecer you're wearing is probably made of polycotton. Or take the project I was working on today. It could lead to new fibers from meristem hairs. Or new building materials that grow in sheets. Or even a new species of food plant—one that only humans could possibly benefit from, I might add."

Pite laughed. "Like Kerthin said, you haven't figured it out yet. But maybe there's hope for you. You keep your ears open tonight, Brammo, and maybe you'll wake up someday."

They walked on in silence. Bram saw that they were

heading toward the older section of the human quarter, where ill-nourished lightpoles cast a feeble glow down the side streets and abandoned, discolored shell structures huddled accusingly among the more viable buildings. A few cheap vending stations were still open, dispensing food, drink, and minor comforts.

Eena moved into step with Bram. "Don't let Pite get on your nerves," she said. "I wasn't politically conscious either when I met him, and honest, you should have heard the way he rode me. So, you never finished telling me. What is this work you do with the decs?"

Relieved at the change of subject, Bram started to explain his part in the new project to provide the space poplar with heterochronic genes that might lead to a new, self-replicating organism at the embryonic stage. He talked more loudly than necessary and kept stealing glances at Kerthin. But her face stayed blank, without even the uncomprehending smile that Eena, at least, was favoring him with.

"And so," he finished lamely, "I guess they'll keep working on it. If this combination doesn't work, there're others we can try."

"How'll you know?" Pite said.

"Huh? Know what?"

"Know if this thing, whatever it is, works?"

"Why—they'll tell me. I'm part of the project."

"Sure," Pite said with lazy sarcasm. "Like the thing-amajigee you tried to look up, and they tell you the records aren't available to humans."

Bram was almost too flabbergasted to reply. "They weren't keeping anything from me. From me as a human, I mean. I had some trouble interpreting the touch reader. And when I asked for help, I got it."

"You're being naive, Bram," Eena said earnestly. "They show humans what they want us to see."

"But—but what motive could they possibly have for concealing data?" Bram asked.

Fraz answered him this time. "To keep human beings down, what else?"

"You're wrong, dead wrong," Bram said. "Look here—"

Kerthin nudged him with her elbow to shut him up. "Here we are," she said. "I hope it hasn't started. Now for pity's sake, don't be getting quarrelsome about things you don't understand."

CHAPTER 4

The meeting was being held in a back room of a neglected old building that housed a drink shop. A couple of other ground-level shops had long since crusted over. Pite led them through, nodding at a burly man who was hanging around just inside the entrance.

A few customers still sat in the murky outer room, nursing cornbrew or thickened alcohol at the long tables. The place looked shabby. The biolights were elderly and overdue for replacement, and pitting was well advanced on the wall surfaces.

They had arrived just in time, Bram saw. As if on signal, the loitering customers drained their drinks and began to file into the back room. The proprietor, a pale heavyset man in an apron, locked the door and pulled over the shades before he joined the rest. The burly man stayed behind, presumably to admit latecomers.

The inner room looked like any tired club room, with game tables and a few sagging lounge puffs pushed against the walls. Rows of chairs had been set up to face a small raised platform that once might have been used as a bandstand. A speaker's rostrum had been improvised out of two boxes resting on trestles. Behind the platform was draped a long homemade banner showing a crude representation of two human hands cupping something that looked like a planet.

Forty or fifty people were already seated. Bram was surprised at the size of the crowd. People talked politics all the time at parties and other gatherings—though Bram tried to avoid them—but he had never really thought of political discussions being organized in the sense that plays and concerts were.

He was surprised further to see people he knew dotting the assembly: Dal Terson, the playcrafter, who never talked politics and who, Bram assumed, took a cynical attitude toward such matters; a Resurgist architect he had met at a viewing party Arthe had invited him to; a sallow clerkish man he recognized from the library annex at the biocenter.

"Over here," Pite said, and muscled a way through for them to some vacant seats up front.

Nothing much happened for a while. Three or four people at the rear of the platform were having a whispered discussion among themselves. There was a buzz of desultory, low-pitched conversation in the audience. Bram occupied himself by looking around the meeting hall, but there wasn't much to see.

All of a sudden there was a sharp crack from up front that made Bram jump. The people on the platform had sorted out their differences, and one of them had struck the improvised lectern with a cube of wood. He was a thin, stoop-shouldered individual afflicted with the baldness gene that had not yet been edited out of the human pool because of possible allelomorphic benefits.

"The meeting will come to order," the bald man said. "I see we have some new faces tonight."

Bram looked around again, but he could not tell who the new faces were besides himself.

"We'll clean up some old business first," the bald man went on, "and then we'll go on to the committee reports." He paused for dramatic effect. "I should warn you that we are not going to have the opportunity to vote on the resources allocation resolution tonight, because the resolutions committee has not been able to agree on the wording."

There were groans and catcalls from the assembly. Somebody shouted, "Damned Schismatist sabotage!" The bald man rapped with his wooden cube and waited for the noise to abate.

Bram looked over at Kerthin. She seemed as agitated as the rest of the audience. "What's it all about?" he whispered.

"Shhh," she said. "Just listen."

The bald man waited until his audience was under control again. "But I have another surprise for you that you're all going to like. We have some news from Juxt One—an update on how the struggle is going there and a special message from Penser himself."

The meeting became unruly again. A man stood up and yelled, "Give it to us now, Jupe, and the Inferno with all the other garbage!"

"Now, now, gene brother Hwite," the bald man said. "All in good time. Patience is a virtue. Besides, our guest isn't here yet. As you all can appreciate, he's taking the utmost precautions."

Eena leaned over from the seat on Bram's other side. "Huh, we knew all about the laser message from Juxt One. That's why Pite wanted to be here tonight. Otherwise he wouldn't bother with this bunch of word dribblers."

"Shut up, Eena," Fraz said from the next seat over.

"Shut up yourself, Fraz, honey, and stop trying to act so big," Eena told him.

"Who's Penser?" Bram said.

Unexpectedly, it was Pite who answered. "Just a man. With some good ideas. We could use him here on this planet."

On the platform, the committee reports had begun. A fussy little man in dull-colored pleats was droning on about vote tallies for the planetwide Human Advisory Council and the need to elect representatives who reflected the Ascendist point of view. He read off an endless list of figures from a memory slate, smoothing the surface with his palm at intervals to let the next set of statistics pop up. He was followed by a drab middle-aged woman who reported on the small discussion groups that had been organized to raise the consciousness of politically immature people to the importance of human ascendancy. A fervent young man on the arts and education committee reported on a drive to get Ascendist plays performed. A square-jawed woman with cropped hair reported on poster production and efforts to get Ascendist leaflets into the hands of the human workers at the ethanol plant and other Nar-directed enterprises serving the human quarter.

Bram tried to figure out what it was all about. The concept of a political party was new to him. As near as he could decide, the Ascendists were something like an extended touch group, and the committee reports corresponded to opening amenities. At least the wordage was high and the information content low. A Nar touch group would have disposed of all this, he thought, in a minute or two.

"Word dribblers," Eena had called them. Evidently Kerthin's friends belonged to a faction that favored more direct action of some kind.

There were more words during the discussion period that followed. Kerthin took pity on Bram and explained that it had something to do with a vote that was going to take place on various resolutions afterward.

"We need to demand a greater share of this planet's resources, that's all there is to it," said the square-jawed woman who had given one of the committee reports. "We humans have done very well in small-scale enterprises like furniture manufacturing, for example. We even have Nar customers for specialty items, helping us to pay our own way. But we have no say whatsoever in the large-scale enterprises that affect us directly. For a starter, we should demand that the ethanol plant and the grainworks be turned over entirely to us."

"That will all be in the resources allocation resolution, gene sister," the bald moderator said. "Any comments on that? Yes, gene brother Lal?"

Lal got to his feet, a hulking man in stained workclothes. "Seems to me that's the way to greater dependence, not less. We're just talking about begging for bigger handouts. But the Nar still pull the strings. We need to go where the power is. Get human representatives in every nook and cranny of Nar society. Transportation, energy, spaceflight. Hell, *their* food factories, if it comes to that! Put it to them reasonable-like. A token share of control. Proportional to our numbers. Then we work from inside."

"That's just the same old Partnerite drivel, spinning on a different shaft," another speaker objected. "Working from within is a daydream. We can never get *inside* any Nar institution, let alone influence it. And that's just a biological fact of life!"

"And what would *you* suggest, gene brother Gorch?" the bald moderator asked sarcastically.

Gorch stuck out his lower lip pugnaciously. "For starts, we demand planets of our own. Where the human race can develop without interference. As long as we live on the same worlds with the yellowlegs, our initiative's going to be sapped. We're nothing but pets to them—about on the same level as a muffbeast."

An angry mutter rippled through the hall. Evidently Gorch had struck a raw nerve.

"That's telling it, Gorch," somebody shouted.

"More Schismatist mischief making," a dissenter broke in. "We've got to solve our problems right here on this world and the other settled planets, not go charging off into space and running away from the struggle!"

Voices in the hall shouted him down. Other voices shouted down the shouters.

In the hubbub, Bram turned to Kerthin. She was leaning forward, straining to hear. "That fellow's talking nonsense," he said. "About demanding planets from the Nar. There *aren't* any suitable planets anywhere within a human life span that aren't already populated by the Nar. What's he proposing? That we all chip in and buy a ship and go exploring? There isn't a large enough human population on all the planets added together to command that kind of capital investment."

"Don't be a fool," Kerthin snapped at him.

Hurt, Bram stopped talking. Pite leaned across Kerthin and spoke past Bram to Eena and Fraz. "The guy that called Gorch a Schismatist got it half right. Schismatists don't demand. We take."

That got a guffaw from Fraz and an adoring look from

Eena. Bram hunched in his seat and tried to look neutral. The argument in the hall was still going on.

"I'll tell you where Schismatism leads to," said the man who had disagreed with Gorch. "To outlaws like Penser. Where's he been the last seven years? Hiding underground. What good does *that* do the struggle? We're lucky the Nar permit the Ascendist party to still exist on Juxt One."

There was a scuffle. A chair was knocked over. Bram couldn't see clearly what had happened, but a man in a mono, like the ones Pite and Fraz wore, was being held by two or three men around him. The anti-Schismatist was being similarly restrained. The man in the mono spat, "You say anything else against Penser and you're going to wear your legs for a scarf!"

"Please, please!" The block of wood hammered on the podium. "We mustn't fight among ourselves," the bald man said. "If we divide, it can only hurt the struggle."

"What did Penser do?" Bram asked.

"He took things," Pite said with a mocking smile. "From the yellowlegs."

Kerthin gave a sigh and addressed Bram as if he were a child. "Penser was very high in the Ascendist party on Juxt One. There were some who found his ideas too extreme. They tried to read him and his followers out of the party. But he fought back." She frowned. "There was an . . . accident. Some people got hurt. Died. Including some of his political opponents. His enemies tried to place the blame on him. They tried to get the Nar to do their dirty work for them—have Penser deported to some small colony in the Juxt system where the people are enroofed and he wouldn't be able to move around freely. But Penser went into hiding before the monitors could lay hands on him. He's been underground for seven years. But he's carrying on the struggle till the day he can come out into the open again. He issues manifestos, and his followers distribute them on Juxt One and carry the word to humans on other worlds."

"Including people here on the Father Planet?"

"Yes. He's an inspiration to thousands. Oh, Bram, you'll have to hear his words for yourself. They're stirring."

Eena nodded in solemn agreement, a transfixed expression on her face. "The struggle will be long, the victory eternal," she quoted. "No egg grows until it first divides."

"What did Pite mean—he took things?" Bram said.

Kerthin's tone became defensive. "He took—he takes what he needs to carry on the struggle. Penser teaches that the resources of the universe are there for the human hand to seize. 'Ownership is power,' he says. It isn't fair for the Nar to own it all."

"The Nar share it with us," Bram said.

"To share is weakness," Eena said. "That's another of the things that Penser says. And to accept is weakness."

"I don't understand the reason for all the antagonism," Bram said. "Human beings and the Nar have always existed together in harmony. If the Nar knew how you people felt, they'd be terribly upset. But I forgot. They know about Penser."

"Not everything, gene brother." Pite's colorless eyes flicked over Bram's face. "The little fracas that caused all the trouble was because Penser intended to take over one of the islands that were still under development on Juxt One. To serve as a starting place for his grand plan. There were installations already in place and a fair-size human population to work from, and not too many Nar to get rid of. He had reliable, trained people around him, and he'd already laid his hands on the equipment he needed—a lot of it from Nar warehouses."

"What do you mean, not too many Nar to get rid of?" Bram asked with a growing sense of horror. "You don't mean that—that this Penser actually contemplated . . . *interfering* with Nar physically and removing them from the island?" The idea was almost unthinkable, but Bram was beginning to believe that this Penser person was capable of anything.

Pite gave an unpleasant laugh. "Let's just say that they'd be out of the way."

"It would never be allowed."

"Oh, yes, it would. It would all be over by the time they finished one of their touchy-talky meetings to decide what to do. And then they wouldn't do anything about it, because there wouldn't be any point to it—to them. They'd have let Penser keep his island, you can count on it. They'd probably even feed the animals—at first. The yellowlegs don't fight. They can't. Touchy-talky, touchy-talky—that's how they're made. But we humans know how to fight for what we want. It's in our history. It's all there in the King James book and the Shakespeare plays that the Resurgists are so fond of. Except that they think it's all just words."

"Words fester, deeds cleanse," Eena chanted in what sounded like another Penser quote. "Actions speak louder than words."

Bram was having trouble adjusting to the enormity of what Pite had revealed. "Something like that could—could strain relations between human beings and the Nar forever," he said. "The trust would be gone. It could affect the whole human race."

"That's why it was hushed up," Pite said. "Even those

Ascendist traitors on Juxt One, the ones who opposed Penser and tried to get him deported, didn't want to give the yellowlegs something like that to think about. Or maybe they were afraid of what would happen to them if they did. We have ways of dealing with traitors." The pale eyes bored into Bram again. "You wouldn't inform on Penser, would you, Brammo?" he asked softly.

"No," Bram said. Pite's implied threat had nothing to do with it. Shame alone would seal any human being's lips. Perhaps it was a good thing, after all, that the Nar paid so little attention to human chatter.

Pite settled back comfortably in his seat, thinking that he had won his point. Bram settled back in silence, too. He had a lot to think about.

The squabble on the meeting floor had died down. A new speaker was giving another prescription for human ascendancy.

"Reproductive autonomy!" a red-faced young woman brayed. She looked around belligerently to see if anyone cared to challenge her. "The key is for humans to breed freely. At fifty human generations to one Nar generation, human population expansion would eventually unravel the fabric of Nar society."

Bram was shocked again. The prospect of unrestrained reproductive behavior and unedited genes was appalling. The small human genetic pool, itself stemming from variations of the original metagenome according to a mathematical formula provided by Original Man, needed the constant creation of new genotypes from unexploited alleles. If people simply mated like animals, the species would be endangered by genetic drift.

"Good idea," Fraz muttered. "Outbreed the yellowlegs fifty to one."

Bram refrained from pointing out that even if the human population on all the planets were to double every generation, it would take fifteen generations for them to reach their first billion. It was hardly a solution that one would expect to appeal to a group of people who, like children, wanted everything handed to them right away. But, Bram reflected, Kerthin's odd friends didn't seem to be very good at thinking things through.

At that moment, Kerthin turned to him and gave him the kind of smile he was used to from her. "I know it's hard to get used to new ideas," she whispered. "Give yourself time. When I told Pite what you did, he said that the human race is going to desperately need its own biotechnicians when—"

"When what?"

"When things change," she said. She gave him a pat on the hand and returned her attention to the front of the hall.

A lively debate about reproductive autonomy was going on. Somebody made a motion that a committee be formed to study it, and the bald man called for nominations from the floor.

While Bram was trying to fathom the peculiar ritual, a newcomer eased himself into the meeting hall. The burly man who had been left to guard the door followed close behind. He left the newcomer standing at the back and went up to the platform, where he whispered in the moderator's ear. The moderator let the discussion proceed under its own power for a few minutes while he conferred in low tones with the other people on the platform. Then he went back to the podium and rapped for attention with his block of wood.

"Gene brothers and gene sisters, can we shelve the business at hand temporarily?" he said. "I know you're all anxious to hear the news from Juxt One."

The newcomer came forward. He was a short man who held himself stretched taller at the expense of having to keep his arms crooked stiffly at his sides. He was dressed in one of the petalsmocks affected by public servants. He had a pale meager face that receded from a little red beak of a nose. He kept darting suspicious glances around the meeting room.

"I'm going to ask all of you to be discreet, particularly the people who are new here tonight," the moderator said while the newcomer fumbled with a pouch and extracted a palm-size portable display screen that still had an interface module dangling from it.

There were loud groans from the audience. "Come on, Jupe," somebody called out.

The moderator spread his hands palms out. It was a peculiar use of the gesture, Bram thought. In the company of the Nar, it was a greeting, an invitation to communication. Here, in this segregated human gathering, it was a pushing away.

"I'm not accusing anybody of being low enough to fink to the decaboos," the bald man protested. "But sometimes people like to show off what they know, and things get around to where they shouldn't. So when you talk to people outside, think twice about how much you let out and who you're telling it to. That goes double for those of you with proselytization assignments. Security first, indoctrination second, as the saying goes. Some of you will recognize the gene brother here and know where he works, and you'll be able to figure out how the message came through, so keep it to yourselves."

"What's he talking about?" Bram said.

Amusement showed on Pite's face. "Lot of rigamarole. You piggyback a coded message on the regular commercial laser traffic between stars. Why bother? You might as well get some sympathizer to send it in an open 'gram. The yellowlegs don't give a damn, anyway. But these jokers like to think they're a secret society."

"How did I get in?"

Pite's negligent wave of the hand was almost an insult. "You've been vouched for, Brammo. None of this is worth a bucket of industrial sludge, anyway."

"You said it," Fraz grunted. "The only codes worth worrying about are codes to keep secrets from *them.*" He hooked a thick thumb at the platform.

"You talk a lot, Fraz," Pite said. Fraz's red cheeks got redder, and he slumped down in his seat.

The short man in the petalsmock cleared his throat. "Our gene brothers and gene sisters on Juxt One continue to fight for the cause under great difficulties and despite great personal risk," he said, his little darting glances traveling among the seated people. "But their spirit remains undaunted. There is a smaller human population to work with, resources are slimmer, and travel between the continents and between the planetary bodies in the system is not easy. The unfortunate events of several years ago frightened off many potential converts and made proselytizing more difficult. Membership—" He hesitated. "—has fallen off somewhat." His voice regained its stridency. "But a loyal, dedicated core of those who believe in human ascendancy remains. And frankly, brothers and sisters, they ought to make us ashamed of ourselves."

"Get to the point," a heckler cried.

The short man flushed. He thumbed his hand reader and began to stumble through the words he found there. It was an endless document in stilted prose, full of jargon.

Bram listened, trying to make sense of it. The "struggle" on Juxt One didn't seem to amount to much. An "education committee" had been formed to "augment the awareness" of moon-dwellers. Workers at a human food factory had been organized to request an increase in allowances from their Nar employers. An "informational" campaign had been launched to persuade human dwellers in rural areas to grow their own potatoes, chimeric soycorn, and sunflowers to lessen their dependence on the Nar infrastructure; however, to accomplish this, the Nar would have to be persuaded to condition large tracts of soil with terrestrial-style microorganisms—most of them custom-designed to hold their own in the Juxt One ecology—so that the crops could be grown outdoors. An Ascendist social club had been started in one of the larger cities and was successfully attracting young people to its Tenday evening get-acquainted parties.

The audience sat through about ten minutes of the speech. Then somebody started chanting, "Penser, Penser, give us Penser." Other people joined in the chant and started stamping their feet rhythmically in time with the words. Others in the audience tried to break it up with shouts and slogans of their own, but the pro-Penser faction was louder.

The bald-headed moderator whispered into the short man's ear. The short man held up a hand, looking annoyed. The chanting died down. A few stray voices were heard, but the bald man rapped with his wood block and these too died down.

"Since the last message from Juxt One," the short man said, "there have been several new reports of Penser being seen on some of the moons in the Juxt system. Like earlier reports over the past few years, these could not be verified.

Some of his opponents have suggested that the reports were fabricated—that there was no way Penser could have lifted off-planet, with all space transportation in the hands of the Nar."

"Stuff that," somebody heckled. "There're plenty of loyal Penserites who'd be happy to loan him their identity for an off-planet trip."

"Be that as it may," the short man said stiffly, "Penser's various surfacings all seem to take place within small, loyal cadres of his followers, who then proceed to distribute his texts to a wider circle. Or vidtapes of Penser that could have been made anywhere. One or two of these purported appearances were even in other star systems. If that's the case, we can only conclude that Penser can travel faster than light."

It was too much for Fraz. He jumped to his feet. "Whose side are you on, anyway, you son of a spoiled zygote?" he shouted. "How many legs you got under that smock?"

The moderator banged with his block of wood. "Let the man talk," he said.

"Sit down, Fraz," Pite ordered. "We've got him on our list. The main thing now is the message."

Still glaring, Fraz sank into his seat. His hands still made two big fists.

The short man nodded thanks to the moderator. Looking annoyed, he went on. "There are no 'sides' in the struggle for human ascendancy. Or there shouldn't be. I was signing petitions and working for the cause when some of the people in this room were a blob of jelly on a laboratory slide. And I won't have my motives questioned. I may not agree with all of Penser's positions, but I'm aware that he has a following here and on other worlds and that he is an important voice in the struggle for human ascendancy, no matter what his differences with the leadership on Juxt One. So I'm going to read his statement, and there will be printouts later for those who want them."

He twiddled the control on the little display screen in his palm until it came up with the text he wanted. He cleared his throat again and began to read.

"The universe is within our grasp," Bram heard, "but first we must make a fist. The stars like grains of sand will slip through separate fingers, but the human hand, clenched, is capable of possessing the cosmos."

With the very first words, the image of a fussy little man at a lectern, peering nearsightedly at a hand-held reader and mouthing someone else's message, disappeared, and the room was filled with a powerful presence. Bram could almost sense Penser's forceful personality hanging in the air.

A hush had fallen over the assembly. The others could sense it, too, even those who had been antagonistic.

The words themselves were extraordinary. Taken literally, they made no sense, as Bram realized later when he ran over them in his mind. Penser used a lot of repetition, repeating what evidently were his cant phrases: "No egg grows until it divides." "We shall prevail." "The matter must be forced." "To build, we must first destroy." "Some say there is no goal, only the road ahead; I say the results justify the methods."

But as the phrases mounted, building on simple rhythms, they cast a spell. It was language used as Bram had never heard language used before—not to convey information, but to bend and twist human emotion. The closest comparison Bram could think of was the preaching of some of the prophets invented by King James.

Politics had been among the earliest of the human arts to be revived. It required only three people: two to disagree with each other and a third to be wooed for support. Bram had always thought of it as a dull but necessary instrument used to elect proctors and council members. But until now there had never been a Penser. He had rediscovered the art of demagoguery.

Bram could see tears running down Eena's face. In the seat to his right, Kerthin seemed to be in a trance; she sat like a statue, her face lifted and her eyes focused on an imaginary spot somewhere above the lectern.

"Hold yourselves in readiness, for our time is come," flowed the smooth words, rising now in peroration. "There is a universe to win."

Bram caught Pite nodding meaningfully at Fraz. Pite had been taking notes on the speech, but the notes seemed to consist of short groups of numbers. He saw Bram's stare and buttoned his writing slate up in the breast pocket of his mono.

The spell was broken. The people in the seats began to move and talk as if awakening from a dream. Bram heard the arguments starting to break out.

He turned to Kerthin to say something, but the sound of a chair overturning made him crane his neck. The two who had almost gotten into a fight before were at it again.

"Take your hands off me!" the anti-Schismatist sputtered. "You and your kind are risking all the progress we've made because of the words of that maniac on Juxt One!"

"Shut your traitorous mouth," the other spat.

They scuffled around the floor while others tried to pry them apart, as before. But this time one of them got in a punch. Somebody grabbed his arm, but then another partisan hit the peacemaker, and the fight became general.

"Stop it, stop it!" The wood block pounded on the lectern, but nobody paid attention. A few people made hastily for the exit, but others poured toward the focus of disturbance.

"What are we waiting for?" Fraz cried joyfully, and waded into combat, knocking aside vacant chairs as he went.

Pite gave Bram an ironic glance. "Still sitting on the fence, Brammo?" he asked before heading toward the milling center of the fray.

Bram grabbed Kerthin by the wrist. "Come on," he shouted above the din. "We're getting out of here." She tried to pull away from him, but he held fast. A fist struck him on the shoulder from behind; whether it was a would-be savior coming to Kerthin's rescue or a stray blow from the scuffle going on around him, Bram could not tell. He kept hauling on Kerthin's arm and headed toward the exit.

"We've got to stay and help," Kerthin railed at him, twisting around to look at the little riot. "Where's Eena?"

"She's doing all right by herself," Bram said. He could see Eena, standing on a chair and drumming her skinny fists on the top of the head of one of two men who were trying to throttle each other in front of her. As the locked forms swayed back and forth, shifting position, Eena impartially banged on both heads, first one, then the other.

Bram had gotten Kerthin almost to the door when a chair sailed through the air and there was a crash of glass as it went through a window that some human renovator had installed long ago.

"That does it," Bram said. "We'd better get out of the neighborhood fast, before the monitors arrive."

There was going to be a terrible stink about this. The proctors dealt severely with disturbances that got so far out of hand that they were likely to come to the attention of the Nar. There would be fines, tongue-lashings. As a Nar associate, Bram would be permitted to go to work mornings in order to keep things hushed up, but he didn't fancy spending his nights in polite confinement for a Tenday if the proctors felt tough.

He pushed Kerthin through the door, and they ran. Other people were dispersing in all directions. They were just rounding the curve of the street when Bram heard running feet and the clinking of the little hand bells that the monitors carried, converging on the structure that housed the meeting hall.

"Just in time," he said.

"I don't understand," Bram said. "Why didn't they let him talk? It doesn't hurt to listen to someone's ideas."

"Poor Bram," Kerthin replied. "You're too reasonable. You keep trying to understand everybody else's point of view instead of following the *right* one. Well, never mind, that's one of the things I like about you."

She yawned and snuggled closer to him in the spartan sleeping nest that he still hadn't gotten around to replacing with a double. The fleecy metaplasmic material readjusted its temperature where her hip touched his, to cope with the increase in body heat. On this hot summer night, it felt pleasantly cool against the skin.

Bram was pleased to see Kerthin acting like herself again. He had felt shut off from the tense, humorless stranger who had dragged him to the political meeting. Perhaps it was his fault for not hitting it off better with her friends. But after they had gotten back to his chamber, Kerthin seemed to have shaken off the touchy mood she had been in. She had fixed the two of them a light repast of grainbean flats and sunflower dabs, topped by a sauce of single-cell protein and tomato—rustled up miraculously out of the leavings in his plundered food chest. A couple of cold brews and a lingering nightcap of alcohol slush had mellowed them further.

"Kerth," he said, lying back comfortably. "Why don't we get joined next Tenday?"

"What's wrong with the way we are now?" she asked sleepily.

"No, I mean have a real welding ceremony. Take a pledge of monandry. Throw a party for our friends."

"A what ceremony?"

"Welding or wedding. It's one of the old human forms. They've pieced it together out of the old literature. It's sort of a formal way of bonding permanently, Original Man's version of a monandry pledge. It's becoming very popular. Orris and Marg are going to do it before they emigrate."

"They would," she said. "I've never known a stuffier pair. I don't see why you bother with them."

"Orris is an old friend. He lived across the passage from me when I first moved into my own compartment after I was apprenticed. We used to borrow things from each other all the time." That had been when he was living with Mim, but he did not want to say that to Kerthin.

"You don't have anything in common with him anymore. Honestly, I could fall asleep when we have to go to one of their tastings."

"Marg's on the culinary development project. She's very good at it."

"She's duller than he is. Her head's stuffed full of assimilationist ideas."

Bram retreated from the subject. They lay in companionable silence. "Kerth?" he said after a while.

"Hmmm, yes?" she responded, shifting in the nest.

"How about it? Getting welded, I mean. If we signed the pledge, we could join a gene co-op, and if we added up to twenty-five percent and nobody else was higher, we could get custody of the baby."

"I'm not ready to be tied down yet," she said lazily. "There are too many things I want to do."

"Like politics?" he said, and instantly regretted it.

But they were not going to have an argument about it this time. She started to giggle. "Did you see Eena, pounding with both fists on those two heads? They were so busy fighting, I don't think they even noticed. I wonder if she got out all right."

"She's probably cooling off in the proctor's lockup right now."

"This is a bad time for Pite to be attracting attention," she said. "It's that Fraz. He was the one who got him into it. He's very hotheaded."

Please, Bram wanted to say, let's not talk about Pite right at this moment. But he didn't want to have another bout with Kerthin, so he bit off the words. "Pite looks as if he can take care of himself," he said.

"I'm awful, aren't I?" Kerthin said with a laugh. "Forcing you to sit through all that soft-headed drivel and then getting you involved in a fight. But at least you got to hear Penser's declaration. Don't mind Pite. He's that way with everyone."

Bram hesitated. He didn't want to seem to be lecturing Kerthin. The one thing he feared was having her call him stuffy, like Orris. Finally he said, as mildly as he could, "I know Pite is your friend, but you mustn't let him get you into trouble."

There was a long silence, and he was afraid that he

had muffed it, but Kerthin was still in an affectionate mood.

"Don't worry, Bram, sweet. We won't go to any more meetings like that."

They made love again, then Bram made one more try. "Will you at least go to the gene co-op with me and have them look at a sample? No strings attached."

"Mmm, we'll see," she said comfortably. "Anything to shut you up. Now, go to sleep."

CHAPTER 5

The library annex was tucked away on a lower level near the siphuncle tube. It always smelled a little dank to Bram. Here, near the windowless inner core of the orthocone, one could place a hand flat against the shell partition and feel a deep, slow rhythmic throb as the creature's mantle alternately dilated and contracted to pump water through its funnel.

The librarian was bare to the waist for convenience in consulting the annex's sole Nar-style reading machine. He was a large, ruddy, hairy-chested individual named Hogard. He was the only human person Bram had ever met who could get more out of a body reader than Bram himself.

"Well, Bram, you don't ask for help very often," he said jovially. "What can I do for you?"

"I'm having a little trouble tracking down some historical data," Bram said. "There's a set of artificial genes I've traced back to an early stage of fabrication. But I've only got the conserved variations, not the discards. I'd like to trace the lineage a little further back. I was wondering if there might be a natural prototype somewhere among the antecedents."

The librarian gave a nod. "Like the nitrogen-fixing plasmids from terrestrial bacteria that were found in the original corn genome. Well, let's have a look and see what your problem is."

He squeezed out of his cubbyhole and accompanied Bram to the row of alcoves that held the visual interface readers that let humans use the Nar library system. The reading machines were a patchwork of individual design, reflecting the varied off-the-shelf components available to the human computer buffs who had volunteered their talents and time over the years. Some of the rigs dated back more than a century. At least half of them could be counted on to be out of commission at any given time.

About a dozen men and women were hunched over the reading screens at the moment—some of them bioresearchers, like Bram, from the center; others, browsers from outside, interested mainly in the historical and cultural material. One of them looked up as Bram and Hogard passed. It was the sallow-faced man whom Bram had recognized at the political meeting.

The man's eyes encountered Bram's and instantly darted away. Had there been a flicker of recognition in them? Bram was sure of it, but the man had gone back to his screen without a sign.

Hogard seated himself at the console Bram had vacated. The screen was still on, the image flickering. Hogard hit the device with the heel of a meaty hand to steady the picture. Bram's index symbols came into view along with a boxed message that said NO FURTHER RECORD in Inglex and Chin-pin-yin.

Hogard fiddled with the finger bars for a minute or two,

following Bram's references and punching in alternate codes. There were blinks of meaningless text and the reemergence of the boxed message.

"It may be this machine," Hogard said, frowning. "Did you try one of the others?"

"Three of them," Bram said. "Same result every time."

"You understand that the translation program is very basic," the librarian said. "We couldn't possibly transcribe the Great Language in anything but a simplified form, because the ultimate limitation is the human sensory apparatus and the human nervous system. Oh, the computer boys will keep working on improved programs, and maybe someday there'll be computer-mediated brain implants and genetic enhancement of the deep brain structures. Some of the wilder visionaries talk about it, anyway. But for now, what we've got is mainly a system that's good for hard technical data, things that can be expressed in numbers, visual data, human-loaded references, and so forth. And a sort of precis of everything else."

"I'm not asking for anything subtle," Bram said. "It's all perfectly straightforward—just nucleotide sequences. I've got the right reference tabs. I know that, because I've been following them through."

"This research program goes back five or six hundred years. In fact, here's your foster tutor's name on one of the reference tabs. Voth-shr-voth. Maybe the early work was too inconclusive to enter. Or it's floating around in another file. We don't have the resources for locating *everything*. I'll tell you what. Why don't we go back to the message of Original Man. There's a log reference. Maybe you can trace it from that end."

"There's a gap there, too."

Hogard looked up alertly. "Are you sure?"

"Yes."

"Well, there's some kind of glitch, then. It may have been improperly entered. We'll have to try to bypass the interface program and go direct to the source."

"I've already taken a crack at the body reader upstairs, but I didn't get anything I could make sense of. I've had trouble with that file before."

"Let's give it another try, shall we?"

Hogard led the way back to his cubbyhole and invited Bram inside. It was a rare honor. Few people were allowed behind the swinging gate. The burly librarian clambered up a step stool and streched himself full length on the star-shaped surface of the body reader. Bram was glad to defer to him. Hogard's hairy chest and arms, so the joke went among the envious, were really covered with excessively long and curly cilia.

He lay there a long time, his brow knotted with concentration. When he climbed down, he wore a thoughtful expression.

"I don't understand," he said. "As far as I can make out, it's not cataloged."

"But there's that log reference," Bram said.

"Yes," the librarian agreed. "It goes back half a millennium. It must have been withdrawn from circulation for some reason."

"But why?"

"I don't know. The only thing I can think of is that somebody must have borrowed the file while it was still at a temporary memory address. And that it's been gathering electronic dust in a private file all these centuries. Why don't you ask Voth-shr-voth?"

"I suppose I'll have to. I didn't want to bother him. He has a lot on his mind these days."

Hogard nodded in understanding. "When he goes into the change, a whole era goes with him. He may be the last living member of that touch group. He was one of the youngest associates."

Bram ran a fingertip along the tens axis of the Nar-style waistwatch he wore for a belt. "It's almost quitting time. I'm supposed to meet someone at the gene co-op. I'll talk to Voth tomorrow."

"You're already registered, of course," the gene broker said. "At birth. We've called up copies of your charts from the central files. But we like to do our own mapping. You'd be surprised at the discrepancies that can crop up when you're dealing with more than a hundred thousand genes per person, to say nothing of the chromosomal protein factors."

He was a plump-cheeked young man in a high-collared tunic that looked uncomfortable where it cut into the underside of his chin. He had turned on a practiced heartiness as soon as he had seated Bram and Kerthin opposite him at the little round console that, Bram supposed, controlled the wall screen.

"Is it legal?" Bram asked.

The broker gave him a pained look. "My dear friend, of course! The Nar reproductive monitors are perfectly happy to have us act as their agents in these matters. After all, human beings are not cabbages. They understand perfectly that an element of free choice must be preserved. All we're required to do is to stay within the parameters."

"*Their* parameters," Kerthin said scornfully.

Bram's heart sank. He had hoped Kerthin would be on her best behavior.

But the gene broker was used to coping with difficult clients and their doubts. "Very broad parameters in our generation, fortunately," he said smoothly. "Essentially, all we're doing is following Original Man's plan for avoiding the dangers of genetic drift—extrapolating from the master genome in an orderly mathematical progression. By now we've derived enough new genotypes and expanded the human population sufficiently to give us considerable latitude. In fact—" His face took on an expression of professional benevolence. "—our chief function these days, I sometimes feel, is to assign custody of the children. And the Nar very wisely agree that those decisions are best left to a human agency."

Kerthin's face softened at the mention of children, and Bram gave a silent sigh of relief. "And what would our chances be of getting jurisdiction of a construct?"

The broker pursed his lips. "Excellent, I'd say. I can't see that any question would arise. You're both young, healthy, with no obvious heterozygous matching problems in your charts. You'll almost certainly qualify for the twenty-five percent minimum, so that if the young lady opts to exercise her prerogative for host mothership as well as gene mothership, that should clinch matters. You understand, of course, that every human child must be assigned a Nar proxy parent—just as we ourselves were—but the baby would be yours to raise."

"What about it, Kerthin?" Bram asked, looking into her eyes.

She bit her lip. "I'd like time to think about it."

"Of course, of course, take all the time you wish," the genebroker boomed. "There's no hurry."

"I suppose," Kerthin said slowly, "that other bits and pieces of our gametes will go into the construction of other babies?"

"That goes without saying," the broker said. "Look at

it this way. Your primary offspring will have dozens of partial brothers and sisters running around the Compound." He assumed an expression of piety. "When it comes to that, we're all brothers and sisters in a sense—every human being alive. We all share nucleotide sequences in some degree from the metagenome and its appendices."

"I don't know," Kerthin said. "It seems to me that Bram and I ought to be able to have a child all our own if we want one. The way Original Man did in all the books and plays we have. Without having to get a license from the yell—from the Nar. You said yourself that the human race is large enough now so that we don't have to worry about losing genes through genetic drift."

Bram was astonished. He had never thought that Kerthin was capable of being so sentimental. "Twenty-five percent would be fine, Kerth," he said. "And more than likely, it would be over fifty percent." He appealed to the gene broker. "Isn't that so?"

The gene broker grew sober. "Gene sharing goes back a long way in the history of Original Man," he assured Kerthin. "At least as far back as Shakespeare."

"I thought that was before their technological era," Bram said.

The gene broker smiled broadly and took out a well-thumbed book that had the look of a training manual. "They practiced some primitive form of genetic engineering even then," he said. "There's a reference here in *A Midsummer Night's Dream* to a group of three couples contributing genes to a construct in order to edit out genetic defects. Let me just find the passage . . . hmm, here it is."

He spread the book flat on the console and recited aloud:

To the best bride-bed will we,
Which by us shall blessed be;
And the issue there create
Ever shall be fortunate.

So shall all the couples three
Ever true in loving be;
And the blots of Nature's hand
Shall not in their issue stand.
Never mole, hare-lip, nor scar,
Nor mark prodigious, such as are
Despised in nativity,
Shall upon their children be.

"So you see," the broker said, triumphantly snapping the book shut, "the tradition of gene sharing is a very ancient one for humanity. Our prototypes invested it with special ceremonies: visiting the molecular engineering facility as a group rather than separately, swearing oaths of friendship, and conferring their 'blessing' on the compound nucleotide matrix—or 'bed,' as they termed it."

Bram nodded, impressed. "We were thinking of going through one of the reconstructed welding ceremonies ourselves," he admitted.

He turned to Kerthin for confirmation, but she was already rising to her feet.

"Well, thank you very much," she said. "Bram and I will discuss it and let you know."

The broker was taken by surprise, but recovered nicely. "Would you like to leave a tissue sample before you go, so that we can at least begin some of the preliminary classification work? It would save quite a bit of time later on. It's quite painless, and it would only take a few minutes."

"We can see about that later," she said. "Are you coming, Bram?"

"Uh . . . yes," Bram said. He smiled apologetically at the broker.

"I quite understand," the broker said. "One doesn't want to hurry a decision like this." He bestowed a firm handshake on both of them. "We're available for counseling at any time."

Outside, Bram turned to Kerthin. "What's the matter, Kerth? You haven't changed your mind?"

"I *said* I'd come," she said. "And I did.""When will you go back with me to give a specimen?" he said.

"I don't know. Let's not talk about it right now."

Later they fed at a repast house that everybody had been raving about in the new extension of the Quarter. The architecture was human-style, designed with straight timbers and sheathing material plastered with a lime compound. Even the roof line was straight. The architects had cleverly braced the beams at right angles, avoiding the more familiar curved vault made of bowed poplar timbers that were planet-grown in great cradles that were progressively tilted as the tree developed.

Everything had been lovingly researched by the proprietors, two young men whose previous enterprise had been a neoteric gallery. The item being served this evening was "steak"—a slab of pressed bacterial protein reinforced by fiber and molded into the shape of a four-legged, bilaterally symmetrical creature with curved antennae, copied from a line drawing in the Inglex dictionary. With it were served potato slices sautéed in sunflower seed oil, baked soyatash, and a tomato compote that Kerthin pronounced too sweet.

"Unusual," Bram said. He broke a leg off the sculptured steakbeast and bore it to his mouth with his eating tongs. Something inside, tasting suspiciously like soycrisps, provided a crunch. "It's hard to believe that Original Man actually ate little creatures that looked like this."

"I've heard that there's a genetic template for this type of food creature in the Nar archives, but that it's being suppressed," Kerthin said. "That's part of the Ascendist program—to demand that it be released. After all, eating animal life is part of the human heritage."

The idea made Bram lose his appetite. He pushed the soyatash around with the bowl of his tongs. "I'm sure there's nothing to the story," he said mildly. "I work at the biocenter. I'd know."

"Oh, Bram, you're so naive. What about the egg creature? *That's* being suppressed."

"There's no secret about it. It's not Nar policy to reproduce it, that's all. Anyway, what do we need it for? We've got eggs."

"You let them lead you around by the nose," she said, more sorrowfully than accusingly.

Bram did not reply. If Kerthin was working up to one of her dudgeons, he wasn't going to help her. He looked around at the crowd in the big limed and timbered room. They all seemed to be enjoying themselves, laughing and talking while they stuffed themselves with the exotic food.

He said as much to Kerthin in an effort to steer the subject to neutral ground. "I'm surprised they can attract a crowd as large as this, when you think of the size of the allowance transfer it takes to eat here," he said. Then, suddenly realizing that Kerthin might think he was complaining about the price, he tried to turn it into a general observation: "When you think about this place and some of the other businesses in the Quarter, it sometimes seems as if half the human species exists by selling things to the other half."

But once again he'd said the wrong thing. "And the other half," Kerthin said bitingly, "lives on the bounty of their masters. The human species will never get anywhere until it controls its own capital."

He finally lost his patience. "Kerthin, we're supposed to be having a good time. What's got into you lately? Is politics all you think about?"

"One of us had better think about it," she blazed.

"There are more important things in life."

"There's *nothing* more important. All life *is* politics, whether you realize it or not."

"A lot of people in this world seem to get along nicely without it."

"Like your old artsy-crafty friends, like that little girl from the music department? People who call themselves human Resurgists but who are content to stick their heads in holes in the ground and let themselves be manipulated by external forces! I'll tell you this—an absence of politics *is* politics. Noncommitment is a conscious choice. It says that you've given up on the idea of being in control of your own destiny."

"Calm down, Kerth."

She realized she'd been raising her voice and glanced around at the other diners to see if she'd attracted attention. "Listen, Bram, my innocent swain," she said, leaning forward. "Like it or not, politics rules your life. And it's going to become even more important in the times ahead. There are changes coming. And it's going to be important to be on the right side."

"Your friends' side?"

"When it comes to that, yes. But more important than that, to be on your *own* side—to realize where your own interests lie. Not with a species that's so different from us that they don't even have a centralized brain! On the side of the human race!"

"We don't have to pick sides. We're all life forms together."

"More of that soft-headed assimilationist nonsense," she said scornfully. "We'll get rid of *them* when the time comes. Open your eyes, my dreamy pet. The Nar work in their own interest, not ours. They'd be stupid if they didn't, and they're not stupid. They *have* to be worried about what would happen if our numbers got out of hand, for example. We're controllable now. We have no ecological niche. We're nothing but potted plants. And they'll do whatever they have to do to keep us in the pot."

"The Nar don't think that way, Kerth," Bram protested.

She paid no attention. "So it's perfectly natural for them to want to control information. Information is power. But the great message of Original Man is our property, not theirs. It belongs to humanity, to use as we see fit."

"Kerthin, you keep seeing plots where there aren't any. How can I convince you that the Nar aren't keeping secrets from us? There's a tremendous amount of data in the archives. Decades and decades worth of transmissions. A lot of it hasn't been digested yet. But it's all available.

Scholars—both human and Nar—are digging into it all the time."

"You said yourself that you sometimes have trouble finding the information you want."

"Sure, but that's because humans have difficulty using the Nar library system. There's nothing sinister about it. The cultural package is fairly simple, but a lot of the other data was simply packed away till someone could get around to it. There was a codicil to the first cycle of transmission that lasted fourteen years—apparently additional scientific data and an historical update—that's hardly been more than cataloged."

"That's what we've been told, anyway."

"Kerthin, there's generations worth of work there," Bram said, exasperated. "Anybody who wants to is welcome to track it down, if he wants to spend the time." Seeing the stubborn look on her face, he poured out the tale of the elusive historical data on the heterochronic gene project. "So you see," he finished, "a little sniffing around will generally lead you to the file you want. I'm going to ask Voth about it in the morning."

She was instantly alert. "Don't," she said.

"Huh?"

"Don't ask him about it. Could you get access to Voth's files without him knowing about it?"

"Well, sure. Everything's right out in the open. But I don't see—"

"How can anyone as intelligent as you be so dense? If they know you're after it, they'll take steps to conceal it."

"Don't be ridiculous."

She reached across the rickety eating stand and took his hand. "If I'm wrong, it doesn't matter, does it? But you have an opportunity to show your loyalty to the whole human species. And if that's not important to you, do it as a favor to me. Promise?"

"Kerth, you're asking me to spy on my own adoptive tutor, the being who brought me up!" Bram exclaimed. Spying was one of the most universal human activities if one could believe fifty centuries of literature, and most of the authors, from Homer to Jarn Anders, didn't appear to think too highly of those who practiced it.

"How can it possibly hurt Voth—unless *he's* deceiving *you?*"

"But—"

She withdrew her hand. "And to think I was considering sharing genes with you!"

"Don't be like that, Kerth."

"Promise?" she asked.

"All right," he said miserably.

She settled back in her seat. "Let's have another drink before we go home," she said. "See if you can catch their eye."

Voth glided out of his private chamber and headed across the atrium toward the elevators. He paused when he saw the reading light in the human end of the spectrum shining in Bram's alcove. With a corkscrew swirl of his upper structure, he reversed polarity and retraced his steps.

"You work late, Bram, my child," he said. "Everyone else has gone."

Bram looked up at the sound of the words. Voth's voice was becoming deeper; it was almost as deep as a female's now. The other Nar tiptoed around him with exaggerated deference these days.

"I . . . I'm just catching up on a few odds and ends," Bram said.

He had been within a hairbreadth of getting up and leaving when Voth had finally decided to call it a day. It had seemed almost providential to Bram that Voth had picked this particular night to linger; Bram had been almost grateful to have an excuse to change his mind.

"Are you having difficulties?" the old decapod asked. "I can stay to help."

"N-no, there aren't any particular problems. I just want to clear up some work."

"Your contribution to the embryonic stem project is causing much favorable comment," Voth said. "The work goes well in the biocrafting department. Soon, we believe, we will have some good news to pass along. I am proud of you, Bram."

"Thank you," Bram replied, feeling worse than ever.

"But you ought not to work so hard. You should be at home to give time to the young woman you contemplate pairing with."

How had Voth known that? Of course! The gene coop would have requested records from the Nar reproductive monitors, and Voth—as preoccupied as he was with the approaching change in his own life—still took the trouble to keep up with the lives of his human foster children.

"I won't stay long," Bram said wretchedly.

133

CHAPTER 6

Bram lay spread-eagled across the prickly surface of the pentacle, calling up demons.

He might have thought of it that way if he'd been familiar with the old superstitions, because the data he'd summoned gave off a definite spirit of evil. Evil was the only way to describe the overtones of revulsion, horror, and fear that crawled through the factual coordinates of the touchdocuments.

There was no such thing as neutral data to the Nar. A human being might have written down these documents in the impersonal medium of words and numbers, keeping his feelings to himself. But the Nar who long ago had committed the information to machine memory had written with his living body. And now the machine was reproducing every ripple, every tremble of vibrissae, every chemical nuance, at an information rate that no human brain could absorb even if the connections had been there.

Bram pressed his cheek harder against the palpitating sheet of artificial villi, trying desperately to extract sense out of it all. A scratchy many-legged shape—the ghost of a visual image?—scuttled past his face and disappeared into the broader surface that his body couldn't cover, leaving little multiplying echoes of itself in the other four points of the star under his forearms and naked thighs. Sweat trickled off Bram's body, confusing the chemical cues, but a faint acrid whiff traveling past his nostrils made him press his tongue flat against the surface at that spot. He knew he risked being poisoned by Nar proteins if he used his tongue and lips too much, but sometimes a human could pick up more details that way than with less sensitive parts of the body.

At last he rolled off the machine, exhausted. He sat on the floor with his back against the pedestal, resting until his strength came back. He'd been on the body reader for more than two hours by then. He'd had to run it at slow speed, repeating sections over and over again, to riffle through what a Nar might have covered in five or ten minutes.

Was this whole area of information under interdiction?

Bram thought it over. He didn't think so. Nothing was specifically forbidden, or he wouldn't have been able to delve farther into layer after layer of the material. But there was something about this area that made the Nar shy away from it. Out of distaste. Out of fear. Out of whatever negative emotions whose blurred phantoms had lapped at him these past two hours.

But, naturally, any human attempting to enter this system through the crude interface program would run up against a confused and ambiguous interpretation of the Nar warning flags: "Stay away." "Caution." "Dead end." "Unclean." "Proceed at your own risk." "Adults only." The "records not available" borderline he'd skirted previously was one of those ambiguities.

What it meant was that you pushed your way into this area while figuratively holding your nose.

But Bram had learned one thing while racked on the star-shaped machine—there were visual records associated with this file. And he thought he knew how to get at them.

He put his clothes back on. From somewhere within the great hollow structure he heard the collective patter of Nar footsteps reverberating through the central shaft and then the whir of a descending elevator, but the wing he was in was silent. He felt a stab of self-reproach as he let himself through the oval opening to Voth's sanctum and reminded himself of what Kerthin had pointed out—that it was not as if he were doing something to hurt Voth. It was not even as if he were doing anything wrong. He used Voth's vidlink and other peripherals all the time, with invitation and without. He had always felt free to use Voth's private files whether or not Voth was there, and Voth had encouraged him.

Why, then, should he feel guilty now?

There was a one-tentacle touch pad mounted on a swinging bracket over Voth's desk—a narrow triangle about three feet long. It served both as an input device and a small-screen tactile reader. It was a good enough computer link for all practical purposes; the Great Language was not petal-specific but was dispersed through all five points to add up to optimum sharpness and clarity, and if need be a one-tentacle reader could be scrolled to build up a five-point impression one point at a time.

The vidscreen was a concave curve with about ninety degrees of arc—adapted to the triple-perspective vision of a Nar using three of its five evenly spaced eyes. But Bram was used to such screens and had long ago found that binocular vision was no obstacle once the initial feeling of disorientation had passed.

He lowered the triangular plate face down on its bracket and inserted his bare forearms beneath it, elbows and wrists pressed together to give him the maximum continuous surface for feedback. His fingertips danced with practiced agility across the input wedge at the tip, smoothing down areas of cilia in complex, shifting patterns and teasing other areas upright. Human fingers were clumsy but good enough to call up menus and submenus and respond to them with yeses and nos and supplemental queries— rather as if he were using his elbows and knees to punch in a few basic routines on a human-style keyboard.

Colors swirled across the curved screen, and images began to take shape. With a thrill, Bram recognized the characteristic loop of a terrestrial DNA strand, enormously magnified.

A moment later he had lost it. Abstract representations of molecules, brightly colored, streamed past at high speed. Bram recognized protein and lipid structures. After another ten minutes of tickling the touch pad, he got more microphotography showing lipids forming a membrane that enclosed DNA and the dark specks of proteins that had to be primitive enzymes.

A simple protocell was being assembled before his eyes. In due course, the protocell divided, then divided again. A viable life form had been created.

He knew he was on the right track then. Protocells like this had no utility except as student exercises. The file he had tapped was very dusty indeed.

For the next two hours, while his arms and shoulders screamed in protest at their cramped position, he browsed through the records, watching as the Nar molecular biologists, lifetimes ago, learned how the terrestrial-style information molecules, enzymes, and lipids worked together to make living organisms. They were practicing for the reinvention of man.

It was strange to think of a young Voth, a Voth without an honorific in his name, as one of those researchers. Long as was the Nar life span, there couldn't be many survivors of those original teams. At what point had Voth split away to follow other byroads, eventually to found the touch group that had given him his present eminence, while newer teams sprang up and fused and split and recombined to take up the ever-multiplying branches of research? There was a biological treasure trove to explore—a wealth of possibilities that had transformed Nar civilization. They were in no hurry to get to man. The Nar sense of time, with its enormous scale, was not conducive to urgency. Things could be put down, laid aside. Everything was always there, spread out in eternity, to be taken up again by one's future self or by the future self of some touch brother's spawn, nearing sentience and ready to be adopted into the touch group.

Bram got up, stretched, and felt his joints crack. Outside, the city was sleeping. Through the clear elastic window, the sprawling lacelike patterns of boulevards, plazas, and junctions glowed with the pale blue biolight of the wee hours. A single strand of bubble cars crept through the black sky, carrying late commuters. A preoccupied snuffling and scraping from somewhere below told where a streetcleaning behemoth was pulling its flat bulk along the avenue. In the human quarter, which was visible as a ragged patch of brightness in the distance, even the most tenacious reveler would long since have staggered home by now.

Bram, stiff and aching, turned back to the visual display where a mini-ecology was suspended, waiting for him to animate it again.

He could only guess at the scale; a few simple multi-celled organisms wriggled through greenish water, but one of the swimmers—though its organization was complex enough to provide a whiplike tail and an unarguable gullet—was obviously single-celled. Bram could easily see the shadow of a cell nucleus and several organelles within the translucent form.

The frame of the picture jerked, and the magnification changed. Bram gasped at the teeming life he saw there. A segmented creature with long feelers darted past at close range. A flattened ribbon with a deltoid head and eyespots undulated through feathery green bottom plants. There was something like a tube or sac with a cluster of waving tentacles at one end, much like some of the small aquatic forms here on the Father World. There must have been, Bram realized with wonder, at least fifteen or twenty separate varieties of plants and animals represented in the picture.

There was a puzzle here. The creatures didn't exist. Or at least, if they once had existed, they were no longer being manufactured. They had no obvious utility, of course. Were they steps on the road to man? It seemed unlikely. Not all of them, surely.

The senders of that stupendous genetic message from the dim past had necessarily been parsimonious. It took a thousand genes or more to specify the enzymes for a single cell, such as a simple soil bacterium. To construct a human being, one needed more than a hundred thousand genes adding up to well over a billion nucleotides; Bram had seen the cupboards where copies of those magnetic storage records were kept, and they contained more shelf space than the cabinets for all the cultural records combined.

Potatoes were simpler than people, of course. The limited selection of food plants needed to support reconstructed man, the necessary microorganisms, the handful of useful life forms like the poplar tree—none of them had required anywhere near as much transmission time. And additional variations, even new species, could be derived from short nucleotide inserts and from protoplast-derived clones that were somatic variants. But it all added up in terms of transmission priorities.

So there didn't seem to be much point in making an aquarium like the one Bram saw before him.

Perhaps only visual footage had been transmitted. Maybe the aquarium had existed on man's world. Even so, it seemed profligate. It had been running for some minutes. How many thousands of color frames had been lavished on this presentation? The art historians would have given their eyeteeth for a fraction of this precious time.

Bram rotated his forearms slightly, trying to pick up additional clues. The prickly sensations continued; they constituted a running commentary on what he was seeing. And they contained the same overtones of dread that he had detected on the whole-body reader.

And something else.

This section of the record came from the codicil he had imprudently mentioned to Kerthin—the supplement that had added fourteen years of transmission time the second time around, before the message had been cut off. So whatever genetic information was contained in this electronic bin could not have been needed to draw up the blueprint of man.

It was an afterthought.

An afterthought somehow connected with the idea of heterochronic genes and with man himself.

The sense of dread built. Bram's trembling arms strained to hold their position. On the screen he watched a scuttling multilegged creature whose resemblance to man was poignant.

Discount the armor-plated body, the segmented legs, the feelers it waved ahead of itself as it climbed a green blade. It possessed bilateral symmetry, paired eyes in a sort of face, and, obviously, some sort of central nerve pathway instead of a neural net.

More to the point, it possessed the same sort of DNA as did Bram himself, not the Father World's sort with its uracil-adenine pairs and reversed sugars. Bram could not take his eyes off it. He realized that tears were running down his face.

And then the water exploded into motion.

A nightmare creature filled the screen, all head and hairy legs, with a long slender body trailing behind. Its eyes were like green tomatoes, its mouth a vertical cleft. The armored creature was gone, simply vanished. Bram had just time enough to glimpse a twitching leg disappearing into that strange maw, and then the two hemispheres of the face snapped shut again.

An afterimage lingered in Bram's vision. He could not be sure he had really seen it, but there was the impression of something long and scooplike that had whipped out of that bisected face and drawn the segmented creature inside.

Bram blinked again, and now the monster itself was gone, flicking itself away by some process too fast to follow.

His fingers scrabbled for the touch pad, trying to bring the picture back so that he could study it one frame at a time. But the machine misunderstood his human input. Somehow he had triggered a search program. He could feel the successive ridges of raised pinpricks marching across his joined arms, the forward edge of a great arc of rotating wheel. Random images flashed across the screen. But try as he might, he could not call up the sequence he had just seen.

He was back on the fringes of the heterochronic egg project, following one branch after another—decades, perhaps centuries, of diverging data. None of it told him how the long codicil was supposed to be connected with the genetic program for man—a program that already had been complete in itself. What kind of synthetic gene, destined for man, was supposed to come out of these tomato-eyed horrors? Bram shuddered.

He tried for the next couple of hours to backwind the search program to the point he wanted. He got back to the assembly of the early terrestrial protocells without any problems, but then the database began skipping all over the place. When daylight began to show through the window, he gathered up the holo printouts he had generated, cleaned up, and went back to his own cubbyhole and sat down at his desk.

He was still sitting there when the orthocone awakened to morning life. The elevators hummed, daylight flooded through the oval ports and washed out the bioglow, and the resonant thrum of Nar voices spread through the passages. A pair of co-workers came in, holding hands in conversation—early arrivals from the proteins assembly subgroup. They saw Bram sitting at his desk and, after a twitch of surprise, saluted him with a flared tentacle apiece.

"Greeting, Bram-brother. You are at work early this morning."

Voth came drifting in about midmorning, large and imposing with hydrostatic pressure. He was gaining actual mass as well, with his increased appetite these days. He gave a preoccupied top flutter to the juniors in the atrium and sailed past them to his office, moving in the absent-minded spiral gait of five-way equipoise.

Bram gave him a few minutes to get settled, then followed him inside. Kerthin would have seventeen fits at what he was about to do, but he could not leave the matter as it now stood.

It went against his grain to behave conspiratorially, as Kerthin wanted him to do. He could not bring himself to believe that there was anything sinister in Nar motives. If anything, the Nar were paternalistic and overprotective toward their human wards. Bram had never known anything but affection from Voth and his touch brothers.

He didn't care if Voth knew that he had dipped into forbidden knowledge—if it *was* forbidden. The only thing that bothered him was that he could not now be totally forthright with Voth. It would have been too embarrassing to admit that he had succumbed to Kerthin's suspicions—that he had gone sneaking about in the middle of the night.

But he could be oblique.

"You're tired, Bram," Voth said, turning a couple of eyes on him. "It is not good to stay awake nights."

Bram gave a guilty start, then realized that Voth merely had interpreted correctly his bloodshot eyes and stiff movements. Voth, even for a member of a naturally empathetic species like the Nar, was a superb reader of the human body.

"I'm all right," Bram said.

Voth, noticing his hesitation, beckoned inwardly with his crown if tentacles. "Don't hang about by the door, youngling. Come over here."

Bram perched beside Voth and let him wrap a tentacle around his bare forearm. It was the only comfortable way for a Nar to talk, even in the Small Language. Bram needed

143

the contact almost as much; it was how he had been raised.

"Now, tell me what is troubling you," the decapod said before Bram could speak.

"There is a thing I do not understand," Bram said.

Hesitantly at first, then with increasing fluency, he let his doubts pour out. He summarized his problems in retracing the origins of the heterochronic genes, told of his encounter with the warning bells in the file from the codicil and the elusive footage of the voracious underwater monster. He left out the circumstances under which he had run across it and hoped that his blush would not betray him.

"What *was* it, Voth?" he concluded lamely.

The old decapod was silent for several seconds. The wrapped tentacle gave a little squeeze, as if Voth were trying to hold onto him more tightly. It recalled for Bram the way, when he was a small child, that Voth had restrained him in the presence of moving machinery or dangerous heights.

"I am surprised at your interest," Voth said finally. "Those archives have been untouched for centuries. I had almost forgotten that they exist."

"It was a terrestrial life form, wasn't it?" Bram prompted. "It had six legs. But they were paired."

Voth sighed: a rush of wind and a relaxation of muscle. "It is called a nymph."

The word, as Voth pronounced it, had an Inglex ring to it. After a moment, Bram remembered. It came from the translation of Homer. A nymph had held Odysseus prisoner in a cave.

"It is a stage in the development of a particular terrestrial life form," Voth went on, as if the words were painful. "The adult form is quite different—an air breather with wings. It lives for only a brief mating season. But the immature nymph form may persist for two or three years. It is one of the most dangerous creatures in its particular ecological niche. It exists only to eat other life forms—some of them as large as itself. Swimmers, crawlers, even small manlike amphibians." Voth broke off, as if the subject were distasteful.

"What was the adult form called?" Bram asked.

"A dragonfly."

Bram knew about dragons. He shivered. The adult form must have been a fearsome creature indeed.

"Why . . . why would the message senders have expended data time on such an organism?"

"As a warning."

"Warning?" So the source of all those danger flags had been Original Man himself. The Nar records would have amplified them, adapted them for Nar sensibilities, and spread them through the associated data frames.

"A warning to whomever might have received the first cycle of the message."

"It was in the codicil, then?"

"Yes." A fountaining wave front of cilia movement showed that Voth was uncomfortable with the subject. "The dragonfly genetic information—not complete, fortunately—had been sent earlier as part of a particular genetic exposition. Fifty years later, they had . . . cause to regret it. They decided to communicate their . . . second thoughts."

Handle with care. That was the meaning of the warning flags that had kept Bram at arm's length from the data.

"May I know the nature of this genetic exposition, Voth-shr-voth?" Bram asked formally.

"Of course." Voth's fibrillar membranes dilated contritely. "When have I kept anything from you, even as a child? You are entitled to the information available to any junior of good sense and judgment."

The juniors in the department were at least a couple of centuries old. The implicit meaning of what Voth had just said was best passed over, and he went on quickly.

"The dragonfly was one of a number of earthly life forms with extended immature stages. Only the imago—the adult form—reproduced. The humans conducted experiments to modify the cellular timing mechanism, to see if sexual maturity could be induced in the aquatic form."

"Heterochronic genes," Bram said, beginning to understand.

"Their purpose was to make the arctic regions of their home planet more habitable. A modified nymph, they thought, would control small biting insects called blackflies and mosquitoes that still inhibited full exploitation of these regions, even at the height of man's technological prowess. Such organisms, it seems, were also water-breeding. And the nymph devoured anything that swam."

Voth's sensitive tentacle lining fluttered in a manner that in a human being would have been called a shudder.

Bram could empathize with Voth's instinctive revulsion. Voth was visualizing the tiny swimmers that would be his own children, after he had expended his life in mating—and imagining a creature like a dragonfly nymph gobbling them up.

"The key to a synthetic heterochronic gene was found in a peculiar creature called an axolotl," Voth went on. "The axolotl was the larval form of a kind of animal known to humans as a salamander. But unlike other salamanders, the axolotl spent its entire life as a larva. It was able to reproduce without undergoing metamorphosis to its adult stage. It retained its gills and lived and died as an aquatic form.

Human scientists believed it to be a separate species until, by chance, some axolotls on exhibition changed into air-breathing adults, as axolotls cut off from water will sometimes do."

Bram furrowed his brow. "The heterochronic mutation would have to be a dominant one. But if it could be turned off, it means—"

"Dominant heterochronic mutations cause particular cell lines to repeat immature patterns *instead* of developing. Recessive heterochronic mutations, on the other hand, *cause* premature development of other cell lines."

"Yes, I see. Axolotls were a sexually mature larval form. So when those exhibit specimens completed their metamorphosis, something had happened to turn *off* the dominant mutant genes that had prevented cell differentiation in those cell lines *not* concerned with reproduction, though leaving the reproductive system itself to mature normally. But dragonfly nymphs were sexually *im*mature. So somehow the mechanisms of a *recessive* heterochronic mutation would have to be mimicked in order to turn *on* the genes for sexual maturity. While at the same time acting as a *dominant* mutation to suppress adult development of non-reproductive cell lines."

Voth gave a confirming squeeze to Bram's arm. "Precisely. A set of synthetic chimeras was contrived by man and spliced into a dragonfly sequence. The container and the contents were inseparable, unfortunately. Further species-crossing capability had to be determined by trial and error. That merged set of genes was the one we were given to work with. By the time of the warning in man's codicil, we were already well along with our work on the heterochronic hen's egg."

"Why was a warning necessary?"

"An unstable allele was found at a key junction. It made the gene vulnerable to point mutation caused by random radiation. A chemical regulator related to thyroglobulin was no longer suppressed. And, like the captive axolotls, the mutated nymphs lost their gills."

"They became air breathers," Bram said grimly.

Voth's organ voice carded wheezing overtones of stress. "The result was an organism that got out of control, spilling out of the ecological niche for which it had been intended. The ground-dwelling nymphs were large and active. Formidable enough to prey on small mammals called rodents. Vicious enough to attack even larger mammals, including man. They were a greater danger than the blackflies and mosquitoes they had been intended to control. They were exterminated with great difficulty. It took decades. And when it was over, whole regions of the arctic were so poisoned as to be economically useless."

Bram thought of the footage he had seen. Voth had avoided being explicit about its origin. "Was the nymph recreated here on the Father World?" he asked.

Voth gave a shuddery fibrillation. "No. It was an incomplete genome, fortunately. It might have been possible to construct a close analog by filling in the gaps. There were some who actually wanted to do such a thing. They argued that even if the creature were to escape from the laboratory, it could not have survived, because it would have been poisoned by the proteins of our life forms."

Bram felt the hairs on the back of his neck rise, in the human analog of Voth's reaction. "There are single-celled planticules here on the Father World that produce terrestrial-style right-hand amino acids," he said. "There are other organisms that have evolved to metabolize all sorts of poisonous substances into simple abiotic organic compounds. There are higher life forms that live in symbiosis with colonies of protozoans within their digestive organs and are nourished by the breakdown products. Even we humans utilize some Nar food sources by using them as feedstocks for industrial microorganisms." His voice dropped to a whisper. "If a creature like the nymph ever learned how to use the native-style proteins and amino acids and then somehow got out of the laboratory . . ."

"That was exactly the argument of those who opposed the creation of a nymphlike construct, myself included," Voth said. "There was already too much terrestrial DNA around, particularly in the tailored microorganisms associated with our infant cellulose industry. If there was even the most astronomically remote possibility that some mutated form might colonize the nymphs and act as a metabolic buffer for them, then we dared not risk it."

"No," Bram agreed fervently. "You couldn't."

"We held an all-world touch conclave to consider the matter. We waited two years for Juxt One's touch transcription, even longer for the farther stars. No world or moon that had even a few thousand Nar living on it was left out. The vote was close. But the touch union makes us all one in questions affecting the entire race, so the decision was thereafter binding on all Nar."

Bram drew a breath. "There are other terrestrial life forms on the shelf, aren't there, Voth?"

He did not use the word "suppressed," but the nuance hung between them.

Voth gave a little contraction of embarrassment. "You know of the egg-creature called a hen. We believed it wrong to raise any organism possessing a nervous system for mass slaughter. But the hen genes live on in the self-dividing egg."

"And there were others, too, weren't there?" Bram persisted. Kerthin's accusation about the steakbeast sprang into his mind.

Voth was definitely on the defensive. Bram could feel the searching patterns in the field of cilia. "We created a limited number of terrestrial animal forms before attempting man and allowed them to live out their lives after their usefulness was gone. They were mostly simple creatures—wormlike forms, a mollusk similar to the ancestor of our orthocone creature, a small amphibian called a frog. They were necessary steps in the learning sequence provided by man. But Bram, Original Man used mollusks for food. Would you and most of the human people you know, raised apart from that custom, do the same?"

"No, I guess not," Bram admitted. He felt deflated. "Still," he said wistfully, "I can't help thinking about what a precious reserve of data remains locked up in the archives. Even the dragonfly nymph. Think of what you already got out of it before you slammed the door. The heterochronic egg. The work that's going forward now on embryonic stem tissue in the poplar—"

"Nothing is lost, my Bram," Voth said, hugging him. "Knowledge awaits, as it always has. All will be explored in the fullness of time. Research will continue. But under the provisions of the touch concordance. Under the scrutiny of our species. With safeguards."

"I won't be here to see it."

"Nor shall I," Voth said.

"You didn't come home last night," Kerthin said as Bram popped the door shut behind him.

She was kneeling in front of the stove, putting on a pot of brew. Her overcape was flung carelessly across Bram's writing stand; she must just have come in herself. She twisted around to look at him questioningly, tossing back the thick rope of hair.

Bram sank wearily into a seating puff. His eyes were scratchy, and his limbs felt like lead. "Is there anything to drink?" he said.

She got up without a word and poured him a measure of ethyl, neat, over a scoop of slush from the cryobacterial coldbin. She handed it to him and waited while he took a thirsty sip.

"Well?" she said.

"I traced the file back," he said. "It took me all night."

"Was I right?"

"Kerthin, your steakbeast is just a fairy tale, but yes, there's a certain amount of genetic information that isn't generally available to researchers—human *or* Nar."

"I *knew* it!" she said.

"You don't understand, Kerth. There are no secrets. Not exactly. The whole Nar commonwealth is aware that sections of the great transmission have been put aside for the time being. For good reasons. Humane reasons. Reasons of safety. Eventually researchers will get around to reopening some of the material on a file-by-file basis, under proper supervision."

"*They* know! *They* decide!" Kerthin's voice dripped scorn.

"It's a Nar world, Kerthin. They're doing the best they can for us, by their own lights. But there are obstacles that nobody can do anything about. Like the human life span. Even with cloned transplants, even though the genes we carry were selected for longevity and good health, none of

151

us can expect to live much beyond our allotted sevenscore and ten. There isn't *time* for us to do things on the Nar scale. Like my little project running up against the nymph cross-file. If you ask me, the Nar've been low-key about its existence out of simple tact."

"The nymph file?" Kerthin's gray eyes became alert.

Bram explained about the dragonfly nymph and about the belated warning the long-ago humans had tagged it with. "Voth was perfectly right about it," he finished. "It might have been a danger to the Father World's ecology. And when you come right down to it, we're a part of that ecology too, in our little artificial bubble."

"You went to Voth-shr-voth about it?" she asked incredulously.

"What's wrong with that? I *told* you Voth was perfectly open with me."

"How could you do something that stupid? After I explained everything to you. You were supposed to let him go on thinking he was flimflamming you. People like you are a threat to the movement. At this stage we're still trying to lull the Nar. We don't want them to suspect the extent of human dissatisfaction."

"There isn't any dissatisfaction. Except for a handful of people like your friend Pite. And this Penser. Most of the people I know are happy just to go on living their lives."

"I was right about man's heritage being suppressed, though, wasn't I? You said as much."

"Kerthin, let's not go through all that again."

"Never mind." She bit her lip, thinking. "This dragon thing. Can you find out more about it?"

"Of course. I can look through any file I want to, and Voth will help me get into it. In fact, I plan to *tell* him I intend to go on reading a little further. I just can't work with the genetic material without a license, that's all. No one can, not even Voth himself. Whoever tried would need the resources of the whole biocenter, anyway."

"Hmmm." She pondered further, "This . . . dangerous life form. It might make a good weapon in the coming struggle against the Nar." Her eyes lit up. "Anyway, Pite will be interested in the information."

"Kerthin! I thought you gave all that up!"

"I told you you didn't have to go to any more meetings. But who can tell when I might happen to run into Pite or one of the others again?"

"All he can do is get you into trouble."

She laughed. "Did you hear what he said to the proctors? He gave them better than he got. They didn't know what to do with him. They threatened to lock him up for a week. He said he'd welcome it. In the end they let him go. He refused even to acknowledge their warning."

"Kerthin, I don't want you mentioning what I told you to Pite."

"Oh, don't be tiresome."

"I mean it."

She tossed her head. "Oh, all right, if it means so much to you."

"I don't want you telling *anybody*!"

"I *said* I wouldn't." She turned away from him. "There are some messages on the screen for you."

Bram went to the viewer and ran his eyes down the message list. Nothing required immediate reply. He opened a few electronic envelopes at random.

"Hey, Kerthin, how about this? There's an invitation from Orris and Marg. They're already aboard their tree. It's in a parking orbit. All the human passengers are throwing a farewell party. Arrangements have been made with the Nar to lift the guests."

"I thought they weren't sailing for a couple of months."

"They aren't. They're living aboard while the tree's being outfitted. It's never carried humans before. The purser wants to make sure the ecology of their branch is adjusted properly, and it'll give them a chance to settle in. Give everybody a chance for a last-minute change of mind, too!"

He looked at her hopefully. He supposed he could go alone if he had to, but he didn't relish the thought.

"I'd love to go."

"Hey, that's great." He gave her close scrutiny, but she seemed genuinely enthusiastic. "I thought you didn't care for them. Dull, you said. Stuffy."

"We'll never have to see them again, will we? Besides, I've never been in orbit."

CHAPTER 7

The orbital ferry was a sandwich of three flattened, sleek craft standing on their flipperlike tails, wrapped in a close embrace that turned them into a single deltoid shape. It was only a shiny toy in the distance, until one's eye took in the mitelike crowd swarming about its base and adjusted for scale.

"Is that what we're riding in?" Kerthin asked doubtfully. Her fingernails dug into the meat of Bram's arm.

"The ferry's the one in the middle of the stack," Bram said. "The two outer vehicles peel off and land again after they've finished giving us a boost."

"Let's take the next one," she said with a shiver. "We can go back inside the terminal and have a drink while we're waiting."

"We're already booked," Bram said firmly. "Come on, it's perfectly safe for humans. Hundreds of people get boosted into space every year."

"They made that thing for themselves," she pointed out. "*They* fly it, *they* ride in it. And *they* don't have any bones

155

to get broken. And *they're* not as fussy about breathing as we are. And *they* don't even *care* if they die."

Kerthin was at her most petulant. But behind the petulance was a genuine anxiety that surprised Bram. He had never known Kerthin to be at a loss before. There were people who were afraid of flying, he knew, people who were afraid even to step into a bubble car, but he would not have placed Kerthin among them. It made him feel responsible and protective.

"There's every provision for human beings," he soothed her. "Special safety couches. Everything. Even the amenities, like the little lounge in the terminal. They take good care of us."

"How do you know?"

"I looked into it. They even spend extra fuel to boost at low g for us."

"I'd still like to have a drink first," she grumbled.

"There'll be plenty to drink up there. Half the crowd'll have to be poured back into the ferry, I'll bet." He smiled reassuringly. "And by the way, it's not true that the Nar don't care about dying. They care as much as we do. Until the end, when they're through with life."

A spread Nar with one of its arms in a computer sleeve stood in their path.

"May this one know your names, brother persons," it said in fair Chin-pin-yin except for the gender confusion.

Bram told it, and it waved them on after presumably checking them off through its portable relay. There were no seat tokens—not even the simple plastic counters sometimes used to keep high-density systems like the bubble cars flowing smoothly during rush hours. The Nar did everything on the honor system.

"Is that all there is to it?" Kerthin exclaimed. "Anybody could have taken our places."

"Who'd do a thing like that?" Bram asked.

"How do I know?" she said peevishly. She turned half away. "Somebody who wanted a free trip into orbit so they could get a close-up look at a tree."

Bram laughed. "I don't think that anybody who wanted to crash the farewell party would have to go to lengths like that. I don't imagine the guest list was checked too carefully. The only reason they took our names here was to give the flight crew a little advance notice that our seats would be occupied on this lift."

As if to punctuate his words, a great shuddering roar filled the air as some ferry farther down the line took off. Bram looked up and saw a column of yellow fire paint itself across the clear violet sky. He couldn't see the craft itself, only its blinding tail.

"There goes the first section," he yelled against the deafening rumble in the sky. "We're probably next."

Kerthin clutched at his arm. Her face had gone pale.

"Easy," he said. "You don't have to take this ride if you don't want to. We can still turn back."

"No." she said. "I'm going."

She released his arm. Her lips were compressed with determination. She gave him a forced smile and moved quickly ahead of him toward the waiting jitney. It was an electric vehicle, not one of the big living walkers the Nar usually used for short and intermediate distances. Bram wondered if that was in deference to human sensibilities—a lot of people were made nervous by tons of living flesh that they unreasonably imagined might get out of control—or if mechanical systems were the norm here in this place where enormous energies were dispensed as a matter of course.

He got his answer when they boarded. Except for the three or four Nar sprawled out on splayed bases in the cleared center of the vehicle, all of the passengers were human, sitting around the perimeter on molded benches that had been temporarily glued to the floor alongside what had been the usual pedestal mounts. Thirty or forty people were already in place, dressed in festive multicolored clothes. A couple of preliminary parties were in progress among people who had brought jugs along, and a number of people had used their baggage allowances to take what looked like a variety of housewarming gifts scattered at their feet.

"Hi, over here!"

Bram waved back at the pair who had spotted him and pushed his way through with Kerthin to the empty seats.

"Kerthin, this is Trist and Nen," Bram said. He didn't know them very well; Trist had been one of the fellows at the bachelor lodge when he had been staying there, and he had met Nen several times when she had been Trist's guest at one of the Tenday breakfasts or evening shindys.

"I know," Kerthin said shortly.

"Kerthin and I were in the same division at middle school," Nen explained with a quick smile. She was a trim, rangy girl, not quite as tall as Kerthin, with pleasant, freckle-dusted features. "I haven't seen you for pentayears. Are you still keeping up with your sculpture?"

"I don't have time for that anymore."

"I was going to be the world's greatest actress," Nen said with a laugh. "I'm working as a med tech now. At the Compound infirmary." She shrugged. "It's useful work, and it's interesting. Better than hanging around on allowance, anyway."

"She's too modest," Trist said. "She practically runs the place."

"What are you doing these days?" Bram asked.

"I'm in the physics group," Trist said. "With our old friend Smeth."

"How is he?"

"You'll see him at the shindy. Grown oracular beyond his years. He's trying to calcify himself into a monument, and you know, given a few more feathers in his cap and *a lot* more gray hairs, he might just do it."

"He's doing well, then?"

"He has a first-rate mind for plasma physics, you have to hand him that."

"What's happening in your project lately, anyway?"

"I'll let Smeth tell you that. And tell you and tell you and tell you. If you're unwary enough to get collared by him, that is. No shoptalk right now. We're here to have fun." He slipped an arm around Nen and gave her a fond squeeze.

"Who do you know in the tree?" Bram asked.

"One of the fellows in our team decided to emigrate. Giving up the rigors of intellectual pursuit and signing on for the bucolic life."

"Juxt One is hardly a frontier society."

"No . . . they've had several centuries to become civilized. But there's a lot more openings for humans lately."

"We brought Lilla and Jao a little going-away present," Nen said, partially unfolding the wrappings around a cylindrical object and unfurling a couple of feet of it. "It's a wall hanging to brighten up their quarters during the trip. We got it from an art shop in the new extension. It's painted with hibernating pigment fungi. Each layer is activated by the decay products of the previous layer so that over a period of several years you get eight different designs. All of them planetary scenes to remind them of home."

"That way there's a new picture before you have time to get tired of the old one," Trist offered. "If the humidity in the tree isn't too different from what the art shop calculated, then the last design shouldn't appear till they reach their destination. Keep 'em from getting bored on the trip."

"I'm afraid we didn't think of anything as imaginative as that for Orris and Marg," Bram said. "Just a candy plant."

Kerthin was carrying the covered pot in her holdall. Bram glanced her way, expecting her to show it, but she was staring glumly out the viewdome, paying little attention to the conversation.

"If I know Orris, though," Bram said hastily, "he'll tap it for the ethyl."

They laughed politely, and then a few last-minute passengers came aboard and the jitney started up with a mild hum of electronics.

The trip into orbit was uneventful, made up of bland routines designed to tell passengers that it was no more exciting than being reeled across an ocean in a cable pod. Trist, whose job had taken him to Lowstation before, actually napped. But to Bram, who had never been in space, every moment was an adventure.

First he was led to a yielding nest that accepted his contours and, once a little shifting and wriggling had provided an average, jelled into shape. In the nest beside him,

Kerthin lay rigid. By craning his neck over the edge, Bram could look down at rank after rank of similar nests projecting like paddles from what would become the deck of the ferry during reentry but was now a sheer cliff of dizzying height, ascended in an openwork elevator cage. Transferring oneself from the cage to the couch was the tricky part for some humans; Kerthin had kept her eyes squeezed shut, but the Nar flight attendants had been very helpful. Bram supposed that all the nests swiveled to the horizontal when the craft changed attitude. The safety nets between the levels of nests—rigged, Bram was sure, to assuage human anxieties—would then become irrelevant curtains dividing the rows and probably would be drawn open.

The giant palm that pressed him into his nest during takeoff was gentler than he had expected. There was a moment of weightlessness after the outer craft separated—a restraining web kept him from floating away—then the ferry engines kicked in. He was lucky enough to have a window near his face, and he strained to catch sight of the leaflike boosters as they tumbled away and looped over for the long glide down.

Then, half an orbit later, the ferry caught up with its target, and Bram caught his first glimpse of Lowstation.

It was a gigantic hexagon some two thousand feet across, suspended in the blackness and turning with slow deliberation. In the naked vacuum of space it showed stark and clear. He could easily pick out the lines of the main timbers where the sheathing material had been seamed to them.

Lowstation was a real antique—one of the first of the wood-framed space stations to be built after the Nar had acquired the code for the poplar genome from Original Man. It had started life as an equilateral triangle with thousand-foot sides. Even then, it had given good service with temporary environmental shells attached at the three points. Five identical triangles had been knocked together out of additional thousand-foot timbers floated in from the nursery wheel that grew them. Then the six wedges had been fitted together, and Lowstation was in business—still skeletal, to be sure, but starting to enclose itself a little at a time.

In those days, they had still bothered to square off the timbers, in imitation of man, and that had been the biggest part of the job. Even so, assembling large space structures from ready-made framing elements that could theoretically be miles in length was still easier and cheaper than lofting flimsy plastic girders into orbit from the planetary surface.

Poplar had not been much used as a building material on that long-vanished planet of man. Hardwood had better lateral strength and made better posts and beams. But poplar had one advantage: It grew fast and it grew straight, provided that it didn't have to compete for its little piece of sky.

It grew even faster in the low simulated gravity of a space wheel, and it grew just as straight: pointing itself at the hub along the lines of force. In a closed spoke of such a wheel, provided with air, water, and sunlight, its ultimate height was limited only by the radius of the wheel.

Tensile strength is more important than rigidity in space construction, anyway, and a poplar trunk certainly could not be pulled apart by the usual one-g forces; plastic girders, assembled in segments, were more likely to do that. In fact, the poplar's relative elasticity, adjusting to longitudinal stress, was an advantage.

Later, the Nar learned to grow curved beams for arches and the curved perimeters of space wheels. You simply enclosed a wedge of a space wheel and moved a tubbed sapling in gradual stages along a straight floor that made a chord along the curved perimeter. The poplar, always yearning for the hub, would keep changing its direction of growth.

Man, it was known from the records, had made woodframed space stations and other structures the norm by the end of his twenty-first century. Even the larger ships used for intrasystem voyaging were wooden vessels fitted out with rocket units. For man, the space-grown poplar had brought about an era of cheap interplanetary expansion. And for the Nar, in the early stages of their own space age, it had done the same.

But man had never taken the next obvious step. To teach the poplar tree to live and grow in vacuum.

He would have been surprised to learn what the Nar had done with his gift.

"Please fasten your harnesses," the Nar attendant said gently from his pedestal in the center of the transfer vehicle's oval cabin. "We will begin to decelerate shortly."

An obedient rustle of movement ran around the circlet of seats lining the cabin. A few adventurous souls who had been swimming in midair—to the annoyance of their fellow passengers—hauled themselves back to their seats along the lines they had been clipped to.

The attendant waited until everybody had settled and announced: "I'm afraid that there will not be much to see during most of the approach, since we will of course be decelerating floor first."

There was a groan of disappointment from the passengers. The attendant, with a sympathetic swirling of arms, continued. "But our pilot has promised to invert us briefly at some point between deceleration thrusts so that, for a few minutes at least, you should have a fine overall view of the tree through the overhead dome."

Bram turned to Kerthin in the seat beside him. "Won't that be marvelous?" he asked.

She nodded without answering. She had regained her color, Bram was glad to see. The trip in the ferry up to Lowstation had been the worst part of it for her. The paneled corridors and reassuring solidity of the orbital facility had acted as a tonic. The Nar personnel had gone out of their way to make things comfortable for the human party during their wait for transportation—two loads of earlier arrivals had already been delivered to the higher orbit where the tree had parked itself—and the window-filling view of the Father World from the passenger lounge had been spectacular. Kerthin had ignored the splendid scenery and instead had given her nervous attention to every human drifting in and out of the lounge, as if searching for the reassurance of a familiar face. Bram or Trist had waved at several casual acquaintances, and some of them had come over to chat briefly with the foursome, but Kerthin had remained preoccupied and aloof. She had glanced up sharply once at some people returning from the rest room—Nen had seen it and reminded her that there would be no facilities on board the transfer vehicle—and later had excused herself to use Lowstation's amenities herself. When she rejoined Bram, she seemed more relaxed, and Bram wondered if she had been sick all this time. At any rate she seemed more herself now and showed signs of looking forward to her visit to the tree.

"Ready to fire," the Nar attendant murmured from his central post, keeping watch with all five eyes on his ring of human charges.

There was the gentlest of nudges, then the stars outside the plastic dome turned as the craft flipped over. A moment later there was a small steady push from the floor, and Bram felt a pound or two of weight return to him.

There were four or five firings at intervals, then a period of coasting, while Bram wished that someone had thought to install a window in the floor. Finally the Nar attendant spoke again. "We're less than a thousand miles from the tree now, and if you'll keep your eye on the overhead dome, you'll be able to see it in a minute."

Bram glanced at Kerthin. She was immersed in a printout of Shaw's *Saint Joan*, which she had brought along for the ride. She appeared not to notice the tiny jolt when the attitude jets began to roll the vehicle over on its back again. Bram got her attention with a nudge of his elbow, and she put the printout down and looked up.

The great living starship that was the tree swam majestically into view through the overhead bubble and came to a halt as the transfer craft steadied itself.

Bram gaped unabashedly. Beside him, he heard Kerthin catch her breath.

The star-traveling organism resembled not at all any tree ever seen on land or even the giant trees grown in space stations. Vacuum-poplars spread outward, not upward.

Its form was that of two umbrella-shaped masses held apart by a trunk that was relatively too short to be seen between them at this shallow angle of approach. The trunk would, Bram knew, be some eighty miles long and twenty or more miles thick. But it was dwarfed by the twin wheels of growth that it had given rise to after it had done its essential work.

The immense silvery crown of leaves, some three hundred miles in diameter, was a flattened dome—almost a disk—whose irregularities were canceled by distance to make it as round and symmetrical as any artificial object.

The foliated root system at the other end of the hidden stem was an almost exact match in size and shape to the crown. A living system like a vacuum-poplar had exquisite feedback. It had to. Spinning at one gravity at its twin rims—slowing its spin as it grew outward in order to maintain a constant one-g level—it had regulated its growth over the centuries for balance and symmetry.

It was hard to detect the spin at the tree's present enormous diameter, but spin it must, Bram knew, unless it wanted to lose its shape. A space poplar started life as a seedling on one of the billions of snowballs in the cometary halo at the outskirts of the system, feeding on water ice and the inevitable carbon and nitrogen compounds. When it had used up its comet—rarely more than a few miles in diameter—it was still a fairly orthodox looking tree, with leaves at one end and roots at the other. Long shapes tumble in space, and the random rotation encouraged the tree to continue to grow straight—much like the trees grown in space stations—except that centrifugal force pulled it in both directions. The roots foliated, modified themselves to take advantage of random traces of water and organic molecules floating around in the shell of unborn comets. The true leaves, with the help of a little biological engineering by the Nar, learned to conserve water rather than respire it.

And like all plants, it reached out for water in the only way it could.

The leaves were dark on one side, silvery and reflective on the other. With the cunning phototropism of plant life, the leaf system used available starlight to change the tree's direction of spin. Instead of rotating end over end, the tree began, over a period of years, to twirl on its axis. That encouraged the branches and roots to grow out laterally—to spread its sails and enable the tree to move by the pressure of starlight. At the same time, the axial rotation put a stop to the tendency of the trunk to grow taller and instead made it grow thicker—better able to support the opening umbrellas.

Now the tree was a true spacefarer—able to follow the tenuous currents of life-giving vapor wherever they led, engulfing new cometary cores and sucking them dry, building its own tissues in the process.

The cometary halos of neighboring stars are contiguous. The vacuum-poplars were seeding themselves outward. Already, thinly spread forests of them grew around Juxt One, with little help from the Nar, and they had been found in the cometary shells of stars as distant as twenty light-years.

When the Nar needed a new starship, all they had to do was tag a likely specimen, tow it to planetary orbit, and outfit it with living quarters, a parasitic ecology; and simple biological controls to make it deploy its foliage as commanded.

Man, for all his technical superiority, had never brought his own space-grown trees to their full potential. With his shorter life span, man had to hustle between the stars. The Nar could afford a leisurely sail, pushed by the gentle pressure of starlight.

"I . . . I've seen pictures of trees," Kerthin breathed in wonder, "but I never expected . . ."

"It's hard to grasp," Bram agreed. "Lowstation looked

pretty big to me. But it would just be a speck next to that thing. You wouldn't notice it at all. You could hide it inside a twig at the end of the branches."

As they watched, the moon-sized disk underwent a startling change. It was growing darker on one side. A wave of dark green rippled across its face until, within a few moments, it was neatly bisected by a geometrically straight line—silver on one side, green on the other.

"We've all been very fortunate to see that," the Nar attendant said. "Our timing is lucky. We've just seen the tree decide to make a small attitude correction."

"What happened?" Kerthin said.

"The leaves," Bram said. "It turned its leaves over on half the reflecting surface. Over the next few days, it'll get a small push that'll—" He checked the cloud-marbled surface of the Father World below. "—line up the trunk vertical to its orbit. I guess it doesn't like tidal forces."

"You are correct," the Nar attendant said. "The star trees are uncomfortable in the vicinity of large planetary gravitational fields and try to avoid them unless they are forcibly guided."

Bram turned mildly pink. He hadn't meant to be overheard.

"How do they do that?" somebody asked from the other side of the cabin.

"We can deceive the tree with various synthetic hormones," the attendant said. "There's a pumping station in the trunk. There are also simpler means. We can throw bait—release water vapor ahead of it. Or use artificial light."

"Poor tree." Someone laughed. "The carrot leading the stick."

"I'll have to learn that trick," Nen said, twisting around in her seat to face Bram and Kerthin. "About the hormones, I mean."

"Don't pay any attention to her," Trist said. "She's been doing it for years. She's got all the hormones she needs."

"Where the hormones—" Nen started.

"There moan I," Trist finished for her. "How about you, Bram?"

The line had been shamelessly stolen from some ancient author; Trist had used it years ago in the bachelor lodge during his ribald period. Bram smiled helplessly at Kerthin, apologizing for Trist, but Kerthin wasn't smiling. Bram tried to think of something lighthearted to say before the mood got too chilly.

"We're about to turn over for our final approach now," the Nar attendant said. He must have received a signal from the pilot through his glove.

A murmur of disappointment rose from the passengers. Trist raised an eyebrow at Bram and turned around in his seat to adjust his safety harness.

The two-tone crown of the tremendous tree began to slide from view. The line of green, Bram noticed, was keeping pace with the ponderous rotation as millions of leaves turned over ahead of it and turned back again behind it.

Kerthin seemed just as fascinated as he was. She kept her eyes on the colossal shrub until it was gone. She licked her lip and turned to Bram with moisture glistening on it. "If only *we* had one of those," she said.

"We?"

"The human race. We could migrate to another star and start out again on our own. Away from the Nar."

"We'd have to travel at least a hundred light-years to

get to a habitable planet that wasn't already settled by the Nar," Bram said reasonably. "At no more than about seven percent of the speed of light. And when our descendants got there, fourteen hundred years later, they'd probably find that the Nar had arrived there ahead of them."

She gave him a strange look. "Maybe there's someplace closer," she said.

"We'll land on the trunk," the attendant was saying. "It would be too dangerous to attempt to dock on the outer branches. At one hundred and fifty miles from the axis of rotation, we'd acquire one gravity immediately, at the moment of contact. I'm sure you can all appreciate the wisdom of avoiding that kind of brush. But the trunk is only twenty miles in diameter at its thickest, so that no point along its surface is more than approximately ten miles from the center of rotation. For all practical purposes, gravity—if we can call it that—is negligible anywhere along its length. We'll be landing at about the midpoint, by the way, so you needn't worry about our colliding with either canopy. We'll have miles and miles of leeway for maneuvering."

"How are we getting to the tip, then?" somebody grumbled. "Do we have to transfer to another vehicle?"

"No, we'll stay inside this one all the way," the attendant said in a voice that, despite the nonhuman way in which it was produced, suggested smugness.

"But how?" another passenger cried.

"You'll see when the time comes," the attendant replied. "If you'll all think about it, I'm sure you'll realize that there's a very simple method by which we can acquire the one-gravity force of the outer rotation period gradually and then dock at our final destination. I think I can promise you an interesting experience."

"How? Tell us!" several cries went up. But the attendant was enjoying his little moment of suspense.

"Like children," Kerthin said. "Guessing games and treats. That's what they've brought us to."

"He's only trying to make it more fun for us," Bram said.

The passenger boat continued to drop.

Dropping was the way Bram's perceptions interpreted the motion now, as did the perceptions of the people around him. The up-down sense had been reinforced by the feeble but regular bursts of the braking jets under their feet.

So the astonishing horizon that now began to rise through the clear viewdome became the distant edge of a flat plain—a green and silver forest that stretched for hundreds of miles before it was cut off by the black knife-edge of space.

He knew it was an illusion. He was looking down a vertical wall of greenery, not across a forest landscape. The g forces were outward from the center of that vast canopy of leaves. But the seat of his pants kept contradicting his common sense.

The horizon marched toward him as the passenger boat continued its descent. There was enough curvature across the tree crown to do that. Now the down-sloping plain was hidden behind the skyline. He appeared to be looking uphill toward the shallow arc of the crest. But the passenger boat was not going to land among those mighty branches. It would fall past the fringes of the crown at a safe distance.

The mound of silvery green rose up and filled the universe. They had dropped past the edge. Now Bram could see the flat underside of the umbrella. Close up, the circumference wasn't the geometrically perfect curve he had seen from afar. Great twisting growths poked into space, any one of them big enough to have swallowed up a small city in its foliage. But the tree averaged out the mass.

The boat dropped another forty miles and, with a long, finely tuned burn of its thrusters, hovered. Bram drank in the tremendous sight.

Above, the roof of foliage stretched for three hundred miles. Below, the tangled root system formed what at this distance looked like an equally flat and solid floor, Its modified structure drank in and conserved every molecule of moisture that escaped from the miserly canopy above and sent signals to the living light sail to keep it on course in its search for water ice. it dwarfed all but the largest comets. When it caught a comet in its fibrous net, it shed its adventitious leaves within the circle of contact and sent out root hairs to melt and drink every last drop. And the tree celebrated another minute fraction of growth.

"It's a *world!*" Kerthin exclaimed in awe. "But it's *alive!*" Her hand clutched Bram's.

Trist's head bobbed in her direction. "Think of them, spreading slowly outward between the stars," he said cheerfully. "Acquiring their own ecology. Parasites like us, for example. They could make planets obsolete."

Kerthin did not rise to the bait. Bram knew that Trist had overheard her remark about migration and was teasing her.

"You may have something there," Bram said, keeping his voice serious.

"Sure, back to the treetops after forty million years," Trist said.

The boat's attitude jets coughed diffidently, and the cabin made a quarter rotation. Bram's orientation changed. He was no longer looking down at a floor of roots, up at an umbrella of leaves. They were now the walls of an impossible chasm, and he was looking up through the top of the viewdome at it.

This time his senses agreed with his intellect. What he viewed as "up" was "up" for the tree, too. One hundred and fifty miles over his head was the axle that spun the twin disks.

Others had the same thought. "There's the trunk," Trist was telling Nen. "Can you see it?"

Bram peered straight up at the slice of night visible between the two living walls. The trunk could be seen as a mottled gray bridge that joined them. It was as straight as centrifugal force had grown it, except at either end, where it fanned out gracefully to give rise to the circles of reaching growth.

The thrusters gave the hovering craft a measured kick and sent it rising up the living canyon.

"It's a yo-yo," Trist said suddenly.

"Huh?"

"The tree is shaped exactly like a yo-yo. Didn't you ever have one when you were a child? And now I bet I know how we're going to get transferred to the rim."

It took another hour to reach the trunk. For the last twenty miles, the pilot sent the craft rolling and timed each small burst of the braking jets for the moments when he was pointed toward his destination. He finished up nicely with his trimming nozzles aimed for the vertical—compressed gas jets that wouldn't hurt the tree.

The tumbling had disoriented some passengers and produced nausea. Somebody across the way was being sick in one of the pinchbasins that had been provided for that purpose. "First casualty," Trist said.

Bram looked at Kerthin. Her face had gone the color of putty, but she swallowed hard. "So much for the consideration of your five-legged friends," she said.

"Be fair, Kerth," he said. "This is the way they always do it. The Nar don't get motion sickness with their kind of nervous system. They can't change their touchdown routines just because they've got a load of human passengers."

"Or maybe they could, if it had occurred to them," she said angrily.

The tree trunk hovered overhead, a solid wall of patchy gray bark. Bram could see Nar in space suits clinging to it, moving like disembodied claws along the surface. They didn't seem to be at all inconvenienced by the fact that they were hanging upside down off a spinning cylinder that could hurl them off into space. This close to the center of rotation of the tree, centrifugal force was so small as to be almost negligible. If one of them lost his grip and started drifting outward, he would have ample time to make a grab for it.

And the Nar were better suited for space work than humans, anyway. Even leaving the prehensile legs aside, they could hold on with two arms and still have three to work with at any given moment.

Two of the space-suited figures deliberately broke contact with the rough expanse of the trunk. Several passengers gave a gasp as they saw them drifting downward like five-pointed snowflakes.

But not quite. One of them was trailing a gossamer cable attached to a great curved hook cradled between two of his tentacles. Bram followed the line with his eyes to where it ran back to a massive spool mounted within a skeleton housing on the bare trunk. There were several bubble structures seemingly growing out of the bark at that point, and dozens of space-suited Nar swarmed around the spot.

The two decapods landed with the tiniest of jolts on the overhead dome and clung to one of the radial struts that framed it. Some of their momentum must have been transferred to the passenger craft, but it was so relatively slight that Bram, though he was watching for it, could not detect any alteration in the boat's hovering position.

The workmen waved at the passengers inside the cabin and got friendly waves in return. They set about attaching the hook to the large ring at the top of the dome where the struts met. Bram had noticed the ring when he had boarded the vehicle, but he hadn't been able to figure out what it was for. He had thought it might be an antenna.

The cable that he saw looping away from the hook did not seem particularly thick. It was about the diameter of Bram's thumb. But if it was made of the same long-chain viral filament thread that was used for bubble car trams, then it had strength to spare.

The space-suited pair got the hook attached, then retreated hastily along separate struts to the perimeter of the cabin. They were showing the cable a lot of respect.

The looping thread slowly straightened itself out. So some of the workmen's momentum *had* been transferred to the boat. Bram glanced at the trunk overhead and saw that it was indeed some tens of meters farther away.

There was the smallest of jolts as the last of the slack was taken up, and the passenger boat began a pendulum swing that carried it to a point below the opposite side of the giant spool above and then back again. The cable must have been winding out somewhat to ease the shock, because Bram could see the ceiling of bark retreating farther before there was a final jolt. And now, he realized, he weighed something again. Not very much—probably not more than a few ounces. But it was funny the way the body could tell.

In the seat ahead, Trist was testing the sensation by letting a small object from his pocket drift to the floor and timing its fall. "Don't mind me," he said cheerfully. "We physicists are a compulsive lot."

The work crew above reeled them in partway so that the hook handlers would have less distance to climb. The pair gave a final wave to the occupants of the cabin, then swarmed up the cable.

The boat hung there for some minutes while the pendulum motion damped itself out. The Nar attendant had a dialog with the pilot through his glove. Then the descent began.

Yes, Bram agreed, it *was* an eminently simple and straightforward way to match rotational forces gradually with the outermost branches. And yes, it promised to be an interesting experience.

The attendant was being bombarded with questions from his passengers.

"What happens if the line breaks?"

"It never has."

"Yes, but what *if*?"

The Nar laughed: an explosive exhalation of air from the modified alveoli that formed the vocal syrinx. "The transfer vehicle can develop accelerations of up to one-fifth gravity. At this point we could easily cancel the outward motion. We would simply start over again."

"What about when we pass the one-fifth-g mark?" This

was from Trist, pausing in his experiments to help the attendant with his lecture.

"There are crews waiting at the rim who could snare us and reel us in. If worse came to worst, they would send a rescue ship after us at several g's acceleration. Our direction would be along a choice of degrees in the known plane of a circle. They would catch up in a few hours. I assure you there is no danger."

Everybody was watching the wall of greenery slide by, some twenty or thirty miles to the side. Bram could pick out no details at this distance other than the half-buried contours of the main branches, radiating outward like gargantuan spokes. If there were any artificial structures tucked among them, they were invisible to the naked eye.

Trist whistled. "If you hollowed out just one of those branches it could house a population of millions. Hmmm. Think of it as a tower, a hundred fifty miles high and maybe five or six miles in diameter at the roof and tapering to a half mile at the base. Conic sections. Remember your middle school math? Figure fifty-foot levels—fifteen thousand of them, with a floor area of . . . care to do the honors, Bram, old chum?"

"They don't use the branches," Kerthin said unexpectedly. "Except for travel tubes and way stations. They leave the tree mostly alone. It's a life-support system. It has to stay healthy. They probably use less than one percent of it. The trunk for low gravity. And the tips of some of the twigs and branchlets for living space. But its mostly wild growth in between."

Bram looked at her in surprise. "I didn't realize you knew so much about star trees," he said. "I thought you weren't interested."

"Oh, I heard someone talking about them," she said, and fell silent.

Some of the other passengers were still pestering the attendant. "When we reach the end of the line, we'll be dangling in midspace, between the roots and the crown. Miles and miles from anything. What happens then?"

"Wait and see," the Nar said.

Kerthin made a disgusted sound. "More guessing games," she said.

The boat picked up speed as the cable unwound, almost—but not quite—failing. Descent had to be somewhat slower than what would have been the normal rate of "fall" in order to maintain tension on the cable. The differential was great enough to give the passengers noticeable weight—weight that increased proportionally—as the great circle around which they were being swung grew in diameter.

They had not made a full revolution when the line played out, buffered by the skill of the winch operator one hundred and fifty miles above them and by the elasticity of the viral filament itself.

The boat swayed gently at the end of its line, an upsidedown captive balloon straining for the stars. Everybody craned for a look at the strange, green, topsy-turvy horizon that was their destination.

Its curvature was quite noticeable, of course, dropping off sharply in either direction. But the diameter of the foliage crown still put it in the same class as a good-sized planetoid.

Or would have, if it had been a complete ball instead of an oblate hemisphere. The boat was suspended midway between two such slices of world—the halves of a yo-yo, as Trist had described the shape—and it was rather like hovering within some enormous canyon. A canyon with a log bridge across it halfway up and stars at the top *and* the bottom.

"Yggdrasil," Trist said.

"What?"

"Don't you know your Norse mythology? Yggdrasil, the world tree."

"There are so many different legends," Bram apologized. "I'm afraid they all got mixed up in my head when I was a child."

"Its roots spanned the earth and the heavens," Trist said. "And when at the end of the world the universe was devoured by fire, a new race of men emerged from its wood."

"Thoughtful of Original Man to give it to us, then." Bram laughed. "But you've got the story wrong. We emerged from radio waves."

"The tree *could* nourish us through a transition, though, couldn't it?" Nen said, joining in. "Yggdrasil was supposed to have given the water of life."

"Well, this one will certainly do that for the Juxt One colonists," Bram said.

"Look, they're coming for us," Kerthin said, touching his arm.

Bram followed her gaze and saw a bright dot of flame perched on the inverted horizon. It moved to a point fractionally within the green arc, burned for another minute, and winked out. He kept his eyes on the spot where it had been, trying to hold his line of sight, and after a few minutes was rewarded by the appearance of a polyhedral framework that had moving dots clinging to it. The dots resolved themselves into a Nar work crew dressed for space.

Some day, Bram thought, someone would design a space suit for humans—if humans ever became numerous enough to be more than mere baggage! What would it look like? It would have to have a transparent dome at one end, for the head. Accordion joints for knees and elbows. Twisting around might be awkward. The Nar anatomy was better designed for space. A Nar space suit looked for all the world like two silvery gloves joined by a transparent wristlet that provided 360-degree vision. No sore necks for them!

The service frame floated past at a respectful distance. Why weren't they braking? Of course! For the same reason they weren't being swung outward by the line they must be trailing. Having canceled their own centrifugal motion with respect to the tree, they wanted nothing to do with the one-g force the passenger boat had picked up during its long unreeling.

Bram squinted and confirmed his guess. The line the service frame was hauling behind it had plenty of slack, bellying outward at an arc that must have carried its invisible portion at least fifty miles into space. Though tethered at its point of origin, and obeying the laws of physics itself, the minute tug it exerted had not yet materially altered the trajectory of the service frame.

The passengers waved as the frame drifted by, but the work crew was too occupied to wave back. "Why aren't they stopping?" Kerthin asked.

"You'll see in a minute," Bram said.

"Oh, good gods, you too?" she exploded.

A Nar crewman clinging with all five legs to the putative top of the polyhedral frame was swinging a length of free line with a grapnel hook attached to it around and around his splayed top. Skillfully he played out the line little by little, keeping it safely away from the outward-looping portion of the cable. He'd timed the arcs nicely. Bram watched as the line intersected the cable from which the passenger boat was dangling and wrapped itself around it. The grappling hook fetched up against the cable in a final spasm of angular momentum, and then the low-friction filament began to slide. The Nar roping artist hauled in smartly, keeping tension on the unwinding line until the grappling hook engaged. Now the service frame moved outward with a quick spurt of its jet, while the Nar let the guy rope slide through his grip. The bellying line, whose far end was attached to the rim of the tree crown, straightened out as somebody began to winch it in.

The Nar lasso specialist let go at the last possible moment and allowed the line to twang taut. The little shiver of momentum was hardly noticeable within the passenger cabin; the tether lowered from the trunk had already matched g-forces.

It took the high-speed winch at the rim less than a quarter hour to reel the boat in while the service frame followed behind. Willing tentacles snagged the lines and made them fast. It was a primitive way to bring in a spacecraft for docking, but when he thought it over, Bram had to concede that it made sense. It was simply the application of known forces, just as was maneuvering by rocket power. In fact, brute muscle power and simple mechanical forces were probably more accurate and economical. It was a good thing the Nar hadn't forgotten the skills learned in their days of wind-driven sailing vessels.

The boat was resting on a wooden ledge carved out of the trunk. When the Nar ground crew was satisfied that all was secure, they cast off the hawser bound to the faraway trunk. Released from its vector of forces, the cable began a slow pendulum swing outward.

The boat was winched from the ledge into a dome-shaped vacuole that was a hundred feet across. Airtight hangar doors in the shape of vast triangular sections flapped shut and sealed at the center. Air billowed into the vacuole with a force powerful enough to rock the boat and knock one unwary Nar workman off his tentacles before he could latch on to something. Bram knew it was safe when the Nar crew began peeling off their double-ended space suits. A moment later the flight attendant announced that they could leave the vessel.

A welcoming committee was waiting for them inside the next chamber: a half dozen men and women in scanty shipboard attire. They looked for friends among the several dozen disembarked passengers and in a few minutes were exchanging multiple embraces.

Orris and Marg had not been among the greeters. Trist's friend Lilla was, and Trist and Nen were babbling eagerly at her. Bram took the opportunity to look around the chamber he was in.

It was vast—bigger than the vacuole that had been converted into an air lock. The tree's simulated gravity had forced a generally domelike shape, and the floor was fairly flat, with a little help from carpenters. The dome overhead had a burnished velvety sheen, lovely in the glow of the biolights that seeded the chamber. The air was clean and forest-fresh.

"What do you think of it?" he asked Kerthin.

"What did he call it—the world tree?"

"Yggdrasil," Bram said.

"It'll do," she said, quite seriously. She sounded like a prospective buyer considering its merits.

"Do for what?"

She presented a face to him that was totally devoid of humor. "As a way to start a new world," she said

CHAPTER 8

Over a thousand people were gathered in the hall of the tree, embarkees and guests, but they seemed lost in hugeness. There were too many echoes, spoiling the spontaneity of the party noises that some of them were trying to make. A few small clusters, mostly twosomes and foursomes, were thinly dispersed across the immense woody amphitheater, but the majority had drawn instinctively into a loose concentration along the part of the wall that held the bar.

"This is going to be a farm chamber when we're fully outfitted," Marg said, "but the party committee thought it would be a good place to hold the bash. I *told* them it was too big, but they wouldn't listen to me. We could have used one of the smaller vacuoles nearer the surface and had a view of the stars to set the mood."

She locked eyes with Bram, waiting for his agreement. Men tried hard to agree with Marg. She was plump and pretty, with wide ingenuous eyes. She was wearing a cleverly simple sleeveless dress that showed a generous expanse of her glowing skin.

Orris, a knobby beanpole in shorts and singlet, hovered at her side, looking proud and possessive and overwhelmed. "You remember Marg's theory of how to throw a really good party," he said. "Crowd people together in a space that's a little too small for them. Make 'em rub elbows. Make sure there aren't enough seats, so they can't take root. Force 'em to circulate. And keep the lights low."

"It's so *bright* in here," Marg said. "I'm going to try to get them to shut down the pumps for the overhead tubes circulating the biolights."

Bram smiled sympathetically and looked around. The lens-shaped cavity was still unfinished. The distant end, leading to the hollowed-out resin canals that had brought them from the outside air lock, still needed a lot of scraping and polishing. Marg was right about the size; the party decorations dangling far overhead looked remote and forlorn.

"The drinks will save the day," Bram said. "And the eats. I've raided the buffet twice. Do I recognize Marg's hand in those swirled yolk things?"

"Oh, it's just something I whipped up for the culinary development department," Marg said, touching her hair. Orris beamed.

Bram listened with half an ear while Orris rambled on about Marg's triumphs. They'd given her a facility in the trunk so that she could experiment with zero-gravity cooking. Under those conditions, one could do amazing things with puff pastry and heat transfer. By the time they arrived at Juxt One, Marg would be the system's expert on it.

Kerthin was nowhere in sight. She had drifted off earlier after a minimum exchange of conversation with Marg and Orris. Perhaps she had found a planetside acquaintance in the mob, or found a volunteer to take her exploring in some of the side tunnels. Quite a few of the visitors were doing that.

A few feet away, Smeth was holding forth to a captive audience that included Trist and his colonist friend, Jao. Jao was one of the red, hairy types that seemed to be popping up with increasing frequency in this generation after having been buried in the master genome for so long.

"You picked the wrong time to quit the project, Jao, old son," Smeth said. "We're on the verge of great things. The hadronic photon theory that our team tossed into the ring is going to mean a real breakthrough in developing a star drive, and the Nar know it. They're inclined to give us more resources and step up the pace of the project now."

He gave a toothy smile, then spoiled the effect of superiority by scratching his ribs. Smeth had regrown his beard since Bram had last seen him; it made a fuzzy round pompon on Smeth's chin, a pompon that despite Smeth's youth had an unexpected streak of gray in it that must have pleased him. Otherwise, Smeth hadn't changed much, except that his gangling frame now carried a small potbelly.

"The hadronic photon came out of Jao's work on photon-proton absorption, remember?" Trist put in mildly.

"Never mind, Trist," Jao said with a large gesture of a furry forearm. "The project can have my little share of glory, and welcome to it!"

"That's what I don't understand," Smeth said. "Giving it all up to go to Juxt One and become a—"

"A brewmaster," Jao finished for him. "There's always work for a good brewmaster anywhere in the known universe." He gave them a wide grin through his red whiskers. "Regular hours and all the brew you can drink."

In the crowd past Smeth's cozy little coterie, Bram

caught sight of Mim. How long had it been since he'd seen her? And even then it had been at one of her concerts; intimidated by the swarm of close friends and admirers around her, he hadn't gone backstage to talk to her after the performance.

Her freshness and energy had always been attractive, but the past few years had given her beauty. Cheekbones, wide and explicit, had carved themselves into the roundness of her face. Her eyes were dark and huge and knew more. She had let her choppy black hair grow, and it hung past the line of her jaw, framing her face. Bram thought she looked a little sad.

Olan Byr was not with her. He had been in poor health lately, so the story went, and his virtuoso concerts were few and far between these days.

"And Marg's pregnant, too, did you know that?" Orris was saying in his ear. "They've frozen the blastocyst for us, and she's going to have it reimplanted when we go back down to the surface for the predeparture leave. The pronuclei were three-quarters ours—the rules for Juxt One are a bit more relaxed."

"And the baby will be born between the stars," Marg said. "It's so poetic."

There were coos of approval from two women whom Marg had collected into her orbit while Bram's attention had wandered. A man with one of them said, "Juxt One *needs* humans; I'd go myself if I were younger." When the conversation grew general, Bram slipped away without being noticed.

Mim was standing alone when Bram came up to her. The young man to whom she had been talking had been pulled away by two people, tree dwellers by the evidence of their bare feet, who wanted to show him something. "Hello, Mim," Bram said.

She looked up, and her new molded face broke into the old Mim's unaffected smile, washing away the tired lines he had seen there. "Hello, Bram."

"It's been a long time."

"Yes, it has." They raised hands and touched palms. "What are you doing here?"

"Orris and Marg invited me. You remember Orris?"

"Always borrowing things. Yes. I hope Marg is feeding him."

"No fear on that score." They looked at each other's faces. "You're not sailing to Juxt One, are you?"

She laughed. "No, I came to see friends off, too. We're exporting a whole string quartet. They've never seen the real thing with the friction wand out there. They've just heard transmissions. The music department there issued an invitation that was hard to resist. Four of our young students decided to take advantage of it. That was one of them you saw me talking to."

"How's Olan?"

She bit her lip. "Not very well. He wanted to come with me today, but he wasn't up to it."

"I'm sorry to hear that. Please give him my best."

"Thank you." She tossed her head. "Are you still dreaming your magnificent dreams? About sailing between the galaxies and finding the worlds of Original Man?"

Bram smiled at the memory. "I guess I've become more down-to-earth over the years. It seems magnificent enough to be sending a string quartet to a star that's a whole light-year away."

"We're all getting older," she said sadly.

Yes, he thought. That was the crux of the matter. Mortality. That was the true obstacle to dreams like the one he'd had. You never thought about mortality when you were a child. Time and distance had been the enemies then.

Bram thought of Olan Byr and felt pity for him. And for Mim and himself and everybody else. The string quartet would spend their youth traveling to Juxt One. Marg and Orris would spend their baby's childhood. They'd decided the bargain was worth it. But in every life there was only so much to spend.

"The dreams get more practical over the years," he said lightly. "I'm quite happy to be working on projects that have some chance of being realized during my lifetime without woolgathering about imaginary thirty-seven-million-year journeys. Smeth was perfectly right about it."

"Of course! I'm *always* right," a voice said loudly at his ear. Bram turned and saw Smeth standing there with a fatuous smile on his face. "What is it I'm right about?"

"The impossible mass ratios for traveling near the speed of light."

"Oh, that." Smeth waved a negligent hand. "Forget about it. We're not going to have to carry our fuel anymore."

"He's going to tell you all about using interstellar hydrogen, depend on it," Jao said, crowding in behind Smeth with a drink cradled in one fist. "Hi, Mim."

Trist followed, raising his eyes heavenward for Bram's benefit.

Smeth scowled. "That's what the probe project is all about. The Nar want to build a probe that can reach the galactic center in a reasonable length of time. On the order of fifty thousand years. And it's beginning to look more and more possible. And yes, we think we can do it by scooping up hydrogen atoms in space and squeezing the plasma to induce fusion."

"Don't fail to tell him about exhaust velocities," Jao prompted, winking at Bram.

"Go ahead, have your fun," Smeth said.

Trist sighed. "The original idea," he said, "was to collect interstellar hydrogen and use it both for reaction mass and for an energy source. But matter is matter, even when you strip it down, and even though you can expel it at velocities brushing the speed of light, all our studies indicated that there was a practical limiting factor of about ninety-eight percent." He turned to Jao. "That about right?"

"Yah. Ninety-eight percent. For plasma and all that junk."

"The ultimate exhaust velocity, by definition, would be provided by a pure photon drive. But that would require the total conversion of matter into energy, and we don't know how to do that. So photon drives of the various sorts we'd been kicking around—mostly they boiled down to turning a fraction of the energy of matter into laser light—are inefficient."

"Yah, weak," Jao said.

"Now we come to the hadronic photon. Under certain circumstances, it's possible to increase the energy of a photon by a factor of from one to ten billion. And when you do, it takes on the properties of a hadron. It acts as though it has mass, like a proton, for instance. It has energy and momentum that are conserved."

"First you have to pump all that energy into it," Bram pointed out. "Ten billion times, did you say?"

"Hey, not bad for a biologist," Jao said. "Yah, all that has to come out of the ramjet fusion reaction in the first place."

"The point is," Trist said, "that we don't have to annihilate matter to get our beam of superphotons. It's done strictly through electromagnetic interactions that we know how to handle. In theory, at least."

"What you do is you swat pulsed laser photons with a high-energy electron beam and scatter them a hundred eighty degrees," Jao said. "They pick up the energy of the swat."

Trist nodded. "Then you focus the back-scattered photons—hadronic photons now—in the electromagnetic throat of the drive, and since they have a temporary nonzero mass, your vehicle not only gets a healthy kick, but gets it at the speed of light."

"Don't forget to mention the four-wave conjugate mirrors," Jao said, pulling at his sleeve.

"Oh, those. Yes. That's how we collect all those muscular photons that're scattering in all directions and herd them into a tight beam."

"It all sounds wonderful," Bram said. "I think."

"Of course, these aren't real photons we're talking about," Trist said.

"What?"

"They're virtual photons. They exist by courtesy of the uncertainty principle."

"Now you've lost me," Bram said. "Mim, do you have any idea what he's talking about?"

"Not a clue," she said, looking amused.

"All physicists are crazy," Jao said. "It's a well-known fact."

Smeth gave a snort. "You two are crazy. I'll grant that much."

"Jao's right," Trist said. "We're all crazy, Smeth included. We believe in things that don't exist. The hadronic photon has no right to be. It's supposed to hold hands with another photon, so that momentum and energy can be balanced. But it doesn't. It lives its brief solitary life, violating all the superstitions of quantum electrodynamics. The universe finds this a very unsatisfactory state of affairs. So our imaginary friend disappears before it can be detected. It materializes into a rho vector meson, which immediately decays into two pions, and those *can* be detected."

"But we don't care by then," Jao said with a red-bearded grin. "Let the universe sort things out. By that time our mythical photon's given its mythical kick to the vehicle."

"What's this about the uncertainty principle?" Bram said.

"That's the beauty of it. The shorter the time the virtual photon exists, the larger the uncertainty about its mass. Theoretically, it can assume a whole range of masses. There's only one problem."

"What's that?"

"The Nar find it hard to believe in imaginary photons. They can't seem to bend their minds around the concept. So they're leaving it to us for the time being. Or rather to these fellows. I'm out of it. I'll be on Juxt One, soaking up the Juxtshine and getting a tan."

"The Nar will come around to it eventually," Trist said. "Through the back door. They have their own way of looking at abstractions. In the meantime, they're giving us the benefit of the doubt. They know that humans have a peculiar talent for physics."

"Very peculiar," Bram agreed.

"I don't know," Mim said. The three physicists looked at

her in surprise. "It's easy for a musician to believe in things that only exist by virtue of other things that they turn into, but that are real nonetheless."

"How so, Mim?" Trist asked.

"It happens all the time in music. Like some of the Chopin pieces. Cascades of unresolved chords that collapse into other unresolved chords linked by carry-over notes and never come to a resting place. If you play them individually, they're all ugly discords. But they imply harmonies that the ear fills in. Harmonies that are just as real as if they existed as actual sound. In fact, you can diagram them if you care to, as a student exercise." She wrinkled her nose. "Olan was always having to restrain students who thought they were 'correcting' the discords."

"I like that," Jao said. "A universe that plays it by ear. That hints rather than states. Matter and energy don't actually exist. They're only implied by the transition states."

"We'll make a physicist out of you yet, Mim," Trist said. "You've got the divine madness."

Mim laughed. "I find it complicated enough sometimes just to try to beat time."

"Beat time," Jao said. "That's what we're trying to do."

"Why do the Nar want to reach the galactic center in fifty thousand years?" Bram asked.

Trist looked him in the eye. "Don't you know? You work at the biocenter."

"Just my own little septum of it."

Trist and Jao exchanged glances. "Are you familiar with the absent tidings paradox?"

Bram laughed. "What's that?"

"If intelligent life arises, and if billions of years have

elapsed since the universe became hospitable enough to give rise to it, where are they all?"

"But that's been disproved. We know it happened at least twice."

"Make that three times," Trist said.

Bram glanced up sharply. "What are you talking about?"

"The big ear that discovered Original Man finally hit the jackpot again. A couple of centuries ago, the Nar gave up on the nearby galaxies and turned the search inward, toward the galactic center. Worse odds, but closer to home, so to speak. They worked out computer techniques for filtering all the isotropic noise, and they used variable search strategies—the hydrogen line, the hydroxyl line, pulsed transmissions at all frequencies simultaneously, and so forth. All very discouraging. Finally, about the time redbeard here began to develop fuzz, they started searching at low frequencies along the magnetic field lines in the galaxy. The theory was that the lines would act as a guide, beating the inverse square rule, and that you might pick up very weak signals at very great distances."

"How great?" Bram said.

"They don't know. Maybe thirty or forty thousand light-years in toward the core."

"What's in the signals?"

"Pure noise. No information content at all. Scraps of carrier waves, maybe. Leaking radar. But there's no doubt that they're of artificial origin."

"I'd have thought the news would be all over the place."

"You know the Nar. They don't go crazy like us. They only started picking up the signals a couple of years ago, and then they weren't sure what they were. It took a while for the implications to sink in, and then the group leaders on the probe project started mulling it over with some of their opposite numbers at the biocenter, and it started to spread to some of the policy touch groups, and it's trickling down. Some of *us* know, and one or two people on the human advisory council have been told, and I suppose some hacker on news net will pick it up, and then everybody will know."

"So that's why the Nar want to reach the galactic center," Bram said. "No—" He remembered that the project had started long before the Nar had picked up the signals that were the evidence of life. Smeth had told him about it years ago, saying that it had something to do with some grand racial purpose of the Nar. "—you've all been working on the project all along."

Trist nodded. "But now it isn't a blind gamble—a leap into the dark. The project's going to have a lot more impetus now."

Smeth's shaggy head bobbed up and down. "That's what I've been trying to tell you, Jao, old son. You picked the wrong time to leave the project. We're going to get more funding, more recognition. And you'll be stirring up vats of yeast on Juxt One."

Jao ignored him. "You see, Bram, Mim,—the probe couldn't reach the vicinity of those radio signals for another thirty or forty thousand years even if it started out in the next century. And then it could miss them by tens or hundreds of light-years. We don't know exacly where they are. So there's not much point in sending back telemetry that wouldn't get here for *sixty* or *eighty* thousand years. Or trying to have a dialog with them at that exchange rate."

"They might not even be there anymore," Trist added. "Maybe their civilization destroyed itself long ago. That kind of radio leakage is the signature of an early stage of a radio age. Temporary. *We* don't—the Nar, I mean—put out that much stray radio energy anymore. Or maybe they're getting more advanced. A few more centuries of listening on their wavelength will tell us more—long before the probe could let us know anything."

Jao's face was flushed. "Or maybe they've been spreading toward us for the last thirty or forty thousand years—just behind the speed of light—and they're about to burst into our volume of space, somewhere out there beyond Juxt One, any day now!"

Bram was caught up in the vision. He could see that Mim was, too. "Or maybe," he said, "they're spreading at the same slow rate as the Nar, in their version of a sailship at fourteen percent of the speed of light, or on a boron fusion-fission drive at twenty percent, and some tens of thousands of years from now the two expanding spheres will intersect."

Trist nodded. "But it's the *fact* of their existence—or their former existence—that's given the probe project more urgency. That's the real significance of those radio noises. Until now, the Nar had only two cases to go on. There was a theory that maybe only one civilization could develop per galaxy—that it might be a kind of natural law. That life was a rare event and that when once it arose anywhere in a galaxy, it would eventually take total possession. One calculation was that a starfaring race can colonize an entire galaxy in about thirty million years. That's extrapolated from the Nar's rate of expansion. So that if there are hundreds of millions, or billions, of years between these events we call life, the number two race becomes clients—"

"Or victims," Jao put in.

"—of the first. But here we have a case of two intelligent races occupying the same time slot in the same galaxy. Even if the Nar were bloody-minded, which they aren't, they can't even *reach* these creatures, whoever they are, before they have time to do a lot of expanding on their own."

"And vice versa," Jao said. "These inner-galaxy types may be way ahead of the Nar by now. Thirty or forty thousand years ago, the Nar didn't have radio."

"Same difference," Trist said. "Then, on the other hand, we have the example of Original Man. He disappeared *before* he totally populated *his* own galaxy, it looks like, in spite of the fact that he was technologically superior at an early stage of his expansion. So maybe there's some imperative that leads to the extinction of intelligent races at that point on the timetable. Maybe *that's* why other galaxies are mute."

"And maybe," Jao mused, "life isn't rare. Maybe it's late. Somebody had to be first. Why not Original Man? And this galaxy is second. And in the next billion years, life will be popping up all over the universe."

"The point is, nobody knows," Trist said. "The data are too few. The Nar aren't willing to risk species extinction. And maybe *that's* a universal imperative. The drive for species immortality. Original Man tried it with the proclamation of his genetic code to the Virgo cluster. And now the Nar are about to do it on a smaller scale within their own galaxy. It's probably a stage that all intelligent species go through when it begins to dawn on them that the means is at their disposal."

"And your hydrogen-gulping probe is that means?" Bram said.

"Yah," Jao said. "They're going to attempt to seed the galaxy with replicas of themselves—using other intelligent races the way Original Man used them."

"Broadcast their genetic code?"

"*And* a cultural package," Trist said. "A race isn't only its genes. It's the sum of its memories, too."

Jao was bursting to continue. "The probe'll zip through the galactic center, broadcasting all the way. The power available to it will be enormous—more than this whole planet could generate. The signals ought to have a range of hundreds of light-years along the flight path. Then it'll zip out the other side, using the core as a gravitational sling-shot. It'll be going too fast to be captured. By the end of its mission, it'll be crowding the speed of light practically to the limit, and time dilation will have lengthened its radio waves to undetectability. But by that time it will have encountered one percent of the stars in the galaxy. Upwards of two billion stars!"

"And if the Nar species survives," Trist said solemnly, "and if their slow expansion someday takes them to the opposite ends of the galaxy, they won't find an indifferent or inimical universe, but their own children waiting to greet them."

Mim had been frowning. "I don't understand," she said. "It's a . . . a staggering idea. But why would they decide to stake it on another race or races that might not even *exist*? Why wouldn't they send automated biological packages instead?"

"A biological package wouldn't survive the radiation aboard the probe," Jao said promptly. "That baby's going to be *hot*!"

"Besides, Mim," Trist added, "the Nar want to cast

their seed on fertile ground. If their children are called to life in the far reaches of the galaxy, it will be because a supporting culture is there, ready to nurture them. A culture that's already made a *decision* to nurture them, as the Nar did with us. And they'll grow up as a *part* of that culture, a bridge between the races. Homegrown ambassadors for that ultimate day when two alien civilizations meet."

"Even if it weren't for the radiation," Jao said, "there's the time factor. Time dilation would help to keep biological samples fresh, sure, but even so we're talking about them having to survive maybe up to half a century of subjective time."

"Yes," Trist said. "And that's with our hadronic photon drive, which wasn't even a glimmer in Smeth's eye when the Nar conceived their project. Without the drive, the ramjet might *reach* the other side of the galaxy almost as fast—add a couple of thousand years to the hundred thousand years or more it's going to take—but with a gamma factor of only about five for the time dilation effect, it would mean an extra *ten* thousand years aboard the probe."

"Why do you need to crowd the speed of light so closely?" Bram asked. "What difference does it make how fast you slow down time aboard your robot probe when the net effect on actual travel time is so small?"

"Operating systems," Jao said. "Human beings are the best engineers in the universe, but it's better to have operating systems that age only fifty years instead of ten thousand."

"Translate that as human vainglory," Trist said. "We want the Nar to know how good we are."

Jao gave a wink. "Get them to subsidize our particle research, he means."

Mim had been following the discussion with widening eyes. Now she said brightly: "This time-stretching thing, the . . ."

"Gamma factor."

"Gamma factor. How high can it go?"

"With our imaginary drive? Theoretically there's no limit."

She turned to Bram with an alarming smile. "You see? Your dream isn't as impractical as you think it is."

"What dream, Mim?" Jao said.

"Mim," Bram warned.

There was no stopping her. "About going back to the place Original Man came from." She gave Smeth a reproving glance. "Now, won't you admit you were wrong?"

Smeth drew himself up to something approaching good posture. "Don't be ridiculous," he huffed. "What I said still goes. All that's changed is the necessity for accelerating fuel. The ramjet idea ought to work fine within a galaxy, of course. There's plenty of ionized hydrogen around. And the H-II regions get thicker and thicker as you steer for the heart of the galaxy, where the stars are packed closer together. Traveling *between* galaxies is a different story. Hydrogen pickings would be slim. No matter how much of a gamma factor you managed to pick up in your home galaxy, you'd still have to spend hundreds of years coasting. And how are you going to stop when you get there? You've still got to *shed* all that energy you've picked up! Besides, didn't you hear what Jao said? The ramjet probe's designed for electronics, not living things. You'd fry long before you got up even to gamma five."

"Oh, you're just trying to be difficult," Mim said.

"I rest my case," Smeth said. "Right, fellows?"

Trist said thoughtfully, "What you really want to do, Bram, is travel faster than light."

"Hey, how about that?" Jao said with a wide grin. "Forget about imaginary photons and all that stuff. Give yourself an imaginary proper mass instead. Still better, forget about relativity altogether. What do you say, Smeth?"

Smeth started to sputter. "Stop talking nonsense!"

"Let's not dismiss it out of hand," Trist said soberly. "We may be on to something."

"Right," Jao said. "Tachyons. In fact, wasn't that a pet idea of Smeth's a while back? They don't even violate the equations. At zero energy they have infinite speed."

"Don't you ever get tired of playing the buffoons?" Smeth said.

Jao smiled hugely at Bram and Mim. "All we have to do is break through the skin of the universe. On the other side, we have the tachyon universe, where *everything* travels faster than light."

"Wait a minute," Trist said. "You can't break through the skin. All you can do is form a diverticulum. But the surface of the diverticulum is still in space-time."

"Oh, yah, I forgot. It's just warped—like your sense of humor. How about this, then? You send a probe ahead of your ship, like a sacrificial pawn. It accelerates until its relativistic mass is enormous. It warps the geometry of space and sinks into a pit, like a neutron star, only more so. The process continues until it's sunk so deep—all the way to the center of the plenum—that the pit closes over it. Pinches off, so to speak. And your ship, following close behind, simply skates over the surface of the dimple, thereby skipping a big chunk of its journey. All without leaving normal space-time. Hey, you could even *maneuver* in space without building up new vectors—just tilt space in the direction you want to go. You could even *reverse* direction in two or three maneuvers without having to go to the inconvenience of decelerating and building up near-light velocity all over again!"

"You've overlooked something."

"Yah, what's that?"

"You're only skipping the part of space that the diverticulum took down to the center of the plenum with it. It may be stretched out to half the diameter of the universe, but you've only saved a few light-hours of travel."

Jao looked crestfallen. "How about this, then? The universe has a fancy geometry, see? It's a Klein universe or a Möbius universe. Inside and outside are the same. Or there's no skin you have to break through to get to your tachyon universe. It's all the same eleven-dimensional space-time, with a twist. You make your double circuit, and everything comes out backward, like a left-hand glove coming out a right-hand glove. Only we don't call it antimatter, the way small minds like Smeth do. We don't turn electrons into positrons, or neutrinos into anti-neutrinos, or anything like that. Shut up a minute, Smeth. No, we do a much cleverer flip-flop. We turn tardyons into tachyons. And vice versa. And there's no *transition* point at which the inversion takes place—it's one continuous circuit. Because tachyons and tardyons are the *same thing*. It all depends on your point of view. Like a sort of superrelativity. No, let me finish! In other words, tachyons and tardyons must coexist everywhere and are merely different expressions of identical phenomena." He paused to gloat. "Thus, one may simultaneously travel more slowly than light and faster than light, depending on the position of the observer."

"And where does that leave faster-than-light travel, you idiot?" Smeth shouted. "You're right back where you started!"

Bram and Mim smiled at each other and left the three physicists arguing among themselves. Their departure went unnoticed.

"It was good to see you again, Bram," Mim said.

"It was good to see you too, Mim."

"Are you ... with anyone now?"

"Yes." He hesitated. "I don't know if you ever met her. Kerthin Quo-willers Hwite. She only goes by her own praenomen now, though; she doesn't believe in bynames." He cast about awkwardly. "It's against her ... her political convictions. She was a sculptress when I met her. We ... we've seen a gene broker. Just to discuss it."

"That's wonderful, Bram. I hope you'll be very happy."

"Thank you."

"I'd like very much to meet her sometime. Olan's very interested in sculpture. Particularly touch sculpture. He says it's the one art form where we share perceptions with the Nar to some degree—other sculpture is meant to be *seen* from a viewpoint or viewpoints, and the Nar don't perceive it the way we do, with their full-circle perspective. Maybe we can all get together one of these evenings."

"Yes, that sounds fine," Bram said without conviction. He found it hard to imagine Mim and Kerthin together.

"I'll tell Olan I saw you. He was very impressed by you, you know. He always said you'd go far." She laughed. "Even though he's prejudiced against science."

Bram laughed too. "I remember."

She twisted her head. "There's Kesper and Ang making signals to me—they're from the quartet. I'm supposed to go over some of the material with them. They're beginning to look impatient."

She stood on tiptoe, kissed him swiftly, and was gone.

Bram went over to the buffet and got himself another drink. Marg's hors d'oeuvres were fast disappearing, and relays of the tree dwellers had put out trays of less inspired finger food. The alcohol was lubricating the crowd by now, despite Marg's fears, and the vast bare reaches of the vacuole had taken on a friendlier aspect—more like the stage for any outdoor party. A female colonist in a scanty costume made out of two fresh-picked leaves worn fore and aft, tied at the shoulders and belted at the waist, bumped hips at the buffet with Bram and said, "All by yourself? I'm Tasi. Would you like me to show you around the tree? The xylem passages in our part of the branch go on for miles and miles, and they haven't finished putting in the trail marks yet. You could get lost without a guide."

"Uh, thanks, I'm with someone," he said.

"Pity," she said, looking up at him through her eyelashes. "I know phloem chambers that no one else has discovered yet."

"I'm sorry."

"Me, too."

She moved away. When Bram saw her again, she was leaning up against another male excursionist from planetside, who was showing his sense of humor by tearing off small pieces from the edges of her leaves and nibbling on them. After a while they departed hand in hand.

Bram looked around for Kerthin, but he still was unable to find her. She'd been gone for over an hour. Drink in hand, he started down one of the side passages, the one that seemed to have attracted the greatest share of the desultory foot traffic. He thought he remembered having seen Kerthin heading in that general direction.

The passageway was roughly octagonal in cross section and huge, its flattened sides as smooth as if they had been sandpapered. Once it had been alive, a conduit for water and dissolved nutrients, but now the tree didn't need it anymore. Side tunnels branched off in all directions at varying angles, a reminder of the complicated changes of up and down that the space-dwelling tree had undergone at various stages of its life cycle; Bram detoured around a tunnel that opened straight down and had a safety fence erected around it.

The light was dim enough to leach the color out of one's vision; the only illumination came from transparent bladders swimming with biolights, which somebody had strung overhead at widely separated intervals. But he could see that this was going to be a main thoroughfare: Bundles of cables, tubes, and optical fibers were loosely strung along the walls, waiting for final installation, and there was a control station, partially assembled. Of course, there would have to be some way of tapping the electrical potential of the tree. And there was a ventilator elbow; the tree was its own atmosphere plant, but it was inevitable that a few adjustments would have to be made for the comfort of the human and Nar parasites who would inhabit it during its long migration to the next star.

Yes, Bram thought, it was no wonder that the Juxt One colonists were so keen on exploring the tree. This planetoid-size organism was going to be their life-support system for the next several years, and they had better become familiar with it quickly.

A tourist party came down the tunnel toward him, chattering and giggling. A barefoot colonist in shorts and a leaf cloak was explaining the sights. As they passed Bram on the opposite side of the passage, the guide called to him, "Don't get lost! Stick to the marked routes!"

"I will," Bram called back.

Not everybody was taking that advice. From the next side tunnel came a sound of heavy breathing and moans from a couple who hadn't taken themselves very far out of sight past a bend. Bram discreetly passed the corridor by and determined to have a look in the next promising tunnel.

He found one going up a slope toward a dim milky light a quarter mile's distance away. This would be one of the lenticels that Orris had mentioned—a round chamber toward the surface made by a raised pore covered by a translucent blister. The treefitters didn't even have to seal it off from space; the tree did it for them. On planetary trees, lenticels communicated with the atmosphere and served for gaseous exchange, but the vacuum-grown poplars conserved every precious gas molecule.

As he climbed toward starlight, Bram saw two dim figures emerge from a branching artery halfway up. A man and a woman. With the light behind them, he couldn't make out their faces with any clarity, but of course they must have had a better look at him.

He read a brief instant of confusion in their silhouettes, and then the man darted back down the tunnel he had emerged from. The woman looked as if she were about to follow him, then changed her mind and continued on down toward Bram.

Bram kept on climbing, and as he drew close, he saw who it was. "Kerthin!" he exclaimed.

"What are you doing here?" she demanded. "Are you spying on me?"

He was dumbfounded. "N-no," he said. "I was looking for you, and then I thought I'd explore some of these branching corridors."

"Well, there's nothing to see up there," she said. "Just some machinery that they haven't installed yet and some chambers they're hollowing out for air locks or something. Come on, let's go."

He took another step upward. "Who was that with you?"

"What do you mean?" she responded angrily. "I don't like this!"

"I don't mean anything," he said, more puzzled than ever. "I just asked who it was."

He wrinkled his forehead. There had been something about the silhouette—the set of the shoulders, the shape of the beard.

"Let's get back to the hall," she said. She tried to brush by him.

He grabbed her by the wrist. "It was Pite, wasn't it?"

"Let me go. What if it was?"

"What's Pite doing here?"

"He can look at a treeship if he wants to."

"No, he can't. He's supposed to be under house arrest after that last fracas. How did he get up here?"

"None of your business. I said let me go."

He released her. "He borrowed somebody else's identity, didn't he? Like his idol, Penser, does."

"What if he did? Pite has lots of friends. It's *their* business."

"You were one of them, weren't you?" Bram said. "That's why you wanted to get to the farewell party—and then hardly bothered to say ten words to Orris and Marg. And that's why you disappeared at Lowstation. You met somebody there. Why is Pite interested in star trees?"

"You're being ridiculous," she snapped.

"No, I'm not," he said. "Pite and his friends are up to something, and you've gotten yourself involved in it. Kerthin, I don't like to see you getting yourself in trouble. I thought you had more sense than that."

"All right," she said. Her demeanor changed abruptly, became affectionate and wheedling. "Pite *did* use somebody else's name, and he had the help of a friend aboard the tree in getting an invitation. And I found out about it, and I helped cover it up. What's so awful about that? It isn't as if Pite was doing anything *wrong*. All he wanted to do was explore this tree. Just like you're doing."

"I'm sorry, Kerth, I didn't mean to question you like that."

"You won't tell anyone, will you?" she asked quickly. "That you recognized Pite?"

"Kerthin . . ." he began wearily.

"You said it yourself. It could get me into trouble."

"All right," Bram said. "I won't say anything."

In the shuttle on the way down, after the reentry trajectory changed the gimballed overhead tiers into horizontal rows on the deck in front of him, Bram saw Pite's shaggy blond head in a nest ahead. Kerthin gave no sign that she knew Pite was there, and neither did Bram.

Just before touchdown, Pite twisted his head around and gave Bram a single hard stare. Bram stared past him, showing no reaction. Pite treated him to a small, mocking smile of approval, not much more than a flicker, and turned to face front again. When the shuttle landed and cooled down enough for exit, Pite was the first one out. Bram looked for him in the electric jitney to the terminal, but Pite did not reappear.

PART II

CHAPTER 9

The library annex was dimming for the night as the over-head tubes drained and the biolight fluid flowed back to its holding tanks. A few diehards were still bent over the screens in the reading booths, waiting for Hogard, the li-brarian, to kick them out.

"Are you all set?" Hogard asked. "You got everything you need?"

Bram glanced at the neat stacks of holos he had arranged in a semicircle around the apparatus that the li-brarian had helped him carry into the cubbyhole and set up. There was an ordinary, rather beat-up, viewscreen that had been cannibalized from an older machine, and a human-style lap console with touch bars, but there was also a jumble of connections slaving everything to a Nar-type desk reader, with curved screen and input sleeve. An-other set of temporary connections led to the librarian's prized whole-body reader on its wooden platform.

"Yes," Bram said. "I'll be all right."

"Be sure to turn everything off when you're finished. How long do you think you'll be here?"

"I don't know. Two or three hours."

Hogard shook his head, looking aggrieved. "If Voth-shr-voth fixed it up, I guess it's all right. But I don't do this for everyone."

"I appreciate that. Thanks."

Hogard pointed at the first stack of holos. "That the new translation program?"

"Yes. An interim realization of it, anyway. There are still years of work to go into it. The hackers who took the job on are working with Voth-shr-voth's second touch brother, and at his request they pasted together a test model from their unassembled routines to date."

"I don't like it. It should have come to me first."

"It was only delivered this afternoon. I'll leave you a copy. You'll find it on your desk in the morning."

"I hope it doesn't blow anything."

"It won't. It's been tested in a closed system."

"That's no guarantee. This library system has been growing for thousands of years. Nobody knows where all the forks and interconnections are."

"Voth's taking full responsibility."

Hogard scratched his chest. "He must sure think a lot of you."

"The results will interest him, too. There's a lot that's still not known about Man's codicil."

"Well, go to it, Bram. Let me know what you turn up."

Some instinct of caution prompted Bram's reply. "Don't expect anything startling for a while. I'll just be noodling my way through the datastreams for the next few months."

Hogard gave a final worried look to the interface bulbs attached to his precious whole-body reader, then set about the task of shooing the late browsers out of the annex. One by one, they reluctantly switched off their reading machines and got up to go. The last to leave was the clerkish, sallow-featured man Bram had recognized from the political meeting where Penser's manifesto had been read. He seemed to hang around the annex a lot. He saw Bram looking at him and dropped his eyes. Bram resolved to find out who he was and if he worked at the biocenter, then promptly forgot about him.

He found it on the fourth night. It was down one of the endlessly dividing data branches growing out of that single muffled reference to the set of synthetic genes that had been derived from the embryonic switching mechanisms of the axolotl and the fearsome dragonfly nymph.

It back-referenced to another tangle of data branches arising from a cultural package that had been included in the monumental afterthought that was the codicil to Original Man's great message, and there was no doubt at all that it had to do with new genetic information for the human genome. And that was odd, because the complete recipe for cooking up a human being had already been transmitted fifty years earlier in the first—or hundredth?—cycle of the human message to be intercepted.

It sat in the center of his screen, a multicolored geometric figure with twenty hexagonal facets, rotating slowly in space to show its three-dimensional structure. A long, hollow tail dangled from it, endlessly flexing as if in search of something.

Bram knew what it was. He had made simpler versions himself many times for projects to inject new genetic information into food plants and industrial crops. It was the protein overcoat for a synthetic carrier virus. Inside that faceted overcoat was a molecule, or molecules, of infectious DNA.

Bram knew nothing about the nucleotide sequence of the viral DNA or what receptor sites in what human chromosomes it was meant to attach itself to. But he knew what it did.

It made human beings immortal.

"You look as if someone just told you that you were going to die!" Kerthin said. "Can't you act a little more lively?"

"Sorry," Bram said.

She faced him, her hands on her hips. "You've been moping around ever since you got back from the biocenter last night. You're no fun at all! Is something wrong?"

"No," he lied.

She peered at him suspiciously. "You found out something, didn't you? Something that you don't want to tell me."

"I'm just working late on a project, that's all."

"You don't want to tell me because you found out that I was right. Your precious Voth-shr-voth has been lying to you."

That stung. Bram told himself that Kerthin could not be right. If Voth had been trying deliberately to conceal the existence of a genetic amendment that kept human beings from aging, then he would not have encouraged Bram to keep on searching through the archives, not have lent his assistance. No. The explanation *must* be that the Nar simply didn't realize the implications of the unculled information in their files, and that was why it had lain there undisturbed for half a millennium. The file was simply a dumping ground for all the dangerous data having to do with that unstable dragonfly allele.

But the fact remained that human beings died after a

century or two—and kept on dying, generation after generation, while the Nar lived for a thousand years.

"The Nar don't lie," he said. "It's physically impossible for them to lie to one another, and they never got into the habit."

"Have it your own way." She tossed her head. "When you decide to join the human race, you can tell me about it. We need all the information we can get to help us in the struggle."

A finger of ice traced Bram's spine. He could imagine what use Kerthin's Schismatist friends would make of the information that human beings were meant to live forever—and that the Nar had not yet gotten around to conferring this gift upon them. He didn't want to think about what such poisoned knowledge would do to the human community once it got out.

He needed more time to think about this, time to decide what to do.

"There's nothing to tell, I said. Anyway, I'm not working tonight." He smiled with an effort. "Why don't we go to that new repast house you like? And afterward they're having a singfest down at the bay. It ought to be fun."

Kerthin was at the clothes chest, pulling an outdoor tabard over her head, an anonymous gray garment that seemed at odds with her liking for color. "I'm going out tonight. You'll have to find something yourself to eat. I think there're some leftover potato cups in the locker. Or you can eat at the bachelors' lodge."

"Where are you going?" Bram said. "It seems to me you're going out a lot lately."

"What do you expect?" She bristled. "You're gone half the night, and when you *are* here, you act all grumpy. I

216

didn't know if you were coming back tonight, and I promised I'd—I'd look at someone's sculpture."

"Go some other time."

She belted the tabard. "I can't. I said I'd be there tonight. Some other people will be at the showing."

"I'll go with you."

"No—I mean it's private. Just for a few artists. They aren't ready to show it to outsiders."

"It's a meeting, isn't it?"

"Oh, why are you acting this way? I'm going. Good night!"

She flounced out. The door fluttered with the force of her exit. Bram stared thoughtfully at it for a moment, then got his own overgarment out of the clothes chest.

Before he left, he checked the food locker. There was nothing in it except a few stale cornflats. Kerthin hadn't been spending much time at home either.

The bachelors' lodge was about two hundred years old, if you dated it from the time its original occupant died and was scraped out of the interior. Thick deposits of lime partially filled in the original grooves of the spiral, turning the basic helical shape into a squat, bumpy cone. Nevertheless, you could easily distinguish the five fat bulges that comprised it, not counting the cap chamber, which was almost too cramped to stand up in and which was used mainly for storage.

Bram felt a pang of nostalgia as he let himself through the outer gate and looked up at the calcified ribs and old-fashioned casements fitted into the reticulated pattern they formed. The manicured grounds looked exactly as they had looked on the day he had first moved in with his few belongings, ready to begin his independent life and uncertain of how the other members would receive him.

Jimb, the old man who tended the plantings, was working with a spade near the path. He looked the same too, bent and ageless, his face a network of unchanged wrinkles, his knotted forearms burned brown by the suns. He was wearing the same stained garden smock, the same shapeless bags over his feet, tied around the ankles to keep out loose dirt.

"Hello, Jimb, how've you been?" Bram said as he approached.

The old groundsman looked up from the hole he had been digging and squinted incuriously at Bram's face.

"Fair enough, young fellow, fair enough," he said, and went back to his work. Old Jimb had seen them come and seen them go for over a century. There had been no glimmer of recognition in the faded eyes.

The anteroom was dark and cool, with heavy comfortable furniture and the worn appointments that had reassured generations of new members. A smell of cooking and a clatter of dishes came from the dining chamber beyond, where they would be having the early serving about now. A few neophytes, too young for Bram to recognize them, stood around, talking in appropriately hushed voices.

He hesitated, wondering if he ought to speak to the steward first, when one of the older members came through the curtain and spotted him.

"Welcome back, Bram. Drop by to say hello to the old fogies? How are you? We've been hearing great things about you."

Bram pressed palms. "Hello, Torm. You're not ready to join the fogies yet, I hope."

Torm laughed. He was a small, neat, pink man who supplemented his allowance by doing free-lance sound transcription for the Nar. "Any day now, but I'm trying to stave it off." He winked broadly. "I've got myself a new girl friend out at the cove. A lady of mature years like myself, but worth the trip every Tenday, if you know what I mean. I'd take the monandry pledge with her and move out of this place if I wasn't so set in my ways."

"Well . . . I'm glad to see you so lively."

"Stay young, my boy. Any way you can. That's my motto. Do you agree?"

"Yes," Bram said, concealing the jolt that Torm's words had given him. The man couldn't possibly have read his thoughts. Bram's eyes strayed to the curtain as he remembered the errand that had brought him here.

"Looking for Smeth? He isn't here tonight. He had a guild meeting."

"No. I was wondering . . . is Doc Pol around?"

Torm's eyebrows lifted. "You'll find him in the common room, same as always. What do you want with the old codger?"

"Just thought I'd have a few words with him. He was very helpful when I was studying mol-med applications. I couldn't have passed my molecular biology exam without him."

"So? I'd have thought his mol-med would have been out of date even then. Don't let him trap you into a game. Smeth's his usual victim, so tonight is dangerous. Shall I tell the steward you're staying for supper? Second serving's in about an hour."

"Thanks, Torm," Bram said.

He found Doc Poi in the corner chair that was reserved for him by the general consent of the members. When an unwary newcomer tried to sit in it, he was quickly set right. Doc evidently had just finished supper, skipping the sweet as usual so that he could plant himself in the common room for the serious business of whiling away the evening. An after-dinner drink was on a small taboret beside him, within easy reach of his hand, and he was reading an old, often-refolded printout of Moliere's *Imaginary Invalid*.

He looked up and brought Bram into focus. "Good halftide, young fellow. Bram, wasn't it? The bioengineer? Pull up a chair, my boy, and sit down."

"Thank you, sir," Bram said, and settled opposite.

Doc Pol had grown whiter and more withered since the last time Bram had seen him. His voice was cloudier, his hands less steady. It was impossible to guess how old he might be. He had been a fixture of the lodge when Bram had first met him—fifty years retired and full of dusty, forgotten honors. Some unspecified disappointment had driven him to pare down his life and consign himself to the lodge. Nobody from outside ever came to see him. Perhaps he had simply outlived everyone close to him.

"You look fit, Bram. Older. Filled out a bit. Let me think. You'd been accepted as an initiate by a Nar touch group. Did you ever get your apprenticeship?"

"Yes, sir. Thanks to you. The help you gave me with human biology. You know more about molecular repair than anyone I've met."

"Nonsense," the old man snorted. But Bram could see that he was pleased. "My practical knowledge was fifty years behind the times. Why, at the time I retired they hadn't even begun to autoclone cortical tissue. Nowadays it seems that every senescent old fool runs to have it done as soon as he begins forgetting a few things. I wouldn't do it myself. We have more than enough brain cells to keep us going until we croak—the trick is to keep on using the ones we have left."

"Well, cerebral enhancement aside, you certainly opened my eyes about how autoclone grafts work on the cellular level. Kidney tissue, lung tissue, intestinal tissue—even the cellular mechanisms involved in regrowing working structures like limbs."

Doc Pol took a small sip of his drink. "Hmph. Clone grafts for injury repair, organ replacement for nonsynchronous wear and tear. That's about all we bumbling medcrafters are good for, apart from broken bones and obstetrics. Original Man didn't leave much work for a doctor to do. Not after he edited out the oncogenes and selected for longevity, good eyesight, good teeth, and the rest of it. And kindly kept his germs to himself. It all catches up with you in the end, of course."

"That's what I wanted to talk to you about, sir."

"Talk about what?"

"Why it catches up."

Doc Pol turned a pair of bright blue eyes on him. "You mean why can't we go on recloning parts of our bodies forever and live on as patchworks?"

"Well . . . something like that."

"Each of us has a fetal analog frozen in nitrogen and put on file before blastocyst implantation. And that's fine in case of medical catastrophe. Particularly when someone needs a new heart or kidney. But you can go back to the well only so often. And even if that weren't so, eventually you'd be stitching your patches to worn-out material." He shook his head sadly. "No, my young friend, if you're looking for a prescription for immortality, you'll have to find it in the cell itself. Our fetal analogs stay young only because they've been arrested by freezing. Thaw them out, grow the

differentiated cells into the replacement part you want—
and your new lung or kidney goes through exactly the
same number of cell generations as the rest of you. It
might outlast you—but not for long."

"How many cell generations, Doc? And why does cell
division have to stop at all?"

The old man looked longingly at the backgammon
board on his chairside taboret. "About fifty cell generations in human beings. You'd know more about vegeta-
bles than I do. As to why they eventually lose the ability
to function and replace themselves, there are different
theories."

Bram leaned forward in an attitude of extreme interest,
chin on knuckles, elbows on knees. "Like what?"

Doc Pol sighed. "One of them is the accumulation of errors. Do you know what collagen is?"

"A large protein molecule. Chief constituent of connec-
tive tissue."

"It accounts for about thirty percent of all the protein in
the body. It supports the skin, separates the spinal disks,
and so forth. Because the molecules are long, cross-links
tend to form over a period of time. The tissue hardens,
loses its elasticity. For a long time, Original Man thought
collagen was the key to aging, simply because the effects
of cross-linking were so pervasive. Wrinkles, stiff joints,
slipped disks, degenerative circulatory conditions, arthri-
tis—the lot! He worked on it for centuries and gave us the
results. Now we know how to dissolve the cross-links, and
that's why, when you're about a third as old as I am, you'll
start to go in once or twice a year for your rejuvenation
treatments." He chortled at Bram. "I passed my sevenscore
and ten a long time ago—I won't say how long, but I'm a
lot closer to two hundred than I am to one hundred and

fifty, and with any luck I'll get there! And I'll tell you this. I look a lot better and feel a lot better than youngsters of ninety did back in the days when Original Man was at the mercy of nature."

"But," Bram prompted delicately, "the human life span still is limited. Even with rejuvenation treatments."

"Yes, yes," Doc Pol said vaguely. "What was I saying? Ah! The accumulation of errors. If collagen is subject to cross-linking, so must other long molecules be. Like DNA. You're a genetic engineer. You can imagine what that does."

"Codons attached at the wrong sites! Inappropriate palindromes! Loops and detours! Wrong enzymes being made, or enzymes not being made at all! That must be it! Suppose you could find some way to tell those codons that they've grabbed a wrong place on a strand—get them to let go and cast about till they hook into an appropriate site? Like what you do in genetic engineering when you fool a stretch of nucleotide into accepting a foreign plasmid. Only in reverse! Dissolve a bond to *undo* the damage!"

" 'Fraid not, son. Cross-linked DNA is part of the explanation, maybe, but it's not the whole story."

Bram exhaled. "What, then?"

"You know that DNA has a great capacity to repair itself."

"Yes, otherwise the stray damage caused by ionizing radiation would begin to add up in a long-lived species . . ." He looked at Doc with new surmise. "Accumulated errors!"

"The ability of DNA to repair itself decreases with each cell generation. By the fiftieth generation it's about gone. You know how redundant DNA is."

"Yes. A given cell uses less than one percent of the information in its DNA during its lifetime."

"Consider the redundant genes to be replacement

parts. If a functional gene is damaged, a spare takes over its job. Over a period of time, all the spares are finally used up."

Bram's face fell. "That would mean there's no hope of reversing the aging process."

"There's one more theory."

"Which is?"

Doc Pol raised a sere hand and held it in front of his face as if studying it. After a bit, he put it back in his lap. "That our cells contain aging genes, just as they contain genes that mediate the various stages of embryonic and adolescent development. A sort of death switch, if you will. These switches tell the cell when the show's over and it's time to shut down. And there's no cure for that, either, son. It would mean that the sequential shutdowns of age and death are just part of the normal biological process, like the genetic programming that shuts down various stages of embryonic development when the time comes. I'm told there was once a creature, called the salmon, that aged and died after spawning, but we've got an example closer to home—the Nar." He shook his head. "No, my boy, if you're looking for eternal life you'd have to imagine something that stops an inherent developmental process and keeps particular genes that are a part of our genetic material from expressing themselves."

"Like the dragonfly does," Bram said, half to himself.

"What's that, my boy?"

"Nothing," Bram said quickly. "I was thinking about heterochronic eggs. The Nar interfered with normal embryonic development there and came up with a single giant cell that absorbs nourishment through an outer membrane and divides when it gets big enough."

Doc Pol looked at him shrewdly. "And you think genetic

tinkering might some day interfere with death genes? That day's a long way off, my young friend. Original Man never managed the trick, even at the top of his form, and we're very small potatoes compared to him. And the Nar, even though they use something corresponding to DNA, never did it for themselves. I'll grant you, of course, the fact that for the Nar to go chasing after immortality would be to flout a biological imperative that's stronger than the sex urge is for us—given the fact that they can mate only once, like a flower going to seed."

"Yes," Bram said. "I suppose you're right."

"I'd rather be told I'm wrong," the old man said. His expression became sly. "Care for a game of backgammon?"

"I'm not sure I—"

"Nothing to it. I can refresh your memory about the rules as we go along."

Doc Pol began briskly to set out the board and pieces. With a sigh, Bram gave in to the inevitable. It was a cheap way to pay for the information he'd gotten from Doc.

Halfway through the first game, the steward sought Brain out in the common room to remind him that the second serving was about to begin. "Torm said you'd be staying for supper," he said.

Doc Pol snapped peevishly, "Bring him a tray! He can eat while he's playing. He's having too much fun to stop."

A new individual was in charge of stores—a young Nar who knew only a few words of Inglex. Patiently, Bram explained in the Small Language and with some creative boneless gestures what he wanted.

"I'll need a container of uranyl acetate for negative staining and some standard head and tail proteins from the multipurpose insertion provirus. And an amino acid kit and some clay substrates—oh, yes, and I'll want to check out one of the small protein synthesizers for a few days."

Sweat broke out on his brow as he waited for the stores clerk to question him, but the slender being merely gave the perfunctory triple unzipping of tentacle edges that was a Nar nod and went soundlessly prowling through the honeycomb spaces of the supply room.

After the clerk had helped him load everything onto the carrystraps and shelves of the three-legged walker that he had borrowed for the purpose, Bram asked casually, "And would you book me some hours on the muon scope?"

The Nar clerk checked a touch list tacked to the wall. "The schedule is filled for the remainder of this quint, but if it is important to a project of Voth-shr-voth, I can get authorization from him to rearrange viewtime."

"No, don't bother," Bram said hastily. "Can you just book me for next Tenday morning?"

"No one will be there to assist you then. Shall I arrange for a technician?"

"No, don't do that. I don't want to put anyone to any trouble. I know how to operate the equipment myself."

He gave the walker a kick to get it started, and the synthetic resilin protein that was its motive power unsnapped and got the tripod legs going in syncopated rhythm. A walker wasn't alive, strictly speaking—it couldn't feel the pain of a kick, didn't take nourishment, and merely went on dispensing the mechanical energy it could store in its fibers until one day it wore out.

With one hand, he guided it through the corridors, nudging it up to a walking speed just short of a pace that would attract attention, and halted it in a small cul-de-sac outside the septum where he worked. Some unused furniture had been temporarily dumped here, and an unattended walker was not likely to be noticed.

Bram draped the upper tiers of the biodevice with a tarpaulin he had brought for the purpose, then went back to his department and plunged into the work he was supposed to be doing. Today he was screening gene libraries for one of the junior subgroups. The job involved using synthetic oligonucleotide probes to trace amino acid sequences of proteins, and Bram was able to sneak in a few side searches of his own.

He waited until past quitting time, when he wasn't likely to bump into anyone who knew him, and returned to the storage alcove. The walker was still there, its tarpaulin undisturbed. Bram triggered the elastic tendons again and got the draped biomachine into an elevator and out into the street.

He was halfway to the hackstand at the crossing when the walker quit on him. He gave it a push; it staggered on a few steps and quit again.

With a nervous glance around him, Bram dropped to one knee and felt under the skirts of the tarpaulin for the tripod legs. The bunched artificial muscles had gone completely flabby. Bram cursed himself for not having made sure the walker was fully wound up before borrowing it; a simple few minutes with a high-speed mechanical flexor would have done it.

He massaged the reselin bundles manually until he felt them knotting up, keeping a jittery eye on the incurious crowds flowing past. The sight of a human using a walker to move his possessions was not that unusual; what Bram was afraid of was that some helpful soul from the nearby biocenter would come along and get a look under the tarp.

A protein synthesizer was not something that one generally borrowed.

He nursed the Walker along for a dozen yards before it came to a halt again, then had to stop twice more to massage it before he could coax it to the transport post. He hired a small pentabeast with a palanquin, heaved the walker aboard when its legs gave out again at the last moment, and high-legged it for home.

Kerthin was not there. She was out almost every night now, going to her secret meetings. She hardly bothered to keep up a pretense any longer; once Eena had come to call for her, and the two of them had gone off together after some unconvincing light conversation and an evasive exchange of glances.

She and her disgruntled friends were up to something; Bram was sure of it. What it might be, he could not guess. Some event was on the way; that was all he could surmise. Kerthin showed a suppressed excitement these days, an excitement that mounted Tenday by Tenday. Bram dated the change in Kerthin from the visit to the orbiting tree, when she had covered up for Pite, and that had been months ago. Now Kerthin kept putting him off whenever he tried to talk about a welding ceremony or a return visit to the gene co-op. She would only tell him, with an impatient toss of her head, that she needed more time to think about things, that she didn't want to make any long-range plans before Yearsend—as if she had some hidden agenda in her mind.

Bram could hardly complain. He was keeping secrets from Kerthin, too.

In fact, he thought as he steered the lurching walker into the little spare chamber where he worked at home, Kerthin's absence tonight had been a relief, in a way. It saved explaining. And, he thought guiltily, her frequent absences would make it a lot easier for him to do what he had to do.

To manufacture an immortality virus—even with the active cooperation of the Nar hierarchy, if he dared seek it—would be a long and elaborate enterprise. It would take a lot of manpower and a lot of Narpower, and it would require the full resources of the biocenter. It was not something to be done by one man in secret.

But he had to make a start somewhere. He could begin work on the outer structure of that tantalizing icosahedral capsid—the protein overcoat worn by the carrier virus.

Even there, Bram knew, he could proceed so far and no farther without medical accomplices and human volunteers. But he would face that problem later.

With a sigh, Bram began unloading the walker. He got out the amino acid kit and unpacked the clay substrates. For the moment, at least, he could begin the tedious job of assembling proteins.

It was after middark before Kerthin got back. She stood in the elliptical opening to the small chamber and looked suspiciously at the run-down walker and the equipment Bram had set up. "What's all that stuff?" she said.

"Oh, just some things I brought home," he said. "There are a few ideas I want to try out. Where've you been?"

She avoided the question. "That doesn't look like the kind of thing you just bring home," she said with a nod toward the synthesizer. "What does it do?"

"It puts chemicals together in different combinations," he told her.

She came farther into the chamber. Her face was

flushed, he noticed. She had come home with a flushed face on quite a few occasions recently, as though she were living at a stepped-up pace on her nights out.

"Bram," she said, moving closer.

He turned the synthesizer off and stood up. He grabbed her by one wrist and pulled her to him. She melted against him. Her body felt hot and feverish, full of untapped excitement that he was expected to relieve. She had been keyed up by something tonight.

Later, lying in the nest together, there was a languid ease between them that had been absent for some time. Bram was almost tempted to bring up the subject of the gene co-op again but was afraid it would spoil the moment.

"Wouldn't it be nice," Kerthin sighed, "if we could stop time whenever we wanted and lie here like this and not worry about anything?"

"Hmmm," Bram agreed. Then, reasonably, "That's what we're doing."

"But then the world always comes into it again." She propped herself on one elbow and looked at him gravely. "I mean, what if we could just float away and start all over again in a perfect world?"

"This one isn't so bad sometimes," Bram said lazily.

"You're too easily satisfied."

"Not that easily," he said, reaching for her.

She wriggled away. "In a world that was run properly, you'd be a very important person. In a world like this, it's the Willum-frth-willums that get the credit for everything. When you know a thousand times more about bio-crafting than he does."

"You're flattering me."

"Maybe you need flattering."

"What does that mean?"

"It means you can't go on drifting through life. Sometimes you have to make choices."

"I make choices all the time," he said lightly. "I do it every time I flush a cloning tray down the drain or decide to pass it on to the biocrafting department."

"For *them* to take the credit," she said.

"That's not the way it works," he said uncomfortably. "Biocrafting's a big enterprise. Everybody does their share."

"What's that stuff you took home with you?"

Disconcerted, he said, "I told you, I just want to work out a few ideas."

"Why can't you do it at the biocenter? Why don't you want the Nar to know what you're up to?"

"Kerthin . . ."

She laughed. "Never mind. It's good to know you're showing some spunk." She rolled partway over to peer at him. "It has something to do with that dragonfly thing, doesn't it?"

Bram froze. "What makes you think that?" he asked carefully.

"Keep your secrets for now, my poor, transparent love. When the time comes, you can share them with those who'll know how to use them properly."

"Like Pite?" he said, and instantly regretted it.

She patted his hand. "You're very nice, and you'll be nicer when you wake up. You need somebody to take you in hand. As Penser says, 'Discipline is better than consensus.'"

The Penser quote depressed Bram. "Kerthin, I don't want you talking to any of those people about what I do."

"Of course not."

"Don't humor me. I mean it."

"Could you make those dragonfly things with that

equipment you've got?" she asked, tracing a circle on his chest with her finger.

"Is *that* what you think?" he said, then checked himself. "Look, you don't understand what I've been saying. To craft any living organism above the level of a virus is an enormous enterprise that requires lots of different specialists. Synthesizing the DNA is only the start of the job. Then you've got to assemble a working cell. Even the simplest bacterium has over a thousand 'small' molecules—sugars, amino acids, fatty acids—and another thousand or two thousand macromolecules—the different proteins and other polymeric chains—that are hundreds of times more complex than the subunits. You've got to have a functioning cell membrane and, once you get beyond bacteria, a structured nucleus that's separated from the cytoplasm. The precise three-dimensional configurations are important—the polypeptide chains have to fold up to form the properly shaped catalytic cavities. Oh, why go on?"

"Poor Bram, now you're all upset."

"Biocrafting is the science of life, not a weapon in some imaginary battle."

"Never mind, Bram, sweet. Go to sleep."

She turned over and curled up with her back to him. Bram tried to sleep, but he couldn't.

It was a couple of Tendays later. Bram no longer worked late at the biocenter, except for those nights when he was able to gain access to the facilities of the library annex. instead, he hurried home to solve protein chains.

He was getting nowhere. It was not a job for the empirical approach. What he needed was a high-powered computer search program. Eventually, he knew, he would have to enlist a hacker—to kindle somehow the feverish monomania that those strange involute creatures thrived on while concealing the true purpose of the program. In the meantime, he plugged away, gaining experience that might translate into a more successful search technique.

Hogard, the hairy librarian, was becoming inconveniently curious about Bram's nighttime researches. Bram fobbed him off with snippets of incidental material that kept him busy collating and cataloging. Once Hogard had buttonholed him and asked, "Did you ever turn up anything further on those egg genes, the ones where the historical references just petered out?"

"No," Bram had answered, startled and wary. "Why do you ask?"

Hogard had nodded in the direction of the sallow man from the Ascendist meeting, who was fiddling with one of the reading machines. "Waller over there asked me what you were up to nights. Said he'd be interested in being kept informed."

"Waller?"

Hogard's curly eyebrows had gone up in surprise.

"Don't you know him?"

"No."

"That's funny, he seemed to know you. I got the impression you had friends in common."

"Who is he? Does he work at the biocenter?"

"Him? Naw. He's a clerk over at the laser comm center. Routes commercial traffic and separates out the human messages for decoding and forwarding. He's a human history nut, though—spends half his life at the annex here poring over *The Lives of the Twelve Caesars,* the sayings of Mao, the entries on Napoleon and Alexander the Great—things like that. Been a help to me, though. He gets me printouts of the new literary works coming from Juxt One and Next so I can enter them here. I enter 'em, but I can't say I understand some of 'em—like this play, *The Interchangeable Man,* where all the characters wear masks and the hero begs a tribunal called the 'control-chorus' to execute him for what he calls deviation. But I guess you can't argue with art."

"You told him about the uncataloged data?"

"Sure, him being interested in history and like that. He says he can't wait till it gets straightened out."

Waller had glanced up and seen them looking in his direction, but instead of responding to Hogard's offhand wave, he had ducked his head and pretended not to notice it. A few minutes later he had switched off his reading machine and, eyes down, left.

Bram had not returned to the library annex since then, but out of curiosity he had gone back to the drink shop in whose back room the Ascendist meeting had been held. He had lingered over a cold toddy and then, on the pretext of looking for the cloaca, peeped into the meeting room. The rows of seats were gone, there was no sign of a rostrum or political banners, and the lounges and game tables had been restored to their places. Two men playing a game with pasteboards seemed not at all familiar.

On this night, some days after his conversation with Hogard, Bram had returned home to find Kerthin away, as she was so often. Half an egg, left over from supper the night before, was in the food locker. He cut off a slice and fixed himself a light repast of yolkballs and cold bean-fry. He had just finished eating and was settling down to work preparing a batch of ribosomes for the protein synthesizer when the door rattle gave an ugly rasp.

He got up to answer, thinking that if Kerthin had decided to spend the evening at home, after all, he would quit work. He could put on some music, make drinks.

The door rattle made another impatient noise. "I'm coming," Bram called. He opened the oval port and saw Pite standing there with two bulky shadows behind him.

"Hello, Brammo," Pite said softly.

"What do you want?" Bram said, not bothering to conceal his distaste. "Kerthin's not here."

"We didn't come to see Kerthin, Brammo," Pite said. "It's you we want to talk to."

Before Bram could do anything about it, Pite pushed his way into the chamber, followed by his two hulking friends. All three were wearing gray monos with the sleeves cut off; it seemed to be an unofficial uniform for Pite's faction. Bram recognized Fraz: red-faced and scraggly-bearded. The other intruder was equally large and muscular, with a broken nose and a bristly head of hair that had been trimmed close enough to show the bumpy contours of his skull.

Fraz clumped past Bram without looking at him and stuck his head and wide shoulders into the little workchamber. "Hey, Pite!" he yelled. "Come take a look at this stuff."

Pite stayed where he was, grinning at Bram. "What about it, Brammo? Doing a little private research that the decaboos don't know about?"

"None of your business," Bram said. "Now get out of here."

"Is that any way to talk to a gene brother?" Pite said. "Be nice, Brammo."

Fraz was rummaging through a basket of Bram's printouts. He lost interest in them and picked up one of the clay substrates lying next to the protein synthesizer.

"Leave that alone," Bram said sharply. He started toward the alcove, and the fellow with the close-clipped hair blocked his path. Bram tried to go around him, and a set of thick fingers wrapped themselves around his upper arm.

"Let go of me," he said.

The grip on his arm only tightened, but Pite said lazily, "Let the man go, Spak. We're all friends here. Fraz, don't touch anything. We wouldn't want to disturb Brammo's work, would we?"

"Sure, Pite," Fraz said, replacing the little tablet. "I didn't hurt anything."

Bram, with a glare, moved back the things Fraz had disarranged and pushed the workbench against the wall. "Why are you here?" he said to Pite.

"It's like this, Brammo. Time's running out, and like Penser says, knowledge is power. We want to make sure that our gene brothers who work with the decaboos aren't holding out on us."

"There's nothing I do here or at my job that would be of any interest to you," Bram said.

"That's not what we hear, Brammo," Pite said softly. "We hear you're sticking your nose into a restricted area. We think you've come up with something that could give the human race leverage against the Nar. Biological leverage or propaganda leverage. We don't care which."

"Who told you that?" Bram said. "Waller?"

"Waller?" Fraz said innocently. "We don't know any Waller. Do we know a Waller, Spak?"

"Shut up, Fraz," Pite said. "The point is, Brammo, if you're not with us, you're against us."

"I'm not against anybody," Bram said. "I just want to be left alone to do my work."

"That's not possible anymore," Pite said with a half smile. "When the struggle comes to a head, very soon now, it'll be too late to choose sides."

"There's no struggle. It's all in your imagination."

"You see, Brammo," Pite said, ignoring the interruption, "we're making our lists now. We expect everybody who's fit to be called a human being to do his part. Especially people like you, who work for the yellowlegs and who're in a position to keep us informed about what they're up to." His lips stretched humorlessly within their fringe of uncombed blond beard. "So do yourself a favor, gene brother, and tell your friends all about it right now. What is this secret from the heritage of man that the yellowlegs are holding back from us? And what does all this scrambling around you've been doing lately have to do with it? It has something to do with the origin of eggs, doesn't it? Where does this dangerous life form come into the picture? Are they dragon eggs?"

Bram was shocked at the extent of Pite's information. Garbled though it was, it was uncomfortably close to the truth.

"How about it, Brammo?"

They were all looking at him. The fellow with the broken nose and the bumpy skull, Spak, edged a step closer, his oversize arm muscles working like independent creatures, and glanced toward Pite as if waiting for a signal.

Bram drew a deep breath. Keeping his mouth shut wouldn't solve the problem now. He had to throw Pite off the trail—concoct some kind of story that would allay Pite's suspicions. And he didn't dare stray too far from the facts; he had no idea how much Pite knew or might find out.

Later, he could face the question of where Pite had heard

about "dragons." Neither Waller nor Hogard could have told him. Kerthin was the only person Bram had confided in. But there was no time to think about that now.

"No, they're not dragon eggs," Bram said. "But they contain a few altered genes from—from the dangerous life form you referred to. All the genes do is keep an egg growing without differentiating, to make it suitable as a food source. A complete genome of the—the other organism doesn't exist."

"Pity," Pite said. "Could you use the genes you have to construct a chimeric analog of one of these flying dragons?"

Bram skipped a breath. Pite was not as stupid as he had believed.

"Dragonfly," he said automatically. "No, it's not the kind of job that could be done with the resources available to humans, like backtracking potato genes to make a simple vegetable organism like the tomato. And it's certainly not anything one man could tackle with the equipment I have in the other room. If it could be done at all, it would need all the resources of the biocenter and dozens of Nar specialists."

Pite nodded as if he had heard it before. "Then what is it, exactly, that you're up to, Brammo, that you're being so cagy about?"

"How much do you understand about genetic engineering?"

"Try me."

Bram made himself look embarrassed, reluctant. "You see, Pite, if I could somehow neutralize the right gene or genes suppressing the embryonic development of the egg, than maybe I could make the yolk give rise to some kind of structured multicellular tissue. Not the original egg creature itself—the egg's been altered too much for that—but mesoderm tissue in the form of fibrous protein. It ought to be similar to spun bacterial protein or textured protein made from soybeans. If I could do that, it would be the greatest bioengineering achievement by a human being since Willum-frth-willum's work with the nightshade family. But the Nar wouldn't like it. It wouldn't involve the exploitation of a living animal as a food source, but it might come close enough to their definition to offend their sense of values." He shrugged. "Once it was done, of course, they'd have to accept it."

Pite stared at him for a moment, then gave a single harsh bark of laughter. "You're after glory, then, pure and simple? Do the yellowlegs suspect you?"

"No."

Pite clapped him on the shoulder. "Go to it, Brammo. I wouldn't have thought you had it in you. But keep us informed."

Bram nodded.

Pite gathered his two henchmen around him and headed for the door. He paused before leaving to give Bram a penetrating stare. "Just don't get tricky and try to hold anything back, gene brother," he said. "Withholding vital information about the Nar is treason. And we know how to take care of traitors."

Kerthin arrived shortly afterward, almost as if she had been waiting for Pite and his companions to leave. She chattered on about sculpture and her adventures of the day, but she didn't seem able to meet Bram's eyes.

"I bumped into Hok-kara—you know, my old teacher, I've mentioned him before—and we went back to his studio. He has a new protégée he wanted me to meet, a girl named Ele, and he showed me some of her work, done in resins, very nice. Anyway, there's exciting news. A starship's arrived from Juxt One—it's been on its way for seven years, and no one's paid much attention to the cargo manifest until now, of course, and it's brought a representative selection of the new sculpture for exhibition. Not holos or laser-pointed reproductions, but the actual pieces themselves. In stone, wood, polymers. And metal casting—they're way ahead of us there on Juxt One—they've rediscovered some of the old methods. They're parking the tree now to refurbish it for the return trip, and they'll be shuttling the pieces down starting in a day or so. I'll be getting a first look at them through Hok-kara, and I may be asked to help prepare them for exhibition, so I'm going to be very busy."

After she ran down, Bram said: "Your friend Pite dropped by, with Fraz and another fellow. He seemed to know all about dragonflies."

"Oh?" Kerthin said vaguely. "Too bad I missed him."

CHAPTER 10

The tree was a silver daystar on the horizon. Bram watched as it crawled up the sky, slowly overtaking its bright twin. It was easy to tell which of the two was the newly arrived starship. It was the one that waxed and waned. It still hadn't quite damped out all its tumble.

As they climbed, the living stars grew brighter, their reflective undersides catching more light from the late afternoon sun. There was a moment when they seemed to pause and almost touch—an illusion, Bram knew, since their orbits had to be hundreds of miles apart—then they began to separate again.

It was a magnificent sight. There were swarms of the great trees in higher orbit, of course, but none could match these two in brilliance. At the moment they were the only two starships in low orbit—the new arrival to discharge cargo and passengers, the outbound leviathan to complete its refitting and final loading.

Bram kept watching through the elastic window until the glinting motes passed from sight overhead; he used a hand to stretch the clear membrane outward for a final neck-craning glimpse. When he could see no more, he let the window snap back and turned reluctantly back to his desk. Voth was standing there with a sheaf of holos.

"You have friends aboard, do you not?" the elderly decapod inquired solicitously.

He was wearing a skirt now for decency's sake, a loose wrapper that concealed the dark inflamed tissue rimming his lower petals. Above the waistband, the lower set of eyes—the lensless ones that sent biorhythm signals to the structures that corresponded to the pineal gland in the human midbrain—had gone milky, signifying a new stage of endocrine changes.

"Yes," Bram said. "They invited me for a visit when the colonists first began to settle in."

"They will be leaving soon. The tree's ecology has been certified for extended travel. I am to be a member of the commission making the final inspection. Bram, you should take the opportunity soon to say a last farewell."

Marg and Orris were, in fact, due to make planetfall in a day or two for a last fling and for Marg's implantation. The tree-to-surface traffic was picking up considerably as sailing time grew near. Bram had hoped to ask them over with a few friends, but Kerthin was being embarrassingly ungracious about the whole thing, and Bram had just about resigned himself to catching the two of them at the round of goodspeed parties the Quarter would be throwing for embarkees.

"Thank you, Voth, I shall," he said.

Voth held out the sheaf of holos. "You may find these of some use. They are early records of some of the beginning investigations of my touch group into the precursor heterochronic mechanisms—from before those lines of research were abandoned. I had almost forgotten they existed." He hesitated, his tentacles delicately weaving. "I have been cleaning out my files and . . . getting things in order."

Bram took the documents. They were stiff with age and moldy around the edges, but that wouldn't affect the readouts. "You are kind, Voth," he said.

"There are many false starts, many failed lines of inquiry. But perhaps you might notice something which we did not." A tentacle, feeling feverish, descended on Bram's shoulder. "There is no one I would rather let have them than you, Bram of my center."

The Small Language sobriquet could not really be translated, but Bram felt the warm lapping contractions on his shoulder. He was profoundly moved by the gift. Voth must have some inkling of what he was up to by now, and the holos were a reticent form of encouragement.

Bram, ashamed of himself, resolved to bring what he had found to Voth, get it all into the open, as soon as he had more to go on.

Voth gave his shoulder a final squeeze and left. Bram had no taste at the moment for working with the holos. He shoved them into a desk iris and brooded, staring out the window, for a while.

Finally he stood up and took his overgarment from the hook. He would explode if he stayed here any longer. He decided to go to the spaceport and see the excitement. Kerthin had said something about being there this afternoon for the arrival of the first crated batch of human-made sculpture from Juxt One. Perhaps he would see her there and have it out with her about Pite.

Five or six shuttles from various parts of the tree had landed already that afternoon. From his vantage point in the observation pinnacle atop the port terminal, Bram could see them floating lazily in the artificial lagoons adjoining the landing channel—flat, sleek, finned shapes that resembled some huge mythical sea creatures come to wallow in the shallows.

Passengers were still flowing in a bright yellow tide down the gangway of the nearest shuttle. A half-mile farther on, an earlier arrival was being hauled by a gigantic crawler up a service ramp to an unloading area where a number of bowl-shaped cargo vehicles waited for it.

Beyond the lagoons, made tiny by distance, still another orbiter was being prepared for takeoff, standing upright on its flippers next to a service tower. The two matching curvilinear wedges that were the ascent stages stood a little apart, waiting for the orbiter to be fitted between them.

A lively traffic in transfer vehicles, both living and mechanical, poured in two contrary streams along the wide causeway that led from the terminal. Outside the terminal, as Bram had discovered when he arrived, was a traffic jam of beasts and machines ranging from one-passenger pentadactyls to multibuses hired by extended touch groups.

Bram savored the colorful spectacle. In spaceports all over the Father World, similar scenes were being enacted as the tree overhead poured out its worldlet's hoard of wealth and living inhabitants. It would be at least a five of Tendays before the transfer was completed and the tree could be allowed to rise to a higher orbit, where it would be more comfortable.

Bram tore his gaze from the outside view and gave his attention to the sunlit interior of the cupola. The terminal was bustling with activity today, its floors and ramps a moving forest of undulating tentacles. Bram was not the only human there by any means. There were hundreds of them scattered through the observation cap—people waiting for the touchdown of a landing craft that would bring them a friend or close gene kin they had not seen for decades, merchants waiting for orders they had placed by laser more than seven years before.

Kerthin was nowhere in the throng. Bram tried to remember what her old sculpture teacher, Hok-kara, looked like.

Finally he went to an information kiosk where two harried Nar were using all five abovedecks tentacles simultaneously to service all comers and stood in line to await his turn.

The information clerk grasped Bram's hand before he realized he was talking to a human. "What do you wish to know?" he boomed in the Small Language, focusing the apposite eye in the general direction of Bram's armpit. He kept his tentacle pressed against Bram's hand for the sake of politeness, though he might, with the split attention made possible by the Nar's decentralized nervous systems, have used it to talk to a sixth customer.

"Have passengers or cargo from the human bough landed yet?" Bram asked.

"Lobe four," the Nar replied. "A carrier is arriving now."

"Thank you," Bram said.

He hurried to the downbelt to beat the stampede that was going to develop as soon as the waiting crowd became aware of the arrival. The terminal had been grown in the shape of a single interior space, a haft mile high and a thousand feet across at the base, with a continuous spiral concourse winding from top to bottom along the conical wall. The concourse averaged a hundred feet across, with plenty of area for offices, shops, passenger lounges, and other facilities, and though there was no such thing as level floor anywhere, that didn't bother the Nar. Bram paused at the railing and looked straight down the spiral to the terminal floor a haft mile below. He was too high to see the ground-level crowds as much more than patches of yellow dust motes, but he could discern the beginnings of movement toward the arrival lobes.

Outside the observation cupola, a speck grew in the lavender sky and spectators crowded the view wall. Bram loitered, a hand poised on the rail, until the graceful deltoid form glided in over the channel waters and skimmed to a stop, its red-hot underbelly sending up a sizzle of steam. Before the ripples died down, Bram stepped onto the moving belt and let it carry him along its corkscrew path to ground level.

By the time he got to lobe four, it was solid with humans and decapods converging on the reception area. Bram searched through the crush for Kerthin. He thought he caught a glimpse of her in the middle of the throng, but when he got to that spot, there was no sign of her.

At that point the first wave of human travelers from Juxt One came through the gates with their hand luggage, and there was a surge to greet them. After some milling around, the place cleared out a bit, and Bram saw her standing with a small group of people.

"Kerthin," he cried, and started forward.

Intent on the arrival gate, she didn't hear him at first. She turned her head and spoke to the person next to her but broke off as she saw Bram heading toward her. The other person said something, then Kerthin nodded, and hurried to intercept Bram.

"What are you doing here?" she said. She seemed nervous.

"I didn't feel like working. Where's your teacher? Is he over there?"

"No. He couldn't come, after all. There was some mix-up about the pieces of sculpture. They won't be coming down for a few more days. Those are just some people who came to meet the shuttle. I got to talking with them while we were waiting. Let's go."

She was edging him toward the lobe exit. Bram took a few steps, then, stopped. "What's the hurry? It isn't every day a star tree arrives."

Another wave of star travelers was coming through the gates. The people in front were leading a pair of exotic pets that were attracting attention—artificial animals that obviously had been bred for conditions on Juxt One. Waist-high and covered with a fine silky floss, they were streamlined, saddle-shaped creatures whose incurvate edges terminated in ten slender legs that were plainly meant for running. A cluster of alert-looking eyes had migrated to what had become, unmistakably, a front end on the Terran plan.

"Sand-runners," Bram said. "I've seen pictures of them. Long-range errand beasts, but they race them, too. Some people turn them into house pets."

Kerthin was not very interested in the sand-runners. "Let's get out of here," she said.

"Just a minute," Bram said stubbornly.

Another passenger had trailed in, unnoticed in the hubbub stirred by the sand-runners. He was a tall, thin man with a pale face and a smear of beard. He kept looking in both directions as he advanced, scanning the place. A group of people—Bram thought that one of them was the man Kerthin had been talking to—surrounded him and, with a minimum exchange of words, hustled him out of the lobe.

Kerthin was staring, wide-eyed. When she saw Bram

looking at her, she jerked her gaze away from the group. "Are you ready to leave yet?" she snapped.

"Did you know that man?"

"What man? What are you talking about?"

Bram gave up. Outside the terminal he left Kerthin standing by the entrance while he went off to look for transportation. He was lucky enough to find a two-passenger jaunting beast outfitted for human riders with a pair of back-to-back chairs and foot rests slung across the creature's hump.

When Kerthin saw him leading the jaunting beast toward her, she said, "Oh, no, I'm not getting on that thing. Can't you find something with wheels?"

"This is all there is," Bram said.

Grumbling, she mounted the conveyance. "This is no way for a human being to travel. *They* don't have any trouble hanging on."

"You can't fall off. And it's a fine way to see the scenery."

"I like to face forward," she said. "Not sideways."

The ride home was a silent one, with Kerthin's tense, rigid back pressed against his shoulder blades and her knuckles white on the gripping knobs. Rocked by the steady, loping motion, Bram let his mind stray back to the scene at the spaceport, when the tall, pale passenger from Juxt One had come through while everybody was being distracted by the sand-runners. Bram kept picturing the way a small group of waiting people had moved with disciplined teamwork to encircle the pale man and hurry him out of sight. Bram had seen their faces only fleetingly, but one of them, he was certain, had been Pite.

"Are you working again tonight?" Kerthin said.

"I'm afraid so," Bram said. "I could—"

"No, no," she said hastily. "Do what you have to. I'm sure it's very important."

"It's repetitive," he said. "And boring." He made a show of setting out gels and filters and arranging printouts in neat stacks.

She bent over and kissed him lightly. "Don't wait up for me," she said. "I may be late."

He sat back, comfortably full of the meal that she had taken pains to prepare. His relationship with Kerthin seemed to have taken a new turn since the visit from Pite. She was solicitous of his comfort, took care not to ruffle his feelings, and was all sweetness and light. And, he noted wryly, she was paying him the courtesy of providing more plausibility for her mysterious excursions.

"What is it?" he asked. "More sculpture?"

"It's a group work. Hok-kara says that collective art is the only kind that makes sense, because it reflects the shared aspirations of humanity. They're doing some very exciting things in ensemble sculpture on Juxt One. Hok-kara's coordinating the creative merger here, and he gave me a chance to be a part of it."

Kerthin's old sculpture tools had suddenly appeared again, and an armature partially covered with clay now stood on a modeling stand in the center of the living chamber. She made a show of working on it every once in a while, but it had been there for several days now, and there was no progress that Bram could see.

As soon as she left, he got up, put on his overgarment, and went out the door. He was not proud of himself for what he was doing, but he could see no other way.

Kerthin's tall, slim figure was ahead of him, already some distance down the thoroughfare. She was walking quickly, looking neither to right nor left. Bram hung back until she turned down a side lane, then darted out of the doorway after her.

The lane was narrow and cobbleshelled, the architecture a sprawling hodgepodge of styles with the newer square buildings of framed lumber or blocks of refractory materials beginning to crowd out the older organic dwellings. Shrill children dashed back and forth, playing their eternal reinvented games and trying to postpone bedtime. Older people sat in front of their doorways to digest their evening meals and watch the world go by. Bram spotted Kerthin's swinging gait and hurried to keep her in sight, then ducked behind a databooth when she paused at the next bisection to look around.

The street plan in this part of the quarter was a net of intersecting rings, and for a moment Bram thought she was going to follow the circular thoroughfare all the way around to its next recrossing, but she turned left, heading for the older part of town where she had taken him to the drink shop that first time for the Ascendist meeting.

She didn't lead him there. He followed her almost to the waterfront, to a dilapidated conchate structure that might once have been used as a warehouse. The evening, was well lit, with the lesser sun, now alone in the sky, casting strong shadows. Bram loitered in the groined intersection of two buildings, where a defective lightpole kept it dark. Kerthin climbed a loading ramp, took a quick look backward, and disappeared through the lip of the main opening.

The building was inhabited; a pale yellow light showed through a blister that provided a skylight on the upper curve. Bram waited a few more minutes, then, feeling foolish, moved quickly toward the building and through the natural opening that had swallowed Kerthin up.

About thirty feet inside the chasm of an entrance, a wail

had once been constructed from the floor all the way up to the vaulted roof, wailing off the interior. There were a number of doors, each with its spiral staircase going up into the various recesses of the converted structure.

He poked his head through each doorway in turn and got an impression of darkness, hollowness, and dead silence from all except one. He climbed the stairs past three deserted landings in a gloom relieved only by the dirty half-light leaking through a semitransparent blister high overhead.

At the fourth landing he heard muffled voices coming through a closed door. Cautiously he mounted the last few steps and listened. Several people seemed to be talking at once. None of the voices was Kerthin's. They ran on, interrupting each other, until another voice, quiet and firm, cut them off. There was a pregnant pause, then the quiet voice continued in the calm, measured tones of authority.

Bram crept quietly to the threshold and strained to make out the words, but he couldn't catch enough of them to make sense.

"... need organization ... not satisfied with what I saw ... secrecy ... but at some point, if we're going to recruit successfully ... have to let them in on it ..."

Bram was so engrossed that he almost failed to hear the footsteps coming up the stairs. Then somebody stumbled and cursed, and from one or two landings below Bram heard someone say, "I don't like it, handing over the organization to him just like that. His methods are too extreme."

"You can't make an omelet without whipping eggs, gene brother."

"I know, but if they find out ..."

Bram barely had time to scuttle out of sight. A doorpeg was by his hand; he pulled on it and stepped inside, closing the door after him.

He was in a storage room lit faintly by a bowl of bio-lights that had been placed on a shelf and left to die. He held himself still and listened while the new arrivals—five or six of them by the sound of their footsteps—tapped at the door Bram had been eavesdropping at and were admitted after a gruff exchange.

Bram looked around the storage room. The objects it normally held seemed to have been pushed against the far wall, carelessly enough so that some of them had toppled and lay on the floor. From his early association with Kerthin, Bram recognized the materials of sculpture: pieces of lumber, lumps of clay the size of his head or bigger, wire armatures, wax blanks, elastic molds.

But the other items were a puzzlement. There were shelves of glass bottles with rags tied around them; a sniff told Bram they were filled with alcohol. There were jars of metallic powder. Wooden billets the size of a man's forearm, which someone had taken the trouble to whittle down at one end to make a grip. Tools—too many of the same kind for anyone to have a use for them: Fifteen or twenty axes, a half dozen sledgehammers, agricultural implements in the form of poles with curved blades attached at one end.

Bram was trying to puzzle it out when the door groaned and a pair of men in monos with the sleeves sawed off came into the room with another load of billhooks. They saw Bram and let the implements rattle to the floor. One of them had retained a hook. The other grabbed for one of the wooden billets piled at the entrance.

"How'd you get in here?" the one with the club demanded.

Bram could think of nothing to say. They grabbed him roughly and pushed him toward the door. "You're coming with us." The end of the club prodded him in the kidney.

He let himself be herded. Voices stopped and faces swung toward him as he was given a final push into the room. "We found a spy in the armory," the one with the billhook said.

"Oh fine, that's just great," a disgusted voice said. "Now he's seen Penser."

"Well, what were we supposed to—"

"Oh, shut up, Chonny. You have the brains of a sweeperbeast!"

Bram looked about with interest. He was in a huge, tall room: the one with the skylight he'd seen from outside. A draped bulk under the skylight, too big to be moved, was a piece of sculpture in the form of a reclining figure; Bram could make out the general form of a head and shoulders under the covering, and a gigantic unfinished bare foot stuck out at one end.

About two dozen men and women were scattered in a loose arc across the uneven floor, standing, leaning, or sitting on whatever they could find. One of them was Kerthin; Bram saw her right away, bunched with a small group that included Pite, Fraz, and Eena. Pite raised his eyebrows in ironic salute. Bram smiled at Kerthin, but she flushed and didn't try to speak to him.

The gathering, whatever its purpose, was focused on the tall pale man Bram had seen at the spaceport. He was sitting at a small table, flanked by two men in short robes and tight legwear that Bram took to be Juxt One fashions.

The pale man studied him with pursed lips. So this was Penser? Bram stared back openly. The splinter faction's notorious leader was not what he had expected. Penser had a pasty, unhealthy face and a body that showed signs of flab under the drab gray garments he affected. The flesh around his eyes looked bruised: heavy lids and bluish pouches. But the eyes themselves were totally compelling. They burned with a dark intensity, an utter certainty. It was impossible not to be impressed by the man.

Chonny, the one who had been reprimanded for stupidity, was whining a protest. "Well what about you, Treg? You were the one who said Penser's name out loud. If the fat wasn't out of the pan before, it is now."

Penser put a stop to it firmly. "That's enough." He returned his bruised gaze to Bram. "What is your name?" he asked.

"They call me Bram."

"How did you get here?"

Bram hesitated. Pite spoke out from across the room. "That's easy. He followed Kerthin." He looked Kerthin over coldly from top to bottom. "You were kind of careless, Kerth."

"Never mind that now," Penser said. "Can he be trusted?"

Pite sucked his cheeks in thoughtfully. "Brammo isn't one of us," he said. "On the other hand, he isn't a member of the Accommodationist wing or some Doctrinalist softhead, so maybe that's a plus. He knows how to keep his mouth shut, all right. I tested him. Maybe he's not committed, but he's got the right number of legs. And he's bonded to a member of the Cause. I don't think he's the type to go running to the council or to the yellowlegs."

Penser's dark-pouched eyes measured Bram. "Pite says you're not a squealer," he said. "Is that true?"

"Yes," Bram said.

One of Penser's flanking confederates from Juxt One, a comfortable, well-fed man with red cheeks and an upward-curving gray beard, leaned over and whispered something in Penser's ear.

Penser listened, pinch marks forming beside his nose,

then said, "I have decided." He fastened his eyes on Bram again. "I've just been advised to have you locked up until it can be decided what to do with you. But I'll take a chance on you for the time being. In view of what you have already seen, it cannot matter a great deal more if you stay." His voice grew hard. "But you *will* stay. I cannot risk having you leave while this meeting is in progress. You will stay, and then you will leave with your friends. Is that clear?"

"Yes."

Penser made a cage out of his fingers and with a curious gesture raised it to his lips. "You are part of us now—Bram, is it?—like it or not. You will not betray my presence here to the Nar?"

"No," Bram said.

He gave his promise without hesitation. Almost, he meant it. Something very peculiar was in the offing, and, Bram decided grimly, he had better go along with it until he found out more.

Penser nodded. "I'll accept that. Remember, you will be watched. And I can promise you that the consequences of treasonable behavior are not pleasant."

Bram made his way self-consciously to the part of the room where Kerthin sat with her friends. He could feel all the silent, appraising eyes on him. Somebody stepped into his path and clapped him on the shoulder.

"Congratulations, gene brother. I'm glad you decided to join us."

Bram looked into the other's face. It was Waller, the man from the library annex. Bram mumbled a thank you.

"Pite told me what you've been doing," Waller said. "But he isn't familiar enough with molecular biology for me to get a very clear picture. You and I will have to get together for a talk sometime soon."

Bram made vague noncommittal noises and walked on. Eena jumped up and squealed. "I *knew* you'd see the light some day! Didn't I tell you? Isn't he marvelous?"

Pite said sardonically, "Welcome to the human race, Brammo."

Bram sat down next to Kerthin. Kerthin looked at him with tight fury.

"Kerthin, I'm sorry," he said. "I had to know."

"Oh, never mind!" she said, and looked away from him again.

Some latecomers arrived, the door was closed and barred behind them, and the meeting began in earnest.

"... and that's about all there is to using firebottles. They're very effective, especially against vehicles, and alcohol and glass containers are available everywhere. Just be sure to remember to soak the wick before you light it and throw it. Any questions?"

The speaker was another of the men Penser had brought with him from Juxt One, a hard-bitten man in his early forties who had given up seven years of his life to accompany Penser here. How had he learned about things like firebottles, Bram wondered, and had he ever used one, and if so, why and how?

A roundish girl with a bowl haircut stood up. "Wouldn't it be dangerous to use one in a tree?"

"Who said anything about using one in a tree?" the man barked. "Where did you hear that?"

"I don't know. I just thought—"

"Too much thinking can get you into trouble. And loose talk can endanger us all. Do what you're told and don't spend so much time thinking."

"Please." The gray-bearded man next to Penser raised a palm. "Gene brother Grome didn't mean that as harshly as it sounded. But we must all learn to be careful. The fact is," he went on smoothly, "a tree does not catch fire as easily as you might think—this is just theoretical—and we believe a firebottle could be used within an individual chamber without endangering the entire tree. Even if a fire were to spread for hundreds of miles along a branch, eventually it would burn its way through into vacuum, and the tree would be able to regrow and reconfigure over a period of time. So we believe—and again, we're only talking theory— that firebottles might be a legitimate weapon against a particular *sector* of a tree. A sector inhabited by an enemy. But if worse came to worst, spin could be stopped, and fires would simply smother themselves." He beamed at them. "But we aren't talking about that, of course. We're talking about ground targets."

Through it all, Penser had sat silent and withdrawn, as if he were not a part of the weapons lecture. Now he raised his chalky face, and the room quieted to hear what he would say.

"We don't seek violence," he intoned as if from a distance, "but we must always hold ourselves in readiness in case violence is demanded of us. We all share the great dream, and that dream may not be denied. Those who attempt to deny us our dream will deserve rightful retribution."

Eena squirmed in her seat next to Bram. "That's right," she whispered in ecstasy. "Burn them. Burn them all."

Bram was appalled. Was this what it was about? Was this why Pite had made that clandestine survey of the starship? Did Penser intend to injure a tree?

There was a respectful silence after Penser's words, and then the gray-bearded man spoke again. "Next, we're going to hear from gene brother Sard on the subject of combat techniques."

Sard was a brisk, stocky individual with close-cropped hair, dressed in the short robe and tights of Juxt One. Like Grome, he was in his forties—a good decade or two older than most of Penser's new recruits from the Father World whom Bram saw about him at the meeting.

"Most of the disabling techniques we've developed were meant to be used against humans," Sard said. "But many of them can be adapted for use against the Nar. For example—" He held up a bottle of an oily yellow liquid. "—the Nar are just as vulnerable to corrosive materials as humans are, and if you splash some into their eyes, or still better, toss it down inside that nest of tentacles, you've got a Nar who's out of the action."

Bram felt ill. On either side of him, Pite and Fraz were drinking in every word.

"Of course, you can't break a Nar's bones because he hasn't any, and you can't kick him in the crotch because he has five of 'em—" He smiled lewdly and got a laugh. "—without anything between 'em. But if you can slash a limb across its hydraulic channels, it's as good as breaking a leg. Now, a Nar has more reach than a man, so remember—when you're fighting against a human traitor, it's clubs and fists, but for the Nar, what you want is a long pole to slash with."

He held up one of the billhooks Bram had seen in the storeroom and feinted realistically with it.

"What about explosives, brother?" someone shouted.

"Not my department. You'll be hearing from gene brother Hyd about that. But I can tell you that explosives are easily made, and you'll be shown how. We'll train explosives teams for the demolition work, but every one of you ought to have a working knowledge of how to make explosives out of common materials and how to use them."

"Aren't explosives dangerous to handle?" somebody else asked.

"Dangerous to enemies and deviationists, gene brother. If you've ever seen a being blown into small pieces, you'd appreciate what potent weapons they can be."

Beside Bram, Eena shivered pleasurably. "I'm going to get on one of those explosives teams," she whispered.

Bram looked over at Kerthin to see how she was taking it, but she was staring rigidly straight ahead. He couldn't make eye contact with her.

"Now, here's an item that's really effective," Sard went on. "We used them in fights against the opposition all the time. Easily concealed and a good way to break up a rally or teach someone a lesson."

He held up a flat gray case shaped to fit a human hand. There was a glint of metal at one end, a ring of short little rods.

"A touch of high voltage that'll knock your back teeth out or turn a Nar into a limp rag. I won't tell you how we got to test one on a Nar except to say that the test subject never told the rest of the decaboos that these things exist. Oh, yes, and they're very good for interrogation, too, when you apply them to the right places. We only brought a few of these with us, but they're not hard to make. Somebody here promised to look into getting hold of a supply of microcapacitors."

He looked questioningly at the gray-bearded man.

"Ah, yes," the gray-bearded Juxtian said. "Pite, what have you to report?"

Pite stood up and struck an indolent pose. "It'll take a couple more days. We've got an inside man at one of the transshipping points. The next shipment to go through will just disappear."

"Can it be done without arousing suspicion?" the Juxtian asked.

"No problem," Pite said, and sat down.

The meeting lasted until well into the sleeping period. There were going to be a lot of red-eyed humans going to work or other pursuits in the morning. Bram sat through the so-called training sessions with mounting horror and revulsion. They were acting as if it were some kind of game, an interesting abstraction: ordinary-looking people talking in reasonable voices about hitting folks over the head and blowing up vehicles and throwing corrosive chemicals at gentle beings who had never done them any harm.

At the end, Penser made a quiet speech, as if he were talking to each member of the audience individually. "Remember, a useful lie is better than a dangerous truth. There is a risk in coming together in large groups like this instead of compartmentalizing our organization so that no member knows too many others, but time is short, and we must come out into the open soon anyway if our great objective is to be accomplished. We will act before serious opposition develops and before our enemies decide to take us seriously."

Then there was the matter of selecting volunteers for further specialized training. "I'm going to talk to brother Hyd about making bombs," Eena said. "How about you, Kerthin?"

Bram was relieved to see Kerthin shake her head.

Pite left the parcel of muscle-bound bullies he had drawn around him and sauntered over to Bram. "How about it, Brammo? Want to get in with my bunch and learn how to break heads?"

"I don't think I'm the type," Bram said steadily.

Pite laughed. "I didn't think so. Go back to your trays and bottles. You'll be called on to do your part when the time comes."

"How can Penser be here," Bram said, "when there are all those reports of his activities in the Juxt system during the last seven years and when he's still beaming laser messages?"

They lay together in the nest, their unclothed bodies not touching. Kerthin held herself rigid, like a block of construction plastic.

"He arranged it before he left," she said indifferently. "It was all carefully thought out—recordings, holos, 'eyewitness' accounts of having meetings with him. He has supporters at every level, I suppose one of them applied for a trip to the Father World and let Penser change places with him. Then they would have arranged for that person to disappear or take on a new identity. Same for the handful of helpers Penser brought with him. It would have aroused speculation if too many of Penser's known supporters traveled here together."

"How long have you known, Kerthin?"

"Not very long. Since just before Marg and Orris invited us to the treewarming. Pite and a few others have known for over a year. They've been waiting for this day to come for ten years, but they didn't know exactly when it would be. Penser left instructions for a coded signal to be sent after he was already in transit. He didn't want the word to get out too soon, but he wanted to give his followers here time to get organized."

"Pite must have known when I met him that first time, the night of the Ascendist meeting."

"I suppose so," she said indifferently.

"Probably the code was in the message from Penser that was read that night. A prearranged phrase, maybe. That's why Pite was so eager to go to the meeting. I don't get the impression that he thinks very highly of the run-of-the-mill Ascendists."

Kerthin made no reply to that. If anything, her body went even stiffer.

Bram drew a deep breath. "What in the name of creation is Penser planning to do here?"

"You heard him. He wants to build up an organization. An organization that's stronger than the rest of the silly factions here. Hold ourselves in readiness, he said."

"He has some specific act in mind. Something violent."

"He doesn't seek violence," she said peevishly. "You heard him say that. Unless he's forced to it."

Bram turned on his side to face her. "How many followers does Penser have in this system? Fifty? A hundred? What could they possibly do against the wishes of the entire human community? And even if he succeeds in bringing another few hundred people over to his side, what then? What, with all this talk of explosives and slashing poles and electric shocks, could he possibly accomplish against a population of ten billion Nar?"

"Numbers aren't important, Penser says. What counts is determination. There's no way a soft, unorganized majority can resist a resolute minority."

"You don't *believe* that nonsense?"

"It isn't nonsense!" she flared. "Anyway, he doesn't have to fight ten billion Nar. He just—"

Bram's skin prickled. "Just what?"

"Never mind."

"Do you know? Or don't they trust you, either?"

"If they don't," she said, "it's because of you. Following me. Spying like that."

"And now you've got to prove yourself to them?" he said bitterly. "Penser said I was going to be watched. Who's going to watch me? You?"

She turned her face away from him. "Go to sleep," she said.

A couple of Tendays passed. It was like living in a nightmare. Bram existed in a controlled daze, going through the ordinary routines of his life by rote. He went to his job at the biocenter every dawn and marked time until the quitting hour, doing enough work to get by. He wasn't remiss enough to cause comment, but he was sure his inattentiveness was noticed. He attended the round of last-minute farewell parties that were being thrown for the departing Juxt One colonists and was distracted enough for human friends who knew him well to sense that something was bothering him.

"You don't look well, Bram," Marg said, peering at his face. "Pale. I don't know, thin. Aren't you feeling well?"

"I'm all right," he said.

"He's working too hard," Orris said. "You ought to ease up a little, Bram. Have a holiday. Why don't you lift up to the tree with us next Tenday? We're having a last blast before departure. The party to end all parties. I'll bet we'll have two or three hundred visitors." He looked around. "Where's Kerthin?"

"She had a sculpture class. I'm sure you'll see her before you leave."

"Think about what I said. Bring Kerthin with you. The

boats are all reserved—plenty of room for last-minute visitors. You can stay overnight. A couple of overnights! Most of the others will. We could sleep half the population of the quarter in the branch that's assigned to us!" He winked. "Maybe you'll like the accommodations so much that you'll stay aboard—sail to Juxt One with us."

Bram managed a laugh. "That sounds tempting." He half meant it. At least Juxt One was a world without Penser.

For the moment he had lost interest in working on the protein coat of the carrier virus. It didn't seem important, somehow. Immortality had waited thirty-seven million years. It could wait a while longer.

The equipment he had borrowed from the biocenter was pushed into a comer or stored in cupboards, out of the way, when his living quarters were invaded by the meetings that were being held there at night. Protesting to Kerthin did no good. "We've all got to do our part," she said. "They needed a place where a study group could meet without attracting attention, and I volunteered. You ought to be grateful you're not living with Eena. They're manufacturing explosive pots at *her* place!"

Bram shuddered. That was true enough. At least he was under no risk of being blown to pieces in his own living chambers. Lethal objects were not in evidence at the study group meetings—unless it was possible to be bored to death by words. All of the rebels seemed to be humorless, excessively earnest people. They held endless discussions on subjects that came equipped with mind-numbing headings: "occupation and reeducation techniques for governing unenlightened populations"; "utilization of the political infrastructure of isolated communities"; "tactical ideology"; "rehabilitating the social defaulter"; "correct principles of

Schismatist thought"; "the practical uses of force in political negotiations."

Kerthin served refreshments while Bram half dozed through the rhetoric. Once Pite and a couple of his bravos showed up. They sat and listened, and at the end of the evening, when people started to leave separately in ones or twos as they had been instructed, they spoke quietly to one of the group members and accompanied him to the door. The man turned pale and went with them, smiling nervously. He did not show up at the next meeting.

At the biocenter, Bram avoided Voth as much as possible. Again, he was deceiving his old teacher, and it was too painful to be in his company.

It was temporary, Bram told himself. He was only waiting for something definite to go on before confiding in Voth. So far, this was only a bunch of people talking—and amusing themselves with deadly toys and deadly fantasies. But he couldn't denounce people for talk and daydreams.

But partly, Bram admitted to himself in the dark and restless hours when he could not fall asleep, he was being dilatory because these were fellow human beings. Maybe Pite was right to some degree. One owed one's phylum a certain loyalty. Bram was reluctant to expose the worst side of human beings to his old teacher.

So he waited.

And then it was too late.

"He's a danger to us all," said the worried-looking Ascendist on the platform. "These incidents can no longer be hushed up or explained away. Last night a young man was severely beaten up in a street fight. Broken fibs, contusions, head injuries. A Nar medical warden happened to be at the Quarter clinic when he was brought in. The victim himself covered it up—claimed he'd been in an accident. But the injuries weren't consistent with his story. The warden didn't pursue the matter, but you can be sure that he's wondering about it."

Bram recognized the speaker as Gorch, the man who had been accused of being a secret Schismatist at that first meeting behind the drink shop. But Gorch didn't sound like a cupboard Schismatist anymore, now that brute reality had overtaken his foggy notions. He sounded like a badly rattled man.

"And that warehouse explosion two days ago," Gorch went on. "Luckily no one was hurt. But you won't find a person in the Quarter who believes it was caused by a gas leak, and the Nar aren't stupid, either. It's time for every faction among us to band together and put a stop to this nonsense. Penser's group is only a small minority. We can't allow it to compromise the party any longer."

Scattered boos and catcalls greeted his words. Jupe, the bald-headed moderator, stepped in smoothly. "I'm sure we all appreciate your concern, gene brother. Now, if there is anyone else who wishes to speak—"

"I'm not finished yet!" Gorch protested. "What we all want to know is, what is Penser up to?"

More boos and catcalls were heard, this time coming with greater purpose from the people Pite had planted in strategic places throughout the audience.

Bram sat at the rear of the hall, with a goon on either side of him. The meeting place behind the drink shop was swollen with people this time. When he first had been here, there might have been fifty men and women in the rows of seats. Now there were ten times as many, not counting the tough-looking men in short-sleeved monos who stood with folded arms at the back of the hall.

Bram had been summoned to the meeting on short notice. He had just finished a frugal supper of soyrice and greens and was putting away his bowl, when somebody began rattling his door impatiently. He had opened it to find one of Pite's bravos standing there: Spak, the fellow with the dented head.

"Pite wants you at the Ascendist hall right away."

"Ascendist hall? I thought all Ascendists are supposed to be deviationists and traitors these days."

"There's a meeting," Spak said without humor. "We're going to take it over. Pite wants the seats filled with our people. We need a strong show of support."

"All right. I'll be along as soon as—"

"Now," Spak said.

He waited, silent and huge, while Bram got his overgarment, then fell in behind him. Outside, a small alcohol-propelled vehicle was waiting. Bram got in the back. Three other people were inside: a man from Kerthin's discussion group and two others he didn't recognize. When they got to the meeting hall, the burly Ascendist door guard opened his mouth as if to say something, but Spak gave him a menacing look and swept past him with his little flock.

Now the place was crammed. Word had gotten out that this was to be an important meeting, and even the idly curious had crowded in. Penser's supporters were scattered through the seats in little self-reinforcing groups. Bram remembered what Kerthin had said about determined minorities.

"We have a resolution before us," Jupe said, pounding for order with his cube of wood, "and we've had a discussion. Before I call for a vote, we're going to hear from the party secretary."

The resolution called for a reprimand of Penser and the

disbanding of his special goon squads, on pain of a request to the Nar for the deportation of Penser and his Juxtian associates. There was a bribe in it too, though, of minor party sinecures for those involved if they pledged to behave. The motion and seconding had almost been drowned out but had gone through.

The party secretary came forward. He was a grave, dignified man with flat cheeks and a pointed black beard. His face was mottled with emotion, but he held himself in check as he spoke.

"We *all* of us here believe in the principles of human ascendancy. We must not forget that basic fact during the vote to come. The human race is small, but its destiny is large. We may reasonably disagree among ourselves on the means of achieving that destiny. But we must disagree without rancor. We must never forget that we are all gene brothers and gene sisters, descended from a single genome—though our genotypes vary—and that the purpose of all of us collectively is the purpose of each one of us individually."

"Bodyrot!" somebody yelled from the audience.

The party secretary blinked mildly and went on. "We are always willing to welcome our strayed brothers and sisters back into the fold, but we must make it unmistakably clear that—"

"Sewage gas!" the same voice shouted.

Bram looked to see where it was coming from and saw that the heckler was one of Pite's plants—part of a little group of mono-clad bullies that included Fraz. Fraz was grinning hugely, enjoying himself.

The party secretary tried to go on, but the orchestrated interruptions came thicker and thicker.

"Gene brother Penser's supporters would do well to remember that he is here illegally and that the Nar as yet do not know about his presence," the secretary said tightly. "But—"

A chorus of boos and jeers threatened to drown him out.

"—*but*," he continued doggedly, "that can be fixed with the Nar through the good offices of the leadership of this party. Therefore—"

"No more Accommodationist poison!" the heckler yelled. "We want to hear from Penser!"

"Therefore," the party secretary said, struggling to control himself, "in the interests of human unity, the party leadership asks each one of you to vote for this resolution. We hope that it will have the effect of chastening—"

"No more talk!" Pite rose to his feet from his seat in the front row. Spak and another bullyboy rose with him, pulling concealed clubs out of their monos.

"You're all through speaking," Pite ordered. "Clear the platform, all of you."

The party secretary sputtered, but by that time Pite and his two thugs had leaped up onto the platform and seized him by the arms. More of Pite's mono-clad roughnecks converged on the platform from either side and began pushing and shoving the moderator and other functionaries. One of the younger party officers tried to resist and got himself whacked across the abdomen with a club. He sat down slowly on the floor, his face gone white, holding himself tenderly.

That was a signal for a surge from the anti-Penser elements at the meeting. But Pite had planned his strategy well. The small, disciplined groups of agitators that were dispersed throughout the rows of seats were in position to stop each surge as it started, sometimes by clubbing an opponent from behind. A dozen small scuffles broke out, and the rest of the audience began to stir belatedly into life like a rippling bed of ocean weed.

Suddenly there was the crack of an explosion and a bright flash at the front of the hall. Out of the corner of his eye, Bram barely caught the blur of movement that preceded it—an arm tossing a small round object onto the platform.

All the small straggles in the hall ceased. In the shocked silence that followed, Pite stepped forward with a grin.

"All right, it's all over," he said. "We're going to hear Penser speak, so everybody just sit down and keep quiet."

The bomb had only been a noisemaker, but it had done its job. There was a rising murmur that quickly died down as people settled in to make the best of it. The man who had been hit in the stomach was helped off the platform and given a place to sit. The other party leaders were escorted to one side and kept in a group, surrounded by a small bodyguard of strong-arm men. They took their seats with injured dignity, but they did what they were told.

Penser came down the aisle from the rear with his honor guard of Juxtians in their short robes and tights. Bram had not even seen him enter the hall. Penser looked neither right nor left. There was not a flicker of expression on his pasty face; it was as if nothing in his surroundings was worth his notice. Penser himself was not wearing Juxtian costume. He wore a plain, decent gray garment that was gathered at the wrists and ankles and covered any looseness of neck so that all that could be seen of Penser himself was pale hands, pale face.

When he took his place at the improvised podium, his claque stood up en masse and clapped and cheered. He stared out over the audience, appearing not to hear.

Bram got a poke in the ribs from the goon next to him. "On your feet." Bram stood up obediently and cheered with the rest.

It was not only Penser's faction that was applauding. Others in the audience joined in—some with patent enthusiasm, some because they were being prodded by monoclad agitators—until a good half of the meeting was on record as showing support for the gray-draped figure on the platform. The other half, intimidated, kept silent and neutral.

Penser waited until the prearranged demonstration ended, then began to speak, simply, and quietly.

"The time has come to stand up and be counted. The time has come to prove your allegiance to the great idea which is the human race. The time has come to make a choice. And that choice will be judged harshly. There will be no forgiveness for those who make the wrong choice. For the universe does not forgive. I tell you the time is at hand. The time has come . . ."

The simple sentences and the repetition had a hypnotic effect. There was an impression of untapped power behind them. And, Bram had to admit, Penser had a magnificent speaking voice and knew how to use it. As Penser gathered force, the crowd was visibly swayed. Even Bram, much as he now detested the man, found himself responding on some primitive level.

". . . Man was made by Man. Man made Himself. The Nar were merely his instrument. The Nar were his tool. And how were the Nar made? By the accidents of organic chemistry in a primordial soup. They are accidents of creation. But Man was created with a purpose. *For a* purpose. To master the universe. To own all of creation . . ."

It was obvious that if Penser went on, he was going to carry the meeting. Some of the members who had previously spoken out against Penser grew visibly agitated, muttering among themselves and wriggling in their chairs like schoolchildren. The toughs in sleeveless monos who were monitoring the crowd's behavior moved in a little closer, watchful and alert.

Gorch, the man who was worried about violence in the Quarter, was speaking in low tones to the person next to him, a large raw-knuckled man who looked as if he did a lot of outdoor labor. Bram remembered his name: Lal. At the previous Ascendist meeting, Lal had spoken in favor of a peaceful infiltration of Nar society. He had advocated token human representation in Nar institutions proportional to human numbers. At the time, Gorch had accused him of being a Partnerite. Now it looked as if Gorch and Lal were on the same side.

"Unfortunately, the human species is not united in its aspirations," Penser was saying, the model of reasonableness. "There are destructive elements among us..."

It was too much for Gorch. Gathering courage from the mutterings of the cronies around him, he lurched to his feet and shouted, "The destructive elements are those who're risking forfeiting the good opinion of the Nar with this violence in the Quarter! Why are we letting this Juxtian interloper intimidate us? Let's get back to the business of this meeting and vote on the resolution!"

The goons moved in joyfully. Shoving people aside, they grabbed Gorch. Bram saw one of them produce the electrical shocking instrument that had been displayed to Penser's troops.

He didn't see it actually make contact. But it must have

touched Gorch somewhere—Bram heard a mindless reflexive cry of pain, and Gorch went down, flopping.

The man who had applied the dose of current turned Gorch's body over with his foot. Gorch's mouth hung open; his eyes stared unseeing at the ceiling. You could tell he was still alive because his arms and legs kept twitching minutely and a feeble gargling sound was coming from the back of his throat.

Lal had his big workman's hands around the throat of the Penserite who had shoved him aside. A couple of the others were struggling with Pite's henchmen, too, and getting the worst of it. Another young man, inspired to do battle by their example, leaped up. More of the Penserite strong-arm men moved in.

On the platform, Penser waited, detached and distant, for the disturbance to end. The blue-ringed eyes showed no interest. To Bram, Penser's aloofness was more chilling than any show of impatience would have been.

Somebody clubbed the young man who had tried to join in. The sound of the club against the side of his head could be heard at the back of the hall. He sank to his knees, blood streaming down his face.

Their other opponents disposed of, the bullyboys converged on Lal. They didn't bother to try to pry his fingers from around their friend's neck. A club struck Lal between the eyes, right across the bridge of the nose, and he let go, staggering. Another club thudded across his ribs, and somebody else took a lick at his skull.

A woman screamed, and people scrambled to get out of the way, knocking over chairs. Lal had somehow stayed on his feet until now, but with the last blow he sagged and went down. Bram could not see him. Burly men in monos surrounded him completely, bent over him like a circular, many-legged beast. All you could see was the clubs, rising and falling, and the feet, drawing back to kick.

Pite and his two lieutenants had bounded to the spot and were trying to pry their cohorts away. The attackers seemed to have lost all control. "That's enough," Pite was saying. "Take it easy."

The frenzy subsided, and at last there was a ring of monos standing quietly around Lal's blood-spattered form. Lal wasn't moving at all. Nor would he ever move judging by the huge mushy depression in his skull.

The hall was filled with an underwater silence, with little currents of whispers running through it, dying out, and starting up again. Gorch's stertorous breathing could be plainly heard. Every once in a while it would stop and, after a frightening interval, go on. Some people came over to help him. They partially raised his limp form and dragged him off to the side, trailing a set of flexible legs. Nobody moved to stop them.

On the platform, Penser had enough sense not to resume speaking. He stood with his arms at his sides, still as a statue. He showed no reaction to events in the hall. He seemed merely to have switched himself off.

There was a sense of expectation in the hall, a vacuum to be filled. Afterward, Bram felt that Penser had, with his uncanny instincts, correctly gauged the situation—that his unnatural immobility had created a negative force that provided the impetus for what happened next.

The party secretary stepped forward. The Penserite strong-arms assigned to watch him made no effort to interfere. Penser watched aloofly as he approached the platform.

"Listen," the party secretary said in a ragged voice.

"Everybody listen. We've all witnessed a terrible thing. A man is dead."

A woman started to cry. A male voice choked: "Damn you, Penser!"

No attempt at retribution was made by the Penserite goon squads. The imprecation stirred an angry murmur of agreement through the hall.

The party secretary raised both palms in an attempt to restore calm.

"It's no good talking about who's to blame," he said, pleading with them. "And the one thing we don't want is more bloodshed. We can't afford to let this enmity continue. As far as the Nar are concerned, the human race is one." His voice shook. "We all have blood on our hands. If they ever find out about this, they'll step in and take charge of us—for our own good. None of us want that. Do you all want to be children again, with a Nar guardian to supervise you?"

That got to them. A babble grew, then subsided as the secretary held up a hand again.

"Or maybe they'll decide that humans can't be trusted to have a society at all. Maybe they'll curtail breeding, get us down to manageable numbers, separate us, turn us into individual pets, like muffbeasts. Does anybody want that?"

Another brief uproar arose. Bram sucked in his breath. Around him he heard cries of "No, no!"

"Then there's only one thing to do," the party secretary said. He looked directly at Penser. Penser met his gaze imperturbably.

The party secretary bit his lip. "We'll bury Lal," he said in a hollow voice. "We'll undertake to explain it away somehow. We'll see to the medical treatment of the others. No one in this hall will ever mention what went on here tonight to anyone outside—not to a close friend, not even to a mate if he or she is outside the party."

There was a pause while that sank in. A subdued ripple of voices swept through the audience, and Bram knew that the party secretary had them with him.

"In return," the party secretary said, trying to hold his voice steady, "these violent activities must cease. The Quarter is no longer to be a battlefield for internecine conflict. And one more thing. We are aware of these anti-Nar training exercises. They have almost reached the point of open scandal. They must cease, too. No whisper of such activities must ever reach the Nar. Is that understood?"

Penser gave the barest nod. The two locked eyes for a moment.

The party secretary was the first to drop his gaze. "All right, then," he muttered.

Somebody had already covered Lal's body with a blanket. Now, as if recovering from paralysis, people became busy. A couple of men started to improvise a litter, while others stood by, waiting to take the body away as soon as it was finished. A medhelper who had been in the audience was administering aid to a weakly flopping Gorch, and a number of Good Samaritans were helping the other injured to hobble over to await their turn.

The toughs who had wrought the havoc had drawn back into a loose group, looking defiant or abashed or sulky, whispering among themselves. No one would look at them. Bram saw Fraz among them, the front of his mono splattered with blood. Presumably Fraz had been a part of the thicket of legs that had surrounded the fallen Lal.

Bram caught Kerthin's eye across the room. She was sitting with Eena. Bram thought that Eena looked pale and drawn and even thinner than usual. Her right arm was missing. It had been blown off in a small mishap at the bomb factory that had been set up in her living quarters. A little bud had already formed, but it was going to be some time before the arm grew back.

Kerthin got up and made her way toward him. She didn't speak. They left together, both of them thoroughly subdued. Nobody was guarding the doors anymore. The meeting was definitely over.

CHAPTER 11

Y ou're sure you won't come?" Bram said.

"No, you go alone. I've already seen the tree. And they're your friends, not mine."

Kerthin was slapping wet clay on the armature, building up a figure that was beginning to resemble a rather pyramidal human with enormous feet, a tiny head, and huge, clump-fingered hands hanging down somewhere about knee level.

He looked at her doubtfully. "I'll be back tomorrow. Is everything all right?"

"Everything's fine," she said bitterly. "Isn't it?"

Bram sighed. He put down his little overnight pod and went over to her. "It's all for the best," he said. "The Quarter's been quiet. Everything's getting back to normal."

"Normal?" she said. "Back to the hypocritical status quo, you mean. All those hidebound party hacks are all puffed out with self-importance over having put Penser in his place—or so they see it. And the fair-weather converts falling all over themselves to desert the cause when they saw the wind blowing in a different direction. Everyone back to foot-licking the Nar again. The great dream of winning the cosmos destroyed!"

Bram understood Kerthin's feelings. He had gone back with her for one more of Penser's meetings at the former sculptor's studio and found a much-reduced membership of dispirited people. Two-thirds of the new recruits had melted away, leaving only a hard core of dedicated fanatics like Pite. Penser's pep talk about human supremacy had been perfunctory. His mind seemed to be elsewhere. There had been no talk of weapons or violence. Bram had managed a peek into the storeroom off the corridor and found that it had been cleared out.

"Dreams can't be destroyed," Bram said. "Penser'll have to pick up the pieces and start over again, that's all. But without all the destructive elements. He has the same chance as anybody else for political influence. All he's got to do is behave himself. The Ascendists are willing to forgive and forget—in spite of a man's death. They've already said they're willing to intercede with the Nar and take steps to legitimize Penser's presence here. Maybe he turned himself into a fugitive on Juxt One, but now he has the chance for a fresh start."

"Pygmies," Kerthin said. "They're pygmies tearing down a giant. Now, if you'll excuse me, I've got to finish roughing this out." She savagely slapped more clay on the form, patted it into place, and began to pare it down with a knife.

Bram watched her for a few minutes, then shook his head and left.

Through Bram's port, Lowstation loomed ahead, a six-sided piece of carpentry that some giant had left hanging against the stars. It was doing a lot of business today. A dozen or more ferries hovered like tiny barbs around the common apex of the six wooden triangles, waiting their turn at the hub docking facilities.

"I'm afraid they're going to leave us parked for a while," he said, looking across to the adjoining acceleration nests where Marg and Orris were lying. "There's quite a jam ahead of us."

"They may take us out of turn," Marg told him. "They do that sometimes. Passengers first, freight second."

Orris was unfastening his webbing and struggling to sit up, though it wasn't strictly within the rules. As an old hand of five or six round trips during the past months of acclimatization, he didn't take the gentle accelerations of docking maneuvers very seriously.

"Last minute rush," he said. "It's mostly freight an this voyage. All the things you need to open up a new world—even though Juxt One's been settled for generations. Seeds, tools, frozen soil organisms, heavy machinery. It never stops. There're still whole undeveloped continents, new moons to get started on, and the industrial base there just can't handle it yet."

"How many Nar are making the trip?" Bram asked.

He gave half his attention back to the window. The great timbered hexagon filled half the black sky. Bram could see the wriggling silver specks swarming around the parked shuttles: space-suited Nar manhandling the cargo flats out of the bays and lashing on the booster units that would send them along to the tree.

"A couple of thousand," Orris said. "Close to the minimum for their kind of social dynamics on a seven-year trip. Most of them are still planetside for final touch ceremonies. They'll be ferried up en masse just before the tree spreads its leaves for departure."

Marg gave a tinkling laugh. "At this point, we humans

have the tree practically to ourselves. There's only a skeleton crew of Nar aboard."

"That's right," Orris said. "With two hundred colonists and all the well-wishers, we outnumber the Nar temporarily."

"Do they have their own branch?" Bram asked.

"No, they're several miles upstairs from us—same branch, closer to the trunk. Ecology control and life support are more efficient that way—just one set of lines to the sapwood. They'll be living at about nine-tenths of a gravity. They've got a cross section of three or four miles with I don't know how many levels. Of course, they need a lot more living space than we do."

"Well, you'll have plenty of time to get acquainted," Bram said.

"Good distance makes good neighbors," Marg said, quoting a Quarter poet who was known for his crusty Resurgist views.

Bram was shocked. In his involvement with the Ascendists and with Penser's Schismatist extremists, he'd forgotten that there were others in the human community who had their own reasons for wanting to have little to do with the Nar.

"Well, humans have their own social institutions," Bram said diplomatically, "but as kids we all had Nar playmates."

"Oh, I have nothing against the Nar," Marg said hastily, belatedly remembering Bram's friendship with Tha-tha and his close relationship with Voth. "It's just that we have our own lives, don't we?"

"What Marg means," Orris said, laughing, "is that she doesn't really trust anyone she can't cook for."

Outside the port, the enormous mitered joints of the space station's hub grew until they filled the view. They were among the parked shuttles now. Bram saw a cluster of space-suited Nar dockworkers, like a bouquet of double-ended flowers, swimming outward on their thrusters with the wide circular mouth of a docking tube. But it wasn't meant for Bram's ship. As Bram watched, they hitched the free-turning collar of the tube to the nose of a shuttle that had just arrived.

Orris was beside him at the port. "They're going to make us wait," he said. "You might as well get out of your webbing and move around."

"The human traffic was heavier than anticipated," the Nar attendant said apologetically. "And now I'm afraid there'll be another wait while additional transfer vehicles are brought over."

Orris sighed. "We might as well go to the passenger lounge. There's a fairly good human canteen there. Though from the look of this mob, it's going to be overcrowded."

Bram looked at the crowd that was swarming around the attendant to ask questions. But they were not the ones who were worrying him. He was disturbed by some of the shuttle passengers who came through the disembarkation tube one at a time and avoided the reception area, swimming along the walls toward the drop chutes, carrying oddly shaped luggage—long narrow parcels or bulbous padded shapes that even in free fall could be seen to mass a lot for their size. Bram didn't know any of them by name, but he recognized two or three faces from Penser's earlier gatherings.

He considered saying something to the Nar attendant, but that being was busy with other passengers, and besides, there was really nothing definite Bram could say. At any rate, the stopover at Lowstation would last at least a couple of hours, and there would be time to find out more.

"This way," Orris said.

They joined the rivulet of mostly Nar passengers heading rimward. There might be a temporary jam of human stopovers bound for the Juxt One tree, but Lowstation still carried its usual quota of intrasystem traffic and traffic to Ilf and the moons of the lesser sun's system.

At the heads of the drop chutes, friction mittens had thoughtfully been provided for human transients. The Nar had ten braking surfaces to alternate with, but human beings had to make do with hands and feet unless, of course, one panicked and wrapped oneself completely around the pole.

Orris made a protective fuss over Marg, though the implanted blastocyst that she was host-mothering could scarcely have been causing her any inconvenience yet. But she would have none of it. She jumped into the tube without hesitation, caught the central pole with her mittened hands, and drifted blithely downward, her opulent body buoyed horizontally against the air resistance. Orris gave Bram a proud smile and jumped in after her.

At the quarter-g level they transferred to a bucket and rode the rest of the way sedately to the rim. The passenger lounges were near the spokes, fortunately. The gradient in the artificial gravity caused by the difference between a spinning hexagon and a spinning wheel could be a bit disorienting for a human being; besides, there was that uphill walk back to the spoke just when one was in a hurry and trying to get out.

The lounge was a dramatic slice of the thousand-foot triangle, rising all the way to the hub, with a cliff of solid wood for one wall and two window walls looking out on space. Seating was arranged in tasteful conversational groups—multipedestals for Nar, banquettes for humans.

"We're not going to get into the canteen," Orris said. "Look at that howling mob around the entrance." He scanned the lounge. "There're some empty seats over there next to the vertex. Why don't you two grab them? I'll see if I can fight my way through to the service font and bring back some refreshments for us."

He scurried off. Bram smiled at Marg and steered her over to the vacant banquette. Halfway there she stopped and put a hand on his arm.

"Look," she said. "Isn't that Kerthin?"

Bram's smile froze in place. He looked across the crowded lounge and saw her, standing next to the group with the oddly shaped luggage.

"Yes," he said, hiding his dismay. "She must have made it, after all. You go on ahead and claim those seats. I'll go get her."

Marg gave Kerthin a broad, unreturned wave and proceeded onward. Bram, feeling hollow, walked with a heavy step over to where Kerthin was standing.

"What are you doing here?" he said.

She gave him a sullenly defiant stare. "I left about an hour after you did. I didn't think there'd be this jam at Lowstation. I thought I'd see you at the tree and everything could be explained then."

"Explained? Explain what?"

"Relax, Brammo," a detested voice cut in. "You're right on schedule. When Kerthin told us you'd be coming up to the tree under your own power, it saved us the trouble of coming to get you. We're going to need a biological technician."

Bram whirled to face him. He wouldn't have recognized Pite at a casual glance. The short blond beard had been shaved off. Pite looked a lot older, with a tight little V-shaped mouth and a pair of deep lines coming down from the corners of his nose.

"I'm having nothing to do with any of your schemes. Penser promised to drop them, whatever they were. Where is he? Is he here?"

"You don't have any choice, gene brother," Pite said softly. "You've been conscripted. So have your friends over there, though they don't know it yet."

"I don't know what you're talking about," Bram said. "But a man's dead back in the Quarter, and there's not going to be any more violence. I think the Lowstation authorities need to know you're here."

One of the Penserites, a large man carrying a long cylindrical parcel with a bulge at one end, moved closer and put a hand on Bram's arm. It was Spak. He looked different, too. Instead of a mono with sawed-off sleeves, he wore ill-fitting holiday garb.

"That's not a good idea, Brammo," Pite said, smiling with his new, narrow little mouth. "You wouldn't want to make any of the gene brothers nervous. Think what a firebottle would do in a crowded place like this."

"You're crazy," Bram said. "You people are crazy."

"Now, there's a useful thought, gene brother. Keep hanging on to it in case you're tempted to do something foolish. We'll see you at the tree."

Bram shook off Spak's hand and took a backward step. "Are you coming, Kerthin?" he said stiffly.

"That's right, Brammo," Pite said. "You just go back to your friends there and keep your mouth shut, and no one will get hurt. Remember, you're being watched all the way. Why, if you got any wrong ideas, there's no telling who might get in the way while you were being dealt with. That pretty little lady over there, for instance."

As Bram walked back across the teeming floor with Kerthin at his side, he felt his heart pounding. He would have to wait his chance, that was all. Perhaps he could manage to slip out of Pite's surveillance long enough to slip a warning to a Nar officer later on—while boarding the transfer vehicle or docking at the tree. Till then he would have to be cautious.

"How could you do it, Kerthin?" he said, shaking his head. "You've been lying to me all along, haven't you? I thought you'd come to your senses. You saw what happened back there in the Quarter. These people are outside any concept of interspecies or even human comity."

She gave her bronze hair a toss. "You can't make an omelet—" she began.

"I know," he sighed. "Without stirring an egg. There's Marg. Try to put a smile on your face, if you can."

There were no opportunities to break away and inform Nar personnel about the dubious nature of some of their human transients. One or more of Pite's spurious merrymakers seemed to be at Bram's elbow at all times. They mingled with the other tourists and tree dwellers, bearing their odd packages, bunching up in groups of not more than two or three. Bram thought there had been nine or ten in his own shuttle load and probably about the same number in the shuttle that had ferried Pite and Kerthin. How many other shuttles had contained a contingent of Penserites, he could not guess.

Once, as his group of passengers filed through the embarkation area for the orbital transfer vehicle, Bram had caught sight of a Nar communications officer with a portable sleeve slung from his waist in one-tentacle conversation with a pod-festooned port official, and he had tried to edge out of the flow toward them. But Spak was hovering close behind him, and another burly Penserite moved up, hemming him in.

"Pite doesn't trust you," Kerthin said with something like entreaty in her voice, "but he says it won't matter after we get to the tree. They're not going to let you out of their sight till then. Please don't do anything foolish. I'm—I'm afraid of him."

"Why won't it matter?" Bram said. "What's going to happen in the tree?"

"It'll be all right, you'll see. Nobody has to get hurt."

"You're having second thoughts, aren't you? What did Pite mean about all of us being conscripted?"

She opened her mouth to reply, but at that point Orris bumbled over to them and said, "Don't let's get separated. We can get seats together on the transfer boat."

Orris bobbed impatiently around them in the almost nonexistent gravity of the departure bay and, lifting them delicately off the floor with a hand under their elbows, towed them over to where Marg was doing an efficient low-gravity shuffle toward the tube mouth. Three big Penserites closed in around them and moved right along with them. One of them bumped into Marg, but she didn't seem to notice.

During the long process of matching orbits with the

tree, Bram had no chance to talk to Kerthin alone. Orris babbled on unchallenged about the marvelous qualities of the blastocycst that Marg was carrying and its glorious future on Juxt One, while Marg glowed at them, looking smug. The three Penserites hemmed them in, sitting stiffly and trying to look like tourists. Bram tried to pick out other Penserites among the passengers. He counted up to eleven—about half the number he'd seen at Lowstation. Pite was not among them; they must have split up into different contingents again. Bram wondered how many Penserites were already aboard the tree.

He thought he might have another chance to alert the Nar authorities when the ground crew wrestled the transfer boat into the hangar in the tree. There would be a certain amount of confusion as the vacuole repressurized and the passengers disembarked. He watched tensely as the silver-suited Nar winched the boat inside and the great living doors flapped shut and sealed the chamber off from space. The tree breathed air into the chamber, and the passengers were on their feet and milling around impatiently before the hurricane ceased. Bram spilled out of the vehicle with the rest and with incredible luck managed to find himself separated briefly from Orris, Marg, Ker, thin, and his watchdogs.

The Nar personnel who had jockeyed the boat inside were still swarming around, casting off hawsers, checking the boat, assisting passengers. But they were all still in their space suits. None of them would have been able to hear a word he might say.

A Nar dockworker saw Bram looking around distractedly, glided smoothly over to take him by the arm, faced him in the right direction, and started him on his way to the inner lock door. Bram looked helplessly at the row of mirror eyes behind the suit's waistplate and tried to pantomime the idea that the Nar should lift the visor. But the dockworker didn't understand human body language. He guided Bram firmly toward the open lock, and then the Penserites had caught up with him, and Orris was loping toward him, yelling, "Hey, wait for us."

And then the door closed behind him, and his last chance was gone.

The great hall had been fitted out as a farm chamber since the last time Bram had been there. Tall aisles of sunflowers quested toward the lightpipes overhead. A potato field was a grid of burgeoning dark green foliage. Tanks of lettuce marched in multilevel rows along the borders. Winged beans climbed the stalks of the soycorn.

"We'll have our first crop in a few more Tendays," Orris said. "I'm on the pollinating committee."

"Of course, we're self-sustaining already," Marg said. "We grow enough microbial protein and industrial fungi to feed an army."

"I'll take you through later and show you the brewvats," Orris said. "Jao's in charge. He'll want to give you the grand tour."

"But first we'll show you our quarters," Marg said. "I'll whip up a little something for us."

They strolled down an avenue of squash tubs that were already spilling a profusion of growth over the edges. People sat around on the rims of the tubs talking and sipping drinks. The enormous chamber still seemed to be the favorite gathering spot in the tree. All the greenery made it a pleasant place to loiter. It would do until the voyagers got a proper park going elsewhere.

As they walked, Bram took stock of the vacuole's bright interior, listening with half an ear to what Marg and Orris were saying. Several hundred people were scattered among the garden patches or ambling along the paths. He could see Penserites everywhere among them, identifiable by their purposeful demeanor and by the parcels most of them carried.

The three who had been shadowing him seemed to have disappeared. Maybe it was because they had nothing more to fear from him. There were no Nar in the human sector of the tree. At least Bram hadn't seen any so far.

"We live just a little way down the main tunnel," Orris said. "Our quarters face a courtyard with its own lenticule—so we'll have real sunlight for at least part of the trip."

"You'll have to excuse the mess," Marg said. "I haven't really got it fixed up the way I want it yet."

Three oversize Penserites were lounging in front of the tunnel entrance. One of them stepped into Orris's path. "You can't go through here," he said.

"Huh? Why not?"

"Nobody's allowed to leave. You'll have to go back inside and wait."

Orris peered at the man, more puzzled than annoyed. "Who are you? I don't think I ever saw you before. I live down there."

"Better do as he says," Bram said.

"Don't be ridiculous," Orris said. He tried to brush past the other and found a meaty hand clamped on his arm. The two remaining Penserites moved to block the entrance.

"What do you think you're doing?" Marg said in a tone of steely reprimand. She tried to take a step forward, but Bram held her back.

"Don't, Marg," he said. "Orris, come back here with me."

The big Penserite gave Orris a shove that sent him off balance. Orris caught himself, looking bewildered. Bram, with Kerthin's help, got Orris and Marg to move a little distance away.

"Do you know those people?" Marg said with outthrust chin.

Bram squinted at the other tunnel entrances spaced out around the wooden cavern. All of them were guarded by Penserites, who were turning people back if they tried to leave. A real struggle was going on at one of the openings, where six or seven Penserites had converged to rough up a couple of stubborn cases.

"They're political zealots," Bram said. "They're followers of a man named Penser."

"Penser?" Marg said impatiently. "Who is he? I never heard of him."

Kerthin opened her mouth incredulously, and Bram cut in. "The Penserites are a kind of extreme offshoot of the Schismatist faction. They've been disowned by the main body of the Ascendist party."

"I don't understand this at all," Marg said. "They can't go around behaving this way. I'm going to complain to the ship's governing council."

"Wait," Bram said, putting a hand on her arm. "Something's happening."

There seemed to be a general movement toward the large open space in the center of the farm chamber, where bean fields and cabbage patches converged in wedge-shaped plots around a tiered circular service platform that formed a natural stage. Penserites were fanned out throughout the vast bowl, herding groups of stragglers, most of whom seemed to be taking the whole thing good-naturedly.

"But what's it all about?" said somebody from an unruly group of merrymakers who were dragging their feet as they passed, most of them still holding on to the drinks they'd had with them.

"You'll find out," said one of the Penserites who were urging them along. "Keep going. Down this way."

As the group drew abreast, a Penserite made flagging motions. "You people over there. Come on. Everybody's assembling down there."

"I don't think . . ." Marg began. Some of the Penserites were spreading out to include Bram and the others in the befuddled little flock.

"Do as he says," Bram said. The Penserites were carrying sticks, lumps of metal, and tool handles. Nobody here had seen such things in use. Bram had.

They let themselves be drawn along in the group's wake. 'It's some kind of announcement," somebody said knowledgeably. "Something important."

More people were trickling into the farm chamber from the connecting tunnels, with small teams of Penserites prodding them along. Strays were being rounded up. The movement was all in one direction. No one was being allowed out. The potential troublemakers were quickly singled out, grabbed, and hustled forcibly along or, in the worst cases, given a corrective punch in the belly or a tool handle in the kidney that quickly sapped the inclination to resist.

By now, even the dullest-witted and drunkest realized that something odd and unpleasant was going on. A crowd murmur began to grow in the packed center of the mass of people in front of the tiered platform that had been selected as a focal point. Armed Penserites were spotted through the crowd, with more around the fringes to keep order.

Penser stood gravely on the platform, talking to some of his Juxtian lieutenants, his hands clasped behind his back.

He was wearing the same simple gray costume with the high neck and the gathered sleeves. A runner hurried up to him, spoke urgently while Penser nodded, then hurried off.

The front ranks of the crowd, spilling up over the lower tiers of the platform, seemed to be composed entirely of Penserites—the rank and file members who were not part of the muscle squads. It was good strategy, Bram had to admit. They made a solid phalanx, conspicuously visible to the rest of the crowd, lending legitimacy to Penser.

Even so, of the more than a thousand people present, not more than two or three hundred could be Penserites. But they knew what they wanted. And they were prepared to work in concert.

Bram picked out Eena, a thin one-armed figure perched on the rim of a planting box. It was hard to tell at a distance, but he thought he recognized a number of people who bad dropped out of the organization after the death of Lal. Either they had rejoined or they had only pretended to drop out in order to lull the suspicions of the Ascendist leadership.

Orris had drawn protectively close to Marg. "As soon as this is over and the ship's council can get a message to Lowstation, these people will be removed," he said confidently. "Forcibly, if necessary."

Kerthin darted a look at Bram's face, but neither of them said anything. It was getting increasingly difficult to be heard in the babble that was growing around them.

A bomb went off, another noisemaker like the one that had been used at the Ascendist meeting. It produced the same result. The babble died down. People focused their attention on the platform, where it was evident that something was about to happen.

Penser looked out over the multitude as if he had all the time in the world. After a while he began to speak.

"Some of you know me, some do not. It doesn't matter. In myself I am not important. I am here to give you freedom. I am here to give you pride in yourself as human beings, the rightful owners of the cosmos. I am here to give you the universe!"

He did not raise his voice particularly. People at the edge of the crowd had to strain to hear all the words. It got their attention. There was no whispering, no foot shuffling.

"The days of man's servitude are over. They are finished. Today we make a new beginning. Today man will claim his destiny. Beginning here. Beginning now." His voice began, calculatedly, to rise. "And each and every one of you has a part to play in that glorious fulfillment. Make no mistake, you are all volunteers in humanity's greatest undertaking. You will be judged sternly. And traitors will not be tolerated."

The people in the crowd exchanged uncertain glances. What was Penser talking about?

Another minute of resonant generalities and he would have lost control of the situation. But with consummate timing he paused, took a breath, seemed through some trick of posture to grow taller. His face, from where Bram stood, was only a white blob with two black holes bored into it, but somehow the lines of Penser's body communicated an intensity of purpose as he leaned toward his audience. The crowd, unconsciously, leaned forward to meet him halfway.

"We have taken possession of the tree," Penser said.

There was a moment of astonished silence, then things exploded. Everybody seemed to be talking at once. From the front of the crowd, questions were vainly hurled at the platform.

"What does he mean?" Marg said. She looked from one face to another. "Orris, what does he mean?"

"Shh," Bram said. "He's not finished."

Penser waited out the uproar with folded arms. After a while it died down, broken against the rock of his immobility.

"Guards are posted at all air locks and access ducts in the human sector of the tree. No Nar may enter. We are sealed off."

Again there was a hubbub, which died down as Penser raised his hands for silence.

"The next hours will be crucial. We have ascertained that only a handful of Nar are now present in their sector of the tree, which is situated several miles from here, farther inward along this major branch toward the central trunk. Our sources have given us their number and approximate location."

"What does he mean, sources?" Marg demanded petulantly. "Can't anyone tell me anything?"

"I'd guess that there are Penserites among the Juxt One colonists," Bram said. "In fact, it would be surprising if there weren't. There must have been a certain number of his admirers who made plans to ship out without knowing that their idol was already in passage here. They would have been contacted, told to lie low. Isn't that so, Kerthin?"

Kerthin confirmed it with a shrug and a toss of her head. Bram smiled sadly.

Marg, her voice growing shrill, said, "That's impossible. I know everybody here. I would have known."

Penser paced the platform, his hands clasped behind his back. "In addition," he said, "there is the Nar docking crew. We don't have to worry about them for the moment. They have returned to their central station at the trunk, one hundred and fifty miles from here. No vehicle is due to arrive from Lowstation until tomorrow. By that time we will have the leaves unfurled and will be on our way. They are welcome either to abandon ship or to stay aboard for the ride, until their air and water run out. We have the means to shut down the tracheids and resin ducts serving their life-support facilities."

A horrified gasp went up from the crowd. "That means killing a part of the trunk," Orris said grimly. "The tree will seal off the living cambium there with a protective barrier. If the crew can't get into a habitable zone of the tree from outside . . ." He trailed off.

Penser continued to pace. He might have been thinking aloud, except that his voice was pitched like an actor's to carry.

"That leaves the Nar operating personnel at various points in the tree. There are no more than twenty of them, performing caretaker services, and we know where their stations are. We will move to gain possession of these control points. We have key people of our own—human beings—who are able to monitor the tree's functions."

He paused. Bram, though he was too far away to see the expression on Penser's face, could imagine him smiling thinly. "We had seven years to study the problem, you see, on our journey here from Juxt. The Nar crewmembers were most obliging about showing passengers around and explaining how things worked. Running a tree is not at all complicated. For those metabolic functions where we *will* initially require some slight assistance, we will retain the Nar technician and persuade him to help us. As for the others, we will dispense with their services."

There were shouts from up front, and Penser cocked his

head. The questioners sorted themselves out, and Bram heard someone yell: "What do you mean, dispense with their services?"

Penser raised his hands and quieted everyone down. "We will harm no Nar unless it becomes necessary," he said. "They will be put in space suits and cast overboard. They may have an uncomfortable time of it, but eventually rescue craft from Lowstation will pick them up."

"I don't like the sound of this," Orris said.

"Neither do I," Bram agreed. Orris had not seen how ruthless the Penserites could be. Bram had.

There were more yells from up front. "Where are you taking the tree?" someone demanded.

Penser was patient. Questions at this point created a certain level of involvement that made it possible for him to stage-manage events the way he wanted them.

"To a world that will be humanity's own," he said affably.

"There's no such world! Not close enough, anyway! We'd be old or dead by the time we got there!"

A man sprang to the base of the platform, shaking his fist. "That's what you want, isn't it? To have us bye and breed aboard this tree and sail on into space forever! Never to set foot on a world again!" He appealed to the crowd. "I know these people! They're fanatics! They make the Resurgists look like Partnerites. They'll do anything to get away from the Nar!"

Bram waited for the bullyboys to drag the man away and club him into silence. But Penser was still being expansive. He waved the crowd into silence. "There is such a world, I promise you," he said. "And you will not have to spend your lifetimes getting there. You will have your new world in no longer than it would have taken you to reach Juxt One."

"Where?" the calls came. "Where is it?"

"It is not time for you to know that," Penser said. "When the tree is secure, when I can be sure that no one can inform the Nar of our plans, when we have broken loose from planetary orbit and are beyond any danger of interception—then you will all be informed."

"Where is it?" Bram asked Kerthin. "Is it a moon in the Juxt system?"

"N-no," she said. "He tried that. It all fell apart. That's why he came here. He didn't have the right population base, the right conditions to make it work. He's thought it out very carefully. It's one of the worlds of the lesser sun. Even without building up to interstellar velocities, we'd be there in less than a year."

"It's not Ilf?" Bram said in amazement. "Ilf's more heavily populated with Nar even than Juxt One."

"No," Kerthin said. "It's one of the moons of the gas giant. It's only a mining world, but it's already been partially terraformed by the sulfur-and iron-metabolizing mining bacteria it was seeded with. It has a very small Nar population. The human population is even smaller, but it's mostly bunched together in a couple of settlements. The Nar population is dispersed all over the moon. Penser thinks he can strike quickly before they have time to get organized. He'll have had months to whip the passengers on this tree into shape, and he'll have the two human bases on the mining world to work from. He says the key is speed and surprise. He says he can take over before the Nar realize what's happening."

"Kerthin, what is this?" Marg said peevishly. "How do you know about these things?"

Orris was staring at Kerthin and Bram. Bram set his lips in a grim line and turned back to Kerthin.

"Penser can't get away with it," Bram said. "How many people has he got here? Not much over a thousand, even if he got everybody on the tree to go along with him. How many people on this mining world? Another few hundred? A thousand? He's got the whole Nar population of Ilf to contend with. To say nothing of the billions of Nar inhabiting the Father World and the other bodies of this primary, only light-hours away. They'll remove Penser and his gang like a—a plant wart and keep him under hasp and bolt for the rest of his days."

Kerthin shook her head stubbornly. "He's explained it all. By the time the Nar decide to act, it will all be over. There will be a human community on an unimportant little world, threatening nobody. There will be a few thousand Nar prisoners, well treated, who will be allowed to leave in an orderly fashion—provided Penser's demands are met. Penser will show that he's willing to be ... reasonable." She bit her lip. "There'll have been a few deaths and injuries, of course—that's inevitable. Both human and Nar. And that will serve as a warning. The Nar won't want to risk any further ... difficulties. Penser says the Nar commonwealth will accept the situation. They'll let the humans have their one little world. They'll even help us with food and technical equipment while we're trying to get on our feet. It will be a problem that is solved. A problem that is over."

Bram could recognize Penser's syntax in what Kerthin was mouthing so earnestly. He shook his head resignedly. "What then?"

"Penser's studied the ancient history of Original Man," Kerthin said, eager to convince him. "Hitler, Napoleon, Alexander. Jones and the neoamerican takeover. Digest each bite before you take the next one. Let your opponents think each nibble is the last—not worth taking action against after the fact. Penser will build up his strength. Attract like-minded human immigrants. Step up the human breeding rate without bothering about gene editing. Reproductive autonomy! Bram, do you realize that the human population of the universe could be *doubled* in twenty years?"

"And then?" he prodded.

Her eyes were shining. "And then, human beings will have a power base. We'll be ready for the next step. And the step after that. We can grow and expand, always on our own worlds, until we rule the universe for as far as we can reach in a human lifetime!"

"But the Nar were here first," Bram said. "Do we share it with them?"

She scarcely heard him, caught in her secondhand vision. Her eyes strayed past him to the milling crowd up front.

Marg was fretting. "Look at that! They're trampling all the seedlings. Isn't anyone going to stop them?"

At the center of the great wooden bubble, Penser was still fielding questions but getting tired of it.

"And what are the Nar going to be doing in the meantime?" demanded someone with a foolhardy edge of scorn in his voice. "Do you really think they'll be willing to stand by and let a few people with sticks in their hands take a tree away from them?"

"The Nar won't be able to do anything about it," Penser said. "By Tenhour tomorrow we'll be beyond their reach."

"I've always gotten along well with my Nar supervisors," said a querulous middle-aged man who looked like one of the visitors. "I don't hold with this. I live a pretty good life here. What's it going to be like on this new world of yours, I ask you?" He licked his lips nervously. "I'm not opposing you, you understand. No, sir. All I'm saying is I want to be sent back to Lowstation."

Penser's voice dripped with scorn. "Who among you is so base as to willingly be a *possession* of another life form? Perhaps such parasites deserve their chains. And if you're so worried about your comforts that you're willing to lick the gullet of a tenfoot for them, then perhaps we can oblige you. We can push you out of an air lock and let you find your own way back to their so-called Father World."

But the querulous man had stirred something up. The import of all that Penser had said was dawning on everyone.

"I've *got* a new world to go to!" someone yelped. "It's called Juxt One, and there's a whole new life waiting for me there. Steal the tree if you think you can get away with it. But I want to be sent back to Lowstation, too!"

"Why are we standing around listening to this stuff?" growled a young man with two or three friends around him to egg him on. "There's more of us than there are of them. Let's get 'em! We'll tie them up and hold them for the Nar inspection team!"

A clump of earth flew past Penser's ear, just missing him. He didn't even flinch.

"Get that man," he said.

A flying wedge of Penserites armed with clubs and chunks of rock forged through the crowd and descended on the dissenter. Arms rose and fell. Grunts of effort were mixed with howls of pain.

Orris strained forward, his eyes dilated with horror. "They'll kill him!"

Bram grabbed a handful of singlet. "There's nothing you can do."

Up front, the Penser supporters had formed a solid phalanx to prevent anyone from getting through to the platform. The crowd swirled in confusion. There were little eddies of activity where the Penserite forces had previously marked out potential trouble spots and now moved in to quash resistance before it could get started. Nothing much had a chance to get started. The crowd was disorganized. Until an hour ago they'd been having a party. They were deprived of anyone they might have rallied around as soon as he raised his head. The Penser minority had the advantage of a single purpose. People dodged the clubs, glad to get out of the way. Debating societies got started on the fringes. There was a babble of voices, randomized crowd motion.

Then four Penser minions appeared from a side tunnel, carrying a curious long bundle. Other Penserites cleared a path for them, and they dumped the bundle on the platform, almost at Penser's feet. The bundle writhed and showed itself to be still alive.

A horrified buzz went up as the bunched limbs untangled themselves and people realized that they were looking at a Nar. It was in a bad way. It didn't seem to be able to move purposefully. It tried to raise itself a couple of times and flopped down again.

"We found it in one of the branching xylem passages," said one of the men who had brought it. "It was on its way down here from the Nar sector. There were two of them."

"Did the other one get away?" Penser said.

"No, gene brother Penser."

The dazed Nar by now had succeeded in getting its lower limbs underneath itself. But they remained weak and flaccid, without the hydrostatic stiffening needed for walking. A peculiar wail came from the being's central orifice— a sound Bram had never heard from. a Nar.

"What's wrong with it?" Orris said in a whisper.

"I think I know," Bram said.

The decapod, if it was regaining its senses, must have been bewildered at suddenly finding itself in the midst of a huge mass of human beings. It managed to drag itself along feebly on three arms toward the nearest human it could see—Penser, who stood with folded arms watching it while it inched toward him, reaching out pitifully with the two remaining tentacles, forgetting that it could not make meaningful contact that way with a man.

Bram held his breath. Everyone else in the vast wooden amphitheater seemed to be just as mesmerized.

And then Pite stepped forward out of Penser's ring of advisers, holding one of the flat gray cases that Bram had seen before—the device that had needed the high-voltage biocapacitors. Pite touched the thing to the Nar, somewhere near the waist, and the graceful many-limbed body jerked in reflex agony and went limp again.

Penser stepped forward and gestured scornfully toward the mass of mindlessly weaving limbs. "Behold your master," he said. "Does anyone doubt now that we shall prevail?"

A prolonged sigh went up from the human spectators. Somewhere nearby, Bram heard a woman sobbing with emotion.

Any remaining resistance collapsed at that moment. The sight of the helpless Nar quivering at Penser's feet subdued the onlookers as nothing else could have done. Quiet, stunned, they allowed themselves to be rounded up and herded into small groups under guard.

The young Penserite in charge of Bram's group turned out to know Kerthin. He was friendly to Bram. "It won't be too long," he confided. "Penser apologizes for any discomfort, but he can't have people wandering around until the tree is secure. Everybody stays in the farm chamber till then. There'll be food, water, and we can rig up some kind of privacy for the women. Kerthin's gone with a search team to the living quarters to requisition blankets for everybody for tonight. And the commissary people will set up a soup kitchen as soon as they round up cooking utensils and things. Pick yourself a good spot to camp. How about that sheltered corner over by the hydroponic tanks? There's a threefamily taking it over, but I can roust them out if you and your friends want it."

"N-no," Bram said. "I could help with one of the collection teams. There's going to be a few thousand bowls and other necessities to lug back here." He added hastily, "You've seen me at some of the meetings, haven't you?"

In the back of his mind was a vague, half-formed idea of somehow getting away, finding his way to the Nar sector, warning them.

The guard shook his head. "Sorry. Word's come down. Not that we don't trust collaborationists like yourself, but Penser doesn't take chances. Only the actives allowed out for now, and believe me, even they're going out in mutual-watch groups. Later, maybe, there'll be something for you to do. Can't have a friend of Kerthin's assigned to digging latrines."

He laughed, and Bram smiled weakly.

He was helping Orris hang plastic sheeting to enclose a small area for women with small children when the expeditionary force filed by on its way to the tunnel entrance. It consisted of more than half of Penser's available personnel—the fittest and toughest-looking men and a handful of women. Evidently Penser's judgment was that about fifty of the trained combatants, plus the more sedentary reserves, would be sufficient to keep the cowed tree dwellers and their junketing friends under control.

The formidable-looking troop was loaded down with makeshift pikes, clubs, axes, bottles of inflammables, and lumpy sacks containing what Bram supposed were the claylike balls that exploded when you lit the wicks that were embedded in them. The section leaders carried the gray hand-held electrical devices—evidently there weren't enough of them to go around.

Pite was among them, a club in his hand and a knife lashed to a short stick dangling from his belt. The electrical weapon was looped over his shoulder.

He saw Bram and came over.

"Sorry we can't take you with us, Brammo," he said, mockery in his voice. "I don't know if you'd fit in just yet. But it won't take us long to clean out the yellowlegs. Then we'll send a couple of the lads to fetch you. We might need a biologist to tell us if the Nar at the pumping station in the trunk is feeding in the right hormones to make the leaves spread for travel."

"That was a filthy thing you did to the Nar you captured, Pite," Bram said evenly.

"He was the lucky one," Pite said with a V-shaped grin, and rejoined his men.

Bram watched them march off down the broad main corridor until they were out of sight around a bend. His stomach was churning. He looked down at his hand and found that he had made a fist.

"Don't let it get you down," a voice said behind him. "There's nothing you can do."

Bram turned and saw Jao, the red-bearded physicist who was migrating to Juxt One to become a brewmaster. The jaunty smile was in place, but it seemed a bit forced.

"There has to be a way," Bram said.

It occurred to him that unless something was done

soon, Jao would not be seeing Juxt One. But then, it must have occurred to Jao, too.

Jao gave a hairy-shouldered shrug. "I was down a secondary branch working with my yeast vats when they took over. They sent a couple of very competent fellows to come get me. It took about ten minutes for their team to empty out all the subbranches in that area. You don't argue with those fellows."

"You look as if they scuffed you up a little," Bram said. "You should have gone quietly."

Jao had streaks of dirt across his forehead and forearms, and his singlet was marked with grimy spots. "Me? No. I've been digging latrines. They put them in the cabbage patch. After all the care we gave those seedlings. I tried to tell them, but they wouldn't listen. We won't be able to grow anything there but bush crops now." He heaved a mighty sigh. "I suppose when you haven't had the experience of living aboard a tree, things like that don't matter to you. But they'd better learn fast."

"How are they going to get to the Nar sector?"

"There's a transportation system through the tracheids and dry ducts. Not continuous, because the treefitters used existing channels, but it won't take them long to find the transfer points."

"How long will it take them to reach the Nar sector?"

"With a gang that size and the need to maintain surprise, probably ten or twelve hours. They'll be doing a lot of it on foot, taking detours. If you or I were to go straight up by crawlbubble and cable pod, we could do it in an hour."

"If there were only some way to warn the Nar."

Jao shook his fiery mane. "The communication line's under guard, and all the radios've been confiscated."

"The Nar they took prisoner!" Bram said desperately. "He'll be missed."

"Maybe," Jao said. "After six or seven hours. If he was due back, that is. And by the time they spend the next few hours looking for him, it'll all be over. As for me, I'm going to get myself a bowl of soup over at that pot they've got going and let the big brains worry about what happens next. Coming with me?"

"Not right now," Bram said. "I'm going to see if I can get permission to help that Nar prisoner."

The decapod's name was Sesh-akh-sesh, and he was in a bad way. Bram propped him at an angle and poured a trickle of water down his gullet from a bucket he had found. After a while a little color came back to the ciliated lining, and Bram felt the tentacles stiffen a little.

"Thank you," the Nar said. A couple of the primary eyes focused cloudily on Bram. Bram could see the burn marks from the electrical device Pite had used near the lower waist: a circle of round dots that were raw purple against the yellow skin.

"I'm sorry, but there's no food here that you'd be able to eat," Bram said. "I'll see what I can do about that later on."

The food, Bram thought somberly, would have to come from the Nar sector of the tree. One way or the other.

"I do not desire to eat," Sesh-akh-sesh said. "But you are thoughtful."

"I'll try to get something from the human medical supplies to treat that burn, though. A nonorganic ointment ought to be all right."

He wondered how much success he'd have persuading his captors to get him a medical kit from the living quarters. They had allowed him to drag Sesh-akh-sesh to a spot where he'd be more comfortable and to do for him whatever he could, but they had declined to give him a hand. They didn't seem to care at all what happened to the injured Nar. And Bram's fellow detainees were skirting this section of the platform or looking on furtively from a distance, afraid to get involved.

The decapod struggled to raise himself slightly. "You are the Bram who is the protégé of Voth-shr-voth, are you not?" he said.

"Yes," Bram said, startled. "I am that Bram."

"He spoke to me of you, and from the core. You are as harmonious as he said you are. One has the illusion almost of touch behind your words in the Small Language."

"You know Voth, then?"

"I have that honor. We both were chosen as members of the certification commission making final inspection of this tree."

"What? Voth here, on the tree?"

"Surely you knew that?"

"N-no. I mean I didn't realize..." Bram remembered that Voth had said something to that effect, but he hadn't paid much attention at the time. All of a sudden a terrible thought struck him.

"Sesh-akh-sesh," he said urgently. "The humans who attacked you said there were two of you. That you were the lucky one. Is Voth... did they..."

The decapod began trembling. His nervous system had been overtaxed by the electrical shocks. He must have been under considerable strain trying to preserve the normal Nar amenities with Bram.

"I don't understand..." Sesh lost control of voice production for a moment, and there was that peculiar wailing sound again as his vocal syrinx went flabby and wind sighed at random through its air passages. "We saw the humans and greeted them, but they did not reply, and then they were on us like omophage beasts with sticks and sharp things. My touch fellow tried to flee, and they hacked him down. I tried to speak in comity, but then, at the touch, I was helpless . . ."

"You got a severe electric shock. Then they did it to you again, here. Sesh-akh-sesh, you must tell me. Was your companion Voth?"

The decapod recovered from his momentary confusion. "No, Voth-shr-voth did not come to the human zone today. He was to inspect the biological systems at the central pumping station."

Bram felt his knees go weak with relief. But it was only temporary. Voth was in great danger. He leaned over the shivering decapod. "Thank you, Sesh-akh-sesh. This is a terrible thing. Please believe that all humans are not to blame. These creatures that attacked you are indeed like phage beasts. But they prey on us as well as on you."

The decapod repeated, "I do not understand," and Bram knew that whatever the outcome of Penser's mad adventure, the Nar would never look at their human creations in the same way again.

Pseudonight obscured the far reaches of the immense xylem cavity and turned the huddled shapes of sleeping people into vague silvery silhouettes. The bright tubes needed for photosynthesis had dimmed about an hour ago, leaving only a tracery of biolights providing enough illumination to mimic a fabric of spun stars. Here and there a sudden brutal dazzle of uncovered biolanterns showed where Penser's jailers were checking on sleepers.

Bram lay motionless under his blanket, waiting for his guard to doze off again. He'd seen the man's head nodding twice, but both times the guard had jerked himself awake again. He was about twenty feet away. He'd made himself comfortable, too comfortable, with his back against a plant tub and his hand resting lightly on the end of the club that he'd laid conveniently on the ground beside him.

Orris had been a nuisance. He had come to squat beside Bram after the lights went out, to worry out loud about the effect that all the excitement might have on Marg's pregnancy. Bram was a biologist. Did he know if stress and the hardship of sleeping on the bare floor could cause her to lose the implant? Bram had soothed him, but had intimated that it could not hurt to return to Marg's side and give her a sense of security. At last Orris had taken the hint and stumbled off in the dark to rejoin his bride.

There were two guards at the tunnel mouth nearest Bram's spot, one on either side. One of them, Bram had noted, was restless. He kept deserting his post to talk to the man opposite, or to wander a little way uptunnel, or to visit the latrine. The latrine was on the opposite side of the tunnel mouth, and people from Bram's side had to cross in front of the two guards to get to it. They received a desultory glance in the subdued glow of the biolight tube that traversed the lower reaches of the dome in the area unless they stopped to loiter in front of the entrance or look down the tunnel. In that case, one or the other of the guards would tell them to move on.

Bram had a secret—a small knife he had found in the medical kit that the Penserites had grudgingly allowed him to borrow from the miscellaneous supplies that had been retrieved from the living quarters. If the Penser people had seen it in the kit, they hadn't paid any attention to it. As a weapon it was worthless: The blade was blunt-pointed and only an inch or so long. It was made for slicing or scoring, not stabbing. But the blade was very sharp—sharp as a razor. Bram had it hidden under his garments, along with a roll of bandages.

Bram's chaperone let his chin drop to his chest again, and this time it stayed there. After a moment, Bram heard a strangled snore.

He got to his feet carefully, leaving his blanket crumpled in a not very convincing semblance of a prone shape. If the guard woke up now, he would say that he had to visit the latrine. But he did not want the man wondering why he was taking so long. It would be fatal if the guard came after him to check and alerted the tunnel guards.

Trying not to look furtive, he navigated his way through the field of sleeping bodies. Someone else was coming back in the same direction, diluting any attention Bram might get—that was good. The restless tunnel guard gave Bram a cursory glance, then went back to talking to a female colonist who didn't seem to mind consorting with her captors; perhaps she was one of the Penser sympathizers who had scouted out the layout of the tree for him.

Bram crouched behind the improvised screen that had been erected around the ditches in the cabbage patch. The screen consisted of black plastic tarpaulins draped over an arrangement of garden poles. Cautiously he worked one of the poles loose. The tarpaulin sagged a little at that point but was otherwise undisturbed. He peeked between the plastic sheets. The guard was still talking to the girl. So far Bram had attracted no notice. He got out the little knife and lashed it to the end of the garden pole with a length of bandage.

Now he had to wait. He put the pole down where it would be partially obscured by the skirt of the tarpaulin.

A colonist, half-asleep, came to visit the latrine. He looked curiously at the loitering Bram, but he didn't say anything. When he left, Bram peeked through the curtain again. The tunnel guard was still preoccupied with his female hanger-on, but he looked up briefly to give the departing colonist an indifferent glance. The interruption had probably been a help; the guard had seen someone leave the latrine, giving Bram more grace in case the guard was counting.

Now the guard dragged the girl by the hand over to the other side of the tunnel mouth; he was going to pay a visit to his colleague. It was now or never. Bram stood up with the improvised spear in his hand. The biolight tube dipped quite low here, on its way to the reservoir that must be just on the other side of the chamber wall. The circulating pump that sent the living solution through the pipes would be close and strong; Bram could see the pulsating surges that made the light alternately blaze and fade.

He could just reach the transparent pipe. No good trying to puncture it with the squared-off blade; he slashed and sawed with all his might. The tough chitinous material resisted, and if it had been granted days, it would have repaired the scratches. But at last Bram got a groove going, and he began to saw steadily without the blade slipping. It seemed to him that every eye must be on the waggling pole protruding above the screen, but he dared not stop to take a look.

A few fiery droplets of cold light rained down on him, and with a savage thrust he pushed the knife all the way through, twisted, and pried the lesion wide open.

The fluid with its glowing microscopic life spilled out, and the overhead pipes near the tunnel began to drain. The circulating pump worked vainly, forcing a stream of fluorescing solution through the severed end, to splash on the ground and collect in a pool.

Another sleepy colonist came blundering through the partition at that moment. It couldn't be helped. Bram pushed past him, almost bowling him over, and ran into the darkness with his spear.

The biolights faded and died all through the dome. A garish flood of illumination seeped through the plastic partition, dazzling anyone who looked at it. Bram hoped all the guards would be looking in that direction, the light wiping out their night vision. The man he had knocked aside had somehow tangled himself in the plastic sheeting and was tottering around, pulling tarpaulins with him. The sleepers nearest the latrine were up, milling around and adding to the confusion.

Dim shapes collided with Bram. Feet pounded past him. "Get him!" a hoarse voice shouted. The unfortunate man who had enmeshed himself in plastic and was blundering around at the focus of the spilled light was the object of attention.

Whatever Penserites were among those who brushed past Bram in the dark must have assumed that, with his weapon, he was one of them. He slipped through the tunnel entrance, keeping close to the wall on the side opposite to where the guards had been chitchatting with their female friend. But by now, Bram reasoned, they would be converging on the center of the commotion, anyway.

A thousand yards down the tunnel, he paused for breath. When he looked back, the tunnel mouth was a cold flicker of light from the spreading pool of spilled biofluid. That would grow dull and die soon. No one was coming after him. Any minute now someone would think of plugging up the cut pipe and turning on the artificial sunlight.

Bram darted down the first side tunnel he came to. After traveling another hundred yards and going around a bend that cut off his line of sight, he felt safer.

The tunnel didn't seem to be in use, but it was being worked on. A large, multilegged construction machine whose forward end was an enormous auger was half embedded in an unfinished e_cavation in the wood, and there was some casual litter that had been left behind by the workmen. In a stroke of good fortune, Bram found several jugs of biolights that still had some life in them. He picked one up, peeled back enough of the hood to cast some light without giving him away, and moved on.

He chose a branching passage that seemed to slope slightly upward. Since he didn't know his way around the tree, it was the best course of action he could think of for the moment. If he kept climbing, he would eventually have to reach the Nar sector, closer to the center of spin. The problem was that it was miles and miles above his head. He'd never be able to reach it on foot—not in the time he had available. But there was no alternative. The tunnel moved laterally, too, and perhaps he might luck into some kind of transportation.

The passage got steeper. He did not know how long he had been climbing, but his legs ached and his breath was short. He paused to rest and heard his pounding heart—and then he heard a sound in the tunnel behind him.

He covered the jug of light and listened. The footsteps had stopped when he doused the light, and now they came forward again, cautiously. Whoever it was, he was feeling his way along in the dark and making better progress than Bram was.

Bram stumbled along, not daring to use the light again. He kept close to the tunnel wall, feeling his way with one hand. After a while it came to him that he was betraying his progress as much by sound as he would have done by sight. He paused again and heard the footsteps gaining on him. There might be more than one; it was impossible to tell.

He groped his way along the resinous wall for a few more feet, and his hand suddenly slipped off into nothingness. Another side passage. Or an alcove. It didn't matter. He edged his way inside, careful to be quiet, and stopped a few steps from the entrance.

If his pursuer were armed with one of the electrical devices, Bram would be finished at the first touch. Even someone with a club or a pole would have an edge over him; the Penserites were used to using such weapons, and he was not.

Bram had his makeshift spear—a spear not meant for stabbing—but he didn't know if he could bring himself to use it against another human being. He had never consciously tried to injure anyone before. The thought of using the blade against flesh revolted him. His best bet, he decided, was to wait until he heard the small sound that would mean that his pursuer had reached the side passage. There would be an indrawn breath as a groping hand encountered empty air. A small scuff or the sound of hesitation. Then Bram would snatch away the cover of the biolight jug and in that moment of surprise swing the haft of his spear. Perhaps he could knock the breath out of the other or knock aside whatever weapon he might be carrying.

He put the jug down on the smooth floor and waited. After a while he heard labored breathing that somebody was trying to suppress. It had been a long climb so far. But the person was not taken by surprise by the side passage as Bram had been. He came to a halt, as far as Bram could tell, just short of the opening, and then the breathing stopped. Bram's nerve broke; in the dark the man might be coming in after him, holding his breath. He whipped the cover off the lightjug and in the same instant swung his spear, haft end first, at what he thought was rib level.

In the sudden burst of light he saw a startled red-bearded face poking itself around the corner, and then Jao ducked his head back in time to avoid getting brained. The pole smacked against the edge of the entrance with a smart crack that left Bram's hands tingling.

"Hey, hold it!" Jao yelped.

The covered jug he had been carrying shattered against the floor, spilling luminescence that ran quickly downhill and faded out.

"Jao!" Bram exclaimed in relief. "I thought they were after me."

"I don't think they know we're gone," Jao said. He grinned widely. "You're pretty good with that thing. Maybe you ought to join Penser's militia."

"What—how—"

"I saw you slip out. I sneaked away too in all the confusion. For about five minutes there, there wasn't a guard in sight anywhere near the tunnel entrance." He looked at Bram more soberly. "I figured out what you were up to. From the way you were talking before. thought you might try something like this. I lost you at first, but I took a chance on this side tunnel, and I saw your light way ahead. I didn't want to use my own light in case a search party followed, and I was afraid to yell out to you, but I was able to keep your little glow in sight until you covered it up, and I figured I'd catch up with you sooner or later."

"Now what?" Bram said bitterly. "Penser's probably

halfway to the Nar sector by now, and we're off the main routes."

"Don't give up, my friend. I thought you might need help. I know the tree inside out. Remember, I've been living here for the last couple of months."

"Where does this channel go?"

"It's an old resin duct they're converting into a secondary thoroughfare. They can bore through to the adjoining tracheids like this one for apartments and workshops. Eventually it'll intersect a vascular ray with a bucket shaft in it. First, though, let's find ourselves some transportation."

The crawlbubble Jao found for them had seen a lot of hard use, but it was still in operating condition. Workmen had been using it to explore some of the branching vascular rays and had left it parked in a hollowed-out cell that was being used as a toolshed.

"Not the most elegant way to travel, but it'll get us there," Jao said cheerfully. "You know how to drive one of these things?"

Bram shook his head. He had seen crawlbubbles in operation on the Father World on projects where rough or hilly terrain made other work vehicles impractical, but he had never actually ridden in one. They were squat, six-legged things with a transparent cab big enough for one Nar or two cramped humans. Essentially they were a larger and more sophisticated version of a tripod walker—a form of pseudolife operated by synthetic reselin protein.

"Nothing to it," Jao said. "Just point it where you want it to go. It can't tip over—there's always three legs in contact with a surface—and it feels out its own footholds."

He twanged one of the tendons anchored in the metal-framed control pyramid, and the little biomachine scuttled forward. The basic control was a sort of tiller shaped for a Nar tentacle, but a human being could operate it one-handed by fitting an elbow into the groove at one end; the tiller worked on a universal joint, and one could steer and tilt it forward for more speed at the same time or tilt it backward for reverse. A synthetic electroluminescent organ, focused by a lens and mirror, cast a high-intensity beam forward.

The resin duct grew steeper, and the crawlbubble dug in and braced itself as it climbed. "Hang on," Jao said. "It's going to get worse before it gets better." After another hour of climbing, the duct abruptly came to an end, plugged up by a hardened amber material. "There should be an opening about here," Jao said. "They hadn't gotten around to enlarging it yet. There it is!"

A jagged hole in the smooth wall was just big enough for the crawlbubble to squeeze through. The electroluminescent headlamp threw its light down a long, bare horizontal passage.

"There ought to be a bucket stage a couple of miles in that direction," Jao said. "We'd better leave the crawl-bubble here and walk the rest of the way. We don't want to give ourselves away in case they've posted a guard there."

"I hate to think of what I might have done if you hadn't come along," Bram said. "I probably would have just gone blundering onward."

"I don't know," Jao said. "You might have blundered your way to the Nar sector by yourself. Then again, you might not have. That's why I followed you. It was a chance I didn't want to let you take."

"Well, thanks," Bram said.

"Don't thank me," Jao said with a gesture of dismissal. "It's my tree."

They climbed out of the crawlbubble and stared down the length of the transverse passage. Lighting had not been installed, but there was a dim, pearly visibility anyway. "This tunnel's still alive," Jao said. "That's sunlight we're seeing, what's left of it after being pumped through the tree's own optical fibers. A plant the size of this one has to figure out new ways of carrying on its photochemistry."

Bram, after a moment's hesitation, took his spear with him. Jao produced a wicked-looking curved knife from under his clothing.

"Where did you get that?" Bram said.

"It's a garden tool. From the farm chamber. I was able to lift it without being noticed."

"Could—could you use it?"

"I don't know. But it feels good in the hand. We're killers, you know. That's what you learn if you take a hard look at the literature our unedited forebears sent along with us. Maybe it wasn't apparent to the Nar when our numbers were small and we still hadn't formulated anything resembling a real human society. But maybe the Pensers are going to be the natural order of things from now on."

"I don't believe it," Bram said. "I wouldn't want to believe anything like that."

"Suit yourself." Jao shrugged. "But you have to admit that Penser wouldn't have been possible if there hadn't been large numbers of people dissatisfied with the shape of things in their happy little enclosures down below."

Bram was surprised at the unhappiness that suddenly showed in the jovial, red-bearded visage; then he realized that Jao would not have become one of the Juxt One émigrés in the first place If he had been entirely content with his lot.

"Not so many people," Bram said. "I still think Penser's an aberration."

They moved down the dim corridor, their unfamiliar weapons at the ready. It was a long walk in an echoing silence. You couldn't see all the way ahead; the slight irregular curvatures limited visibility to a few hundred yards at a time. But after a mile or so, something—a change in the illumination, a change in the echoes, a different feel to the air currents—told Bram that they were approaching an open space. He and Jao moved more cautiously and pressed closer to the wall on the inside curve. Another few minutes of walking brought them to a tremendous hollow space with the squarish cross section of a tracheid. They stepped out onto a wide natural platform rimming the xylem cell all the way around. A yawning abyss stretched beneath their feet; muted yellow light filtered from somewhere high above. There was no guardrail, and they both instinctively drew back a little.

"It's a bucket station, just as I thought," Jao said. He pointed across the chasm to where a series of filaments were threaded through circular holes in the rim on the opposite side. Buckets rested in several of the wells.

"They've passed through here," Bram said, looking at the charred pits in the living wood where Penser's army had carelessly lit cooking fires and at the litter that surrounded them. "But how long ago?"

"Not too long," Jao said, sniffing the ashes. "They had a head start of three or four hours on us, but they must have used most of it up. Stopping to eat. Being held up by the discontinuities in the shaft, then hoisting people a few at a time and regrouping. Sending out scouts along the side passages to make sure they're not seen."

They hurried around to the opposite side of the great shaft, where the bucket cables were stretched.

"Look, one of them's moving," Bram said.

He could see the slight telltale vibration blurting one of the threads. It was the trailing cable, the one that was anchored to a winch below to keep the bucket from swinging out of control; the hoisting cables were triple, with a pair of safety cords to catch the bucket in case the viral monofilament ever were to snap. That meant that the moving bucket was overhead, not somewhere below.

"There's your answer," Jao said. "You're looking at the last bucketful of stragglers."

"Then there's still time to warn the Nar!" Bram cried.

"There ought to be a communications line on the platform." Jao looked around at the natural pits lining the tracheid walls. "Ah, there's one with a door on it." He disappeared into the hole, holding his knife, and reappeared a moment later. "Line's cut," he announced. "I guess they didn't want to bother leaving a guard behind."

Bram stared hopelessly at the bucket cable. It had stopped vibrating. "If there were only some way to get past them," he said.

"There is," Jao said.

"Huh?"

"Come on." Jao took him by the arm. "How do you think they traveled before they hung the buckets? There're some leftover climbers through there. I hope you're not afraid of heights."

He pulled Bram through the pit opening he had emerged from and led him through the cell wall to an adjoining tracheid. The climbers were there—simple, round-bottomed cups with stiff wiry limbs radiating horizontally in two rows, at brim and waist. The nearer ones stirred as Bram and Jao approached.

"I guess there's still a few breeding colonies of them here and there," Jao said. "They have a commensal relationship with the tree—live on water and dissolved nutrients in the vessels. The tree hardly notices. The climbers give back the nutrients, anyway. They may even do some good—when their cups fill up, they move liquid through the vessels faster than the tree could do it."

Jao climbed into a cup and motioned Bram to join him. It was a tight fit and not very comfortable; the narrow cup was shaped to fit a Nar's bundled lower limbs, and there was no way to brace one's feet. "Hang on!" Jao said as the climber responded to their weight and dragged itself through a tube opening.

The ascent was terrifying to a human though not, apparently, to a Nar. Bram clung to the muscular ridge around the cup rim and tried not to look downward. The climber was choosy about the route it took. If it encountered an artery whose diameter was too large for its bristling array of limbs, it backed down and tried an alternate path. It apparently was unwilling to climb unless it could brace itself all the way around. Under the circumstances, Bram found that comforting.

"We've got a xylem wall between us and Penser's expedition," Jao said close to Bram's ear. "They won't see us. From here we just climb all the way to Nar country without stopping. Penser won't do that. It would take too many bucket trips for his whole crowd, and he'd lose the element of surprise. He'll regroup, give them a pep talk, and take them the last quarter mile on foot. We'll have a chance to beat them."

The climber doggedly scrabbled upward through a tan darkness punctuated by occasional blotches of light that marked cross sections of transverse channels. Once, when it tried to abandon its climb for something enticing down a side channel, Jao corrected its course by reaching over the side of the cup and doing something with his hand that Bram couldn't see. Enough moisture was being collected from the dewy trickle along the woody shaft so that Bram found himself standing in a small warm pool. "Should have brought something along to bail with," Jao grumbled. "But we won't be using this thing long enough to get wet past the ankles."

"I can see the drawbacks in using climbers as your elevator system," Bram said.

"Most humans won't use them at all," Jao told him. "Prejudice about animate machines with independent nervous systems. That goes double for anyone leeward of the Ascendists, like most of Penser's crowd. Actually, I think the climber genome was put together at least partly from plant genes. But you'd know more about that, being a biologist."

"You seem to be more politically aware than most of the people here," Bram said, remembering Marg's blank puzzlement about the differences between Ascendists, Schismatists, and splinter groups.

There was a pause. Bram could imagine Jao grimacing in the darkness. "No, I don't suppose most of my fellow passengers have ever devoted much time to political thought," Jao said at last.

The climber was rising toward a region of amber light.

Bram saw fluid moving sluggishly through translucent walls. Above, the vertical shaft widened slightly. Transverse openings on opposite sides of the shaft were linked by a narrow catwalk that was obviously the result of deliberate carpentry. More catwalks and openings could be seen farther up. But there was still plenty of room for the climber to get by.

"The threshhold of Nar country," Jao announced. "Penser and the others ought to be on the other side of that wall at about this level."

He reached over the side of the cup and did something to slow the climber down. Bram would have preferred to get past the catwalk quickly, but he supposed that Jao knew what he was doing.

Then, as they drew abreast of the opening, Jao reached down again, and the climber stopped, hooked several limbs into the lip of the opening, and began to drag itself inside.

"Where are you going?" Bram said. "This will take us into Penser's hands!"

"I know," the redbeard said.

He plucked Bram's spear from its resting place against the side of the cup and tossed it overboard. Incredulously, Bram watched it tumble down the shaft.

"You're one of them!" he blurted. "You've been a secret Penserite all along!"

Jao nodded. "Kept my opinions to myself. Jao, the happy colonist, without a serious thought in his head. More useful to the cause that way, you see."

Bram tried to scramble over the rim of the cup. The cup bobbed alarmingly as the climber's wiry limbs clawed for support. Jao wrapped his arms around Bram's waist and hauled him back inside. "Stop it, you fool!" he panted. "You'll get us both killed!"

The climber got itself over the edge of the pithead. Bram stared at Jao. "You were Penser's source of information on board the tree, then! That's how he knew about the layout and the movements of the Nar!"

"You're giving me too much credit. There were several of us. We applied as colonists over a year ago, as soon as we knew that Penser was coming. To prepare the way for him." Jao chuckled. "Smeth couldn't understand why I was willing to give up a promising career as a physicist to go to Juxt One."

The climber was on level ground now, hoisting itself along the sidewalls of the connecting duct. Bram looked back at the catwalk bridging the way to the adjoining tracheid.

Jao read his mind. "Don't bother," he said. "You wouldn't get very far."

Bram gathered himself anyway, tensing to give Jao a sudden shove and vault over the edge of the cup. But he had waited too long. Just then, he and Jao had to duck their heads as the climber squeezed past the springy guard cells at the end of the duct, and then the climber broke through into bright light.

There was about an acre of polished floor, bristling with armed men who came running toward the climber as Jao brought it to a halt. At least twenty hard-looking individuals with pikes and bludgeons surrounded the vehicle while one of the section chiefs sauntered over.

"Brought you a little present," Jao said. "He was on his way to the Nar sector to warn them."

Bram found himself staring down into the flushed, sweat-streaked face of Pite. "Hello, Brammo," Pite said. "You're just in time for the fun."

* * *

Bram had no idea how much time had gone by. He couldn't reach his waistwatch with his hands tied behind his back, and though its face was in plain sight, he couldn't distinguish the changes in the texture of its surface by eye.

The man who had been left to guard him was an uncommunicative sort with thin lips, thin nose, and little eyes. He did not respond to Bram's attempts to find out what was going on. He stared wistfully across the wooden plain at the comings and goings of his compatriots. Bram had the feeling that the man resented him for keeping him out of the action.

Only a handful of people were visible in the lofty outer chamber. In the middle distance two or three Penserites tended a depot of indefinable goods heaped in neat arrangements on the ground and dispensed them to the runners who came in pairs with baskets and carrypoles to fetch them. At the base of the wooden cliff beyond, several people squatted in a loose semicircle and watched one of their number trace diagrams with a stick and do a lot of pointing.

Bram looked up as somebody came jogging heavily toward him, a chunky figure weighed down with bouncing gear. Bram's guard stopped picking his teeth and surveyed the newcomer with mild interest.

"On your feet. Penser wants to talk to you."

Bram struggled up. His legs were numb. "What about?" he asked.

"You'll find out from him."

Bram's uncommunicative guard broke his vow of silence. "He's gotten around to sentencing you to death, that's what," he said with moderate malice as he rose to his feet.

"Get going."

Bram stumbled along between the two of them. They went through a cleft in the wall of wood and down an avenue of tall compartments. The signs of destruction were everywhere: charred doorways, splintered rubble, heaps of smashed furnishings. They passed a dead Nar who lay across a threshhold with three spear handles sticking out of him.

"I thought you weren't going to hurt anyone," Bram said.

"Shut up," his guard said, prodding him.

"It's gone wrong, hasn't it?" Bram said, and got another jab with the end of a cudgel for that.

They shoved him through into a large hall that was littered with overturned equipment. A lot of wanton destruction had gone on. Bram saw a touch reader, smashed apparently for the fun of it, and its library of holos piled in a charred heap. About a hundred people were milling around—the greater part of Penser's force. A stink of smoke and chemicals hung in the air.

Pite came striding toward Bram and his captors. He was festooned with equipment: club, short spear, a mesh bag of doughy balls garnished with long wicks dangling from his waist. The nasty little electrical weapon was stuck carelessly into his belt.

"Got him? Good," he said. "I'll take him in to Penser."

The other two left. Pite gripped Bram above the elbow and led him through the hall. Bram saw people pouring clear liquid from demijohns into glass bottles, while others stoppered the containers, wrapped them with impregnated strips of cloth, and bore them away. Quite a collection of them was growing. Bram smelled the agreeable aroma of grain alcohol. "What are they doing?" he said.

"Making firebottles," Pite said. He seemed edgy, over-stimulated, his color high and his eyes shining.

"What's happening?"

Pite stopped him and swung around to face him. "Nothing that's going to change anything. Penser caught them by surprise, the way he figured. We took the whole lower level on our initial sweep. But the place is too big, and the yellowlegs were too dispersed. They reacted faster than we thought they would once they figured out what was going on. I've never seen anything move as fast as the ones that got by us. They've barricaded themselves in one of the upper levels."

"They've probably reached the outside crew by radio by now, haven't they?" Bram said. "And the outside crew will be able to get in touch with Lowstation."

Sweat glistened in the yellow stubble over Pite's upper lip. "There's nothing the outside crew can do to stop us," he said. "There aren't enough of them. And if one of them did get in here somehow, we'd kill him before he got ten feet. They're no match for us. You saw that. They don't know how to fight. They don't get the idea of it." He wiped a hand across his forehead, making a smudge. "As for Lowstation, they can't get here in time. As soon as we get past those yellowlegs who've barricaded themselves, we'll get the tree moving."

"What are you going to do?" Bram asked, feeling a chill start down his spine.

"We're going to burn them out," Pite said, showing his teeth. "We'll burn out the whole Nar sector and get every last one of them."

"You can't be serious! What if it spreads? If you don't care about anything else, there are hundreds of people living in this branch?'

"Fire spreads upward. Inward in this case. And so does smoke. We can keep any downward movement under control. Wet the lower level down with water from those veins. The Nar sector only goes on for a few miles, anyway. After that, it's all living wood. Penser says a fire can't sustain itself in living wood. After a while it'll smother itself, and we get past to the control center. Jao says there's a high-speed tube that goes straight through the heartwood."

"Penser is out of his mind. There's deadwood and discarded ducts all through a branch. Maybe a fire would smother itself when it got high enough for diminishing gravity to squelch circulation, but what if the support wood was so weakened by that time that centrifugal force sent the whole branch flying off into space? With all those people in it?"

"Enough talk," Pite said. "Penser's waiting."

He pushed Bram along to a line of suites that adjoined the large chamber. The Nar had done well for themselves over the many years since the tree had been commissioned. It was a comfortable habitat, with pools, basking slopes, and garden spots planted with the brilliant yellow foliage of the Father World's native plant life with its sulfur-based photosynthesis. Real sunlight poured in through the translucent lenticels along the outer walls—sunlight that would turn to starlight as the tree left a system.

"What does Penser want with me?" Bram asked.

"It seems," Pite said, "that you've become the indispensable man. Nice of you to come join us on your own."

He led Bram to a sunny room where Penser stood staring through one of the tall translucent blisters with his hands clasped behind his back. The room was pure Nax in style, but Penser had taken possession of it by creating a spartan corner with an improvised wooden table surface that had writing materials laid out on it.

Penser turned, though he could not have heard their approaching footsteps on the spongy material of the floor. He wore the same loose gray costume. His dark remote eyes bored into Bram.

"Bram," his hollow voice said. "I gave you my trust, and it seems you have betrayed me."

Bram's throat was desperately dry. He was astounded that Penser could remember his name out of so many. He stood there and said nothing.

"Untie his hands," Penser said.

Pite undid the cords. Bram flexed his fingers, feeling the circulation come back.

"I'm told," Penser said, "that you are a biologist."

Bram found his voice. "I'm more of a molecular artisan," he said. "I haven't really done much work in macrobiology."

"No matter," Penser said. "I'm also told that you are able to read the touch language."

Bram swallowed. "No human can do that," he said.

Penser gestured toward the waistwatch that Bram was wearing. "And yet you use one of their instruments," he said.

"Telling time is easy," Bram said. "It's only a matter of feeling the position of numbers. Simple outlines that don't change. Any human child could be taught to do it. It's not the same as understanding the Great Language."

"Don't lie to me," Penser said softly.

"I'm not lying."

Behind Bram, Pite sighed. "Brammo, we know about all the time you spent stretched out on those tickle machines. Remember? Waller was keeping track of you."

Bram tried to make them understand. "I can pick out broad areas of cilia movement, that's true. Outlines that *enclose* meaning. Maybe that's not a common talent. I guess it isn't, though it ought to be. That's good enough for numbers, some names, general subject headings that give me the drift of things. I can detect some nuances of emotion that surround the . . . the *essence* . . . just as you could tell that a man was angry about a particular something by the tone of his voice and his gestures, even if you didn't understand language, and from that infer some of his meaning. It's—it's like a child who's too young to read being able to look through his picture book and recognize the shapes of the letters and the limited number of things they're associated with—'P' for 'potato,' for instance. But he still can't read. I guess what I'm saying is that I have a certain amount of pattern recognition, even though the patterns aren't compatible with the human nervous system."

"That may suffice," Penser said.

It was hard to resist Penser. As unprepossessing as was his appearance, the man radiated an uncanny force of will that made you want to please him. Bram had to remind himself that Penser's reasonable tones stood for dead Nar, broken heads, Pite's firebottles. He shook his head angrily to rid himself of Penser's influence.

"I won't help you," he said.

"What did I tell you?" Pite said. "Want me to give him a touch of current?"

"I don't think that's necessary yet," Penser said. The bruised eyes regarded Bram sorrowfully. "Bram, I hope to persuade you that whether you help me or not will make no difference to the outcome of this affair. You may tell yourself, if you wish, that helping to move the tree out of Nar reach sooner rather than later may save Nar and human lives in the long run. But one way or the other, you *will* be persuaded."

Bram said thickly, "I'm not cooperating, whatever you do. Anyway, I don't know anything about moving trees."

Penser seemed not to have heard him. He turned and stared out the lenticel again with his hands clasped behind him. It was night again outside the oval transparency, after the quarter turn the tree's crown had made on its axis since Bram had entered the room, and a blurred dappling of stars could be seen through the membrane.

"It's a simple matter, really," Penser said almost to himself, "just a question of overriding the tree's own tropisms. The first problem is to get it out of low orbit. Light pressure isn't strong enough for that. Nor can I use the rocket engines of the various vehicles garaged here; the tree's far too massive to move that way. The tree itself uses its own gases—builds them up and spurts them out under pressure, always orienting itself to break out of orbit. Ordinarily it would have done so by now—trees don't like to linger near planetary masses. But a chemical inhibitor's being metered into the tree's circulatory system through the pumping station. We have to find it and turn it off. But first we have to identify it. We don't want to go into retrograde orbit and fall through the atmosphere."

He said it calmly. Bram was appalled at the risks the man was prepared to take. It was as if Penser wooed death.

"The next problem," Penser continued dryly, "is to point the tree where we want to go. To do that we must induce a secondary phototropism—get the sun behind us and head for the second brightest light source in the sky, as trees tend naturally to do when they migrate from star to star."

"The lesser sun," Bram said, and immediately snapped his mouth shut.

"You know that?" Penser gave him an incurious glance. "Ah, yes, the young woman would have told you. One cannot do without such enthusiasts, but one uses them sparingly. No matter. The Nar will be tracking us soon enough. But when they see that we are headed for the lesser sun, they will assume that our destination is Ilf."

Behind Bram, Pite growled, "The trouble is that our time's running out."

"I thought you said you knew how to operate a tree," Bram said, unable to keep the hostility out of his voice. "That's what you told the people down below. Do you mean to say you've killed and injured folk for nothing?"

"We have our own biologist and computer technicians," Penser said. "They'll be fully competent to sail the tree once we get started. But there isn't time to rewire the systems for human operation."

"It's the computer that runs the chemical synthesizer at the pumping station," Pite said unwillingly. "It only talks the yellowleg language, and we need a yellowleg to feed it the right data out of the operating library."

"We were in the process of persuading a Nar biologist to assist us," Penser said, "but something . . . unforeseen happened. So you see the problem. We need someone who can understand the touch language to select the right programs for us."

"That's you, Brammo," Pite said.

"No."

"Let me give him just a touch," Pite begged.

Penser sighed. Day broke behind his gray figure as the tree rotated back into sunlight again. "Bring him along, Pite."

With Pite prodding him from behind, Bram followed Penser unwillingly to another chamber in the suite. This one, too, had a lenticel in the outside wall, sending light streaming through the interior. A recessed pool added a further note of luxury to the place.

An extensive holo library covered one wall, and there were rows of body readers on pedestals, computer terminals, and workstations for joined touch groups. A few items of equipment were overturned, and a few shelves of holos were spilled on the floor, but somebody had stopped the vandalism before it had gone any further. A half-dozen armed men stood around uneasily, as if on guard.

But none of that was what caught Bram's attention. The only thing he had eyes for was the dead Nar who lay sprawled near the pool, leaving a trail of violet ichor behind.

"Very annoying, indeed," Penser was saying. "We had intended to keep the thing alive, but it reacted badly to electrical shock."

"So now it's your turn, Brammo," Pite said. "Why don't you save yourself some grief."

Bram hardly heard them. He started forward with a cry. He knew before he reached the now pale yellow form who it was.

"Voth," he choked, kneeling.

Voth lay in a purple mess, the ruptured follicles showing on the indecently exposed undersides of his lower tentacles. The electric shocks had hastened his time. He had tried, evidently, to crawl to the pool in time to save his children, but he hadn't made it.

Blinded by tears, Bram turned his head and saw a pale blob that was Penser's face. With a low growl that he would not have recognized as his own, had he been aware of it, he hurled himself at Penser. His fingers were satisfyingly around Penser's throat when there was a flash of astonishing pain that became Bram's entire universe, and then there was nothing at all.

* * *

He was in a darkness filled with blinking lights. He seemed to have no body, except that there was a generalized sense of hurting. A continuous buzzing sound came from the distant places in his head. After a while, the sounds became externalized, and he was aware of strained, urgent voices around him, the coming and going of footsteps, rattles and clanks.

He opened his eyes, and harsh sunlight stabbed his brain. His body returned. He was lying curled up on one side, his hands bound behind his back again. His legs seemed to be tied, too. An area of pain localized as a burn under one shoulder blade. Someone seemed to have kicked him while he lay unconscious; at least that was how the bruised ribs and upper arm on his unprotected side felt.

Bram struggled to sit up. He inched himself up against the wall at his back. The movement brought a wave of headache and nausea. After a moment the headache subsided to a steady throb. He inhaled and tasted smoke in his mouth.

He was in the same chamber, the one with the deep-set lenticel and the workstations, but now it was full of people. There was activity all around him. People with soot-smudged faces kept running in and out, exchanging scraps of hurried conversation and brief flurries of gestures. They bore axes and sledgehammers. A few carded smoldering bundles that must have been torches. Somebody was passing out firebottles. A thick, wet smoke billowed in through the arched openings that led to the inner suites and the chamber beyond. Nobody paid the slightest attention to Bram.

Through his headache, he located Penser. Penser was at the center of all the movement, the only one in the room who was weaponless. He stood with his hands behind his back, head lowered to listen to the reports of the runners, occasionally lifting his head and raising an arm to call someone over to him.

Voth's corpse was still there, too. Bram forced his eyes to find it. It lay near the pool, the outflung tentacles still reaching. Nobody had bothered to move it.

Bram felt numb, unable to summon his feelings. Voth's body seemed curiously flat. The settling and draining of tissues had given the symmetrical decapod form two sides in death—something it had never had in life. The mirror eyes were nothing more than dull pits around the waist. Bram's head buzzed and throbbed. None of this seemed real. After a moment he realized that he had forgotten to draw a breath for too long; when he did so, it was like a knife along his bruised ribs.

Pite came over, an axe slung across his back, one side of his mono scorched.

"Waking up, Brammo?" he said. "You better hope we need you. Penser's mad, really mad. You shouldn't have gone after him that way. You're lucky my little galvanizer happened to be on a low setting. If it had been set for Nar, you'd have been fried."

"How long has that been going on?" Bram croaked, pointing his chin at all the frantic movement in and out.

"About an hour. You weren't out long. We've broken through one compartment wall and burnt out a whole section along one gallery. The yellowlegs've barricaded themselves farther back, but we'll smash through and roast the lot of them. We caught two of them trying to slip away. Got 'em both with firebottles. Know what happens to a yellowlegs when it burns? It sort of pops."

He threw back his head and laughed.

Bram felt ill. "I wish I'd killed him."

"See, Brammo." Pite grinned. "You're just like us."

Bram was opening his mouth to reply when there was a sound like a great *whoof*. It came from the direction of the inner chambers, where the fires had been burning.

At the same time, Bram saw the drifting haze of smoke in the room suddenly give a jerk in the direction of the exits, as if somebody had given a sharp tug to an invisible sheet that it was painted on. Then the ribbons of smoke began drifting lazily toward the inner suites.

An eerie silence descended. Everybody had stopped moving at once. The crackle of flames that had been heard in the distance had abruptly stopped. Then there were cries of alarm and another great *whump*.

Pite, Penser, and everyone else were staring toward the exits. Bram was the only one who saw the shadowy blurs on the membrane of the lenticel blotting out the pearly ghosts of stars.

The blurs were moving purposefully. Bram could not give a shape to them yet. This side of the tree presently faced night, and the interior biolights had flared up to compensate.

Bram looked away from the lenticel. He didn't want anyone to notice him staring.

Penser was barking orders, trying to organize his troops. "Trog, take some men and find out what's going on! Pite, never mind the incendiaries for the moment! Get your people together and have them prepared to move quickly! Hust, how is the large aggregate coming? We may have to blow another opening!"

A man stumbled into the chamber, his forehead bleeding from a large gash. "No air there! The next chamber's all vacuum! It put the fire out! No sign of the yellowlegs! They must have gone farther inside!"

"Did we lose anybody?" Penser asked.

The man was weaving and confused, trying to stay on his feet. "Jupe was inside when the air went—he's dead. I saw somebody else sucked in. I don't know what happened to him. People hurt." His hand went to his forehead and came away bloody. He gave a foolish; inappropriate grin. "Hard to stay on your feet. That's how I got this."

Somebody caught him before he fell. The fifty or so people in the chamber milled about uselessly, but Pite and another section leader were gradually whipping them into shape.

"What happened to Trog?" Penser seemed to be losing control. Bram was surprised. The man had seemed invulnerable to emotion. "Why can't anyone tell me anything?" Penser complained. "How fast are we losing air?"

More people from the inside battleground were drifting in, gradually filling up the place. One of them answered Penser.

"The chamber sealed up again somehow after it drew in all the air. Otherwise, we'd all be dead. Great big floating things, like sticky balloons, slapped up against the hole. I think the tree makes them. Now you can get into the chamber again. Fire's snuffed out. But there's air leakage into the *next* chamber through all the little cracks and breaches!"

Everybody's eyes went to the drifting smoke in the air again. It didn't seem so frightening now. It was still clearing itself out, but the rate of flow was nowhere near the great gulp of air the evacuated area had taken at that first thunderclap.

Penser's confidence returned. "Break through the next wall!" he screamed at them. "There's nothing to worry about. That one will seal itself, too. We won't lose more air than we can afford. This is only a small pan of the tree. It will replenish itself. Keep going. They can't keep retreating forever! I don't care how many walls you have to blow! Keep going till you get them all!"

A cooperative babble broke out. Penser had them all in the palm of his hand again. Pite had his thugs assembled. They were testing the sharpness of spear points, weighing clubs. The person in charge of the explosives yelled that he was almost ready. Bram, with a sense of shock, saw that one of his helpers was Eena, molding the claylike balls together into a new shape with her remaining arm.

Dawn broke through the lenticel as the tree rotated into sunlight again, and a giant many-legged shadow was suddenly thrown across the room.

Bram turned his head with the rest. He saw a decapod silhouetted against the light. More silhouettes, less sharp than the one pressed against the membrane, filled the translucent window, making a flickering shadow play inside.

Somebody gave a strangled cry. "They're trying to get in!"

A nipple appeared in the exact center of the membrane and bulged inward. The sharp point of an instrument broke through, and there was a terrifying hiss of air. The people in the room recoiled, drew back. A few broke and fled.

"Stay where you are!" Penser ordered hoarsely, checking the human movement. Bram watched in fascinated dread.

The silvery tip of a space-suited tentacle followed the sharp instrument, and the rest of the decapod oozed in against what must have been impossible air pressure. The boneless body seemed to elongate, corking the air. The last tentacle to be drawn in was joined to a limb of another Nar behind him, who squeezed through the elastic opening in an uninterrupted flow.

Air kept hissing, but Bram did not feel the radical decompression he feared. More Nar continued to ooze through in a continuous chain that was like a single, endless living creature clad in silver. The last one through slapped some sort of seal on the puncture. The seal fastened with a huge sucking *whoosh,* followed by little bubbling sounds around the edges. Bram could appreciate why the skein of decapods had remained twined together; it must have taken the combined strength of all those tentacles, first to hold the frontrunner down and shove him inside, then to brace themselves and draw the rest in after them.

It had taken less than half a minute for that silver stream of Nar to gush through the opening. Now the multiple creature broke up into units that quickly dispersed into a chess pattern of tall pieces that moved to engulf the still-paralyzed humans.

There were about twenty of the space-suited Nar. It had to be the outside docking crew and maintenance personnel, Bram thought, his mind racing. There couldn't have been time enough for reinforcements to arrive from Lowstation—though, he was sure, they had been getting advice by radio.

And they must have been in contact with their barricaded brethren, too. The diversion that had put out the fires and let space into the inner chambers had been too well timed to be a coincidence.

"Kill them!" Penser screamed. "Kill them all."

Bram strained at his ropes. There were only twenty Nar against more than a hundred armed and desperate humans in this chamber, but they moved with a bold confidence that seemed to unnerve Penser's minions.

The flanking Nar threw scoops of powder at the human crowd. People began coughing and scratching. The other Nar advanced with nets and cords.

Pite was the first to recover from his paralysis. He ran forward, coughing and wheezing, wiping the tears out of his eyes with the back of his hand, and tried to reach the nearest Nar with a spear thrust.

But at least twenty tentacles from a half dozen decapods acted in concert to grasp the shaft of the spear, pluck the little electrical device from Pite's other hand, curl around his ankles and wrists, lift him bodily off the floor, net him, and tie him into a neat bundle.

It was all done in about five seconds.

The four or five attackers immediately following Pite received the same treatment. The Nar dispatched them with unhurried ease, acting in unison, as if they were a single creature with two hundred limbs, each of which always knew where the other limbs were and what they were doing. They didn't split up to take on multiple opponents, and no Nar had to fight alone. It was a case of a limb that had taken a moment to disarm an enemy now being free to hold two ankles together while another Nar tied a knot; of a limb that a second earlier had thrown a net immediately being available to deflect a pike aimed at a brother Nar. Seen that way, limb against useful limb, it was the humans who were outnumbered.

A bare minute later, with eight or nine humans already trussed up and laid aside, Bram understood why.

One of the Penserites, gasping and blinking from the powder the Nar had sprinkled, managed to light the wick of a firebottle and hurl it. It whizzed past a Nar and shattered on the wall behind him, drenching the decapod with flame. Twenty silver-clad tentacles instantly shucked the burning Nar out of his space suit and tossed the garment in a flaming arc into the pool. The Nar who was left standing there in his yellow skin wore a portable touch sleeve, the kind that outdoor crews used to communicate with each other by radio.

The sleeves were both sender and receiver, output and feedback. Wearing them, despite the complaint of some aesthetes of coldness and lack of nuance, the twenty Nar of the work crew were effectively linked into a single extended organism that thought, felt, and acted as one. And, if one theory about cross-connections in the Nar nervous system was correct, they were seeing with one another's eyes as well.

The bare Nar immediately took a new place in the pattern of decapod chessmen where he would be shielded from thrown objects. The aggregate organism learned quickly. Subsequent flung bottles of alcohol or corrosives were snatched out of the air and set gently down or, if they were flaming, doused in the pool.

One of the missile throwers was Eena. Bram, lying helpless, saw her light the wick of the composite bomb she had been molding and, despite the handicap of her half-grown flipper, chuck it high over the toiling mass of decapods and humans.

Bram, every nerve taut, waited for the explosion that would kill or maim everyone in the room, Nar and human alike, but a dozen silver sleeves rose out of the turmoil, caught the object, snuffed the fuse, and passed it along over everyone's head to be deposited carefully in a safe spot.

The phalanx of Nar had chewed halfway through the human ranks by now. Scores of trussed people lay in rows, ankles and wrists lashed together to turn them into convenient basketlike objects to be carried away. Penser's rear guard was turning into a panic-stricken rabble that fragmented and tried to escape through the inner chambers.

Penser himself was backing away from the advancing Nar, arms raised as if to ward off a nightmare. The Nar weren't paying any special attention to him. It was doubtful that they knew who he was. At the rate they were working, it would be another few minutes before they got around to him.

"No," Penser said, as if he were speaking to children. "The universe belongs to humankind. Can't you see that?"

He began edging sideways along the outer wall, skirting the struggling mass. He was not an object of immediate concern to the Nar, since he was not attacking them.

Bram watched his crablike progress. Penser seemed to be mumbling to himself. His eyes were half closed and his face even puffier than usual from the powder the Nar had scattered. Bram wondered what the powder could be. It was not totally disabling, as one would expect of the choice of a chemical pacifier when the stakes were so desperate; it was simply a low-level inconvenience to humans, intended to make the Nar's work easier. Probably, Bram decided, the powder was simply the first harmless irritant the Nar docking crew could grab from their own food stores or cleaning supplies; Nar proteins could be murder on human beings, and vice versa. Some of it, he knew from the way his eyes and nose were stinging, must have gotten to him.

Penser paused for a moment to survey the bloodless battle. Tears ran down his doughy cheeks from the chemical irritant, and his lips were pursed in disapproval.

"The universe must be cleansed, you see," he said in clear, reasonable tones. "Surely everyone understands that. It must be purged of the foul corruption of other life. Their worlds must be cauterized. The universe must be purified before I may possess it."

Nobody except Bram was paying attention to him. The Nar would not have distinguished Penser's ramblings from the general human babble in the chamber.

Bram saw a man who was disintegrating before his eyes but whose pieces were still held approximately together by the glue of long habit. It all must have been more than Penser could bear. Penser's insane vision was crumbling around him. He had seen twenty ordinary Nar workmen, using improvised tactics and with no other tools than their sleeve links, cordage, and other everyday equipment, destroy his empire before it could get started.

What, Bram wondered, would the wrath of the entire Nar commonwealth have been if it could have been brought to bear here?

Penser had picked up a knife somewhere, a great sharp thing with a blade as long as his forearm. What could he have wanted it for? He had seen how easily the Nar had disarmed his followers.

Bram watched as Penser reached the lenticel and hoisted himself up onto its broad sill. The modified gas-exchange pore was deeply inset, and if the Nar noticed him, he must have seemed to be another human looking for a place to get out of the fight. For a moment Penser stood there, flooded from behind by light, and watched the destruction of his dream with dead, meaningless eyes.

By the time Bram realized what Penser intended to do, it was too late. "Stop him!" he bellowed, but the Nar weren't listening to human voices.

Abruptly, Penser whirled and plunged the blade of his knife into the patch over the lenticel membrane. A Nar detatched himself from the linked group and galloped on five legs toward the lenticel, but as quick as he was, he could not reach it in time.

There was a howl of escaping air and the raucous bray of flapping membrane. Everything must have happened in a moment, but to Bram it had the measured eeriness of a dream.

First Penser's arm—the one holding the knife—was sucked through the puncture up to the shoulder. There was a brief delay while the rip enlarged. The trumpet blare of membrane edges climbed shrieking up the scale. Then the shoulder and head popped through, followed by the other shoulder and arm. Penser's broad hips were next to get stuck. There was a brief razz of tearing membrane, and the rest of him whipped through and was gone.

The Nar who arrived then was in danger of being caught in the screaming hurricane himself. Bram saw him cling to the lenticel frame with seven tentacles while three more limbs slapped another seal over the gap. The whistle of air stopped. The space-suited Nar pressed his waistplate against the membrane, trying to see out. If Penser's body could be seen, tumbling through space, it would be rapidly dwindling. Bram wondered if it would ever be recovered.

Penser's dream of possessing the universe was over. The universe had possessed him instead.

Why had he committed that last mad act? Bram tried to puzzle it out. Penser could not have hoped to kill the Nar, most of whom still had their space suits on. He could only have killed himself and his followers. Perhaps, like a child with a broken toy, he had tried to pull down the remnants of his dream in a rage.

Or perhaps he was mad enough by that time for his overloaded brain to tell him that he was escaping that way—as if he could breathe vacuum.

Or perhaps he wasn't thinking at all; maybe it was only

a random act of mischief and destruction by a man who had always been a vessel of death.

Only a few Nar were left in the chamber, mopping up, tying up the last prisoners. The rest had departed to round up the humans who had fled and most likely to liberate their Nar brethren who had barricaded themselves behind vacuum.

Two of the remaining Nar were standing over the outstretched body of Voth, their limbs folded, communicating—if they were talking at all—through their radio sleeves. Bram could not read their posture.

One of them came over to examine him. Bram was a loose end. He had been tied up when they had arrived.

The tall shape loomed over him. Bram looked up into the dispassionate saucer eyes. "You mustn't think that all human beings are responsible," Bram said in the purest Small Language he could utter.

The Nar turned away. He was not going to bother to talk to the animals.

CHAPTER 12

The sea of flesh parted before Bram and closed up again behind him as he and the other prisoners were herded forward. His legs ached; he'd been walking for miles through the crowd. The walls of livid tentacles rose on either side to let the procession of dispirited humans and their grim Nar escort pass, then settled back into the seething golden tide to resume the linkage that was turning the race of Nar into one vast interconnected organism.

The hard-packed sand of the cleared lane was cool and gritty under Bram's bare feet. He raised his eyes and tried to peer past the living palisade. He could see no end to flesh, except for a hint of dark ocean in the distance, where the shoreline indented the boundaries of this awesome convocation.

By now, he estimated, the immense circular pulsing mass must contain more than a billion individuals and it was still growing, as fliers, ground vehicles, and watercraft deposited more Nar at its perimeter.

The weeping girl trudging along beside him stumbled, and Bram reached out to catch her. "Easy," he said.

347

"I'm all right," she said. "I only stubbed my toe." She turned a tear-streaked face to him. "You're Mim's friend, aren't you—Bram?"

He took a closer look at her. She was a solid, rosy-limbed young woman with a round serious face, now puffy with misery, and thick untidy swirls of bright yellow hair. Her name escaped him. "Uh, you're . . ."

"Ang," she supplied. "I was part of the string quartet that was going to Juxt One."

"Yes, of course."

"Why are we here, Bram? This is some sort of trial, isn't it?"

"Not exactly," he hedged. "Not in the human sense. The Nar want to understand what happened, and decide how they feel about it."

"But I didn't have anything to do with it," she wailed. "We were practicing in one of the spare chambers, when those . . . those Penser people broke in and ordered us to go with them. They—they *shoved* Kesper, our violist, when he didn't move fast enough for them. It isn't—isn't *fair* for the Nar to blame us!"

Bram said lamely, "The Nar haven't made any distinctions among us yet. I suppose it's hard for them to understand how one group of humans could coerce another. So for now, everyone who was aboard the tree is a part of . . . this."

He tried to conceal his dismay as he looked around at the throng moving past them. Penser's people were here and there among them, tending to keep apart—even from one another, as if they were ashamed to be seen in the company of their former accomplices. The colonists clustered together in small, stunned groups for mutual comfort. But the vast majority were people who simply had been visitors to the tree—friends and gene kin from the planet's human compounds who'd had the misfortune to attend the *bon voyage* party.

His gaze passed over a number of litters that were held high aloft in the raised tentacles of Nar attendants—people who had been injured in the fighting aboard the tree and who had not yet recovered sufficiently to walk. Most of those were Penser's followers.

He also spotted Marg, being carried in a chair sling rigged on a three-legged walker; a silent Nar with its upper tentacles tightly closed in an aloof vertical bundle was leading the little biomachine on a rope. Orris, a wiry jumping jack in grimy shorts and singlet, danced around the walker, keeping close. Marg slumped in her seat, wan and listless. She had lost the blastocyst implant during the retaking of the tree, Bram knew.

"How much further do we have to walk?" said an ashen-faced man limping along next to Bram and Ang. He was middle-aged and not very fit, by the look of his paunch. Bram saw the sweat trickling down the flabby cheeks, though the principal sun had not yet climbed high enough in the violet sky to make the day hot.

"We must be getting close to the center," Bram said. "You can ask for a litter if you need one."

The man glanced at the litters bearing the injured combatants. A look of distaste crossed his face. "Have them carry me? No thanks. I'll get there under my own power."

He squared his shoulders and put on a burst of speed that pulled him ahead of Bram and the girl, but he couldn't have been able to maintain the pace for very long, because they overtook him shortly thereafter. Chin thrust out, he pretended not to see them at first, but soon gave it up and fell in step with them again. When he caught his breath, he introduced himself.

"Theron's the name," he said. "Theron Chen-martiz Tewart. Maybe you recognize the internomen. I have a demiclone on the council."

Bram diplomatically acknowledged recognizing the name. The council's Chen-martiz was a blustery fellow who hogged meetings with long, pompous speeches of vague purpose.

Theron turned a plump, pleading face to Bram. "It must be some kind of mistake. I'm very well thought of in the Compound. My Nar supervisor thinks the world of me. He's *said* so, more than once. He's told me they *depend* on me to keep my section of the Works humming. They can't think I have anything to do with *that* rabble!"

He jerked a thumb toward the litters carrying the disabled Penserites. Bram saw Fraz, head bandaged and face blistered from the effect of his own firebottles, raise himself on one elbow, stare blankly at the horde of moving humans that he was a part of, then sink listlessly back.

Ang was weeping again. "Why did those awful people have to h-*hurt* Nar?"

"They'll be punished," Theron said, his voice rising shrilly. "The guilty ones will be sorted out and punished, and then things will get back to normal."

Bram said nothing. There was no point in frightening them further. It was impossible to believe that this extraordinary convocation of the Nar race had been called to concern itself with questions of individual guilt. By now that vast congregation must have shared every scrap of background information about every human here, including their pedigrees all the way back to gene assembly. Theron's supervisor would be out there somewhere, as would Ang's childhood tutors.

Bram's throat choked up; his own touch brothers would be out there, submerged in the collective consciousness, a few billionths of the whole. He swallowed hard as he thought of Voth. The universe had become strange now that it no longer contained the being who had raised him. He thought he had been prepared, in his human bones, to lose Voth one day—but not in a manner that deprived Voth's life of its final flowering.

He marched wearily forward, watching the yellow carpet of decapods peel back to let the bedraggled human host through. No, the Nar, in the awful grandeur of their deliberations, would not be concerned with anything as petty as vengeance.

Or forgiveness.

Centuries earlier, such a convocation had been called to consider the creation of man. And the Nar had concluded that it was their obligation to the vanished race whose works, in bioengineering and the basic sciences, had profited them so greatly. Now the debt had been paid. And repaid.

Now the question would be, what is the nature of this alien race we have fostered, and what is their place among us?

An image came unbidden to him: an image from his work at the biocenter with his touch associates. In the laboratory, when a culture went bad, you didn't bother to pick through it to retain individual organisms. You dumped the whole tray.

The Chen-martiz demiclone, Theron, marched stubbornly along at Bram's side, still justifying himself to the empty air. "They can't possibly blame all of us for the actions of a few—why, most of them were foreigners from Juxt One anyway! We'll simply explain the situation to them and set things right."

The path before them started to slope upward, and the damp sand under Bram's feet was replaced by something hard and smooth. Fused glass.

He raised his eyes to the summit of the tremendous structure whose sweeping contour made its own horizon—a horizon that was delineated by the overlapping blanket of Nar spreading over the craterlike rim.

The people around Bram began to hang back, and Bram had to force himself not to drag his own feet. A whimper escaped the blonde girl. Even Theron was subdued enough to cease his chatter.

They had arrived at their destination.

The ancient vitreous bowl had rested on the tidal flats since before the dawn of Nar history. No one knew its origins, though it was generally believed that the surrounding skirt had accreted gradually, through many generations, as the numbers of the Nar increased. The central cup itself was more than a mile in diameter arid could contain two or three million individuals. Once it must have held the entire Nar race.

Now that was no longer possible. But ancestral custom dies hard. The packed, intertwined assembly overflowed the broad rim and spilled across the denuded landscape to make a circle with a diameter of more than twenty miles. A billion folk had become one at this time-hallowed site.

Spaced around the great, throbbing perimeter were scribes, each lending a spare limb to the sleeve transmitters that linked them to the edges of similar gatherings all over the Father World, its inhabited moons, and the nearer planets.

The scribes were living conduits who transmitted the sense of the convocation through their averaged tactile impressions. The chroniclers at the other end became the boundaries of new circles of communion that washed inward in slow, lapping tides of cilia movement. But there was feedback as well. The tides washed back to dilute and modify original apperceptions, until gradually a grand racial consensus could emerge.

Two-way communion, of course, was impractical for the more distant worlds of the companion sun, where the time lag—even for radio waves traveling at the speed of light—began to be measured in hours rather than minutes. And for the colonized stars, a true exchange would mean a delay of years. Those distant outposts would receive touch transcriptions only. But their populations were still scanty compared to the billions of the inner system, and the power of the consensus would carry them along.

Even with modern technology to help, the size of the great primary convocation stretched ancestral custom to its limits. No human gathering—even one of only a few hundred individuals—could have achieved such intimacy through eye contact and vocal communication alone.

But information content in the Great Language was high. Its richness and nonlinear nature more than compensated for the relative sluggishness of those peristaltic ripples of meaning and allusion that took so many minutes to sweep across the packed miles.

The activities of the entire Nar commonwealth of planets would grind to a halt while the deliberations went on. The billions of participants would not eat, would not leave their gathering places. Those who could not attend—mostly because they could not be spared from vital caretaker functions—would be glued to their tactile receivers, adding to the brew of communion through a nexus of averaging computers.

But Nar were never in a hurry. Their civilization would skip a beat while they attended to this matter, then resume its stately tread.

Bram paused at the rim of the bowl and let the rest of the crowd stream past him while he looked out over the living skin that covered the earth. He could see the whole panorama from here, all the way to the horizon. The tesselated ranks of Nar tiled the landscape in an intricate mosaic until distance made them merge. The arrival of the humans in the inner circle was causing reticulated patterns of purple lines to spread outward in concentric rings, as the undersides of tentacles briefly flashed. Bram wondered if the Nar, with their crosslinked senses, were actually seeing what the inner witnesses were conveying by touch and chemical tags alone. No human could ever really know.

He remembered being brought here as a child by Voth to see the great bowl. It had been part of his education. The landscape had been empty then—there had not been one of these great assemblies during Bram's lifetime. Only a few isolated parties of bathers—both Nar and human—had been in view that day, on their way to the beaches some miles beyond. Voth had introduced him to one of the curators, who had shown them around until Voth had seen that the little boy was getting bored; he had bought Bram a sweet then—one of the polysugar confections that were safe for humans to eat—and flagged down an excursion beast to the oceanfront, and they too had gone swimming.

Bram squinted at the band of sparkling water in the distance. The shoreline itself was farther away than it had been during his childhood—pushed back by the expanding system of dikes that held the natal ocean at bay and created the new tidal pools needed by a growing population.

A shadow fell across his face. It was Orris in his grimy singlet, smelling of sweat. Bram couldn't blame him; he was a little ripe himself after being cooped up during the trip back from space.

"Think there'll be showerbaths for us down in there?" Orris asked peevishly. "And maybe a place to wash our clothes?"

Bram looked down past the inner slope of the bowl where Orris was pointing. An inner enclosure of about an acre had been fenced off. Bram saw a circle of benches facing outward, and rows of curtained booths. Some humans were already seated, and there were the tiny dentiform figures of Nar bailiffs moving among the temporary pavilions. "I'm sure they've made some provision for us," he said. "This may go on for days."

"Days!" Orris exclaimed.

"The accused won't be expected to fast with their judges," Bram said with a sudden bitterness that caught him by surprise. He squinted at the bright canopies below, and went on in a more moderate tone. "They realize we'll need to eat and sleep. Those will be cooktents, sanitary facilities, sleeping booths."

"I don't care about myself," Orris said. "It's Marg I'm worried about. She's not in good shape. She'll need privacy, a chance to lie down when she gets tired." His eyes shifted. "She lost the baby, you know."

"I heard that. I'm sorry, Orris."

"Will they let us have a replacement blastocyst, do you think? I suppose we lost our place on the Juxt One list."

Bram mumbled something vague and noncommittal. But he was appalled at his friend's evasion of reality.

Didn't Orris realize that there would never be a shipload of human colonists going to Juxt One again? That human fertility itself would now be evaluated? The easy trust between the Nar and their creations was gone. At best, human beings would have to be restricted, isolated from Nar society, their numbers allowed to dwindle to a manageable level.

At worst . . .

Bram shuddered, seeing again his biologist's image of the dumped tray, the regretful termination of an experiment gone wrong.

He shook off the idea. The Nar were compassionate. Surely, whatever the outcome of this planetwide day of wrath, the existing human beings would be allowed to live out their remaining lives—under supervision and restraint. And if the Nar were generous, perhaps they would even permit the existence of future human beings in small numbers, as curiosities or objects of study, like the dangerous beasts that survived in their zoos.

His eyes were suddenly stinging. Surely, he thought, the human species need not vanish from the universe a second time!

He looked at the straggling file of humans as they picked their way down the slope of the bowl. He hoped they would behave well in the time of judgment to come. He willed them fiercely to understand that they were not there to justify themselves individually, any more than germs in a culture were asked by the pathologist which ones of them were likely to be infectious. The Nar, in this agonized effort at racial comprehension, would consider all these frightened people as a unit. The actions of Pite, who had murdered Voth, would weigh in that collective scale along with the actions of Ang, whose crime had been to play the violin.

His lips tightened with purpose. "Orris," he began.

"Excuse me," Orris said. "I don't want to get separated from Marg."

Orris scrambled down the glassy slope to catch up with the tripedal walker that was carrying Marg. Bram saw him skid to a stop, arms flailing, to avoid bowling over the little biomachine, then fall in beside it with a shambling pace. Orris leaned over to say something, but Marg did not look up.

The last stragglers were flowing past Bram in a trickle. The gap in the solid blanket of Nar was closing behind them, a narrowing furrow between the yellow ramparts of tentacles. A family group went by—a man and a woman dragging a little towheaded girl by the hand. They quickened their steps, not wanting to be left behind. The man glanced at Bram with a look of raw despair. Perhaps he was wondering why Bram was standing there.

A decapod came along, gently urging Bram forward with a fanning out of his upper tentacles. Bram shrugged in an unconscious analog of the gesture, then realized that this Nar was unused to humans, and that the little pantomime of compliance had meant nothing to it.

"All right, I go," he said in the Small Language, and went to join the others.

"There is a sorrow," whispered the little loudspeaker on the top of the post. "There is a regret."

Bram craned his neck to see who the loudspeaker was talking about. It was the second day, and like most of the other humans in the central pen, he was sitting in the circle of outward-facing seats. The weather had held, which was fortunate for the humans. Bram had the distinct feeling that the solid parquetry of Nar, which was all that could be seen in any direction, would not have noticed even the most pelting of spring rains in the intensity of their preoccupation.

A few yards away, he found a small salient of three or four Nar who had stretched themselves toward the fence. The human who had drawn their attention was Eena. She looked even more emaciated than usual. Her ribs stood out plainly under the thin stuff of her upper garment, and her spine traced a series of knobs down to her fleshless hips. She had left her seat to press herself against the grillwork of the corral. She was hanging from the fence with both hands—the normal-size one and the miniature claw of her still half-regrown arm. She was talking earnestly to her interrogators in a voice that was too low for Bram to distinguish the words.

". . . expresses a would-that-it-had-not-been," the loudspeaker struggled on with an approximation in the Small Language of the human idea of repentance. "He pleads that he lived in a false reality constructed of words; that when he saw death he understood that death was not a word, but he remained compelled by fear of what his new brotherlings might think . . ."

The Nar interpreter had gotten Eena's gender wrong—the average Nar had little appreciation of the fact that humans had two permanent sexes—but it wasn't a bad way to put it. "Why did I ever get mixed up with that Pite?" Eena had complained to Bram when they had been thrown together in the food line the day before. "All that talk about human destiny—and all he wanted to do was hurt things. He used to leave me all black and blue sometimes."

The running transcript that the Nar had so scrupulously provided did little to describe what was really happening in the immense composite nervous system that surrounded the human enclosure. Bram knew that if he were to get up and walk around the perimeter, each of the other little loudspeakers would be saying something different, depending on the immediate perceptions of the Nar providing the commentary. Only when this particular scrap of import had traveled through billions of nervous systems and been changed by them would it have meaning.

It was, Bram thought, as if one tried to deduce the shape of an ocean by the waves it deposited at one's feet.

By now, most of the humans had stopped listening consciously to the soundposts. The half-heard murmurings were only the play of the surf, and the prisoners kept their attention on the immense brooding deep around them, as if by staring hard enough they could tell what it contained.

Bram looked around again to try to find Kerthin. He located her a hundred feet away, sitting by herself, her eyes fixed rigidly ahead. She avoided him and everybody else. Bram could not tell whether her behavior was caused by shock, shame, or anger. All he knew was that she had withdrawn totally into herself.

The Nar appeared to have finished with Eena. She turned away from the fence, spotted Bram, and came over. "They wanted to know how I felt," she said. "They know I was one of the ones who manufactured explosive pots for Penser." The embryonic arm made an unconscious half-gesture to conceal itself. "But they don't seem to be mad at me or anything."

"No, they wouldn't be," he said.

"What're they *thinking*?" she said, with a nervous glance at the tiers of overlapping tentacles.

"It's impossible to say."

"You can tell, Bram," she said in a wheedling tone.

"Everybody says you know how to read their machines and everything."

He shook his head. "It's not the same thing."

Eena glanced a few seats away at Ang, who had been staying in Bram's vicinity since their arrival, and dismissed her as not being important. "When it's your turn, you could put in a good word for me," she said, leaning forward.

"Eena, it wouldn't make any difference."

She tossed her head in the direction of the inner enclosure. "We could go in one of the booths. What do you say?"

"Eena, it's not necessary. I'll say something in your favor if you want."

"It's the arm, isn't it?" she said ruefully. "You don't have to tell me, I know it puts you off."

"That's not it at all," he protested.

"Never mind, I understand. Pite didn't want to have anything to do with me, either, after I came out of the regeneration clinic. Of course it was only a bud then. I told him it would grow back all the way, that it was only a matter of time. He said we had to dedicate ourselves to the cause, that there was no time for anything personal any more, but I know he was sneaking around with some of those dewey-eyed woman recruits."

She flexed the little arm and stared at it thoughtfully.

"Another couple of years till it's full-grown, they said. You'd think they could find a way to speed it up."

"Eena—"

"You're still mooning over Kerthin, aren't you? Listen, Bram, she's not worth it, believe me. She was just using you. I'm telling you that even though she's a friend of mine. You're better off without her."

"I don't have much say in the matter anyway, it seems."

What he meant to say was that Kerthin seemed to have taken that decision into her own hands. For himself, Bram did not know what he thought. The image of Voth's sprawled body kept coming between Bram and any thoughts of Kerthin, but the sight of her stiff, withdrawn figure sitting alone on the bench made him feel awful.

Eena misunderstood him. She looked out over the horizon-falling presence outside the penned acre and bit her lip. "Yeah, I guess anything like that may not matter any more after this." She squeezed Bram's shoulder with her good hand. "See what you can do for us, Bram. Not just me. I mean all of us."

She turned away abruptly. Bran watched her pick her way along the curving row of benches until she came to where Kerthin was sitting. He saw Eena sit next to Kerthin, lay a hand on her arm, and try to talk to her. Kerthin listened dully, said nothing, and after a while got up and left.

A rustling noise caught Bram's attention. A few yards away, another small outcropping of Nar stretched itself forward in response to a human who had approached the fence. Bram recognized Theron, the middle-aged man who had denounced the Penserites so vehemently. Theron sucked in his gut and spoke in a loud, clear voice that carried to where Bram sat.

"My name is Theron Chen-martiz Tewart, and you can check my record if you like. I've never caused the slightest trouble, and you can ask my supervisor—"

He stopped as he suddenly realized that his Nar supervisor was certainly out there somewhere, his individuality diluted by the billions of vicarious tentacles that filtered his sensory input.

"Trl-chr-trl," the man pleaded. "You know how hard I've worked trying to get ahead. I've risen higher at the starchworks than any human has done before me. All the Nar there respect me. The Chen-martiz internomen is an eminent one in the Compound." He thumped his chest. "Why would *I* want to be part of some lunatic scheme to change the natural order of things?"

He bowed his head. There was no direct response from the proxies communicating his words, but perhaps somewhere in the sea of flesh Trl-chr-trl was radiating a small circular eddy of sympathy and confirmation that would modify the perceptions of the beings around him until it was finally submerged by other eddies arising from other centers.

A young colonist shouldered Theron aside and addressed the tangled node of decapods before it could withdraw. "We were *prisoners* in that farm chamber where you found us," he said in a voice trembling with emotion. "We were victims of Penser's bullies just as much as the Nar who were attacked."

Bram shifted his attention to another developing bulge in the batter of golden flesh. Spak, the bumpy-skulled thug, edged reluctantly forward to face it. They had called him by name. To Bram's astonishment, Spak broke down and wept. "I'm sorry," he kept repeating. "I'm sorry."

A woman with gray-streaked hair shook off the hand of the man beside her and took Spak's place, her face red with embarrassment. "You can't blame them too much," she said. "Some of the things Penser said sounded good, even to the rest of us. Like taking pride in being human. Like having a place in the cosmos we could call our own.

Maybe some of them didn't realize where all those fine words would lead or how far Penser was prepared to go. I've been an Ascendist all my life, and while I don't hold with Penser's methods, I share some of his ideals."

A gasp came from Ang. Bram got up and sat beside her. "It's all right," he said. "Maybe they ought to hear it."

A ripple of interest went through the packed tribunal, visible as a froth of lavender across the amber surface. A single Nar heaved its central cup above the mass, its five arms stretched to maintain contact. Bram had the impression that it had been deputized by the entire assembly—that it was not just questioning the gray-haired lady on its own.

"We know of your brothers," it said in excellent Inglex. "They are something like an extended touch group, are they not? But do you say that their views differ?"

Haltingly, the woman tried to explain about political factions and got tangled up in a complicated exposition of the differences between Ascendists and Resurgists, Partnerites and Integrationists and Schismatists. The man she had been sitting with got up and came to her aid. The soundposts were generating a fantastic, garbled version of what they were saying.

Around the enclosure a half-dozen other people of various political persuasions gathered their courage and approached the barrier to add their own explanations, making matters worse.

"It's awful!" Ang whispered to Bram. "They're quarreling about a lot of hairline distinctions that don't *mean* anything. What are the Nar going to think of us?"

"Maybe it's all for the best," Bram said.

"How can you say that?"

"It'll give the Folk some inkling of the extent of the yearning of human beings for a place of our own in the universe, make them see that it didn't *have* to express itself Penser's way."

The loudspeaker on the post nearest them sighed on in the soft suspirations of the Small Language. ". . . they differ in their apartness. The one wishes to share in the great concordance though he is mute, the other to withdraw from the sight of the Folk, the next to seize like an impatient fingerling a greater share of goods and habitat . . ."

"I've got to try to make them understand," Ang said faintly. She stood up, her rosy cheeks gone pale, and made her way to the fence.

"I—I'm a maker of music," she began in a small clear voice. "I never thought very much about all these things you've been hearing. I never wanted to take things or smash things or demand things. All I ever wanted to do was to make the beautiful sounds that Original Man left for us in his Message. I don't know if you understand what music means to most of us, but we're all born with it inside us. It's like—like a language. We were learning more about it all the time. We carved the old instruments out of Earth's wood. I wanted to go to Juxt One because I wanted to give those sounds to people there who had never heard them firsthand."

They questioned her gently with a small part of their joint consciousness, while along the perimeter of the pen other outcroppings of decapods continued examining other humans.

"But could you not be happy here? There are more humans here with whom to share your art."

"It's a newer human society on Juxt, away from the old constraints. There's more *room* for people, and I thought that might change the people themselves. That humans might feel freer to be humans—that the music might be freer, too."

"But the practice of the human arts is encouraged by us here on the Father World."

"I know. It's just that—oh, I don't know *what* I mean!" Ang was close to tears. She excused herself with the remnants of her Nar-instilled courtesy and sat down.

Bram became aware that while Ang had been talking, other members of the string quartet had been called. He could see Kesper, the violist, some distance away, gesticulating earnestly. The Nar immediately opposite seemed to be quite interested in what he was saying. Bram had no clue as to what it was all about; the soundpost nearest Kesper doubtless was giving an approximate version.

More names were called. The pace seemed to be speeding up. Every human being in the enclosure was known personally to at least several Nar out there, and the aggregate of those crosslinked nervous systems was able to shuffle names better than any computer for whatever purpose it chose.

Bram tried to find a pattern in the types of people being summoned to the fence, but gave it up. They seemed to represent a cross section of human society—from colonists still clinging to the tattered remains of cloaks and tabards made from the leaves of their tree to once-fashionable Resurgists from the Compound, wearing the bedraggled finery of Earth's presumed past.

"What's happening?" Ang asked.

"I don't know. There's some kind of change going on out there."

"Wh-what kind of change?"

"Don't you see how the color's deepening? There's more

purple in it. That's caused by tentacles flattening out more—showing more of the underside along the edge."

"But what does it mean?"

"In this case," he said slowly, "I think it signifies empathy."

"I—I don't understand."

"Haven't you ever noticed that when two people want to open out to one another, they tend to show it by the way they hold their bodies. It's the same with the Nar. Unconsciously they're saying, see, I'm offering you a greater communicating surface."

He grinned at her suddenly. "I think the Nar have decided they want to get to know human beings better."

The declarations went on through the long day and into the time of double shadows. They seemed to feed on each other as more and more people, not waiting to be summoned, were moved to explain themselves.

The encircling tide of life bulged at a dozen places to hear them. A number of times Bram saw decapods from the outer layers pick their way through the interlocking pattern of tentacles and take their places in the front row of examiners. What this special interest signified, he did not know.

Twice, Nar bailiffs brought pails of food and ladled it out to the humans where they sat. The benches stayed crowded; people were unwilling to leave to be fed at the kitchen tents.

Bram sipped from his bowl, hardly tasting the thin puree. He turned to Ang and said, "It's going well, think."

She, too, could sense the changed mood of the Nar. "You don't think we'll be punished?"

"There was never a question of that. The Nar don't like to cause pain. They imagine it too well."

No, he thought, whatever has to be done, they will do it painlessly.

But now, he dared to hope, perhaps a limited number of babies would be allowed—to maintain the Compound and its microcosm of human culture at a reduced population level. More supervision and more privileges.

Orris leaned over the back of his seat and said anxiously, "You really think it's going well?"

"Don't get your hopes up, but yes, I do."

"Marg wants to testify."

"Is she up to it?"

"You know Marg when she's made up her mind to do something. Nothing can stop her. She's been awfully depressed, but now she says she thinks someone ought to let the Nar know about how humans feel about parenthood—about raising our own children, not just being part of a pool for genetic constructs."

Orris was still pursuing his fantasy of unlimited reproduction. Bram did not want to dash his hopes. "Well, it can't do any harm," he said.

"I'd better get back to her. I don't like to leave her alone too long."

With a nervous backward glance at the penitents lined up along the fence, Orris hopped away toward the rows of privacy booths in the interior of the enclosure. Bram watched him lift up a flap and duck inside.

For the last hour, the Nar had been summoning Penserites. A few of Penser's lieutenants clung dully to their revolutionary slogans, though disavowing violence, but most were appalled by the enormity of what they had done, and their shamefaced contrition showed.

Fraz, when he had seen how things were going, had not waited to hear his name called. He had risen painfully from his invalid's litter with the help of a couple of colonists and hobbled to the barrier with a little support. Now, leaning heavily on Eena's good arm, he addressed himself to the jumble of eyes and tentacles.

"We were wrong," he said hoarsely. He looked round to see who was listening and Bram had a glimpse of red lips writhing within a scraggly black fringe. "We did a terrible thing. Penser misled us . . . but I'm not making any excuses. We shouldn't have listened to him."

He swayed, and Eena propped him up, bracing her hip against his.

"All we wanted was one little moon we could call our own," he said brokenly. "A home in the universe for human beings. But we shouldn't have tried to take it by force. We should have tried to make you understand!"

Eena led him away. Bram could see tears running down her face.

A stir of interest passed along the benches, and Bram saw that Pite had been summoned to the fence. Pite was someone that all of the colonists and their unlucky visitors recognized by now.

Pite swaggered to the grille, his thumbs hooked into his belt. His beard had regrown itself into a bristly half-inch stubble that gave his face a fuzzy indefinite shape.

"It wasn't our policy to hurt tenlegs, or human beings either," he said cooly in response to a question from the decapod who was the momentary proxy of the assembly. "It was the fault of those who resisted us. They gave us no choice. It was they who were the cause of the violence."

Pite was close enough for Bram to hear him directly. The little loudspeaker at the moment was expressing some abstraction of the merged Nar consciousness. The Nar who was examining Pite stretched toward him in a reflex of communication, then recoiled before touching him.

"To resist the destiny of man is a crime," Pite went on steadily. "The universe belongs to us by right. Those who resisted brought their deaths upon themselves."

"Why is he *saying* those awful things?" Ang asked, squirming in her seat. "He'll get them angry."

"No," Bram said. "He won't get them angry."

Another front-row Nar withdrew a tentacle from the latticed mass to coil it in agitation around the empty air and framed a question in stilted Chin-pin-yin. Pite stared blankly; the Nar received a correction through his leeward limbs and rephrased the query in Inglex:

"Surely the parturient Voth-shr-voth on the eve of his great change would not have resisted your wishes . . ."

"If you're talking about the tenleg biotechnician who was supposed to get the tree moving for us, he didn't move fast enough to suit me. He needed to be taught a little respect. How did I know he couldn't take it?"

A vast yellow and violet ripple spread around the rim of the enclosure and receded into the distance until it was invisible. Bram could smell the acrid tang of revulsion hanging in the sir. It was part of the Great Language, a faint trace that even a human could pick up subliminally if he was enwrapped by a Nar. Here, in the middle of a jammed throng of Nar sharing a common emotion, the odor was almost palpable.

Ang knew what it meant. It must have called up childhood memories of her own adoptive tutor, as it had for Bram.

"What is that fool *doing* to us?" she said in a tiny squeak. "Can't somebody make him stop?"

Pite went on, oblivious of the distaste he was arousing.

". . . we would have succeeded, too, if it hadn't been for the spineless cowards among us—and the traitors who stabbed Penser in the back." He was gaining courage and self-importance with every unreprimanded moment. "They'll be dealt with when the time comes. And the time *will* come. We'll rise again. Penser may be dead but his spirit lives on . . ."

Even in the cowed collection of people within earshot, there were voices telling Pite to shut up. Three tight-lipped men looked at one another, then got up in unison and tried to drag Pite away from the fence. He swung and knocked one of them down. The man got up with a bloody nose and helped the other two to grab Pite's arms. Pite shrugged, gave up fighting, and let them take him away.

One of the men was burly and red-bearded. Bram was momentarily surprised when he recognized him. It had been Jao.

There were more ripples in the sea of Nar, retreating gradually to the horizon, and another odor replaced the acrid one. A memory came to Bram of himself as a very small child, unable to make himself stop misbehaving and trying to understand why he had saddened Voth.

Sorrow. Disappointment.

Around the rim of the enclosure, all the loudspeakers suddenly went silent.

Ang reached blindly for Bram's hand and squeezed it so hard that it hurt. "It's all over, isn't it?" she said. "We've lost."

As the primary shadows lengthened into the half-night and the moons began to show themselves, people continued to try to attract the attention of the brooding presence around them. They stood and pleaded, or harangued at length, and in one case even shouted. But there was no reaction. No Nar proxy spoke to them, and the front rank of tentacles remained unbroken.

Bram saw Marg get up, her face wan and her shoulders slumped, despite Orris's hovering effort to dissuade her. She was too far away for Bram to hear what she was saying, but after a while she threw her shoulders back and faced the unresponsive mass with something of her old self-confidence. Orris stood beside her, holding her hand through it all. After a while Marg gave up; her shoulders drooped again and she let Orris lead her away toward the central rest area.

Bram made up his mind shortly after primeset.

The lesser sun was an orange jewel in the sky, casting soft ghostly shadows and deepening the hue of the brimming tide of Nar that licked at the enclosure. The ringed human seats were half empty; people had left to be fed and to try to take some rest after the long day. Pite had not been seen again; some of the men were keeping him hidden away under guard in a privacy booth.

Bram himself had dozed off once or twice. He had not intended to join the procession to the fence. There was very little point to it, he thought, given the circumstances. But he woke from a dream in which his name was being called, softly and persistently, in the deep pure tones of the Small Language.

He looked over at the wall of shadowed tentacles beyond the fence. There was only silence there, except for the ever-present background rustle of billions of respirating bodies, like leaves in the wind.

He shivered. The temperature had dropped several degrees since the setting of the true sun. He looked around and saw the empty benches and the listless postures of those who remained. They had given up. No one had tried to talk to the Nar in the last hour or two.

Bram got up and went to the fence. There was no answering movement from the other side, no sign that anyone had noticed him.

"I am Bram," he said.

He waited several minutes and thought he heard a change in the rhythm of the vast collective bellows that closeness had made synchronous, but he might have been mistaken.

He spoke again. "I claim the attention of my touch brothers, if they are present."

There was another long wait, but this time a salient of flesh pressed itself unmistakably toward the fence. A row of mirror eyes reflected orange light toward him.

"You are that Bram who was the ward of Voth-shr-voth?"

"Yes," he replied. He was surprised that his voice was steady.

"Speak," said the low resonant tones.

"I am more than a ward of Voth-shr-voth, with touch brothers who have outgrown me as other humans have been outgrown by their touch brothers. Voth-shr-voth adopted me into his own touch group. And though I am mute in the Great Language, I claim membership in this assembly."

Some of the people drowsing on the benches noticed that a human had succeeded in initiating an exchange with the Nar, and nudged their neighbors. A couple of people ran toward the interior rest area to spread the news.

A stirring of limbs caught Bram's attention and he looked across to see an unattached Nar stilt-walking on stiffened points through the shadowed mosaic of star-shaped forms. The tall being settled down in the front row without any fuss and plugged two or three tentacles into the group.

"Hello, touch brother," the newcomer said in a familiar half-human patois.

"Tha-tha!" Bram exclaimed. Then he remembered and corrected himself. "Excuse me. Tha-shr-tha."

"We are Tha-tha and Bram," his childhood playmate said. "We swam as fingerlings together under the shelter of the same foster limb, and that cannot change."

A free tentacle extruded itself and wrapped itself around Bram's shoulders, with its final two feet coming to rest along one arm and clasping his hand. Another tentacle snaked through the grillwork of the low fence and slipped under Bram's shirt to curl around his ribs and cover his bare chest.

The familiar warmth was almost too much to bear. He knew Tha-tha was thinking the same thing, because he could feel the involuntary cilia movement trace a childish outline of Voth's name.

"Can you bear to touch me, Tha-tha?" he whispered.

"Hush, touch brother. Whatever may be, Voth's limbs lay across us."

The feather touch of the fuzzy undersurface was being modified by the input of the Nar to whom Tha-tha was connected, including Bram's original inquisitor. Bram could feel the overtones of distaste and incomprehension, and Tha-tha's own constraint in the face of it.

But for whatever it was worth, the surrounding Nar were also straining to accommodate Tha-tha's perceptions of Bram. Bram could make out secondhand traces of Tha-tha's name in the Great Language as reflected in its owner's reaction to its recognition by others. Tha-tha was very young to have been given an honorific. Bram had not seen him in recent years, but he had gathered that Tha-tha's touch symphonies had marked him as one of those prodigies who come along only once in a Nar generation.

Tha-tha's presence was only a single bucket of warmth poured into a chilly ocean, but Bram was grateful for it.

"Sesh-akh-sesh spoke of your kindness to him," the designated inquisitor said unexpectedly.

Bram remembered the trembling decapod whom Pite had turned into jelly with his electric shocks. The image had caused a flutter in the surrounding Nar that Bram could sample in Tha-tha's tentacles.

"How—how does Sesh-akh-sesh fare?" he asked, swallowing.

"He grieves." The term in the Small Language denoted a kind of funk into which the Nar sometimes sank, leaving them apathetic and incapacitated. "His touch brothers now try to heal his spirit."

"I'm sorry," Bram said miserably.

In counterpoint, Tha-tha was telling the assembly about Voth's great affection for his human adoptee, reminding them that Bram had not been responsible for Voth's death or other events on the tree. He stressed that the awful circumstances of Voth's premature dissolution had been a horror to Bram, too—insofar as human beings, whose reproduction was apart from their lives and deaths, could intuit such things.

There was no vocal transcript from the soundposts, perhaps because Tha-tha wished none, but Bram was utterly sure of the subject matter because of the traces of gross meaning he was able to fit together from Tha-tha's tactile patterns.

Tha-tha fed him back some of the assembly's reaction,

too. But Bram was unable to make anything of the crawling sensations and the chemical astringencies except for one puzzling moment when the symbolic outline of a human—standing for himself, he was sure—tried to change its shape into the symbol of a decapod. It writhed, failed, and turned into a distorted abomination. That too dissolved, leaving an evaporating impression of a remote, monumental pity.

It was too much for him. Hot tears stung, and without pausing to weigh the consequences, he let the bitter, bottled-up truth spill out.

"No, we humans are not like the Folk. Though some of us have tried to be—with the tragic results you've seen. Our lives are short—too short for us to make our mark among the Folk—and we have not the gift of Language."

He took a deep breath and plunged recklessly on. "But we don't need your pity. Because we're not failed Nar, not imitations of you. We're the human race, and the heirs of Original Man—though part of our inheritance has been denied us!"

He felt Tha-tha's musculature tighten convulsively. A stir went through the assembly, and then a vast backwash of indulgence. Bram's sting had been received as a datum, not as an affront. The kneading pulse of Tha-tha's mantle was uncannily like a phantom echo of Voth, when the old teacher had decided to be lenient to a small alien creature who knew no better.

"Bram-bram," Tha-tha resonated with the compassion of the gathering filtering though him. "We could not fashion you to be like us, but we gave you existence."

"You gave us our existence," Bram agreed. "But you withheld our immortality."

A shiver went through Tha-tha. There was a long delay while something unnameable surged through the conclave, out to its outer edges, and to the satellite conclaves beyond, then back again, bearing the flotsam of all those decapods who had ever known anything about the creation of man.

"What is this?" Tha-tha asked, speaking for them.

Haltingly at first, then in a fluent torrent that could not be denied, Bram told them all about it.

It took a long time.

A small moon set and another rose while Bram talked. Outside the fence, the dappled expanse of Nar lifted like a tide as each separate decapod strained involuntarily to give full attention.

Within the island of humans, a crowd quickly gathered around Bram in a huge crescent as the word of what he was saying spread. The soundposts remained silent; Bram's revelations were passed along by word of mouth. Messengers ran to the inner area to carry the word to those who had not yet heard.

Man was meant to live forever.

And the secret of eternal life was locked somewhere in the dusty Message of Original Man.

Bram left nothing out. And he did not spare himself. He told his silent judges how he had deceived Voth, the being who had raised him, and how he had pursued his researches with stolen materials. He told them of Kerthin's ugly suspicions, and how he had been infected by them. And how he had withheld the knowledge of his discovery from Kerthin and Penser's other acolytes for fear of the consequences.

"Penser would have used such knowledge to inflame all mankind. But I myself came to believe that it was within the power of the Nar to confer the gift of immortality on humanity."

The assembled nation of Nar listened in silence. Bram could not tell whether they had guilty knowledge of human immortality or were learning about it for the first time.

When the first human ovum had been assembled, Voth had been the youngest of apprentices. Were other members of that long-ago touch team still alive? Still out there, listening to Bram with the rest? If so, their memories were available to the assembly.

Tha-tha oozed more of himself through the fence, enwrapping Bram more closely and amplifying his imperfect human speech for the multitude. Bram could sense his touch brother's unease, but he could not even tell if Tha-tha had known. All he knew was that Tha-tha had shared tentacles with Voth.

"You believed," Tha-tha said, cradling him, "that Voth deliberately withheld this information from you, and that the whole race of Nar kept it hidden for all the generations of man?"

"I—I did for a time," Bram replied in a shamed whisper. "I could see no other explanation. But later I came to believe that Voth and his touch brothers of long ago had simply turned away from the implications of what they found."

There was no word for "turning away" in the Small Language, but Tha-tha remembered his childhood Inglex.

"Perhaps," Tha-tha said, "they did not wish to look closely at what they had found because they feared further understanding, as one fears to put a single limb on a dangerous path because it may tempt the other limbs to follow."

"I believe that Voth had already put a foot on that path before he died," Bram said in bitter self-reproach. "He—he gave me the help I needed. He . . . looked the other way while I did things behind his back."

Again, Bram had to substitute an Inglex idiom. Tha-tha gave the decapod equivalent of a nod: a brushlike strum of encouragement.

"I think . . . Voth wished me success, so that there could be no turning back." Bram said. "But it must have been . . . painful for him to come to grips with the realization that the sentient beings he had helped to create had been condemned in all their generations to brief, unfinished lives."

"It is painful for all of us to face, Bram-bram, my brother," Tha-tha said softly.

The petals enveloping Bram conveyed a strange and complex mixture of emotions from the Nar nation beyond. The eerie realization came to Bram that it went both ways: that all the billions of intertwined Nar on this planet and its neighbor worlds were feeling his body through Tha-tha's perceptions, knowing what it was to caress a human with their tentacles.

He wondered what they could possibly glean from his mute, alien body.

When he had been a child, wrapped in the cloak of Voth's limbs and feeling the warm surges of the Great Language against his bare skin, he had sometimes believed that he was transmitting his inner thoughts through the surface of his body to Voth, just as if he were a Nar, too. Now, knowing that the eavesdropping billions could feel his every slight shiver, every droplet of perspiration, his goose bumps, the raising of each individual hair, the very pulse of blood through his capillaries, he had the same mystic illusion of tactile speech.

Understand, he willed them fiercely. *Understand!*

The crescent of humans contracted more closely around him as he went on talking. Whispered accounts passed through the crowd to the outer fringes. Bram finished by confessing his scheme to assemble the immortality virus with the clandestine help of human specialists from the Compound if that became necessary. "I believed the knowledge was forbidden," he said, "and that man would have to reach out with his own hand and pluck the gift of eternal life for himself."

He listened with his skin to the ghostly touch whispers filtered through Tha-tha, but he could not tell if he had swayed the Nar or made matters worse. He had gained their sharp attention—that he did know from the sudden stillness out across the narscape as billions of decapods forgot to breathe.

After long minutes, Tha-tha let out a protracted sigh. "We did not know, Bram," he said. "No one remembers this knowledge being shared. If Voth knew, he was the last one."

The living landscape sighed all at once. The strangeness of the moment passed.

"It is a very great burden," Tha-tha said distantly. Bram felt his touch brother's attention slip away as Tha-tha submerged himself in the mass conference.

Bram lifted his eyes above the living horizon and found the familiar constellation of the Boat. Using the point star as a reference, he located the patch of night sky that held Original Man's invisible home.

"When I was very small," he said quietly, "I dreamed of returning to the place where humanity began. And I was told that the twin barriers of time and space made such a dream forever impossible. Now, at least, time can be conquered."

He returned his gaze to the tribunal. Several score mirror-eyes changed color as they returned his stare. They could not avoid hearing him, at least.

"Whatever you decide to do about us, everything is changed now," he said. "If you allow human beings to continue to exist at all, we can never go back to being exotic seasonal blooms in your perennial society. Not now that you know, and we know, that we need not be condemned to wither and die. But be warned! If you allow humankind to reach its full potential, one day we will stand beside you as equals."

He stood breathing in the moist night air, wondering if he had gone too far. Was that gigantic entity out there now reflecting anew on the dangers of human fecundity and human aspirations?

He became aware of movement behind him and turned to see the red-maned Jao emerging from the waiting crowd. The ex-physicist was subdued, all his former ebullience drained out of him.

"I'm sorry, Bram. For everything," Jao said. "Do you understand me?"

"Yes."

"Hard feelings?"

Bram thought of Voth, lying in a puddle of violet dissolution. He blinked back the scalding tears.

"No," he said.

Jao faced the expanse of close-packed forms and bellowed at it. "Did you hear him, damn you? He's given you half of the solution, if you'll only realize it! Immortality for humans! Now the question is, what do we do with it?"

The carpet of Nar recoiled visibly at the violence of Jao's outburst, then settled down again. Some of the people around Jao began edging away.

Jao grinned through his beard. "I'm talking about your robot ramscoop that some of us ephemeral humans have been working on for you. The marvelous implement that's supposed to seed the galaxy with replicas of yourself. That's not so very different from what Original Man set out to do, is it? Life seeking to perpetuate itself when its time is ripe. Well, if it's your imperative to exist, it's ours, too. Remember *that* when you judge us. What happened on the tree was a terrible thing, and maybe the ones I'm ready to take what I have coming. But don't judge the entire human race by what a few of us did. Because what we did was only a perverted, misbegotten expression of the same impulse that's driving you ten-limbed wonders to claim your own rightful place in the universe!"

He broke off, breathing hard. "Sorry," he said with a lopsided grin at Bram. "I never learned how to be diplomatic."

Bram, standing with the warm cloak of Nar flesh draped across his shoulders, said, "It's all right. They took it. They just want to understand."

"So?" Jao said. "In that case . . ."

He turned again to the Nar assembly, hands on hips. In the first hundred yards or so, tufted humps rose and fell like wavelets as individual Nar rose up to get a good look at him through their own eyes.

"Listen to me, you lords of creation," Jao roared at them. "Eighty thousand years from now—if your precious robot probe ever reaches the center of this galaxy and you start getting radio signals from your artificial children to tell you that it worked—just remember that we humans were a part of getting it there. Maybe you'll have canceled us out by then. But by the Allfather, you'll owe us! Because the hadronic photon drive that's going to make your messenger possible was born in the human imagination. Not yours."

A soft rustle of uneasy movement spread through the expanse of Nar. Presumably those who knew the details of the probe program were explaining the hadronic photon drive to those who didn't, and it was diffusing gradually through the whole audience of laity.

Jao waited it out, his expression fierce. When he resumed, it was in a more pensive tone.

"Bram, here, told you his dream. The biggest dream that any of us had. To go home again. When I first heard it, I put it down for a kid's fantasy that he never outgrew. But I didn't know he was on the track of immortality. If human immortality is possible, then all of a sudden the long trip home becomes more possible, too."

He raised his eyes to the crowded sky and stared a long time at where the bridge of stars led to the Bonfire.

"Oh, not now," he said. "We've got a lot of work to do first. As Smeth told Bram, ramscoop robots are not for living things. And there's not much hydrogen in the void between galaxies for a ramscoop to gulp. But who cares?" His negligent shrug was probably wasted on the front-row decapods. "Those are mere details! Hell, I can think of a couple of possible ways around the problem right now. Give us *time* and we'll find a way to make that jump." Jao made a gesture that included the people who were crowding excitedly around. "We've got the motivation now. You see, Bram's given us all his dream. It can never be bottled up again. And, damnation, it's a better dream than any of the ones we've had so far. Better than the Ascendists, better than the Resurgists, and especially better than the Penserites!"

A low murmur of assent came from the human crowd.

"Bram gave you half the solution to your little dilemma, and I'm handing you the other half," Jao boomed at the Nar. "Turn your probe over to us. We'll do your work for you. We'll do it better than machines could. And when we're finished, we'll take the damn vehicle for our pay! We'll leave the galaxy and go where you won't have to worry about us. We'll go home!"

He turned to go, then checked himself. "Think about it," he said with another bold grin. "It'd be a good way of getting rid of us."

He shouldered his way through the human crowd, ignoring the attempts to ask him questions. His brows were knit in concentration, as if he were doing mathematical problems in his head. Bram could hear him muttering to himself.

After several minutes, Tha-tha spoke sadly. "It is true, then, Bram-bram? All your life you concealed a dream of going to your human home? You were not happy in your life; you felt you had no place here?"

"Yes," Bram said. "I'm no different from the others."

"Voth would have grieved for you."

"Voth understood my dream, I think. When I was small, he tried to spare me pain by discouraging it."

"It is too late for that now."

"Yes, it is."

Tha-tha held him through the long night. Bram was glad of the warmth of the velvety mantle. The lesser sun cast enough light to read by—if you didn't mind straining your eyes—but no heat.

The loudspeakers stayed off. There was no way to translate what was happening into words. Even the Nar could not have said what was starting to result from the vast exchange that was taking place now, any more than a human being could have predicted what patterns a handful of straws would make when it was cast to the ground. The individual straws might be there, fixed and immutable, but the way they would fall out after a shuffle was the sum of too many variables.

Bram felt the shifting patterns in the velvet pile, caught scraps of emotion from Tha-tha, and waited in silence.

An equally silent semicircle of waiting humans stood nearby, shivering. They probably thought that Bram could in some way follow the deliberations that were taking place—word of his prowess with touch readers had gone round the enclosure—and that they could glean some clue by watching his reactions.

"No," he had to say over and over again to those who edged forward to quiz him. "I can't tell you anything."

Sorrow, he felt, and regret and distress. But it could mean anything. Sorrow over what had happened or sorrow at what they were going to have to do about the humans. Distress over human behavior or distress at the Nar role that was now crystalizing.

And then he became aware that something new was happening.

Several times during the vigil, the carpet of Nar parted to form an aisle and let through people from outside. They were humans from the Compound—folk who had not been involved in the events in the tree.

They spoke to the assembly briefly or at length, then left while the aisle closed up behind them. They would have to walk for miles through that teeming plain back to whatever vehicles had brought them here. And the gaps and neural rerouting that they caused at this stage of the game—after deliberations had already begun—must have been troublesome for the Nar.

Bram huddled within the shelter of Tha-tha's clasp. The new arrivals could mean only one thing.

The stakes had gotten bigger. The inquiry had been widened to include the entire human race.

Mim and Olan Byr were among those who came. Olan had to be brought in on a walker guided by a solicitous Nar. He got out of the seat nimbly enough, but Bram was shocked at his appearance. Olan seemed to have aged tremendously, and he seemed very feeble.

Afterward, they came over to see him.

"Hello, Bram," Mim said. "Some people told us we'd find you here." She looked at the nest of tentacles entwining him, not at all intimidated. "Hello—Tha-tha, isn't it? I'm sorry to meet you again under these circumstances."

"It's Tha-shr-tha," Bram said apologetically.

"Oh, of course. I'm sorry."

"Hello, Mim," Tha-tha said. He did not remind her that he had been part of the group consciousness that had interrogated her a few minutes ago. "Yes, this is a time of sorrow. But I am glad to see you. Hello, Olan Byr."

Olan gave a nod of acknowledgment. The handsome face was a thinner sketch of its former self, drawn in vertical lines, and the dark sleek hair had gone white. Bram saw the quick look of affection and protectiveness from Mim.

"What are you doing here?" Bram said.

Mim answered for them both. "Nobody's sleeping tonight in the Compound. Some Nar came to fetch a few people. I guess they were mentioned here in one connection or another, and the Nar wanted to hear what they had to say. And some of us asked if we could speak, too."

"Quite a few, actually," Olan said. "Not all of them were brought inside; some of them gave depositions at the edge."

"But why?" Bram said. "You're not involved."

Olan smiled with effort. "We're all part of it, all humans. We can't hide behind our music anymore, can we? Not after this."

"What . . . what did they ask you?" Bram glanced at Tha-tha, but the mirror-eyes were reflected inward, listening to the soundless murmurs from beyond.

"They wanted to know how we felt," Mim said.

"What we live for," Olan said. "And what we hope for."

"They know Olan is our greatest musician," Mim said.

Olan gave a wry smile. "They asked me what it means to a human creative artist to die young—young to them! I told them about Mozart."

"Good-bye, Bram," Mim said. She leaned past Tha-tha's tentacles and brushed his cheek with her lips. Then she led Olan to his carryseat and got him settled. A group of about twenty was leaving. The sea of yellow flesh rolled back to pass them through, and they were gone.

Once, in the pale half-light, Bram saw Smeth. The lanky physicist was talking a mile a minute, his hands making violent gestures, his head tucked deferentially between his shoulders. He broke off a couple of times to confer with Jao, then continued with his presentation. He left immediately afterward without seeking Bram out.

Jao was called a couple of times after that to be asked some question or other. He answered laconically and returned to his seat. He did not come over to Bram to volunteer information.

After that, no one else came from the Compound and no

one else was called. Bram found himself nodding off several times. When the sky started to lighten, a number of people left their places to get something to eat. Somebody woke Bram out of a light doze and handed him a cup of something warm. He looked up, thinking for a moment that it was Kerthin, but it was the string quartet player, Ang.

"When do you think they'll decide?" she said.

"Soon."

He could feel some kind of process coming to a head through Tha-tha's blanket of cilia. For some time now the crosscurrents had been seeking to merge, and now there was a steady procession of wave fronts, tide after tide, rolling on and gathering force. He had tried several times to speak to Tha-tha, but he could get no response. Except for the activity of the inner surfaces, Tha-tha's limbs had gone slack, and he seemed to be in a sort of trance.

Dawn broke. Bright sunlight spilled over the tremendous arena, and the Nar nation, acre after acre, shook itself like an awakening waterbeast.

The little loudspeakers on their low posts hummed to life, and the humans throughout the enclosure stopped whatever they were doing and looked at them. One by one, the seated people at the rim rose to their feet.

A few preliminary warbles came through the background sizzle—the Nar equivalent of throat cleaving—but no intelligible sounds could be discerned as yet.

Tha-tha stirred to life. The deep, long rhythms of racial communion had abruptly ceased, and though Tha-tha was still plugged into the whole, the random patches of movement on his inner mantle—thinking aloud—showed that he was once more aware of his surroundings.

"Good morning, Bram," Tha-tha said, and Bram could sense a wave of compassion from him. "The time is here."

"I know," Bram said.

All the loudspeakers began to speak in one voice, first in Inglex, then in Chin-pin-yin.

"Hear us, for we would have you understand . . ."

("*Ting wo men, ni-man pi hsu dong . . .*")

"Humankind has multiplied beyond our custodianship, and the nature of man has become apparent . . ."

("*Jen djang gwe kuan-wo, shung-djir jen-chung hsien jan te . . .*")

"Therefore, this is what we have decided . . ."

"Congratulations," Bram said, lifting his cup. "Here's to the new head of the physics team."

"Not *the* physics team," Jao protested. "A physics team. More of a task force. The task being to keep our vehicle from frying us. The head of *the* physics team is still Smeth. The Nar are being scrupulously careful not to step on human toes now that we've shown ourselves to be such sensitive creatures."

"But you're going to work independently?"

"Yes." Jao grinned wickedly. "And the first thing I'm going to do is to steal our friend Trist from under Smeth's nose."

"It must be good to be back in physics, though."

"Beats going to Juxt One. The best part is the total independence I'm going to have. Smeth may be a sensitive toe, but he's still only an appendage on a Nar foot."

Mim choked on her drink. "*Stop* it!" she said when she was able to stop laughing. "I'll *never* be able to get that image out of my mind. A swollen red toe with a little Smeth face where the toenail ought to be!"

She broke into peals of laughter again. The long night

without any sleep had made her a little giddy. Most of the people at the impromptu celebration were acting a bit too animated. Collapse would come later.

Similar parties were taking place throughout the Compound and wherever human beings lived. The Nar verdict had been more than compassionate; it had been magnanimous. A generation of Nar had grown to midlife taking human beings for granted as a fact of their environment, like house plants and touch pets. When one did encounter the occasional human being, it was as a handicapped creature incapable of true speech, abroad on some errand and asking directions in a halting approximation of the Small Language. One knew, of course, that they lived pitiably short lives without the final flowering that gave existence meaning, and so one was as kind and helpful to them as possible.

Now, all of a sudden, human beings had proved to have free will and murky purposes of their own. And they could sting.

The grand touch conclave had for the first time given the entire Nar nation the opportunity to share the perceptions of those few thousand Nar who had known human beings intimately—raised them as foster children, grown up with them as touch brothers, worked with them in joint enterprises. The sentience of these queer boned beings could no longer be ignored. And a great injustice had been done to them.

And so things had to be set right—at whatever cost. The first item of redress was to help them, with all the resources of Nar civilization behind them, achieve the longevity that was their due. The second was to assist them to full citizenship, despite their handicap. Immortality would help. Who could say what a human being might achieve in a thousand years of learning—even though biologically mute?

And finally, this newly surfaced wish of a majority of humans to go "home" could not be denied—any more than one could prevent a Nar, at the final fruition of his life, from reaching a spawning pool. The interstellar probe project would have to be speeded up and adapted to the purposes of the humans. The probe represented a stunning gift, but fortunately it was a gift that could be repaid: The newly immortal humans could use the vehicle to perform an errand that the Nar, with their mere thousand-year lifespans, could not do for themselves.

Olan Byr gave a small cough and got everybody's respectful attention. His face was drawn. He hadn't held up under the lack of sleep on this festive day as well as some of the younger people. Mim had settled him in a comfortable chair and seen to it that his needs were attended to.

"While we're passing out the congratulations," Olan said graciously, "let's save a few for the new director of the immortality project." His eyes, keen as ever, came to rest on Bram. "I never thought I'd have a good word to say about science, Bram, but it seems that it's good for something, after all."

"Thank you, Olan," Bram said, uncomfortably aware of everybody's eyes on him.

All of a sudden, he and Jao had become the first citizens of the Compound. The celebrating populace hadn't had time yet to absorb the full import of the Nar decree, but word had gotten around that Bram and Jao had been instrumental in the reprieve. Olan and Mim had had to rescue Bram from the jubilant mob that had spilled over the tidal flats in the wake of the dissolving Nar assembly. They had been waiting for him in a small groundcar as the exhausted defendants trudged wearily out. "Get in, Bram," Mim had said, holding the door open. "We're just having a few friends in. Nobody will bother you, and you won't have to talk if you don't want to."

"Hurry up and take their offer," Jao had said, hiking along beside Bram. "Think of my feet."

"Is human immortality really possible, do you think?" Olan asked now, his thin fingers drumming on the arm of his chair. The chair was a poplarwood replica of a gothic seat from a Dürer cartoon; Olan had hired a Resurgist craftsman to copy it.

"Yes," Bram said. "We know that Original Man achieved it. All we have to do is unscramble it from the Message archives, and after that it's just a lot of dull, hard, grinding work. It's going to be a strictly human-run project. The Nar insist on that. In case difficulties crop up along the way—and they're sure to—the Nar don't want to take the blame. They don't want the slightest imputation that they're suppressing anything or dragging their limbs. But they're throwing the full resources of the biocenter at our disposal. And we've got absolute priority. It's better that way. Humans work faster than Nar. We've always had to."

Some of Olan's and Mim's other guests moved closer to hear what Bram was saying. "They feel guilty," the violinist, Ang, said indignantly. "At having withheld the gift of eternal life. It doesn't matter if they intended to or not."

"We'll never know that," Bram said. "And I suspect that the Nar will never really know it, either. The Nar are generous, but all living things have an instinct of species survival, and maybe deep down they were afraid of the fast-breeding pets they'd conjured up."

"Exactly how does one go about cooking up immortality?" Olan Byr asked.

Bram tried to keep his explanation simple, conscious of Olan's ignorance of scientific matters. "It'll be a combination of several different approaches, I think, including a way to coax the cell to manufacture an enzyme to unsnarl cross-linked DNA. I got that theory from a wonderful old character named Doc Pol. But the real key, I think, is something else that Doc Pol put me on to. A sort of . . . of death gene that we carry around inside us. A switch that's programmed to turn itself on after a certain number of cell generations."

"I know Doc Pol," Olan mused. "I had no idea the old fellow was still alive."

Bram finished quickly, knowing he had lost Olan's attention but not wanting to disappoint the audience he had acquired.

"At any rate, Original Man devised a synthetic virus to . . . to infect us with the disease of immortality, so to speak. I've seen schematics of it. The viral DNA becomes part of our own genetic material and hides there quietly until the time comes to keep the death gene from expressing itself. The groundwork must have been laid early on, when they discovered how to suppress human oncogenes—cancer genes. We still have them. There's no way to get oncogenes out of our DNA. They're thoroughly mixed with our genetic code, and they may even do useful work—like a rotten timber still helping to support a bridge. But we simply don't get cancer anymore. Because we've also got an added plasmid to keep oncogenes from ever expressing themselves." He finished lamely, "Anyway, I think the mechanism is similar."

"What about brain cells?" Jao put in. "Turning off the death switch wouldn't affect them. They don't divide anyway. You just keep losing them one by one after birth. We know how to autoclone cortical tissue, sure, but there has to be a limit to brain grafts. I don't want to be walking around without a brain a million years from now."

"I told you it's not a simple problem," Bram said. "My guess is that there's a separate nucleotide sequence to induce the periodic renewal of fetal neurons—at a replacement rate mediated by the loss of our old ones, so as not to disturb our memories."

"Well, it all sounds very wonderful," Olan said absently. "Imagine having an eternity to delve into Bach—not that you'd ever run out of new things to discover."

He seemed to retreat into himself. Two of the music students had found a corner at the other end of the room, had broken out their instruments, and were playing something intricate together. Olan slowly nodded in time to the music.

Mim watched him silently, then turned her huge dark eyes on Bram. "How long will your project take?" she asked.

"It isn't only a matter of following Original Man's blueprint, Mim," Bram said. "We've got to devise our own procedures every step of the way. The Nar took centuries to create the first viable human ovum, centuries more to learn how to bring it to term." He smiled. "But this is a simpler job, and we've got a little more incentive than the Nar had. We'll do better."

She glanced at Olan again and bit her lip. "Don't take too long at it, Bram. Please."

Bram opened his mouth to reply, but Jao's booming voice interrupted him.

"Oh, Bram's got the easy part of the job! He's going to be in complete charge of a human-run program with human concepts of time. Pity *me*, Mim! I'm autonomous, sure, but I'm an autonomous bump on a big, slow-moving Nar project that they thought was whizzing along with a completion date of one or two hundred years in the future." He struck a mock-tragic pose. "*I'm* the one who's got to talk them into speeding up their timetable."

Mim smiled wanly in a pale reflection of her vivacity of a short while before. The lack of sleep was starting to catch up to her.

"Oh, dear," she said gamely. "First Smeth as a toe, now Jao as a bump."

"Isn't that asking a lot, Jao?" Bram said. "The ramjet probe project is going to represent a tremendous drain on the resources of Nar society as it is—even spread out over a century or two. We . . . can afford to wait."

"No!" Jao roared. Several more people came over from the thick of the party to be entertained. "We're not going to wait a year longer than necessary! We humans come cheap at the price. We're going to operate and maintain their roving beacon for them—much more satisfactory than robot systems. We're going to exercise *judgment* in their behalf." He smiled crookedly. "The Nar always preferred living things to machines."

"How did you ever persuade the Nar to turn the project over to us, Jao?"

The question came from one of the people who had drifted over. Soon Jao was happily holding forth about hadronic photons and the uncertainty principle and the gamma factor. Bram and Mim locked eyes.

"So it wasn't a dream, after all," she said softly. "After all these years, it's all coming true."

"It wasn't only my dream, Mim," Bram said. "A lot of people had it. They just didn't know it till now. They had to be told that it was possible."

She looked across the room at her friends and Olan's— musicians, artists, poets, artisans—people who had spent their lives walling themselves off from the Father World's civilization and had created a cosy facsimile of an imagined human culture instead.

"It's not a dream for everybody, though," she said. "You won't get all of these people to risk their new eternal lives on some crazy quest across half the universe in search of a bubble that for all we know might have burst more than thirty million years ago."

"No," he agreed. "We'll just get the adventurous ones. The troublesome ones, from the Nar point of view. The tame ones can stay behind and spend the next million years trying to learn the Great Language if they want."

He had spoken too vehemently. At the hurt look in Mim's eyes, he backtracked. "The Nar are beginning a program to call back humans from Juxt One and the farther stars, you know. It'll take another three years before the news even *reaches* Next, and then those who want to be included will have to start back without delay."

She looked at Olan, sitting with fragile dignity in his imitation gothic chair. "And those of us who choose to stay behind?"

"They—" He made a point of not saying *you*. "—they won't have a wall around them any more. The Nar are determined to make humans equal partners in their society from now on. One of the two big obstacles is gone now. Mim, do you realize that human beings won't be ephemeral curiosities in a long-lived culture any more—to be pitied and coddled. They'll outlive the Nar from now on."

"Mayflies."

"What?"

"Mayflies. It's a term from the old Inglex literature. It's going to be the Nar who are the mayflies now. That will be very strange."

"Not that the Nar are capable of envy. A millennium or so is quite long enough for them. They don't *want* immortality for themselves—couldn't even conceive of such a thing. I suppose if they could, they'd have mounted their own immortality project long ago. But they have to flower and die to reproduce, and to thwart that would be to thwart their own natures."

"We must have seemed very odd to them."

"Yes, indeed." He scanned the predominately Resurgist crowd to avoid looking directly into Mim's eyes. "The stay-at-homes will have all the time they need to get along in a Nar world. And after a few thousand years of that, who knows? Maybe something could be done about the second big obstacle. Perhaps with a little genetic modification and biological-electronic interfacing, one day the first human will say his first halting word in the Great Language."

"I can't conceive of such a thing. But it's a better solution than Penser's was."

"Yes."

Bram's part as an unwilling accessory remained unspoken between them, but Mim must have been thinking about it because the next thing she said was, "Your . . . friend, Kerthin. Will she go with you?"

"No," he said shortly.

"I'm sorry, Bram." She touched his hand.

"That's all right."

At this moment, Bram thought, Kerthin would be clearing her things out of their quarters. She had spoken to him long enough to at least let him know that she was leaving. The brief, unsatisfactory exchange had taken place during the interval when the penned humans waited for the Nar assembly to disperse. Bram had been glad of Olan's and Mim's invitation. He had no wish to go home while Kerthin was still there.

Jao's voice was still booming over the background conversation. Bram and Mim turned in tacit accord to listen.

"You want to know why we don't simply take the Nar ramjet and run off with it once we're out of reach?" he was saying in response to some question. "In the first place, it wouldn't be nice. In the second place, we *have* to take a detour through the center of the galaxy if we want to get to where *we're* going, so we might as well do the Nar's little chore for them on the way. Right?"

There was a buzz of inquiry around him, and Jao held up a meaty red hand to silence it.

"Why?" he said in mock exasperation. "Haven't you been paying attention? It's because only by diving straight through the interior of the galaxy, where the H-II regions are thickest, we can scoop up enough ionized gas to build up our gamma factor to the point we need. We also get a bonus. We pick up some of the rotational energy of the galactic core itself when we whip around it. By the time we head out of the galaxy, we'll be traveling at a speed of—" His eyeballs rolled back in his head while he mumbled figures to himself. "—call it a fraction of the speed of light represented by a decimal point followed by ten nines. Apply the relativity equations and anyone can see that'll give us a gamma factor of about seventy thousand."

Ang, the blonde girl from the string quartet, was part of the group listening to Jao. She was leaning forward with an adoring expression on her face. Jao winked at her.

"Excuse me," someone ventured timidly, "but what do those figures mean?"

"What do they mean?" Jao bellowed in outrage. "They mean that while the outside universe ticks off thirty-seven million years, *we* make the crossing between galaxies in only about five hundred years, *our* time."

"Plus the detour through the center of the galaxy," someone pointed out.

Jao decided his questioners were hopeless. "The detour will only add about another forty years of subjective time to the journey," he said, spacing his words carefully. "And if you don't like it, I might as well warn you that we'll have to perform the same maneuver at the other end in order to brake. Fortunately, the Milky Way's a good match in mass and configuration."

"Still," his listener demurred, "that's a long time for a bunch of people to spend shut up in a spaceship."

"Want me to skip the detour?" Jao growled. "Fine. How would you like me to drop a couple of nines off that string of figures I mentioned? That'd give us a gamma factor of—" Again, the eyes rolled back. "—seven oh seven point one. And you could spend fifty *thousand* years twiddling your thumbs while we make the crossing."

"He has a point, Jao," Bram said. "No matter how big we build this ramjet—and I'm assuming it might be as big as Lowstation—won't it be rather close quarters?"

"Yes," Jao's blonde admirer said. "What about that?"

Jao scowled, clearly stung by the criticism. He thought hard for a moment or two, then a beatific expression crossed his face. "Why not?" he mumbled to himself.

He turned to them with a broad smile. "We'll travel in style," he said. "We'll live in a tree."

Prologue Two
EXODUS

The passengers who came crowding onto the bridge at the pilot's invitation were mostly elderly. But they all seemed to be in marvelous health, and they were quite as lively and eager as the younger people among them as they grabbed safety lines and hauled themselves to the viewports for a look at their destination.

A handsome, erect old man of about seventy, with deep-etched features and an impressive white mane, took the elbow of the trim, gray-haired woman beside brim and steadied her as she took her turn at the port.

"There it is, Mim," he said. "Our home for the next five hundred years."

She drew closer to him. "Oh, Bram!" she said. "It's beautiful!"

The star tree floated in space before them, looking like a perfect green globe. From the cargo vessel's angle of approach—head on toward the center of the crown—the matching ball of root growth could not be seen, nor could the stubby trunk which connected them.

Hanging beside the green puff was a brassy skewer with

401

a trumpet end—Jao's hydrogen-scooping robot vehicle. The flaring bell looked solid enough from a distance, but Bram knew it was as insubstantial as gossamer. It was hundreds of miles in diameter and had to spin to maintain its shape. Still, its electromagnetic fields would shield the tree from the howling storm of radiation into Which it would sail at near-light speeds, and the tree's own reflective leaves, bred to handle anything up through X-rays, would take care of stray ionization—and even soak up the energy and use it.

Space tugs—tiny motes to the eye—were maneuvering to haul an enormous crystalline tether whose colossal links were forged of viral monofilament; the probe's long shaft would be threaded between the tree's two hemispheres at right angles to the hidden trunk. At relativistic speeds, the probe would tow the tree; for local star-hopping or intrasystem travel, it would be the other way around.

"Jao picked it himself," Bram said. "He insisted on traveling out to the cometary halo with the Nar foresters and choosing the one perfect vacuum poplar in the system."

"I remember." Mim laughed.

"The Nar've spent all these years outfitting it and stocking it for us. I guess it's as ready as it'll ever be. The Nar have been generous. They've given us everything from a fleet of landing craft to ground vehicles and heavy-duty mining equipment. Factories, distilleries, a complete duplicate of the Father World's central library, and frozen cell samples of every known life form. They've thought of everything."

"I hope so." She shivered. "If we're all going to be cooped up in the tree together for all those centuries. I hope we won't get on each other's nerves."

He smiled. "Cooped up is hardly the way to describe it, Mim. The tree's a fair-size worldlet—bigger than any of the

Father World's moons. We'll have a lot more elbow room than we did in our old human enclaves."

Mim brightened. "We will, won't we? And we'll have a bigger population than any we've ever known in any single Compound. We won't get bored with each other."

"No, we'll get comfortable with each other."

She squeezed his arm. "I think I'm going to like eternity."

"We'll live in our own little villages at first, in the branch they've gotten ready for us. But it will take us at least half the trip to explore the tree, develop it, and tame the wild branches for settlement. We'll have plenty to do, never fear."

"And there'll be babies, won't there?" Mim said, softening.

"The tree's parasite ecology ought to support a human population of twenty-five thousand or more," Bram said. "We'll be well on the way to populating our home planet before we even get there. And the ones who've gotten too used to the tree to want to leave it can stay aboard and start exploring our neighbor stars."

There was a commotion behind them. They turned to see Smeth, struggling with baggage that kept floating away from him in the zero gravity and haranguing a long-suffering Nar steward.

"What do you *mean*, you don't know where the rest of my luggage is? I have six walker-loads of priceless records and irreplaceable instruments stowed in the cargo hold, and I *insist* on supervising the transfer personally!"

The years had turned Smeth into a crochety old man with bent shoulders and a frail pipestem neck. He was still a bachelor. Nobody took his crankiness seriously anymore; he held the affection of the human race because of his work on the probe project.

The steward twisted his upper tentacles into a corkscrew and untwisted them again in the Nar version of hand-wringing. "I'll attend to it myself, Smeth-brother," he said, gliding off at the horizontal.

Smeth followed him, grumbling. "Nothing ever gets done *properly* anymore!" He stomped off as well as one can stomp in free fall.

"Poor Smeth!" Bram said.

"Poor steward, you mean," Mim said.

"I never thought he'd come. I didn't really believe it till he actually showed up at the shuttleport leading that baggage train."

"Practically every human in his department signed up for the trip," Mim said tartly. "He *had* to come. He'd have had no one left to *preside* over!" She relented a little. "Still, I'm glad he's coming with us. It wouldn't be the same without him."

Bram's eyes strayed to a viewport farther down the bridge, where Marg and Orris were holding hands like a pair of young lovers. Marg had evolved into the most formidable of dragons these last decades, but Orris saw nothing except the winsome flirt he had first been welded to so long ago.

"Marg's talking about having a baby as soon as she gets young enough," Mim said, following his gaze. "She and Orris are actually picking out names now."

"I'm surprised they didn't have one years ago," Bram said. "When the restrictions were lifted."

"They'd already decided to emigrate by then. I guess like most of the other emigrating couples, they decided to wait till we were actually underway. After all, it doesn't matter if you get too old when you know your biological clock's going to run backward again."

"Still, they must have had a lot of faith in the immortality project," Bram said. "That's surprising, considering all those early setbacks."

There had been a nine year delay in developing one of the crucial segments of heterochronic nucleotide from scratch; Original Man had extracted it from living dragonflies, but the complete dragonfly genome did not exist on the Father World, and the prohibition against it remained in force, with Bram's total acquiescence.

Mim squeezed his hand. "Oh, Bram, it still seems so miraculous. Are we really going to he young again?"

"It's already begun," he said. "Do you remember how sick and miserable you were after the injection? That was your body trying to fight off the virus. By now you're totally infected. The viral DNA's settling into every cell in your body, where your immune system can't take exception to it any more."

"All that sneezing and itching and swelling! I thought I'd die!"

"You took it harder than most." He traced the line of her jaw with his fingertips. "But you've lost some wrinkles in the last year, and we're all a lot more spry than we have any right to be."

"Just when I was used to us growing old together," she said with another squeeze.

"You'll have to get used to us growing young together."

They had been well into their fifties when they finally had become joined—Bram after a second failed marriage with someone who, he now realized, he had become infatuated with while on the rebound from Kerthin, and Mim after ten years of nursing an ailing Olan Byr. They had seen one another around the Compound and had thought that they were merely good friends, and it had come as a surprise to both of them to realize that the old attraction between them had been rekindled. Mim had needed time to get over the feeling that she was being disloyal to Olan's memory. Bram had no such qualms. These last twenty years with Mim had been the best years of his life.

The immortality virus had come too late for Olan, as it had for too many humans. The project had taken almost forty years, and there had been many unexpected difficulties. But a surprising number of oldsters had hung on until Bram's team had finally succeeded. Jun Davd, his childhood tutor in astronomy, had been one of them. And old Doc Pol, who must have been more than two hundred and a patchwork of cloned transplants, had volunteered to be the first human guinea pig and had won his gamble. Bram had seen him board the shuttle under his own power, with two canes.

Jao floated over to them with his arm around Ang. The red beard was pure white now, and looked patriarchal. Ang, who had been bent and frail, had started to fill out again and straighten up almost immediately after her immortality injection a year and a half ago. The two had been separated during their middle years, and Jao had had his middle aged fling, but they had been back together for a decade now. "We went through the best years together," he'd confided to Bram at the time. "Why go looking for something you already have?"

"A beautiful sight, isn't it?" Jao commented, thrusting a bearded chin at the spectacle outside.

"That's what I was just saying to Bram," Mim said. "It's strange to think of that ball of green life hurtling between the galaxies, nurturing almost the entire human race with its air and water."

"It's a well-tested life-support system, Mim," Jao said.

"That's what originally gave me the idea. But I wasn't talking about the tree. I was talking about our relativistic hobbyhorse. Beautiful and deadly. You wouldn't want to be within a couple of hundred miles of it when it's operating, even with all the baffles along the shaft, but of course we won't have to be. And the nice thing about relativistic geometry is that the electromagnetic umbrella that's protecting us up front will automatically open up our cone of safety the faster we go and the fiercer the gamma storm becomes."

"Will that contraption really take us home in only five hundred of our treeboard years?" Bram asked hastily, to prevent Jao from launching into an involved technical explanation.

Jao preened his white beard. "It will after we dive through the center of this galaxy, cut a swath through all the hydrogen clouds we'll find along the way, and use the mass of the galactic nucleus to fling us up out of the plane toward the Milky Way. You know, theoretically there's no limit to how closely we could crowd the speed of light if we had enough hydrogen to gulp, but there has to be a terminal velocity imposed by what we've got available to us, plus the slingshot effect of the core maneuver. But I figure that getting within one ten millionth of one percent of the speed of light ought to do the job."

He gave them a toothless grin. Bram could see the little white dots where a new generation of baby teeth was starting to show through the gums. Bram's own teething, in just the few missing gaps, was still bothering him; he knew now what babies complained about.

"Is this character still bragging about that shiny new toy of his out there?" Bram turned to see Trist hanging jauntily in midair. "That'll give you a sample of what we're in for during the next five hundred years. And does everybody realize that if he's off by *one* decimal point in his calculations, it'll be a lot longer than five hundred years? The time dilation factor will work out to a trip of one thousand seven hundred years."

The rangy physicist had weathered welt over the years; he looked like a somewhat faded version of his youthful self. He was going to be in charge of the program to broadcast the Nar genetic code at all the suns that might be listening as the human expedition, in its queer hybrid craft of living tree and robot ramjet, plunged into the galaxy's crowded heart.

"Hello, Trist," Bram said. "Before all the technical blather, Mim was saying that it's a strange ship we'll be traveling in—a world, really, and one that will nurture us between the galaxies."

"People used to name their ships long ago, didn't they?" Mim asked. "We ought to have a name for this one."

Trist peered out the port. Only a few miles away now, the tree was no longer a geometrically perfect ball. The huge twisting green branches seemed to fill all space.

"Yes," he said. "They broke a jug of wine over it first."

Jao snorted. "Waste of good alcohol."

Bram furrowed his brow. "Trist, didn't you once—"

"Didn't I once tell you the story of the tree that was the world—the all-spanning tree that nourished and sustained the entire race of humankind and protected them from the burning heavens while they made the transition from one universe to another? Yes, I did."

"The burning heavens," Jao interposed. "That'd be the gamma rays and relativistic particles that we're going to have to sail through."

Bram said, "What—"

"Yggdrasil," Trist said. "The world tree was called Yggdrasil."

"That settles it, then," Mim said firmly. "That's what we'll name ours."

Bram's mind drifted seventy years into the past, when a sleepy little boy had assured his ten-legged tutor, with all the certitude of childhood, that one day when he grew up he would find a way to return across the impassable void to the home of the first human race. Never in his wildest dreams had he imagined that it would be like this, in a giant space-dwelling tree towed by a device that shrank time. Now, it seemed, there would always be time to spare; his seventy years were only a prelude.

Mim's voice nudged him back to the present. "What are you thinking?" she said.

He looked at the familiar faces and saw them as they would be again. "I'm thinking," he said, "that we're about to start a great adventure."

The boat settled gently into the gigantic branches. The tree's rotation had been stopped for the probe-threading maneuver, so the swarming vehicles that contained the human race could land anywhere, not just at the docking facilities in the trunk. The immortal people filed through to the airlocks, not looking back.